Resort to Romance

Kacey Sophia

Contents

To those who need to hear it. You are so enough and deserve the love you seek. To my younger self who didn't always believe in herself—you got through it and I'm so proud of you.

Content Warnings

Dear Reader,

This story is full of love and laughter but also has heavy and sensitive topics. This includes:

- Mentions of mental health such as anxiety

- Heartbreak

- Mention of childhood neglect and being in care

- Contains sexual content, explicit language and is not suitable for readers under the age of 18

- Mentions of alcohol

I hope you love Felix and Alisha as much as I do and thank you for reading.

Also by Kacey Sophia

An Artist's Dream
An Artist's Desire

Chapter 1

Alisha

"So you want me to write an article about Austria?" I asked my boss, Grayson, as he sipped his chai, which was one of my favourites. I clutched my nearly full notebook with my trusty gold pen, and my knuckles were probably about to burst through the skin, given my grip. Even my eyes felt like they would pop out of my skull. I felt nervous as I could finally get my work noticed properly. This was it. My big break. Well, hopefully, it was.

"Not just write. You're going to go there too, Alisha." As soon as he said this, I felt as though I was going to faint on the spot. Travelling had never been my forte and getting on planes made me nervous, which was interesting because the company I worked for was heavily invested in that. I had just about managed a few trips to India in the last few years alone to visit my family.

Heaven help me now.

"I am?" was all I could muster as the room had stopped swirling. I tugged at a loose strand of chestnut hair that had fallen across my cheek. I wasn't that tall but I felt like I had suddenly lost a few inches. I needed to somehow keep it together for my boss, who had one eyebrow slightly raised.

"You are so don't look so nervous. It's a ski holiday too–perfect for writing and skiing. Taste some good food, explore the culture. You are very talented, Alisha. Now is your chance," Grayson said, giving me a gentle smile.

He had always been a good boss to me over the years. I started working at Culture Horizon as a part-time copywriter at twenty-two. The company published various articles, focusing on places that weren't often highlighted enough as well as events that took place there. It was a company I enjoyed working for, somewhere I felt my voice was valued. I was now twenty-five and working as a full-time editor, but I really wanted to be a journalist, write with passion, and be proud of something I could call mine. Maybe even have the chance to publish every month. It was a big ambition but no dream was impossible. You just had to work hard for it.

I came from a family of six, being the second eldest sibling. I had two brothers and one sister, all of whom I was close to. We'd experienced a great childhood together, full of laughter and fun. We were very blessed to have a close relationship and most nights, we'd hop on a group FaceTime call to catch up. I knew they'd be excited for me regarding the article and that I'd also be stepping out of Surrey for once.

Grayson was now in his early forties and originally lived in Holland. He was a kind man, with salt-and-pepper hair and dark blue eyes that held a lot of wisdom. He had two kids and utterly adored them. That was a life I envisioned for myself in the future.

However, I had been unlucky in love. My parents hoped I would settle down by now, but thankfully, they never pushed me. They were quite docile and didn't like to be involved in much drama. They were popular with their neighbours in Soho. I lived in a one-bed apartment in Surrey with a tuxedo cat named Chou for company. A cat that I absolutely loved and treated like a baby at times.

"Can I take anyone with me?" I asked Grayson and he took a moment to pause before nodding.

Good, at least that makes it more bearable.

"I'll talk to Ophelia. She's skied before," I said, knowing she would be very excited and start packing immediately.

"Everything will be arranged for you. You'll be flying there next week, on Thursday," Grayson said, checking something on his laptop before looking back up at me. He must have noticed my worrisome expression and sympathetically gave me a smile. It was November 25th, meaning that I had less than a week to prepare for this trip. My family would have a lot to say about it.

"So soon." I hummed and then gave my boss a nod to signal I understood. *So be it.*

I supposed it was a free holiday, with everything paid for. This opportunity wouldn't come around again. Plus, Ophelia had always wanted to go to Austria. She loved travelling whereas me...not so much.

"I know. You'll be going to Ischgl. A lovely town, in the state of Tyrol. It's a very popular ski resort," Grayson said, beckoning me to come over and show me what was on his laptop. He brought up several images of the town as well as the self-catered chalet we'd be staying in. It did look very cosy. One evening, I could imagine myself by the fire, laptop on my lap with a cup of hot cocoa and marshmallows. That didn't sound too bad at all.

Maybe I needed to give myself a chance.

I definitely needed to do my own research and it was my lunch break, so it was the perfect chance to do so. I would rope Ophelia into this, and I already knew that as soon as I told her the plan, she wouldn't need any persuasion to go.

"Thank you. I'll get ready then," I said to Grayson, as he then dismissed me. He mentioned he would email over the flight and accommodation details in the next few hours but not to panic, as I would really enjoy it. The alpine air was apparently something else.

I hummed to myself as I made my way back to my cubicle to pull out my sandwich from my drawer. Cheese and tomato, one of my favourite fillings. In fact, I hadn't changed my sandwich fillings in the last two years. Perhaps I needed to extend my palate and Austrian food was apparently quite tasty.

As I sat in my chair eating, I switched on my laptop to go to Google. I took another bite of my food and searched up the town of Ischgl until I felt a presence behind me.

"Ah, Ischgl. Why are you browsing that?" I turned to face my friend of three years, Ophelia. She had streaks of purple in her chestnut hair and bright sparkling green eyes that could draw you in and make you surrender. She stood tall at five-foot-eight, well, taller than me. She was Greek and moved to England about five years ago. She was a senior copywriter here at Culture Horizon, and we occasionally worked together. She was really the only person I was close to at this company. In fact, the only close friend I had.

Overall, Ophelia was absolutely stunning. A few of the staff members had openly admitted their feelings for her, which she dismissed. She was perfectly content being single and enjoying life. She was quite the opposite of me, alert and extroverted. Whereas I was reserved and introverted. A night out in the town versus sitting on the sofa with a good book and a bowl of chocolate raisins was my idea of fun.

Yes, chocolate raisins. They're delicious, sue me.

"Well...you and I are going there," I said and just as I predicted, a squeal erupted around the room. A few heads peeked out from the cubicles, and a few looks of bewilderment were thrown in my direction, but this didn't phase Ophelia, who had a grin on her face like a mad woman. She was also bouncing on the balls of her feet with her hands clasped together.

"I can't believe it. Tell me the details. Now." My friend gushed and took a seat next to me. So, I told her all the nitty gritty details.

"A two-week holiday? I'm so in! We need to do some shopping!" Ophelia exclaimed, she had pulled up a chair next to me and was eating her lunch.

"It's quite cold there, so we'll need to get lots of warm clothes," I said, taking a sip of my smoothie I had prepared this morning. Mango and passionfruit which felt refreshing on my tongue.

"We haven't had a day out in a while. This'll be fun." Ophelia smiled. She was right, as we'd both been caught up in work for the past few months. Plus, I was getting over a horrible break-up.

"I feel like I need to do something with my hair." I tugged on a strand of my hair, which had become a little frayed at the ends.

"Hey, how about you dye your hair like mine? I think it would suit you." Ophelia pulled at a purple strand of her hair, twisting it around her finger. She had painted her nails a dark red and they were perfectly shaped. I took a moment to glance at my own nails and grimaced; yes, they definitely needed a makeover. I twisted a lock of my dark hair around my index finger and then released it, watching it spiral.

"I don't think I'll dye my hair, it just needs a trim," I said. And if I was going to go all out with my appearance, I'd even get a manicure.

After we ate our lunch, we got back to work, and I did some extensive research into Ischgl and the ski school that was available. I would definitely need to book some lessons and perhaps I would ask Grayson if the company would cover this. I would only really need to book at least five or six. I wasn't planning on skiing for the whole two weeks. There was a lot to see and do in Austria.

As soon as the clock hit four o'clock, Grayson popped his head around to say we could go home. I was relieved, as my sofa was calling me. I was desperate for a takeaway too. I locked my laptop away in my drawer and wheeled my chair under the desk. I placed my bag on my shoulder and turned around to walk to the lift.

"Fancy a drink out tonight?" Ophelia met my side as I approached the lift. I pressed the button and turned to my friend.

"I'm going to order a takeaway. You can join me if you want. I've got wine at my place," I said, not feeling the urge to be in a crowded bar with people I didn't know.

"Okay Ali, sounds good. Let's make it a sleepover. Might as well," she said and I nodded, she already had some spare clothes at mine and whenever she had a few to drink, I always insisted on her staying anyway. We got into the lift as it arrived on our floor and I listened as Ophelia started to talk about her ski trip to Japan last year.

My car was where it normally was and I drove us both back to mine within ten minutes, surprisingly the roads hadn't been too busy. As we entered my apartment, I immediately put on my fluffy slippers and tied my long hair into a bun. My cat Chou was eating his bowl of dry food, meowing at me as I reached down to stroke him. He was the cutest company I needed in my life, and no man could compare to Chou.

"I'll get the wine," Ophelia announced, making her way to the kitchen. We both knew what we wanted to order, Dominos pizza was our usual, with some wedges and garlic bread–delicious. I placed the order online as it was easier plus I often got nervous talking on the phone. I sighed, wishing I could be more confident but I had grown used to my own little bubble. My own haven. *Did I really need to change it?*

Ophelia poured us two glasses of rosé, to which I thanked her before sitting down on my blue corner sofa. My apartment was cosy, with a small kitchen and living room combined. The bedroom was near the front door and the bathroom was just opposite. The rent was decent each month, which I could mostly afford with the salary I was earning.

Our food arrived in twenty minutes and my wine glass was half drained. I wasn't looking to top it up but Ophelia was on it straight away. We dived into our pizzas, a Hawaiian pizza for me (*yes, you heard me*) and a Meat Feast for Ophelia. Both small too, as going for large ones would be a waste.

"So, we get a free holiday AND we get to write. Doesn't that sound amazing?" Ophelia asked as she chewed her pizza. She was more excited than me, and I knew she would have no trouble speaking German while we were there. She was very good at languages.

"A little scary," I replied, finishing my slice after picking at it with my fingers. The cheese had gone a little hard as I was eating it slowly. There were still knots in my stomach as I thought about the ski holiday.

"I think you need to expose yourself a little more to the wide world, Miss Dutta. You'll see Ali. This will be the best holiday yet," she said, reaching over to give my hand a squeeze. I only hoped she was right. These could be either two weeks of heaven or hell.

Chapter 2

Alisha

The next day, Ophelia was nursing a slight headache and I was tidying up the kitchen. We'd gone a bit overboard with the snacks so I was busy throwing empty packets away and swiping up the crumbs.

It was about eight o'clock in the morning and after a restless night of sleep, I felt I needed to get up earlier. I had already gone through two cups of coffee and tried not to laugh as Ophelia let out a groan.

"Need some painkillers?" I offered, throwing the packet to her which she caught with one hand just about. She grumbled a thanks as she took two tablets and gulped a glass of water. She then placed her head back on the pillow and sighed. I was glad to say I hadn't followed Ophelia's lead last night in drinking a few more glasses of wine. I think I just felt so anxious about the trip that it couldn't leave my mind.

My friend soon fell back asleep and I knew it would be rude of me to wake her, so I made some breakfast and started planning my article in advance. I turned on my laptop and stretched out my fingers in front of me.

I was frantically typing away some notes, having come across the official Ischgl promotion Instagram account. I watched a few ski videos and huffed as I would never be at a professional level. My dad would probably laugh at the idea, as when I was little, I would barely leave his side to go to my swimming lessons.

Dear Heaven, what was I getting myself into?

I glanced at my empty cup and decided another round of coffee would do. It was now 10:30 am and Ophelia was finally starting to stir from her slumber.

"Hey, Sleeping Beauty." I switched on the coffee maker and as it whirred to life, Ophelia stretched out her arms and stuck her tongue out at me.

"Mmm. God, what a headache. Oh, are you making coffee? Gimme." She threw the blanket off her and instantly it was as if her headache had disappeared as she skipped over to me. Chou hopped onto the counter and nudged her for a stroke. She gladly obliged and scratched him under the chin. His tail swished from side to side.

Oh, I so wished I could take Chou on the holiday. I needed my comfort and his gentle purrs.

Our coffees were ready within a few minutes, and we comfortably sat at the dining table, staring out into the street bustling with busy shoppers, dog walkers and excited children on scooters.

I was pulled away from my thoughts when Ophelia spoke, "Have you heard much from Caden?"

Hearing his name caused my heart to beat rapidly, the dreaded ex. We split up about six months ago but he still tried to talk to me. He would text me to say he missed me and asked if we could try again. Fat chance at that, the guy had cheated on me with one of my so-called friends, Felicity. I had tried to cut ties with the pair, which absolutely broke my heart. Now, I closed myself off and the idea of falling for someone again seemed far-fetched.

"Nope. I'm just going to continue to ignore him. He doesn't dictate my life anymore," I said truthfully, taking another sip of my creamy coffee. I couldn't lie though, I sometimes missed being adored. The sex itself had been good but clearly not good enough for him to go and sleep with Felicity. She had grovelled for the first month but clearly, I hadn't meant much to her as she stopped contacting me. Losing a friend had hurt much more. It was a whole other level of pain and it took me a while to get through it.

"Too right. Time to start loving yourself now, Ali. You are so much better than that idiot," Ophelia said, and I was grateful for her presence. She always knew how to pull me out of the hole I buried myself deep into. Some days, I had just wanted to stay hidden, but Ophelia was determined to keep me in the open so that I could slowly start to heal.

"Thanks." And I meant it. We finished our coffees and decided perhaps a few hours of shopping would be good. I definitely needed to buy ski-appropriate clothing; I'd rent the skis whilst I was out there as well as the helmet and poles. I could picture myself now on the slopes, probably having a Bridget Jones moment.

The next few hours went by quickly and after selecting a few pairs of trousers, socks, zip-up jackets and a few wool hats, Ophelia and I sat down in the nearest cafe with the cutest name, *Teacup O' Delight*. It was a small but adorable business, with a soft pink roof and a glossy white entrance door that rang a bell as you entered. The seats inside were plush, a mixture of white and pink. The tables also had patterns of roses and love hearts, and I always took great care whenever I went there, avoiding any spills of my hot drinks.

The name was fitting as we had our steaming cups of lattes topped with cream in front of us, with mini gingerbreads on the saucers. Christmas music was playing in the background and the cafe was busy for a Saturday afternoon.

We sipped our coffees and reminisced about the previous week of work, which had been a little quiet. We had some competition with the other local journalist company Capture and they were known for their swanky, lavish building and upend customers. We targeted all demographics, and I found we were much more unique. Our articles were from personal experiences and I was about to go on a scary one.

"Do you think you'll get a promotion?" Ophelia placed her teacup down and bit into her mini gingerbread head first. *Poor little guy.*

"I hope so, I feel it's about time, so this article has to be good though. It could make or break me. I still can't believe we're even going." I grimaced and finished my coffee, trying to shake away the anxiety.

You'll be fine, you'll be fine, you'll be fine.

"Hey, enough with the worrying. You do it too much that you're starting to get wrinkles, Ali." Ophelia frowned, and maybe she was right. I spent most of my time panicking about what hadn't even happened yet, but my brain was programmed that way, it had been for most of my teenage and adult years.

"Got any tips?" I questioned, anything to stop my mind from going overboard.

"Full of them. But you know me, I always say meditation is the best. You should try it later," Ophelia suggested. I pondered on the idea and agreed that maybe I would.

"Ready to go?" I asked my friend, just as she was finishing her coffee.

"Yes, I think I'll head back home and call my family," Ophelia said and I nodded. I would also do the same as Saturday was the day I'd usually call them. I gave Ophelia a hug as we said goodbye and with my shopping bags, I walked home and contemplated how exactly to break the news to my family.

Arriving home in less than ten minutes, I was immediately called by my older brother, Zane, who was in the process of fixing his hair. He was a 6'1" professional hockey player and always wanted to look his best. He was twenty-seven with dark, brown eyes and a sharp jawline. As the eldest, he was the one we'd look up to as a role model.

"Hallo behne, everything okay?" he asked with a slight frown as I was chewing my lip. I placed my shopping bags on the sofa. I'd carried the bags in one hand to take the FaceTime call. I rested my phone on the kitchen table and filled Chou's bowl with some cat food. Due to there being no garden, he had to stay indoors. He had his litter box and I was very glad that he hadn't made any mess. There were occasions where I'd come back home, and he had left a special surprise for me on the kitchen floor. Once satisfied that Chou was happy, I picked up my phone to focus on my brother.

"Totally fine. Are the others joining us?" I sat on the sofa and propped my feet up on the coffee table, my slippers already donning my feet.

"Nahi, they're busy," Zane said, and just as he said this, our little sister Kiya popped up on the screen. She had long, curly hair and had a personality that could melt butter. She had only just turned twenty-one recently and was due to finish university in the summer. She was studying Archaeology and had been fascinated with rocks and fossils from a young age. For her fifth birthday, my parents bought her her first fossil brush, which she took with her everywhere. It was adorable and another reason why I admired our parents, as they understood our passions and nurtured them from a young age.

"I'm here!" Kiya waggled her fingers excitedly and turned the screen to show her housemates as well, who waved at us.

"So guys, I have something to tell you," I said, suddenly feeling a little nervous. I clasped my clammy hands together and tried to shake off the bubbling anxiety that was building up. I tried to use the techniques my therapist had taught me a few years ago, hoping my anxiety wouldn't flare up again.

Deep breaths, one, two, three.

Both my siblings paused what they were doing and stared at me, waiting patiently for my next words.

"We are seated," they both said and I laughed before continuing. Maybe my nerves were easing up now. It helped to talk to my family, and they understood me as best they could.

"So, my boss has asked me to write an article."

"Finally. What will it be about?" Zane asked, his eyebrow slightly raised.

"Austria. And I have to go there next week," I said and then waited for their response. They both took a moment to take in the news and then the two of them simultaneously started asking questions about the whole trip, who would be going with me and for how long.

"We're proud of you, Ali. Just so you know," Kiya said and I almost wanted to reach through the screen to hug her, if I could. They definitely needed to come up with a device like that one day.

"Thank you. How do you think Mum and Dad will react?" I played with a loose thread hanging off my top and then looked back at my siblings on my phone.

"They've always said you needed an adventure, didi," Kiya said and Zane nodded in agreement.

"Absolutely. It's only two weeks and you'll be back before Christmas. This is the boost you need, Ali," Zane replied. After ten more minutes of chatting, I felt a little better. *Everything will be fine.*

It wasn't long before dinner rolled around, and Chou was curled up on my lap, his belly exposed for lots of rubs. I was happy to oblige and could feel the rush of endorphins through me.

"Can you come with me to Austria, Chou?" And in response, he let out a small meow. I wasn't sure whether this was a yes or no, but it was nice to know he could understand me and my feelings right now. One of my siblings would need to look after him whilst I was gone, which I knew Kiya would volunteer for as she was on her Christmas break from next week.

"You'll be fine," I whispered to myself, hoping that these words would ring true next Thursday when I got on the plane. I needed to put the past behind me. Enough thinking about Caden, about Felicity. They didn't deserve a place in my head anymore.

Chapter 3

Felix

All I'd ever known was Ischgl. I lived and breathed this place. I didn't particularly mind, because I was comfortable and to be honest, why would I move? Christmas was just around the corner and although I wasn't a massive fan of it, I still made the effort for my family.

I'd been staring at my reflection in the mirror for probably five minutes now, analysing every inch of my face. I looked tired, but I always did. That's what sleep deprivation did to you. Pair that with heartbreak and you're good to go.

Luckily, I had no work today, so my plan was to ski for a few hours. I usually preferred to go by myself but I'd extend the offer to Mira, my little sister who often worried about me.

I rubbed a hand down my face, wincing slightly at the roughness of my facial hair. I definitely needed a shave and even a haircut, as my auburn hair was a little shaggy. Aside from looking like I needed five years of sleep, I wasn't that bad looking.

The only quality I supposed I liked about myself were my eyes, most often people had commented they were soft to look into and a unique colour. Hazel. Evident bags were under my eyes but I couldn't make them magically disappear.

I could do something about the facial hair, at least. So after about ten minutes of shaving, I let out a satisfactory hum and vacated my bathroom.

I was about to pour myself another cup of coffee when my phone started to buzz and I didn't need to look twice to see who was calling. I answered just as quickly as the phone rang.

"Hey," I greeted my sister in German, leaning my body against the kitchen counter. I winced as I looked at the pile of dishes in the sink, I'd have to deal with that later.

"Why didn't you ring me last night? I was worried." Mira's tone was etched with vivid concern. I hoped I'd ease her worries, but sometimes, it seemed as though the roles were reversed between us. Really, it should be me taking care of her.

"Sorry, Mira. I had an early night," I lied, hating myself for it. But I didn't want to tell her the truth, that I had been tossing and turning all night. Thinking about the last six months and how everything had just fallen apart.

You can't change the past.

"Riight." Mira didn't sound as though she believed me but she let it slide for now.

"How are you anyway?" I switched the questioning back to her, I really didn't want to talk about the past twenty-four hours. If anything, I wanted to start a clean slate today and try to act as though everything was okay. Even if it was playing pretend.

I decided to let my sister speak for the next few minutes, every now and then nodding, although no one could see me. For extra measure, I had to speak a few words so she knew I was actually listening and taking in what she was saying.

"So, I'll see you tomorrow then?" Mira asked, but to me, it sounded more like a statement. Like, I'd be seeing her regardless. Today, I'd be skiing along as she told me she was quite tired. I knew she'd felt guilty about declining to come skiing but at least I'd see her tomorrow.

"Yep. Just text me where and when," I told her.

"I will. And Felix, I can tell when you're not okay but you don't have to tell me. Just know that I'm here, I always will be," Mira said and I squeezed my eyes shut, because even over the phone I couldn't hide.

"Okay," was all I could say but it would do.

"I've gotta go but I'll text you later, okay?" Mira's voice almost sounded pleading. After saying my goodbyes to Mira, the call ended and I released a sigh that I had been holding since the start of the phone call.

"Enough now," I told no one, deciding it was time to get dressed and go for a ski. I needed to clear my head. Whether it would work, well I'd find out.

The walk to the cable car wasn't particularly far, and by 9:30 am, it was already busy. I had bundled up extra warm today, as there was a heavier chill in the air. We'd probably have another snowfall later today at this rate. The residents of Ischgl were used to this but the tourists always found this a spectacle. It was the best time of the year to visit, in my opinion.

Christmas holidays would begin soon and I knew just how busy the ski slopes would get. But I didn't mind, skiing was meant for fun and I'd always thought about teaching my own kids one day. Whether I'd actually have any, I didn't know.

The idea of love these days seemed far-fetched, I'd almost given up on it completely, or maybe I had. I didn't keep in touch with my ex and it was best I didn't. I didn't want to open that can of worms again. My mental health was supposed to be my priority now, even though I really wasn't taking good care of myself. I had thought about speaking to a counsellor a month ago and I'd gone to at least one session. I quickly realised that it wasn't for me and I was better off just speaking to those I was closest to. Mira now acted as though she were my therapist and I hated how that had become the norm. I wanted to be a better brother to her, just to be a better person overall. Nothing was going to change now though, was it?

I scanned my card before going into a vacant cable car, and luckily no one got in with me. I appreciated the quietness and adjusted my helmet on my head, watching the people on the ground get smaller and smaller.

"Well, this is it," I muttered, leaning back in my seat. Hopefully, today would be a better day. But I'd always said this and no day ever seemed to be. I just wanted something different. Something to hope for.

Maybe even *someone*.

Chapter 4

Alisha

Yikes, I thought as I watched yet again another ski video. These people were professionals and looked like they were having a lot of fun. A few days had passed and it was now Wednesday evening. Tomorrow morning, Ophelia and I would be catching our plane to Innsbruck, before getting a private taxi to our final destination, Ischgl.

I was currently eating a bowl of yoghurt and muesli, which wasn't my dinner but I was hungry, as well as pacing the kitchen floor for the fifth time.

"Stop fretting, pyari," my dad said to me. He and my mother had decided to come and visit. My sister Kiya was currently playing with Chou and had brought round her two large suitcases since she was staying in the apartment for the two weeks I was away. My other brother, Aadi, had called me earlier in the day to wish me luck and that he had wanted to come and see me but he was currently working overtime at the hospital. He was training to be a doctor and at the age of twenty-three, he was now starting to settle having moved out of our parents' home and into his own flat. He was often quite reserved, similar to me but he made the effort to see us every now and then. Zane had also stopped by earlier in the day with a basket of savoury and sweet muffins, claiming that he had made them or in other words, our mum had. My brother didn't cook often and loved to visit his local bakery to get some sweet treats.

"Your beautiful face doesn't need any more worry lines." My mum gently tapped my forehead and then pulled me into an almost smothering hug.

"Hmphf," was all I could respond, scraping the last of my food from the bowl and then placing it into the sink. Ophelia would meet me at the airport at nine tomorrow morning, and our flight would be at 11:10 am.

"Seriously, didi. You'll wafting all your worry fumes my way. Being positive is key!" Kiya wrapped her arms from behind me. *If only I believed that, if I could have my younger sister's optimism.*

"I suppose I should take a leaf out of your book, baby sis." I walked to take a seat on the sofa, with Kiya still wrapped around me until I almost sat on top of her. She quickly scarpered and giggled doing so.

Mum had decided to make us malai kofta, one of my favourites so she knew how to cheer me up. I was going to miss her cooking so much as well as her hugs.

"Are you all packed? Passport? ID?" my dad asked. He was more worrisome than my mum and often relied on her to keep things in check. The two of them were very sweet and I hoped one day I could maintain a happy marriage such as theirs.

No, I would not wallow in self-pity again.

"Food is ready, mere bachche!" Mum called out, and an array of delicious food was awaiting us on the kitchen counter. Aside from the kofta, she had made saag chana masala with pilau rice. It consisted of chickpeas, chillies and tomatoes. We were served some Navajo fry bread too. My mind drifted off to what Austrian food would be like and, overall, the locals. I knew I needed to start learning German but of course, I wasn't going to be an expert in the space of a week.

We washed our hands before sitting down to eat our dinner. I immediately went for the bread, shaping it into a boat so that I could add some masala within it. As always, the food was divine.

"Thank you, Maa," Kiya exclaimed between mouthfuls of food, but was quickly scolded. I was grateful for the company this evening, it would keep me grounded for the next few hours. I knew tomorrow morning, I'd be a big bag of nerves. My boss had texted me to see if I was alright and had double-checked I had all the information I needed. Where we'd be lodging was a cosy chalet, not too far from the town centre and the ski school. There were plenty of restaurants to try as well and bratwursts were very popular there.

My parents had kindly given me some extra spending money, to which I had politely refused at first but they had insisted. I would convert this into euros tomorrow and I had set up an international debit card as well. Ophelia had encouraged me to get one so it would be easier to make transactions without extra fees, so I was all set. Everything was ticked off the list. The only thing left was to actually touch Austrian soil.

With our stomachs full, I proceeded to wash up the dishes with the help of my sister. I had bought a pack of strawberries earlier and dipped them in chocolate to which they were probably set now in the fridge. I needed something sweet.

Everything was finally tidied and put away, so I joined my parents back in the lounge to watch some TV. Kiya had started to fall asleep next to me and her head drooped until it was resting on my shoulder. The two of us had always remained close, sharing our secrets with one another and whenever our brothers had annoyed us, we teamed up together to get back at them.

"We shall head home now. You need you to rest, Ali," Mum said, pressing a kiss on my forehead. Dad followed suit, once again reminding me that I would be going on an adventure and that there was nothing to fear.

I needed to remind myself of his words before going to bed tonight. As soon as our parents left, Kiya had woken up and was keen to have a movie night with pear flavoured popcorn drizzled in chocolate.

"Right, little one. I'm off to bed," I told her after we finished the movie.

"Alright, didi, night," Kiya said, letting out a small yawn. She pulled the blanket closer around her and rested her head on a cushion. I pressed a kiss to her forehead as she muttered something incoherent.

I went back to my room and started to get ready for bed. My suitcase was tucked away in the corner, along with my backpack. The good thing about the chalet was that we could wash our own clothes and not have to worry about a huge pile up over the two weeks.

Much to my disdain, I received a text from my ex and I sighed, unlocking my phone to see what the idiot wanted. My heart had already started to race and I needed to remind myself that I was in control, that this man had no hold over me anymore.

> **Caden:** I heard you were going to Austria, good job. I still think about you.

I wondered how the fuck he had found out and by who too. Most likely, someone at work.

I grimaced at his words but decided it was perfectly okay to ignore him. Better yet, delete his damn number. It was time. I needed to leave the memories of the past behind and focus on what was ahead of me.

***

I hadn't managed to get much sleep during the night but as soon as my alarm went off, I'd shot up out of bed and made a beeline for the bathroom. The bags were evident under my eyes but there was not much to be done about that. There wasn't anyone to impress anyway. Kiya was asleep on the sofa, which was actually a sofa bed now, and Chou was curled up next to her. I smiled at the adorable sight and made sure to be extra quiet, tiptoeing back to the bathroom to finish my routine.

I brushed my teeth after taking a quick shower, then checked the time. I'd take a taxi to the airport, the journey would be about forty-five minutes if traffic was good. I'd made sure to pre-book it and would claim this back on the expenses form with work later. Grayson wanted to ensure I didn't spend a fortune on transport but if I had to, he would cover it. He was a good boss who cared about his employees. I was quite happy at my job and also glad he could see something in me, to ask me to write a lengthy article was a sign that he appreciated my work so far. I wouldn't let him or the company down. I certainly didn't want to let Ophelia down and I owed her a lot, since she was coming along to support me.

"Bye apartment. Bye, Chou and Kiya," I said quietly as I pulled the front door closed. I had bundled myself up in warm clothing, a red bobble hat on my head as well as a thick beige scarf. Colour coordination was out the window but I didn't care. I wanted to be ready for the cold weather. The taxi was already waiting for me when I got outside and the driver helped me with my luggage, placing it in the car boot.

Time sped by in a blur and I couldn't get rid of the jittering nerves, no matter what song I listened to with my headphones. They also didn't disappear when I met Ophelia inside the airport and we were due to check in.

"You need some good sleep later. " Ophelia scanned my face. She looked fresh and alert, the complete opposite of me. She handed me a cup of coffee, with a sympathetic look. *Thank you Ophelia. Thank you coffee beans.* It tasted amazing and I almost shivered as the hot liquid ran down my throat.

"Yeah, you're right. I kept overthinking last night." I licked my lips, otherwise the sugar would stick to them. I tried to focus on my breathing but I couldn't ignore the anxiety I was feeling right now.

You'll be alright.

"I can tell. But don't worry, you've got me." Ophelia was bouncing on the balls of her feet and we set off to check in, which was the easy part. The treacherous part was going through security, as it would take an age and even if you were sure you wouldn't set the alarm off, sometimes you would. I wasn't wearing anything with metal anyway, as far as I was aware.

Thankfully, it didn't take more than fifteen minutes and we were now waiting at gate two for boarding.

"I just want to be there already." Ophelia paced back and forth, clearly very impatient. I was in my zen mode, blanking out everyone around us.

"Not long, Lia," I said to her, before finally we were called to board. She linked her arm through mine, sensing that I definitely needed someone to lean on right now. The next few hours sped quicker than expected and it wasn't long before we were in Austria, surrounded by snowy mountains. It looked picturesque, and I knew my family would be jealous.

"First photo in Austria." Ophelia took a photo of us as we entered the terminal, to which I couldn't manage to protest. I let it slide as I needed to let myself loose now that I was in a different country. After picking up our luggage, we were on our way to Ischgl. Our home for the next two weeks.

Chapter 5

Alisha

The chalet was absolutely stunning, it had four bedrooms in total but luckily, Ophelia and I were the only two who had booked. It probably would have been weird sharing the place with strangers. Although, Ophelia wouldn't have minded. She loved talking and meeting with different people.

The two of us stared at the place in awe, this was going to be all ours. It was adorable. There were small steps leading up to the oak door which had a Christmas wreath attached. Multicoloured lights decorated the porch, slowly changing colour every five seconds and I could see in the back that there was a hot tub. We turned to look at each other with a grin. I knew exactly what she was thinking.

"We're going to have a party tonight." She winked at me.

By party, I didn't know if she meant just us. I'd hope so, since we hadn't met anyone yet, apart from the chalet owner who handed us the keys and gave us instructions as to how to turn the heating on, to where the local supermarket was and the best restaurants to eat in. We were now unpacking in our respective rooms and I took a moment to admire the natural decor. I appreciated the pine walls and the smell of jasmine. I had my own wardrobe and chest of drawers, plenty of space. *Perfect.* I would message Grayson later to thank him since he must have stuck his neck out to pay for this. I needed to make sure I wrote the most eye-grabbing and interesting article to date for Culture Horizon.

I had changed into some comfier clothes and placed on my slippers as my toes were a little cold. Ophelia decided to take a small nap but knowing her, she could sleep for hours. I'd packed some tea bags from England as well as my favourite mug so I could make some tea. There was some milk provided by the owner as well as sugar and biscuits. As the kettle was brewing, I walked into the lounge area, which felt very homely.

I could hear Ophelia's light snoring from the next room, and the kettle stopped brewing. After my cup of tea, I'd head to the supermarket and buy us some food as it was getting close to dinner time. I also wanted to explore the area more and take some photos of the mountains in the background.

I made a list on my phone of what we needed and gently rapped my knuckles on Ophelia's door to check if she was awake. *Nope, no answer.*

I knew what kind of snacks she wanted anyway so I would treat her as a thank you for coming on this trip. I'd also buy her a very nice bottle of wine.

Making my way to the shop was a short walk, the large rectangular sign was clear to see as I got closer. On my list were cheese, ham, bread, more milk and eggs, crisps and many other goodies to keep us going. As I entered the shop and grabbed a basket, my phone started to ring and took it out of my pocket to see Zane was calling.

"All okay?" he asked as I said hi.

"Yep. Just shopping right now," I replied, reaching to grab a packet of cheddar cheese.

"Oh, I bet the options are great out there. Bring me back some bratwurst if you can," Zane said. We spoke some more as I sauntered around the aisles, grabbing the things I needed. I'd selected a few snacks as well as several meals I could make. I'd also eyed up the selection of cheeses and couldn't help but put a few in my basket. Melted cheese on toast sounded delicious, it was one of my comfort foods.

My basket was full by the time I reached the check-out and I paid with my card. My stomach was rumbling and I hurried home, strange that I called it that, but nonetheless it was for the next two weeks. Ophelia was now awake as I entered through the door and she had changed into some comfortable clothes, a pink jumper with a pair of grey leggings and slipper boots. She looked right at home.

"Oh, you went shopping? You should have woken me." She eyed up the bags which I placed on the kitchen table.

"Don't worry. You needed your sleep. Tea?" I asked her and she nodded quite vigorously. With the shopping packed away, tea made and heating on, we settled on the sofa and switched on the TV to see what was on. Of course, the channels were in German and I didn't understand a word. Luckily, I had brought my laptop and there was a HDMI cable to plug in.

"Stick on a film. I'll start making us food," I said, grabbing my half empty mug of tea. I was going to make us a carbonara tonight with sausage instead of the pancetta I'd normally use.

"Are you all set for your lesson tomorrow?" Ophelia called out, finally having chosen a film. She'd selected *Easy A*, one of our favourites. Emma Stone was a gift to the acting world. I loved her versatility.

"I think so. It's at ten o'clock and takes about an hour and a half. " I hadn't thought about it much until just now. I'd already researched my ski instructor who was a woman named Hilde, she'd been working at the ski school for nearly five years. So she was very good and highly rated.

"You'll be ace. You'll make me so proud. Maybe when you have your last lesson, we can ski together," Ophelia said, and hopefully I would be confident enough to do so. I felt a little more ambition than I had back in England. Something about being in a different setting was encouraging and all I needed to do was remind myself that I was in control when skiing. Nothing terrible could happen to me. I reminded myself of that as my head hit the pillow after our evening of spaghetti, chocolate mousse and white wine. Our 'party' had ended as soon as it started as Ophelia was more exhausted than she thought.

"You can do this, Ali," I spoke to no one but myself as I closed my eyes and willed myself to sleep. *You can.*

***

The next morning rolled around and I was on my way to pick up my ski boots, poles and everything I needed before getting the cable car up to the ski school. Ophelia had joined me and wanted to ensure I was okay. She'd helped me put on the boots which were a maze at first with the multiple buckles. They felt very strange when I started to walk in them, almost as if I was waddling along like a penguin. I knew Kiya would laugh at the sight of this and Ophelia took a photo, as this was one of my many firsts of our holiday.

I couldn't stop my legs from jiggling as we were going up the wire, higher and higher. On the next stop, a friendly American had joined us and greeted us warmly. He had a Missouri accent by the sounds of it.

"Beautiful, isn't it?" He gazed at the scenery and Ophelia nodded. I couldn't say anything but smile as I was feeling extremely nervous.

Pull yourself together, Ali.

"Absolutely. This one here is skiing for the first time." Ophelia jutted her head in my direction and the man raised his eyebrows.

"Well, I can tell you that you'll have a lot of fun. I've been skiing for many years now. It is the most fun you can have with your clothes still on." As soon as he said this, Ophelia let out a throaty laugh, whereas I let out a more nervous one.

"Right on," my friend agreed.

I hoped he was right. Not that I had done any kind of sporting activity naked before.

After some more talking, mostly between Ophelia and the unnamed man, we finally reached our stop.

"Well, I hope you enjoy your lesson," the man said, giving us a nod before departing. We grabbed our skis and poles, walking over carefully to where the school was. It wasn't too busy and I was glad I had booked at the right time, as I was sure by lunchtime it would be swarming.

Ophelia made sure I got to the school safely and waited as I met my instructor. Hilde was a tall, blonde woman with kind, blue eyes. She exerted confidence and assertiveness but I could tell we would get along.

"Very nice to meet you," she said to me, shaking my hand. She had a soft tone to her voice as she spoke.

"You too," I said nervously.

"Right. Well, I'll meet you back here for lunch?" Ophelia pulled me in for a hug.

"Just remember, you are *that* bitch okay? I believe in you," she finished.

"I am that bitch," I replied, letting out a giggle and Ophelia joined, her melodic laughter filling the silence.

"See you later." I waved as her silhouette started to disappear. I wished I could be as good as her by the end of the trip.

"Right. So we'll walk down to the slope we are learning on. I'll hold your skis for you," Hilde said, reaching out to take them from me.

"Thank you," I said sheepishly, wishing I could say more. She stayed by my side as we walked further down until we reached the training slope.

"So first, we'll get you standing on your skis and then by the end of lesson today, hopefully we'll get you skiing down and into a plough," Hilde said, placing her hands on her hips. It didn't sound so bad and I was comforted by the fact that there were other adult learners around. I inhaled and exhaled, trying to convince myself that everything would be fine. I would conquer this.

As I got more comfortable in the lesson, I was unaware of the time until Hilde said we were now finishing. I'd learned more about her. She had said her partner also worked here and they had met about two years ago. She was twenty-three and he was twenty-four. I'd realised she was the type of person to hype you up as every ten minutes she'd cheer me on.

To my delight, I had managed to ski plough a few times with success and maintain a good speed going down the slope. It actually felt quite thrilling, and also exhausting. My limbs were burning and I definitely couldn't wait to sit down and have a bite to eat. The boots were starting to hurt my feet but I knew I just needed to get used to them.

Ophelia was waiting for me as she had promised, with a proud grin on her face.

"I was watching you for the last five minutes. Look at you!" She beamed and then turned to Hilde to thank her.

"Well, you girls have a nice lunch. See you tomorrow, Alisha. Well done." Hilde gently squeezed my shoulder. I thanked her and said goodbye before Ophelia and I set off to the nearby restaurant.

"Right. Food time." Ophelia clasped her hands together as we entered inside. We had placed our skis on the racks outside. There was a variety of delicious food: schnitzel and fries, spaghetti bolognese, bratwurst, steaks and salad. I had opted for the bratwurst with a bowl of chips.

"Can't wait to tuck into all this." Ophelia piled her tray with savoury and sweet dishes. I also grabbed a plate of cheesecake since it looked so good. We paid and found a table for two, luckily.

As we sat down, Ophelia went through the plan for the rest of the day.

"I was thinking of skiing for another hour or so. I'm loving being in the mountains again. Are you going to head back?"

"Yeah, you don't mind do you? I've got some inspiration for writing," I said, knowing that I needed to type what I had experienced. Writing itself was a creative process and I knew there'd be lots of changes I'd make, but ultimately, I wanted an article that I was proud of.

"Of course. That's what you are here for. But also, don't forget to have some fun," she said, placing a fry in her mouth.

"I know. I've been pleasantly surprised today," I said with a smile and proceeded to finish my lunch. The flavours were amazing and the cheesecake was creamily good. It seemed to melt on my mouth every time I took a bite.

We let our stomachs settle before getting up to grab our skis.

"Text me when you get back," Ophelia said, pulling her goggles down over her eyes. It was starting to get sunnier here and much busier.

"Will do. Have fun," I said, giving her a hug. I watched as she skied away with ease, looking like a gliding angel. As I turned around to head to the cable car, I hadn't realised that someone was approaching behind me. Or let's say, skiing. Before I could even attempt to move, we crashed into one another and I let out a small squeal. The other person let out a grunt and I could hear them hit the ground just as I did. Luckily the snow was soft and I fell on my ass, rather than my front.

"Verdammt, schau mal, wo du hingehst!" a deep, rumbling and slightly angry voice boomed. It was a thick German accent too. I almost jumped out of my skin and tilted my head to gaze in their direction.

"Umm," was all I could reply with and I squinted to get a better look. I was met with a fury-infused glare, hazel eyes met my own brown ones. He was attractive as I continued to scan him.

Stubble peppered his chin and upper lip which had turned into a scowl. He had short, auburn hair from what I could see under his helmet. He was well-built and seemed like he was tall. He validated this by brushing the snow off his trousers and standing up before placing his hands on his hips, shaking his head slightly. The next thing I noticed were his hands, how calloused they were and muscular. I realised I was still on the ground and stood up, dusting my hands on my legs. The man continued to speak with annoyance to his tone, trying to work out what language I spoke.

"Êtes-vous française?" To which I shook my head. I understood a bit of French but not enough to hold a conversation. I didn't know what to say to him. For some reason, the words couldn't escape my lips. I felt like an idiot as my mouth was gaping open slightly and this only made him more frustrated. He let out a groan before speaking again. I really didn't like this man's attitude, even if he was *this* gorgeous.

"English then?"

"Yeah. Sorry I bumped into you," I said and I meant it. I hadn't meant to hurt him and I cursed myself for my clumsiness. I couldn't quite meet his gaze which felt as though it was burning me. I just wished he would stop glaring. Something was stuck up his ass and there was no need to be rude.

"Just be careful. Always be aware of your surroundings on the mountains," he said and before I could utter a reply, he was gone in a flash.

How strange.

I shrugged and continued trudging my way to the cable car, wondering what the heck had just happened, and who that man was.

Chapter 6

Alisha

I was still replaying the event in my mind as I returned to the chalet. I'd left my ski gear in the locker we'd rented out. I was now rather annoyed at the grumpy man I had bumped into. I sighed, shaking the thoughts away and grabbing my laptop to start writing.

I've never been able to step outside of my comfort zone but there's this saying that life is too short, was all I managed to type after some time had passed. Life was too short, yes, but how was I going to attract my readers with something as cheesy as this?

I sighed in frustration as I had sat here now for almost thirty minutes, and nothing was coming to fruition. Thirty minutes turned into an hour and then before I knew it, Ophelia was back and hanging her trousers up to dry.

"Holy moly, it's cold. Cold enough to make ice cream." Ophelia had her arms crisscrossed as she shivered.

"I could eat some ice cream." I chuckled before turning my attention back to my laptop and squinting my eyes at what I'd written.

"Huh, interesting. Is that all you could write?" she questioned as she approached me, taking a peek at my laptop screen. She raised a quizzical brow as she observed.

"Nothing seems to be working in my brain." I shrugged and Ophelia nodded because she understood how it was. Up until last month, she had been staying on at work until late in the evening hoping that she'd get some tasks done.

"Fancy going for a drink this evening?" I suggested, shutting my laptop lid. I needed to get out of the chalet and socialise.

"I'll never say no to a beer and good company," Ophelia grinned before continuing, "you seem different here."

"It's the alpine air," I said, winking at her for effect.

"Give me two or three hours of nap time, then we can go." She let out a yawn.

"Sure. Just shout me if you need anything," I said. I felt like I needed a nap too so went back to my room. My body still felt a bit achy, and after looking at my laptop screen for a while, my head was starting to ache. Sleep came quickly as I tucked myself into bed. I didn't want them to but hazel eyes flashed through my mind as I drifted off.

***

I stretched out in bed and felt well-rested after a few hours of sleep. It was now dark outside and I could see there was light snow falling. I could hear Ophelia singing in her room next to mine and pulled the covers off of me to get ready. I needed a touch of make-up and something needed to be done with my bird's nest of hair. I ditched the T-shirt I was wearing for a cute knit jumper paired with skinny jeans. We weren't going to be walking far, just into town for a few drinks.

I added kohl eyeliner to my eyes, and swept my hair up into a high ponytail to show off my neck. Much better. Ophelia wolf whistled as I met her in the kitchen and she looked pretty good herself. She was wearing a pair of dark brown flares and a sparkling, black top with a cream cardigan. Her colourful hair was straightened even more than it usually was.

"Let's go and mingle." She hooked her arm through mine, grabbing the chalet keys and her purse on our way out. We located a small, friendly bar which seemed less busy than the others nearby. From seven o'clock onwards in Ischgl, most bars would turn into nightclubs, but that wasn't our idea of fun tonight. We just wanted a casual drink together.

The bar was cosy and warm, and also served food which was great since we hadn't eaten yet. We sat down in a booth and looked at the drinks and food menus. Pizza seemed to be the only food that called to me right now.

"I'll order the drinks. Malibu and coke for you?" Ophelia asked, hand resting on one hip.

"Yep, just a single shot please," I told her and watched as she disappeared to order.

As I drummed my fingers on the table, I scanned my eyes across the room until I did a double take. The grumpy man I had bumped into earlier was sitting in a booth opposite, frowning at the people around him.

Why was he here then if he was just going to scowl at people? The worst setting to be in if he wasn't a people person. I hadn't realised I'd been staring at him until my friend reappeared.

"Here you go, Ali." Ophelia placed our drinks on the table and I grabbed mine instantly, guzzling it down quickly.

"Woah, slow down horsey." Ophelia laughed, but was impressed.

"I'll get another," I said, offering to get her one too but she shook her head, tapping to her full glass of vodka and lemonade. I made my way to the bar, acknowledging the assistant with the name tag Jakob. I felt a sudden wave of confidence now that alcohol was in my system.

"One malibu and coke, please. Single shot," I asked politely, then waited as my drink was being made. It had to be one of the best I'd ever tasted, the perfect amount of malibu and fizz mixed together. I hadn't noticed a tall figure was now approaching the bar and I almost choked on my drink when I noticed who it was. I remained glued in my position and mentally cursed because I *really* didn't want to acknowledge him.

"Felix!" the bar assistant greeted him. They started speaking in German and although I had no clue what was being said, I still hadn't fucking moved. Felix was a nice name, but it reminded me of the cat food brand and now, it was all I could picture. Maybe I could gracefully exit and he wouldn't notice me. Until Ophelia decided to call my name.

"Alisha. Hurry up, woman!" she exclaimed, waving a hand in the air. I cursed under my breath because now the *grumpy man* knew my name, and he was looking at me.

His eyes darted from my legs up to my eyes as if he was analysing every part of me and then making his mind up about whether he wanted to associate with me or not. I felt bare under his gaze and I hadn't noticed before, but his eyelashes were long. He looked quite pretty.

"I-I'm coming!" I called back to her, averting the situation I found myself in and his watchful eyes. He still had that same pained expression and I wondered what had made him so upset. He hadn't even said a word to me whilst I was standing there. *Oh well.*

I took my seat in front of Ophelia and decided not to get up again for some time. I focused my attention on my friend, who was excitedly talking about her cousin who just announced she was pregnant. Ophelia loved children and wanted at least five of her own one day if she found the right one. When I was with Caden, I thought that was it. We had discussed the idea of a family but it seemed more what I wanted rather than him. *Definitely need to stop thinking about him.*

"So, are you feeling less nervous now for tomorrow's lesson?" Ophelia queried, bringing her glass to her lips. She was being smart with her drink, taking it easy whereas I was guzzling my second drink like no tomorrow.

"I think so. I feel a little braver than before," I spoke boldly because the truth was, I felt more courage than usual.

"Well, cheers to us." Our glasses clinked together and after another round of drinks, we both were tipsy and laughing over the music. I now needed something stronger so I was the one to buy the next lot. Mr Grumpy was still standing by the bar, looking as if he didn't want to be here. Until a female tugged at his arm and asked him if he was alright.

I edged a little closer, totally not eavesdropping but something about him piqued my curiosity.

The pretty brunette seemed to be trying to convince him to do something and then I realised how alike they looked, with the same hazel eyes and perfectly shaped jawline. As she kept talking and growing more frustrated by the minute, he turned his body around so that he was now facing me. There was about ten centimetres between us but it felt as though it had shortened when his eyes burned into mine. *If looks could kill...*

"Hm," was all he said, as his sister sighed and gave up trying to convince him. I really did feel for her. I averted my gaze from his, and ordered two more drinks for myself and Ophelia.

"You gave me a bruise," a brooding voice spoke and almost jolted me out of my skin.

"Where?" I couldn't see one anywhere and I didn't think I'd bumped into him that hard earlier. Now he was just whining.

"Never mind. It's not that bad," Felix said, he looked as though he was having an internal battle with himself.

"It must be if you felt you had to bring it up. Not really a conversation starter, are you?" I hadn't realised how snide I'd sounded but I loved it. Blame the alcohol. But blame my brutal honesty.

"Sorry. I'm not really...good at talking to people." He hesitated and then looked down at his beer, frowning at it.

Did anything make this man smile? I bet he had a nice smile too.

"Neither am I," I replied, which was the truth. I was often a socially awkward mess which was surprising since I worked in journalism. You'd think I'd naturally be a conversationalist but nope, not at all. Often in social situations, I had to focus on my breathing. But right now, I felt somehow at peace. *Weird.*

"Guess that makes us even." Felix cracked a slight smile and this seemed to tug at my heart strings a little.

"Tell me. What's gotten you so upset?" I blurted the question out before I could stop myself. This caused him to frown again and my stomach did a somersault.

"I didn't come here to talk about that. So, what are you doing here so far from home?" Ah, he was getting better at this now. Less awkward, more human. He was facing me even more now, and I noticed he was wearing a dark green T-shirt with jeans and boots. He was muscular in the arms too and maybe he went to the gym.

"I'm here to write an article, just for two weeks," I said, maybe admitting a bit too much about myself. I should ask more about him.

"Well, there's a lot to love about Ischgl. And Austria in general. I was born here. I've never been anywhere else." This surprised me, he sounded more like an introvert than I was.

"I'm also having ski lessons. My boss wanted me to get the full experience," I said before realising that I needed to return to my friend who I had abandoned yet again.

"I should go. My friend over there is probably wondering where I am." I felt shy and didn't want to have to excuse myself. I almost wanted to stay...

"Okay," was all Felix said and I nodded, the tension was now awkward again. Without hesitation or looking back, I returned to Ophelia who did not look impressed.

"Who have you been talking to and what is his name?" she demanded and I started to tell her about the conversation I had with Felix and how mysterious he was. Maybe I wanted to know more about him if I could.

Chapter 7

Felix

I hated bars and never saw the appeal of them. But for my sister Mira, I had decided to tag along. I wanted to let loose, I really did but everything reminded me of my ex-fiancé, Evie. Sadly, the wedding had been called off as she had suddenly gotten cold feet, literally at the altar. So that was one of the reasons why I hated the world and didn't want to enter into another relationship again. *Trust nobody*, I reminded myself. Only yourself, and maybe my family. I, Felix Bauer, would never fall in love again, I'd swear on it.

Mira was my sweet, twenty-four-year-old sister who looked up to me. There was a three year difference between us. We only had each other growing up as we ended up in care. Our upbringing hadn't been the best and eventually, our aunt Brenna had stepped in to look after us. We hadn't even known about her until our birth mother had mentioned her one day. A sad memory flickered in my mind which I couldn't get rid of.

"When's Mum coming home? It's been hours." Mira said, her eyes wide as we waited at the front door.

"I don't know, Mira. But it's okay, you've got me." I held my sister close to me, her petite, fragile frame pressed against me. Her tiny hands were cold and she was shaking. So was I.

I'd tried to protect her over the years but things had changed. The role was flipped now and it seemed Mira was looking after me more than I was of her.

I took another glance at my sad glass of beer and tried to focus on something else or someone else. The girl that crashed into me earlier was laughing at something her friend said, clearly quite drunk now. I thought back to our conversation, or whatever it was. It had been awkward. I decided to get a better look at her. There was no denying she was attractive, dark eyes with a matching complexion and long brown hair that fell against her back. I glanced at her figure as she stood up and couldn't help but eye up her curves and how her legs were so toned.

She'd said she was here to write an article but didn't specify the details or even tell me much about herself. Not that I cared. I had sworn off women completely. I did find this girl attractive though, I mean who wouldn't? I remembered that her name was Alisha and her soft, British accent. I liked the way her voice sounded. Very calming. I needed calm in my life but everything had been a shit storm lately.

"Do you want a different drink?" Mira pulled me out of my thoughts. I didn't want to ignore her since she'd done so much for me.

"No, it's okay thanks," I grumbled, finishing what was in my glass. Mira sighed and I didn't blame her, she'd been trying her best to get me out of the pit hole I'd fallen into.

"Actually, I'll have another." I changed my mind and gave Mira a small smile for extra measure. She looked pleased and ordered us both some vodka, lemon and lime.

With nothing really better to do, I kept on people watching. There were quite a lot of couples here, looking to enjoy their upcoming weekend. Luckily, I wasn't working this weekend. I worked as a travel agent, which was starting to become a little dull. I was close to handing in my notice, having worked there for nearly six years now. My aunt had always reminded me that I was destined for great things and never to limit myself in a job that doesn't make me happy. Maybe I needed to listen to her more.

"Felixxx," Mira drawled, hoping to spring me out of my state of misery. Hey, I never used to be like this. Despite my rough start in life, I'd been the optimistic one. I remembered when I was seven years old, how Mira and I had teamed up one school morning and set off on a hunt for our dad. Of course, we didn't make it past the school gates as we reached them and we had a stern lecture from the principal about how we shouldn't skive. We had explained that we were going to find our dad but the principal didn't believe us.

Well, that was the past, and I was a different person now—more fucked up than I had been. The vodka tasted strong on my taste buds but it was better than the beer. I downed it in one go and then asked for another, wanting to feel a sense of euphoria even if it would be temporary.

"Sorry Mira. I don't mean to be like this." I sighed.

"You're human. You're still hurting. I get it. But I do think it's time to move on. Forget about her," Mira said, and her words made sense, as hard as it would be to acknowledge them.

"I really want to," I replied, my voice sounding more convincing than usual. I didn't want to ruin Mira's evening with my constant complaining so I shut up for now.

Once more, I glanced in Alisha's direction and noticed the crinkles that would appear around her eyes as she smiled. Her friend seemed more extroverted, with purple streaks in her hair and green eyes. They were clearly close and comfortable with one another as they laughed every so often at whatever was said.

Why did I even care?

By the time the clock turned ten thirty, I knew I needed to get going. Mira also needed to as well since she had a seven o'clock start tomorrow morning.

"Well, I am glad you came out," she said, finishing her drink. I looked at my sister, and felt grateful for her presence. I also knew how tired she was, since she worked crazy hours in a hospital but still managed to find the time to spend with me. Her heartbroken brother.

"Well, I hate seeing the same four walls when I'm at home," I admitted. I lived in a small house with two bedrooms. Well, in fact it was the house that I lived in with my ex-fiancé. It had been gifted to me by my aunt, who was stinking rich and wanted the best for her nephew. I owed her so much for that.

"I can't believe you haven't sold the place. I would," Mira said, raising one eyebrow. She was right. I could sell it and repay my aunt. Or do something useful with my life. I loved Austria, always would but maybe one day I'd be brave enough to go to another country. I just needed that motivation.

My attention was diverted once again, to see Alisha who was now getting ready to leave herself, tugging on her jacket. She must have noticed I was staring as she glanced in my direction and had only managed to put one arm through her sleeve. I quickly turned my head and focused on my sister, who was tracing her finger around the rim of her glass.

"Come on Mir, let's go." I turned to my sister, pulling on my own jacket with a scarf and beanie.

"Ready," my sister replied, grabbing a hold of my arm. We crossed paths with Alisha and her friend, and both our eyes locked on one another's for a mere moment. It was enough to knock the wind out of me but I kept steady on my feet.

As I passed her, I caught her scent. A mixture of jasmine and pine. Even when Mira and I were now walking outside, I could still smell her. And those damn eyes. They wouldn't leave my head.

Mira had decided to stay the night, which was right, as I wouldn't let her go home by herself anyway. I made up the spare room for her, and we shared mugs of hot chocolate and cream before bed. As I was now settling down, wrapped up like a burrito in bed, I scrolled through my phone. I didn't pay attention to short-form content, I never did.

Nothing interesting was showing up on Google, so I placed my phone on charge and told myself to go to sleep.

As I drifted off, it seemed as though I had no control over my mind anymore as images of the mysterious girl flashed one after the other. The way she laughed as she chatted with her friend. The way her jeans hugged her legs. The way she smelt. When we had walked past each other and how instantly our eyes had met. And the way that whatever had happened, I felt compelled to cross paths with her again. I knew I would anyway as this was a small resort. I didn't necessarily need to be her friend but perhaps if I spoke to her once more, I'd stop thinking about her. I would need to work on my conversation skills though.

I stroked the bruise she had given me when she bumped into me, which was located on my arm. It wasn't huge but enough to signify she had somehow caused an impact, both physically and most likely mentally.

Chapter 8

Alisha

I was surprised I managed to wake up today, but I was determined to continue making progress with my skiing. I had even stomached a bacon roll this morning with a cup of coffee. Hilde was now teaching me how to ski from higher up, straight down into a plough position. The boots didn't feel as painful as yesterday, which was a good sign I was getting more comfortable with the whole charade. There was also a shift in my overall mood. I felt a bit more optimistic, and hopefully, I'd get some work done today too.

As the lesson went on, Hilde pushed me further to the limit with gentle encouragement.

"That's it, keep leaning forward," Hilde said, which was something I initially found difficult.

"I feel my limbs burning!" I called out.

"You'll feel less of a burn tomorrow," Hilde replied.

By the end of the lesson, we had done several trips up the ski lift and then skied downward into a plough. Tomorrow, I would be working on turning left and right, which was the bit I was scared about.

I learnt more about Hilde, who was hoping to go to university and become a teacher of PE. This sounded great and she definitely had the knack and patience for it. I once considered becoming a teacher, but then standing up in front of kids, trying to manage their behaviour as well as dealing with my own mental health would be a real task. I was glad I hadn't gone down that path, and I was doing something I loved. Not a lot of people could feel this way.

Ophelia and I had met up for lunch again, this time trying something new. The schnitzel looked pretty good, and we were given a generous helping of french fries. As I sipped my coffee, I noticed someone familiar sitting down a few tables opposite us. I squinted, no idea why as I had near-perfect vision, and realised it was Mr Grumpy No Smiles aka Felix. He was sipping what looked like coffee or it could have been hot chocolate. I didn't really think he was a caffeine person but here he was, sipping away and watching people walk by. He had a rigid frame as he sat, almost like he was zoned out until his eyes met mine. I couldn't ignore the somersault my stomach did as he blinked a couple of times at me.

Ophelia clocked on and cleared her throat, bringing me to my senses. I had to stop looking at his eyes, which were so beautiful.

"I recognise him. He was at the bar yesterday, right?" Ophelia spoke calmly, placing her knife and fork on her empty plate. I wasn't quite finished with my own food yet, so I continued to eat the rest of my fries.

"Oh, yes," I said nonchalantly.

Must not give away that I am slightly attracted to him but don't even know him.

"He looks like he recognises you too. And I've gotta say he's very good looking. Feeling brave enough to go and talk to him?" she asked me rather excitedly.

Ophelia liked to think of herself as a matchmaker and suggested that I try dating apps. I absolutely hated them and if I were to meet anyone again, they'd have to be in person and on my wavelength. I thought Caden had been but clearly not. We were not compatible at all really, now looking at it from a new perspective. We were like oil and water. We just didn't go together.

"Nah, don't think so. I'm here on holiday with you. We've gotta work too. No time for chatting up men." I didn't want to sound curt but I wanted to be truthful with her. I hoped she would move on.

"I'll go get us some dessert," Ophelia offered. I was glad she changed the topic. I was fiddling with the napkin I hadn't used, anything to keep my eyes from deceiving me and meeting *his* gaze. I was expecting to be uncomfortable as I felt his burning stare, almost as if it was scorching my skin. *Don't look up.*

Too late. Another jolt of electricity shot through me as I started to admire his face, the way his Adam's apple moved and the intensity of his stare. He would be even more handsome if he smiled. I wondered what he was thinking and now started to wish he would come over and talk to me. We could have a staring competition at this rate.

But after what seemed like a lifetime, he got up from his seat and walked over to me. His steps were slow, no real sense of urgency but obviously something had connected in his brain to bring himself to my table.

"H-hi," Felix said, and it was easy to tell he was nervous. I found this adorable and tried not to blush.

"Hi there," I replied, trying to sound calm and collected. Trying to ignore the way his thumb kept twitching but it was very fascinating. His body language screamed *get away* but he stood still, rigid and blank faced.

Riiiight. Can we make this any less awkward?

"Um, how was your skiing? Are you improving?" Felix asked. This was good. He was working on his conversation skills. Maybe I could see what he's all about.

"Yes, Hilde is a great instructor," I said blankly.

"Oh, yeah. My sister Mira is friends with her." Felix scratched the nape of his neck. I had thought they were related as they looked similar.

"Oh cool." *Now what to say next?* I hoped he would keep asking the questions as I was sitting here starstruck.

"Did you like the schnitzel?" Felix continued, he seemed less like a stone now and relaxed his shoulders. I always thought posture would change the way a person was perceived. My parents always told me to sit up straight and never slouch, always have your body turned to the person who is talking, show you're interested. I tried to listen to this advice now and leaned forward, so that I was slightly peering up at Felix.

Ophelia was taking a damn long time.

"Yes. It was tasty. I like the drinks here too." I started chewing my bottom lip which was already starting to chap due to the cold weather.

"You should try one of the apres-ski. If you like beer and any kind of alcohol." As he said this, I remembered how tipsy I had been last night.

"Well, if you have any recommendations."

"I'd try these three, Kitzloch, Kuhstalle and Fire and Ice," Felix told me. His pronunciation of these words was like velvet.

I'd research at least one of these today with Ophelia and then add to my article. Hopefully today would be more productive.

"And what about dinner?" I queried. Cooking in the chalet was not the plan for every evening and if I really wanted to talk about the real Ischgl in my article, I needed to try different restaurants.

"Here. Take my number and I can tell you the details later." *I was not expecting that.* Within a space of a few minutes, he had gone from cold to hot. Ophelia had been right and she was going to be so happy when she got back. *Wherever she was.*

Felix exchanged his number with me and then I texted him with my name.

"I've got to go. Nice seeing you again." As he said this, he gave me a nod.

"You too." I smiled for good measure and he disappeared as quickly as I started to inhale a deep breath.

"What the fuck?" I heard a frantic voice and a few people around us looked up from their lunches, some of them frowning and staring in awe at the person. The person being Ophelia, who was now hurrying toward me with a tray of cake and tea.

"Sit down. I'll tell you," I said, and she did, slamming the tray day with force. *Yikes.* She apparently had been watching and had heard the whole conversation.

"I didn't want to interrupt you both. But my intuition was right." Ophelia smirked.

"You must be psychic." I giggled, lifting my fork to take a bit of cake. Ophelia had picked out red velvet for me and chocolate for her.

"I didn't think he had the balls to speak to you. But I've been proved wrong." Ophelia plunged her fork into her chocolate fudge cake. *I had been too.*

"We should try one of the apres-ski he mentioned," I suggested. *Partly, I was hoping if we did, that I'd see him at one of them.*

"Hell yeah! I'm one hundred percent down for a nice beer in the sun. What more could I ask for with my best friend?" She smiled at me and she was right, it was a good idea. I started to realise how exciting this holiday was going to be and the possibilities of promotion that could come my way.

"You're so right. I think it's time I enjoyed myself," I said, and this time, I meant it.

Chapter 9

Felix

I couldn't believe I'd just done that. Something had come over me all of a sudden. It's why I had to escape so quickly, so I could process the line I just crossed.

Fuck, fuck, fuck.

Yes, I wanted her number, but now that meant she'd be expecting a text from me. I couldn't be a douche and not send anything to her. I just had to think how to word it and when exactly to send it.

I didn't want to but all of last night, I had thought of her after our meeting in the bar. I *liked* the way she had dimples when she smiled and I admired the way her brown hair shone. I wondered what shampoo she used as it looked soft and silky. I'd prayed I wouldn't see her today, partly because I knew I'd crumble in front of her, but life has a funny way of shoving things in front of you. I decided to go for a ski today to let loose and feel that familiar rush of adrenaline.

When I'd stopped for lunch, I had spotted Alisha, almost as if I was seeking her out and it then became hard to ignore her presence. I knew she had felt my gaze on her as her eyes had met mine. I felt like my stomach had backflipped and frontflipped all in one go. When I had finally plucked up the courage to go and speak to her, all the nerves came back. But this meeting needed to go better than yesterday's. So when I recommended some places for her to try, that was me being nice. Or trying to be.

When she had sent the first text to me indicating that it was her, I had tried to remain calm and collected in front of her. My phone went straight into my pocket, and I didn't look at it for the next few hours.

Maybe I didn't need to text her. She probably wouldn't care.

At five o'clock, I returned home and needed a long, hot bath to ease my tired muscles and mind. My aunt had called me and asked me to come to lunch tomorrow for our usual roast. I couldn't say no and definitely needed family around me during this difficult time. The bath had helped a little but not enough to block the constant memories of my relationship.

"Fuck this." I sighed and decided I needed something strong in my system. In the kitchen, I pulled out a glass from the cupboard and then some génépi. It was a French herbal liquor which I drank neat. After two more glasses, I started to feel the effect and pulled out my phone. I was feeling even more confident and my thumb hovered over the call button, with my ex's name above it.

No, Felix, you are not doing this.

Thankfully, I still had some control, and I deleted *her* number which was long-awaited. I clicked on the text from Alisha and started typing.

Felix: How was your day?

I didn't think she would reply straight away; probably had better things to do, so I made myself busy by pouring another glass of liquor.

So much fun getting drunk on your own.

My phone lit up when I was halfway through my drink and I almost spat it out when I saw the reply from Alisha.

Alisha: Fine thank you, so what are these restaurants then?

I remembered my initial reason for passing on my number to her and started to type.

Felix: So, I'd try Winkler Pizza, Down Under and Loba if you like ribs. There are some more places in town too or if you want to venture further out, I could take you

As soon as I'd sent this, I internally cringed. *I could take you.*

Alisha: I'm always down for an adventure, let's go somewhere tomorrow evening?

I was surprised she actually took me up on the offer.

Well, you can't back out now, Felix.

Felix: Text me your address and I'll pick you up, does your friend want to come along?

Alisha: Just asked her, she said no as she wants to catch up with her family via FaceTime.

The thought of it just being us two panicked me but also ignited a new feeling within me. Perhaps it could be excitement. She didn't seem repulsed and was genuinely interested in spending time with me, but how could I tell from just a few texts? I almost felt hopeful that I could make a friend and now I was thankful for the alcohol. I almost kissed the near-empty bottle.

"Well, you'd better get your act together," I said to no one in particular and it wasn't long before I got myself to bed for a deep sleep. For the first time in months, I slept soundly and probably because I wanted the next day to come quickly. I wanted to see her.

I didn't know what exactly was happening but I felt drawn to Alisha somehow.

***

After a refreshing sleep, I ate my breakfast which consisted of porridge and bananas with a drizzle of honey. I would be setting off to go and see my aunt within the next two hours and my sister would meet me there.

I was dreading going to work tomorrow and wished weekends would be longer in general. I also had a meeting with my boss too, probably about my work performance, which was pretty average. But in that kind of job, it would be right?

I watched a bit of TV, though nothing interesting was on. The only thing I really enjoyed was Ski Sunday. Christmas wasn't far away and I despised the adverts, especially the romantic, lovey dovey ones. Christmas was supposed to be an exciting time of the year. I knew it would be, since it'd be the first one alone since the breakup. I'd remembered this time last year, I was preparing for the wedding and was at my happiest. Nothing could have ruined my happiness back then.

I decided it was time to pause the pity party and get a move on to my aunt's house. I looked rather presentable, well, I hoped. My brown hair was slightly ruffled and I finally had a shave. As I looked in the car mirror, I noticed how alert my eyes looked. The sleep had definitely helped. My aunt lived in Zurs, which was about twelve miles from here. The radio played quietly in the background as I drove, and I even hummed a little tune, which was a first for me in many months. I knew my two older twin cousins Jakob and Elias would be there, they always came around for Sunday lunch and it was a good time to catch up with them.

I pulled up into the gravel drive, and found a spot next to my sister's ruby red mini cooper, she had a thing for that colour and even her car seats were the same shade. My car was a standard Range Rover, dark blue and comfortable. Nothing too snazzy, and the engine was powerful enough. I switched off the ignition and swung the car door open, instantly meeting the tall silhouette of my aunt. I hadn't noticed she was there and jumped a little.

"Finally!" Aunt Brenna grinned as if she was very happy to see me. She had soft features, long wavy blonde hair, with kind, light blue eyes that never seemed to stop sparkling. I had been so glad she accepted us into her family years ago and she always made an effort for me and my sister.

"Hello, Aunt Brenna." I pressed a kiss on both of her rouge tinted cheeks.

"You look better than the last time I saw you." Aunt Brenna took a pause to scan me and seemed satisfied that I wasn't my usual self. I even cracked her a small smile.

"I got some good sleep last night," I continued the conversation as she led us inside.

"I'm so glad. Well, lunch is almost ready so I hope you're hungry." Aunt Brenna was an amazing cook and I knew that what she'd prepared I'd scarf down.

"Thanks for inviting me over."

"You're always welcome, Felix. You're like a third son to me." She smiled. And over the years, she had been like a mum to me too.

Once inside, the familiar living room greeted me. She'd always had the same two beige sofas, both opposite one another and a wide screen TV was in the back of the room. I questioned her about her room decoration a while back, but she was very keen to keep things as they were. She was rigid about her cleaning, everything had to be stored away. Unused magazines would be recycled, as well as newspapers.

Aunt Brenna liked everything in ship shape, just like her. My uncle? He'd died some time ago, never met him, but from what I'd heard, he was a kind man who looked after his wife well. She missed him, of course, but she had her two sons to lean on when times got rough. And she had me and Mira. We weren't going anywhere, not after all she'd done for us.

"So, what can I help with?" I asked her, walking with her to the kitchen. The tiles on the floor were crystal white, matching the shade of her teeth. The walls were off-white and she had a modern sink installed, as well as a dishwasher, washing machine and tumble dryer. She owned two fridges, one was kept for dairy goods and the other for meats and other food and drink. Aunt Brenna would get frustrated if her sons rearranged things in the fridge, which they had done at times to piss her off.

I could smell what was in the oven, and she had also made two different kinds of potatoes: mashed and roasted. Mira was quite fussy with her food but my aunt was always happy to cater for her.

"If you could take the chicken out, then carve it, that would be great. I'm going to put the other food on the table. I'll call your cousins down. I'm so annoyed that they didn't come down already to say hello," Aunt Brenna huffed, Jakob and Elias were probably playing video games since they were addicts, even at the ripe age of twenty-eight. I supposed my aunt was used to it but she'd had several stern conversations with them to '*get off their asses and do something useful*'.

"Of course," I said, the job I had was easy and I wanted to make things simpler for her if I could. Take the stress off her plate and be a helpful nephew. Even if it was something small, it was showing her my gratitude for looking after my sister and I all these years.

"Get down here now, boys!" Aunt Brenna yelled at the end of the staircase, her voice almost cracking as she did. Very soon, we heard the plop of Jakob and Elias' feet across the floorboards and they made it downstairs within twenty seconds.

"Your cousin is here," my aunt merely stated as she joined me back in the kitchen. My cousins followed behind her, a slight frown mirrored on their faces. They were identical twins, with soft blue eyes, the same shade as their mother and dark brown hair which was from their father's side. The twins were close to one another, we always described them as two peas in a pod. Never could separate them.

Jakob spoke first, "Hi, Feli."

A nickname he had given me when he first met me and I'd remembered that it used to bother me but now, I'd grown used to it. I was glad that I had a good relationship with my cousins, even if they could be pain in the asses at times. But they had accepted me into their family. We all needed one another, due to the loss we had experienced.

"Are you feeling better now?" Elias piped in, slapping his hand on my back as he always did when he greeted me. Both of them were slightly taller than me and I'd remember for the first year I'd gotten to know them, it had been hard to tell them apart. But I'd soon recognised the differences between the two. Jakob had a slight scar above his left eyebrow and Elias has a beauty spot underneath his nose. So now I knew who was who.

"Peachy," I replied, a slight sour taste to my mouth as I said this. Today, I was not going to spend any more time thinking about my ex. She had a whole new man now and it was clear there was no room for me. Perhaps there never had been. I wished I had seen the warning signs sooner.

"Right, please now help me with the table," Aunt Brenna said and we all hopped to it with no arguments. As we were arranging the plates and glasses, Mira announced her arrival.

"Sorry I'm late, the hospital was asking me about doing some more shifts," she said as our aunt engulfed her in a hug. She was already tired enough as it was, so I was hoping she'd say no to it. It was nice to spend time with her.

"You need to take care of yourself, young lady. Take a break," Aunt Brenna scolded her.

"I know." Mira sighed but we both knew she didn't like letting people down, especially her colleagues.

It was time to eat and as always, Aunt Brenna asked us to join hands and make a blessing.

"As always, I am blessed to have four amazing children and happy we get to share this meal together," Aunt Brenna said, a warmness to her tone.

I realised how grateful I should be for her, and for my cousins. I cracked a slight smile as we tucked into our delicious food but the smile was partly because in a few hours, I would be in the company of someone different, someone who seemed like they could be worth it.

Chapter 10

Alisha

For hours, I hovered over the texts from Felix and wondered what the evening ahead would bring. To say I was nervous was an understatement but I felt confident with my decision to have dinner with him. We were going to Down Under, and I was curious to see what the food was like over here. So far I really enjoyed what I'd been eating, and our fridge was now packed with delicious food from the supermarket.

I'd offered for Ophelia to come out this evening but she was quick to say no. "Nope, it's your night. Your date, I'm not being the third wheel." Ophelia shook her head.

"It's definitely not a date," I had retorted back to her and she raised one eyebrow, which meant she didn't believe me.

"An attractive man is taking you out to dinner. I believe it is, sweetie. So *you* will tell me all about it later." Ophelia wiggled her fingers and reentered her room all whilst I was still reflecting on her statement.

Maybe I needed to accept that it was a date.

Reflecting back on my day, it had been productive. My legs were burning less today, which meant my body was getting used to the physical activity. I was also getting better, my balance and ability to make turns were improving. Hilde had captured my success by filming me and I'd already sent the multiple videos to my family.

I had about two hours to get ready and I was glad that Ophelia had suggested a few outfits for me to wear. One was a dark red, tight dress that stopped just above my knees and which perhaps showed too much breast for my liking. Also, was it really appropriate for the weather out here?

The other was a pair of black flare jeans and a white halterneck top. This screamed disaster to me as I was often fickle with my food and I'd probably end up with sauce over my top before the evening ended. There was one final option, though—a comfortable pink jumper that would go well with the flare jeans. This seemed like the right choice.

I would put my outfit on last but what I needed to do first was sort out my face and hair. I didn't want to disturb Ophelia in her slumber, so I phoned Kiya for some much-needed advice. She was quite the make-up guru and always gave me tips to make my eyeliner look better or style my hair in a different way.

"Hello, didi," she said excitedly, and immediately I switched to FaceTime, visibly relaxing as soon as I saw her face. I could see Chou in the background, eating a bowl of dry food. Well rather, chowing down on it like no tomorrow. I was glad he was happy because putting him in a cattery would have been a huge no.

Kiya was grinning widely back at me, her hair slightly tousled, and I wondered how she always maintained a positive, bubbly outlook on life. I needed her to be my life coach at this point.

"Hiya. How's everything?" I asked her, entering my room and falling back gently onto my bed. I held my phone in front of my face and waited for my sister's response.

"Totally fine. I haven't burnt the place down and your cat is constantly sitting on my lap. But I don't mind. How's Austria? Meet any cute guys? How's the food?" Kiya asked, and I wondered what question I would answer first. I decided to go with the first one.

"It's lovely out here. Had some snowfall this morning but not too much. Food is also pretty delicious. Will send you some pictures later," I said, and then realised there was one more question I needed to answer. After all, I had rung my sister for a reason and she would clock on that I would be meeting a guy even if I didn't tell her in accurate words.

"Loooovely," Kiya replied.

"I did bump into someone. He's offered to show me the area and I'm going out to dinner with him tonight. It's *not* a date, though. So don't go getting excited," I said, or rather warned. Kiya rolled her eyes at me but decided to let it go. For now.

"So, I am guessing you need some help with your make-up and hair. As always, you've asked the right person." Kiya smiled and soon, she was picking out the eyeshadow, eyeliner and mascara for me.

"I think since you're wearing a pink jumper, your eye shadow should be either beige or a soft pink. And then your eyeliner, it should be subtle. Then, you can wear a bit of lipgloss," Kiya advised me. I did as she said, all whilst talking to her and getting her opinion about how my hair looked.

"Do I look okay?" I finally said, my teeth nipping my bottom lip and then ending up with lipgloss on them.

"Okay? You look gorgeous, didi, but to be honest, you always do. I wish you could see that more," she said and realised that if my sister could tell me I was, then I needed to believe it myself.

"Thank you," I said sheepishly.

"Now, you are ready. I hope you have a good time tonight. I am rooting for you and what's his name?" she asked, her head tilting slightly to the side.

"His name is Felix," I said and the tingles invaded my skin and corroded within me as soon as I said his name. I spoke more to Kiya and laughed when she told me how Chou had climbed on her head during the night. Sounded like him.

"Gotta go now, didi. Have a good night and give me all the gossip tomorrow." Kiya pursed her lips to blow me a kiss.

"Thanks, bon. Give lots of cuddles to Chou," I said and then waved before hanging up.

I still had about less than an hour to go before Felix would be here, he offered to drive us, and I realised how polite he actually was. Well, he had been over text, at least. My initial impression of him would go out the window tonight. He would possibly prove me wrong about my thoughts of him. I did want to get to know the area more but I also wanted to get to know him too.

I needed a drink of some sort so decided to make myself a small Malibu and Coca-Cola, something sweet to calm my nerves. I topped up the glass with ice from the freezer and poured a double shot of Malibu because, hey, I wasn't driving tonight so I didn't mind drinking a little extra. I took one more glance at myself in the bathroom mirror as I sipped my drink and hummed in approval.

It sounded strange in my head but I almost wished time would move faster so that I could get the initial hellos out of the way and dive into some good food.

Maybe I would watch some TV or go onto my laptop to write a bit. After all, I still had a job to do and I needed to write things down that were fresh in my memory. So, for the next thirty minutes, I decided to go onto my Google Docs and type out the day that I'd had. My fingers hovered over the keyboard as I started typing one word. Or rather, name. It was almost as if I'd had no control over my reflexes but perhaps that was good.

I needed to keep the readers engaged and people loved reading about real experiences and about the locals. Felix was a mystery and perhaps I was too. But maybe we could crack the codes of ourselves together. I was just finishing typing my last sentence as I heard two sharp knocks on the front door. He was here.

I closed my laptop down, placing it on my bedside table and nearly fell face-first on the floor as I sprinted to the door. Then, I realised I needed to compose myself. I was breathing heavily like an idiot and this would not be a good look. After a moment of steadying my breath, I opened the door.

As I met Felix's eyes after staring at the floor or, more so, at the expensive Armani shoes he was wearing, it was as if my breath was knocked out of wind.

He looked...handsome. His hair had been slightly gelled back but not too much to make you think he had slathered oil excessively into it. Just like me, he was wearing a jumper, but his was a dark blue. His clothing was casual but he still looked good.

"Good evening," I said nervously, and I instantly hated how shaky my voice sounded. Felix seemed lost for words himself and it made me wonder why, as in his texts, he appeared confident. But often over a screen, people would be.

Stop thinking about the internet and keep talking.

"Sorry, I'm a little early. I thought I'd get lost trying to find your place," Felix said and I noticed that he was now nervous too, as he wrung his hands together.

"That's okay. I'm ready to go now if you want to set off," I said, with a small but soft smile. This seemed to do the trick of easing his vivid stress and his own lips stretched into a crooked smile. This made my stomach do a somersault and backflip at the same time. I had to admit, I was attracted to him.

"Okay, cool. You look nice, by the way," Felix told me, his eyes scanning me from head to toe, which made me blush. I appreciated the compliment, as he probably didn't give them often.

"Thank you. You look nice too," I said and emphasised on the word 'nice'. He looked so much better than nice but I didn't want to overdo the compliment. I closed the door behind me after having grabbed my bag from the kitchen. Ophelia was still fast asleep but I knew she'd be full of questions later.

Felix and I walked towards his car, a Range Rover, which was impressive. I had almost pictured him driving a Mazda or, in general, a smaller car than this. As we approached the car, he leaned across me to unlock the passenger door. I caught a whiff of his scent- sandalwood mixed with a touch of mint.

I wanted to know what he was thinking as we both got into our seats and he turned the engine on. As I buckled my seat belt on, he also did the same and we locked eyes on one another. If we had more moments like these, I was going to be unconscious by the end of the evening. His eyes were very beautiful and his pupils started to dilate. His thumb and index finger were hovering just above his seatbelt as he looked at me. I almost wished those fingers would touch my skin, specifically my neck and mouth.

Yes, Ali, you are most definitely attracted to him.

"Let's get going," Felix said after what felt like hours of staring at one another and I cleared my throat, nodding in agreement. I couldn't say any more words, so I relaxed into my seat and listened to the tunes playing on the radio. He didn't say anything either, but I didn't mind. It was a comfortable silence and it meant every so often, I could glance at him from the corner of my eye and admire the way he looked and the way he made me feel even though I barely knew him. I was in trouble.

Chapter 11

Felix

The drive to the restaurant felt awkward, or so I had thought. I wanted to ease myself into conversation with Alisha but after our staring match, the words just didn't seem to come out. She looked beautiful. I wished I had told her that when I initially complimented her. I told her she had looked 'nice'. A meagre word for someone who practically caused me to palpitate and lose sense of reality. Absolutely stunning would have been better to say. She looked gorgeous in that pink jumper and her perfectly glossed lips—lips I already knew I wanted to kiss but wouldn't dare tonight.

No, I needed to remain composed. I ignored the strain in my trousers as I started to think about her lips, her skin, and the way she was tapping her index finger on her thigh. I almost wanted to push her hand away and replace it with mine. To stop driving altogether and pull her against my body. It was very clear that I was attracted to her. I had tried to deny it for the past twenty-four hours but now it was painstakingly obvious to me. I tightened the grip on my steering wheel and bit down gently on my tongue, trying to distract myself from my heated thoughts.

"Ah, we're here," I finally said and Alisha blinked a couple of times to focus on our surroundings. Down Under was a restaurant inside Hotel Germania and I had been here a few times with my sister. I was looking forward to having my usual garlic cream soup and then cordon bleu for the main course- a satisfying combination of pork, ham, cheese, French fries and cranberries that I particularly enjoyed. The hotel itself had a black and white exterior and the rooms were rather classic with lots of space. I had stayed here once, a few years ago. It was comfortable and not too expensive.

"Thanks for driving us," Alisha finally said, and whether I liked it or not, I felt as though I was succumbing to the sound of her voice. Her words felt like honey, gliding down my skin.

"No problem," I managed to muster out from my lips and hoped to the high heavens my voice didn't betray the anxiety bubbling beneath the surface.

"Looking forward to a nice slap-up meal." Alisha grinned, revealing her straight, white teeth. I wondered how many men in her life had fallen surrender to her smile?

"Slap-up?" I questioned. I was still trying to get my head around English terms since I'd started speaking the language about five years ago. I'd been dedicated to learning and was grateful that I hadn't given up despite the challenge.

"Means a large and enjoyable meal," Alisha replied.

"I see. I thought it meant something else. I guess there are lots of phrases I need to learn," I said.

Maybe she could teach me.

We'd been sitting in the car for far too long for my liking and the strain in my trousers hadn't eased, so one of us had to make the move to get out of the car. I decided that it would be me, stuffing my car keys into my hand and stepping out of the seat to be greeted by the fresh, crisp Austrian air.

Alisha followed suit and I didn't miss the way her jumper rode up slightly, revealing part of her stomach. As we both were out of the car, I locked it with the press of a button and then shoved my hands in my pockets, angling my head towards Alisha, who was waiting patiently. She had a mysterious look on her face as she scanned my features for something I wasn't sure of. It felt like she was trying to undress me with those eyes of hers, and maybe I could let her. But that was a danger zone I shouldn't enter.

"There's a good choice to select from," I told her as we started to walk toward the front entrance.

"Willkommen." We were greeted by a friendly doorman who had soft green eyes that sparkled under the front door lights and his blond hair was perfectly slicked back. I felt a pang of, dare I say it, slight jealousy as Alisha fluttered her eyelashes at him while he gave her a sloppy grin. Maybe she hadn't done that on purpose but that prompted me to place my hand on the small of her back as we entered inside. We definitely weren't a couple, I had to remind myself. But it was almost like I wanted all of her to myself tonight. All of her attention.

You sound like a fucking fool.

"Shut up," I whispered to my conscious, wondering why on earth he decided to pop up now. I was glad Alisha hadn't heard as she walked by my side, and then, finally, we reached the restaurant itself. My hand hadn't wavered from her back and to my surprise, she hadn't made a move to remove it or even say anything about it. *Maybe she liked it.*

"Welcome to Down Under. May I take your name?" the host asked, and I looked at his name tag, which revealed his name was Leon. I hadn't met him before, given that I hadn't been here in a few months. He had brown, cropped hair, which was dusted with some grey hairs and he seemed to be in his late forties if I guessed correctly. His eyes were a deep, ocean blue, and I could tell he was a well-respected man.

"Felix Bauer," I replied, and Leon nodded, ticking my name off on the piece of paper in front of him.

"I'll show you both to your table," he stated and held his arm out to usher us through. The restaurant was quiet for now but I knew later in the evening, clients would start rolling in. Leon presented a table that was tucked away in a corner and decorated with scented candles, shining plates, and cutlery that looked almost too perfect. I was glad we would be sitting here, away from prying eyes. It wouldn't do my anxiety any good.

"Thank you," Alisha said to the host as he held out the chair for her. He also did the same for me and I thanked him, making a note to tip him later. There was some gentle music playing in the background and it helped to ease the awkwardness I was feeling. I wasn't too sure whether I'd drink alcohol tonight since I was driving, but I felt I needed at least one drink to course itself through my system.

"Wow, it's nice in here," Alisha noted as she glanced around the room, and when her eyes met mine, I tightened my grip on my thighs. *Must relax, don't panic.*

"I've been here a few times. I hope you like the food," I said. *Because maybe we could come here again. And next time, I won't be such a lovesick puppy.*

"I'm sure I will. I'm a girl who always has a big appetite. Plus, I'm writing about the food I've been trying for the article," Alisha said, now playing with her knife and fork on the table. I noticed the way her chest rose and fell in an easy, steady pattern and reminded myself to focus on my own breathing. Inhale and exhale.

"How is that coming along?" I asked her out of curiosity. I could tell she was dedicated to her job. I mean, why else would she have flown a load of miles to be here? She had passion. Something which I was lacking in my own job. I wasn't sure what to do about it but it definitely wasn't a long-term position. I needed something that would help me make a difference. I just didn't know what. I really had been a lost soul for some time. *Enough wallowing now Bauer, and focus on the woman in front of you. A beautiful woman at that.*

"Well, I've been writing snippets here and there. I think there will be a lot of edits with the final draft though. This is kind of my big break, so I really want to do well with this," Alisha said, giving me a wry smile.

"I understand. What inspires you to write?" I asked her, because now I was intrigued.

"I would say the people in my life. I have a loving family and a great best friend," she said and I noticed the way her visage softened as she mentioned her family and friend. It reminded me of my own and how, although my life was a mess right now, at least I had them. That was a treasure I should be proud of.

"And where do you see yourself in the future?" I continued, feeling confident in asking her more. As she was about to answer, one of the waiters stopped in front of the table and was poised with a notepad in his hand.

"Can I take your drink orders?" he asked hesitantly, almost as if he knew he interrupted something. I was surprised he wasn't speaking in German, perhaps he heard us speaking in English.

"Yes, please. May I have a glass of Coca-Cola?" Alisha asked politely.

"The same for me, please," I said, surprising myself as normally I'd go for something alcoholic first. The waiter, having written down our drinks order, scurried off to the bar and then Alisha and I focused back on one another.

"So to answer your question, I'm hoping in the future to be an established journalist for Culture Horizon. And then maybe I'd like to be married with a kid. What about you, Felix?" she asked, and I loved the way my name rolled off her tongue. I wanted her to say it again.

"Well, I don't really like my job at the moment. I feel like I am stuck there. So maybe in the future, I could be working abroad. I'm not sure if I see myself settling down," I trailed off on the last sentence. I didn't want to talk about my previous relationship tonight, I decided. Otherwise, it would ruin the mood. No, I would focus on the woman in front of me who was staring at me with vivid interest. For the first time in a while, I felt as though someone was truly keen to be in my presence. Maybe I needed to drop the frosty attitude I had been maintaining for the last few months and make a new friend. I could handle that.

"I totally know what you mean. I've been in many jobs where I've hated them. But I've realised that you shouldn't waste your time on a job you hate. Life is too short for that. Have you ever thought about quitting?" Alisha asked and as I contemplated the thought, our drinks arrived. I quickly took a swig of my drink and relished the fizz on my tongue. I surprisingly had missed drinking soda.

"I have, yes. I guess it's just hard to find the courage to quit. You get comfortable after some time," I admitted. Alisha seemed to take my words in but said nothing else. I didn't mind that.

It was time to order our food and Alisha asked for the tomato cream soup to start, then chicken breast for her main. Two good choices, and I liked that she was a soup woman. With food ordered, we relaxed back into conversation. *This was going better than I initially thought.*

"Tell me your favourite colour," Alisha demanded.

"I like green. You?" I darted the question back to her. Green, in my opinion, was a calm colour.

"I like blue and gold. My apartment back home has a mixture of these colours," she said. I wondered what home was like for her. Whether she lived alone or with someone. What did she do on the weekend? My mind was now swimming with endless questions but I allowed myself to just ask one.

"So, do you live with anyone?" I asked, taking a long sip of my drink. I noticed the way she touched her hair, slinging it back so that I could see more of her neck.

"Nope. I'm a loner." Alisha laughed, placing both of her hands on her glass and softly gripping it.

"Me too," I said. My mind wandered back to a time when I wasn't living alone, but the more I realised it, living with my ex had been a nightmare. There had been zero communication and most of the time, I took responsibility for things.

"You alright?" Alisha's question pulled me out of my pit of thoughts, which I was very glad for. I focused my attention back on her and willed myself to stop thinking of the past. The present was looking pretty good right now.

"I'm okay," I said and I believed it. For the first time.

"Good. I just want you to know something. I understand whatever it is you're going through. You don't have to tell me. But I get it. So if you need a friend, I am here," Alisha said, and I hovered on the word 'friend'. I needed that. I needed someone to care. And the woman in front of me was showing me that, even if we didn't really know one another that well.

"Dealt with your fair share of heartache?" I queried as, finally, our starters were placed in front of us. After all this talking, I was very hungry but I would wait until Alisha started eating. I wanted to be a gentleman.

"Oh, absolutely. But I've bounced back from it. The past is the past. I'd like it to stay there."

"You're right there, of course," I agreed. Her honesty was refreshing.

"Well, bon appetite." Alisha smiled at me, diving her spoon into her bowl and waiting for me to do the same.

"Genießen," I replied.

"What does that mean?" Alisha cocked her head slightly.

"It means 'enjoy'. Maybe I should teach you some German," I offered, half hoping she'd take me up on the offer. Anything to spend more time with her.

"I'll take you up on that." She grinned, which caused my heart to beat faster.

We tucked into our starters, every so often talking about Ischgl and what it had to offer. Shortly after we finished, our mains came and I tried to ignore the soft moans falling from her mouth as she ate the chicken breast. It was doing all sorts to me as I tried to focus on chewing my own food.

"What are your plans tomorrow?" I asked courageously. I was hinting that perhaps we could do something together. I knew she would have a ski lesson but she probably had some free time after. I would invite her friend Ophelia too, if she wanted to come.

"First thing is my ski lesson. Then I'm free for the rest of the day," Alisha told me, placing her knife and fork on her plate to signal she was finished. I had finished just before her and was relaxing back into my seat, my hands resting on my thighs again. But this time, I wasn't gripping them. I'd noticed that about half an hour ago, I was much more relaxed.

"Would you like to do something?" I hoped she would say yes. I wanted to be in her company again. Over the course of this evening, I'd come to realise how kind she was and how my initial impression of her had been wrong. She wasn't just some nosy tourist. I wished I hadn't been so cold to her but what I did next would make a difference.

"What do you suggest?" Alisha raised one eyebrow as our plates were being taken away.

"How does a hike sound? I'll provide a picnic." I almost couldn't believe the words that had come out of my mouth, but I liked it.

"I do love the fresh air. But I bet it'll be cold," Alisha said, and she was right. It would be. But there was something about walking in the cold air that was refreshing. Plus, tomorrow was going to be sunnier than normal.

"We'll just have to bundle ourselves up. I'll treat you to some hot chocolate too," I said, and her eyes lit up at this.

She was a fan of hot chocolate, good.

"You've convinced me now." Alisha chuckled, a sound I was beginning to really like. *I liked that I was making her laugh.*

"How was everything for you?" The waiter had reappeared and was probably going to ask us if we wanted any dessert.

"Delicious, thank you. I don't think I'll have any dessert. How about you, Felix?" Again, hearing her say my name was causing my heart to beat faster. *I wondered what her lips tasted like, probably as sweet as cherries.*

"I won't have any either. Just the bill, please," I said, and the waiter nodded, heading off to grab the card machine as well as the bill.

"Are we going Dutch tonight, then?" Alisha smirked.

"No, I'm paying. My treat," I told her. It was no problem at all. I was just grateful for her company. For the way she had eased us into the conversation.

"Thank you," was all she said. *No, thank you.*

After paying for the bill, which wasn't too expensive, we walked back to my car and I dived my hand into my pocket to grab my keys to unlock it. I didn't want the night to end but I could tell she was tired, as she yawned and stretched her arms slightly above her head.

"Thank you again. I'm one happy, satisfied woman now." Alisha grinned as we were buckled into our seats. I wondered what *really, truly* satisfied her when it came to relationships. Was she a romantic like me?

"I am glad you had a good time. Thank you for joining me tonight. It has been a while since I've been out with a woman," I said and then instantly regretted saying that. I probably sounded desperate. But to my surprise, Alisha gently placed her hand on top of mine, which was placed on the gear stick.

"It's been a while since I've been out with a man. We've got a lot in common," she said, giving my hand a squeeze. It was maddening, the way her gentle touch was sending me into overdrive.

"We do," I acknowledged. If I didn't start driving now, I didn't know what would happen. Whether she'd make the first move or whether I would have to, but perhaps tonight wasn't the night. I still wanted to get to know her but also, to respect her wishes.

It wasn't long before I parked up in front of her accommodation and the pair of us unbuckled our belts, hopping out of the car quickly. I blew out a deep breath in front of me, and Alisha shivered slightly. The temperature had dropped significantly and all that could be heard was deep breathing and the sound of Alisha's teeth chattering. She needed to get inside before she froze to death.

"You better get inside. You're freezing," I said, glueing my hands to my sides. I was almost tempted to place them on her shoulders and then wrap them around her back to warm her up.

"Would you like to come in?" Alisha offered and fuck yes, I really wanted to. But I needed some self-control. I'd be seeing her tomorrow and I needed to get home and get rid of this raging hard-on I'd had all evening.

"Thanks for the offer. But I'm quite tired. So I'll be going home." I looked down at the ground, not wanting to meet her stare. I heard her take another step closer and unexpectedly, her arms had woven around my body, pulling me into a hug. Instinctively, my own wrapped around her body and I relished the way she felt pressed up against me.

"Something told me that you needed a hug. I hope that was the right thing to do," Alisha whispered.

Yes, it was. And I knew that I would need many more from her.

"Yes," I whispered back. The hug ended sooner than I would have liked, but it needed to before I took her up on her offer of going inside the house and doing what I wanted to do to her all evening.

"Goodnight." Alisha smiled, taking a step back.

"Goodnight," I replied, edging closer back to my car. I watched her retreat and waved at her as she walked through the front door into the warmth. I couldn't help but smile. During the drive home, I kept on smiling. And I didn't hate it.

Chapter 12

Alisha

Tonight was wonderful. Felix surprised me and if anything, I wanted to find out more about him. There was obviously something that deeply affected him, but it was up to him if he wanted to share that with me. I was excited that we would be seeing each other tomorrow. I didn't really like hiking in all honesty but I wanted to be in his presence again.

As I entered through the front door, I was immediately brought into questioning by my best friend.

"So? How was it? Did he kiss you first or did you?" Ophelia grabbed both my shoulders, giving me a gentle shake. "Tell me, woman. I must know."

"Okay, mad woman. Sit down." I laughed, pointing toward the sofa.

"Do I need a drink for this?" Ophelia crossed her arms as I joined her, grabbing a cushion and hugging it to my chest.

"No, we didn't kiss but I wanted to. It was great to get to know him more though," I said.

"What's he like then?" Ophelia grabbed her own cushion and I told her everything, as she gave me a pleased look with the information I was supplying her. To be honest, as I was talking, I couldn't help but smile. The night had gone better than I expected. I just wanted tomorrow to be here already, which sounded crazy. There was something about Felix which was intriguing and pulled me in. Did that scare me? No, surprisingly. Normally, it would.

"Well, you speaking of all that food has made me hungry. I suppose you aren't though. I'm so happy you had a good night." My friend seemed happy for me and I mimicked her emotions. It had probably been the best evening I'd had in a while.

"I'm glad I went. Right, I think I need a bath." I stretched my legs out in front of me before standing up. I needed to relax and wind down for the evening. A bubble bath with a glass of something cold and fizzy sounded good to me too.

"Okay, shout if you need anything then," Ophelia replied. She was already walking toward the kitchen, humming a soft tune that I couldn't quite decipher. I noted that it was probably best to spend some time with her after tomorrow, I certainly didn't want to neglect my friend on this trip.

After I poured myself a glass of Pepsi with ice, I proceeded to run a piping hot bath. I didn't mind my skin being a little red, to be honest I still felt on fire after that embrace with Felix. I definitely didn't regret it. I felt comfortable in his arms. Safe. It'd been a long time since I'd felt that.

The bath was halfway full with the bubbles starting to rise, I added a sweet rose scented liquid. *Perfect.*

I heaved a sigh as I dipped my leg into the bath after stripping myself free of my trousers and jumper. I definitely hadn't ignored the way Felix's eyes trailed up and down my body. I wondered what had gone through his head. Did he feel the electricity I felt? I didn't want to imagine that it had been just me.

"Maybe it is just me," I said, as part of my brain still thought it was too good to be true. I sighed, sinking the rest of my body into the tub. I had tied my brown locks into a loose bun, with some of the stray hairs sticking either side of my face. I had a flannel ready to wipe away my make-up, which remained pristine throughout the evening.

I took a large sip of my refreshment, relishing the way the bubbles popped on my tongue. I allowed myself to soak in the heat, willing my brain to take a break for the next twenty minutes or so. It had gone into overload.

In the background, I could hear Ophelia's gentle singing. I always thought she could pursue a career in music as she was very talented, she could play the piano, guitar and the clarinet. But she insisted that her heart was in journalism, at least for the time being. I knew that this would be the job for me in the long run, nothing would make me happier than having people read my work and being able to relate to it.

After mulling over this in the tub, I decided I didn't want to look like a prune and got out, wrapping the soft, purple towel I'd packed from home around me. I shuffled my feet toward the bedroom after draining the bathtub, I would give it a clean tomorrow if I had the time.

Once I was dressed, I lathered some lotion onto my skin and applied some strawberry scented chapstick as I didn't want my lips to become cracked in the cold air that surrounded us in Ischgl. As I was brushing my hair, my phone lit up and I immediately darted toward it. It was a message from Felix. My heart practically leaped out of my chest. *Calm yourself. It's just a text.*

I typed in my passcode and was greeted with several words from him.

Felix: Hope you're wrapped up all warm, the temperature's dropped

I couldn't help but smile at this before typing out my reply.

Alisha: In my favourite slippers and pyjamas, hope you're nice and warm too!

Felix: Hm, I don't tend to freeze. Always hot.

Alisha: Lucky you! What time should we meet tomorrow?

Felix: How does 11am sound?

Luckily, my lesson had been moved slightly earlier in the morning so I would be finished just before eleven. I found out about it from the ski school earlier today. My legs would probably be sore but I didn't care. I wanted to spend more time with Felix and find out what makes him tick.

Alisha: Fine with me, my ski lesson finishes at 10.30am.

Felix: I'll meet you down at the end of the cable car then, what kind of snacks do you like?

Alisha: Sounds great! I like anything chocolately, so surprise me.

Felix: Okay, at your own risk ;)

I bit my bottom lip as I analysed the emoji he had just sent, wondering whether I could be brave enough to send one too.

Alisha: Willing to take it :P

Felix: Get some sleep, see you tomorrow

Alisha: Okay, head is on the pillow. Night night

Felix: Goodnight x

I was practically beaming as I placed my phone on charge and set it down on the bedside table. I couldn't stop feeling giddy.

Knowing that I wouldn't sleep instantly, I decided to brush my teeth and then grab a bottle of water. As I entered the living room, Ophelia was sitting cross-legged on the sofa with her laptop perched on top of her legs. She must have struggled to get to bed too. She was typing quite vigorously but lifted her head up to give me a smile.

"Can't sleep either?" I asked my friend, as I walked toward the fridge.

"Had a moment of inspiration. Decided to get a bit of work done." Ophelia tucked a piece of her dyed hair behind her ear and then reached across her to grab her half full cup of juice to take a swig.

"I can't seem to find any inspiration," I said, twisting the cap off my bottle and taking a large gulp.

"You know any writer goes through this, so don't beat yourself up. Maybe the walk tomorrow might help," Ophelia replied.

"Here's hoping." I didn't just want to ski the whole of this holiday and stay cooped up in the house afterward. An adventure sounded exciting, and perhaps I could even ask Felix to talk about his life in Ischgl. He held a story behind those hazel eyes and if he would let me, I'd want to hear it.

Chapter 13

Felix

I slept very well last night, so much that I almost didn't want to get out of my soft, warm bed. I hadn't had a single negative thought invade my mind, which was a start. As soon as I woke up, I felt giddy and instantly knew the reason why. I would be seeing Alisha today and really was starting to appreciate her company. She had a kind aura about her, I didn't really know much about auras in general, but she seemed like a person who liked to make time for others and truly take interest in them. I would ask her about her backstory today, her life in England and how she was finding Austria. It wouldn't be long until Christmas was here and of course, the shops had started to decorate and restaurants introduced their Christmas lunch menus.

I was in high spirits, I even made myself a hearty breakfast at 8:00 am and ate it all. No scraps left that I would normally throw away. I felt like I had gained an appetite. My sister would be pleased, as she had spent months trying to persuade me to eat a little more. I decided I would give her a call, since she wouldn't be going to work until this afternoon.

Mira picked up within three things and her tone was ridden with concern, "Felix, are you alright?"

"I'm absolutely fine. Just thought I'd call to see how you are?" I asked and I heard her take a deep inhale before speaking.

"I thought you were in danger or something. You don't normally ring in the morning. I'm okay, Felix. Just cleaning the place up a bit," Mira said in a chirpy tone. I could hear plates clattering in the background, she was probably unloading the dishwasher.

"Sounds like you. I've eaten my breakfast and now I'm just relaxing."

"Wow, I'm glad you've had the first important meal of the day. It helps you function. What are your plans today?" my sister asked me, the background noise had halted.

"I'm going for a hike this morning," I said, and I knew my sister would press for more information. She worried about me, more so than she should.

"On your own?" Mira asked, a slight hint of concern in her voice.

"No. I'm going with a woman." I instantly regretted telling her that.

"Am I really talking to Felix or?" Mira laughed and I couldn't help but mimic.

"You truly are. It's not a date or anything. We went out to dinner last night but—"

"You went out for a dinner date and didn't tell me!?" Mira raised her voice and I squeezed my eyes shut, knowing I wouldn't hear the end of it now.

I listened to her ramble on for almost a minute before finally deciding to interrupt her.

"Well, I decided it was time to make a friend. And to stop feeling sorry for myself. Alisha is nice. But she's only here for a short time. So, we can't really be anything other than friends." As I said the word *friends*, I knew it was a lie but I needed to remain nonchalant about this all.

"Okay. I get it. It's probably wise not to start something. Plus, you're still healing. But good on you, Felix. I'm proud of you," Mira said.

"Thank you. I hope you have a good shift today. Maybe I'll ring you tomorrow," I offered.

"I'll hold you to that. You better tell me every single thing. Alisha sounds cool." Mira was right. Alisha was pretty cool, and as soon as I finished speaking with my sister, it was only 9:15 am. Less than two hours until I saw Alisha, but time couldn't speed up quicker.

***

To kill the time, I'd cleaned the kitchen and the bathroom as it had been a while. The laundry had been sorted, and the clothes were now in the dryer. Every so often, my eyes had drifted to the clock hanging on the wall in the kitchen. I hated the way it would tick, but also relished in the fact that with every passing minute I would finally get to leave the house.

"Finally," I muttered as it was now 10:30 am and it meant I could make my way to the cable car. It was about a fifteen minute walk, no need for a car. I would be a little early but I didn't mind waiting. Many, many thoughts were swimming in my head. I wondered what Alisha did last night, whether she went straight to bed or did she have a moment to think about me, like I had done about her.

When I arrived, I checked my phone for the time and it was about 10:50 am. I had walked a little slower than usual, as a way of calming my nerves. I had ten minutes until I would see her. I gave myself a pep talk, reminding myself not to say anything stupid or weird. Alisha needed to see a calm and collected Felix, someone who had their shit together. I really didn't want her to see the cracks, to see my vulnerability. I needed to put that all behind me, at least for today.

"Fuck," I muttered to myself as I could see Alisha approaching, a few minutes earlier than I had anticipated. She looked glorious, her dark hair was slightly windswept, probably from her ski helmet, and she had already changed out of her ski gear. I hoped her lesson had gone okay and that she was making progress. Maybe I could even take her down the slopes one day, if she felt confident enough. I knew she didn't have very long left here in Ischgl, but if I help her achieve something then I'd do my best.

"Hello," she said calmly, as she stopped a few metres in front of me. She tucked a loose strand of brown hair behind one ear and offered me a sheepish grin. It sent me into overdrive, a mere gesture but that was all it took.

Remain composed.

"Hi. Um, how are you? How was your lesson? You're out a bit early," I spoke rather too quickly for my liking and my voice had a slight high pitch to it. But there was nothing I could do about it. I cleared my throat and waited for her answer, shoving my hands in my trouser pockets.

So thankful for pockets.

"I'm very good. The lesson was really fun today, got to try out a higher slope. Fell a few times so I think my legs will be a bit sore later. Nothing a good bubble bath can't sort out. I wanted to leave a bit earlier so I wouldn't be late meeting you," Alisha replied, taking a small step closer. I couldn't help but lean a little more forward, my body was basically ignoring my mind at this point. She looked so beautiful and I noticed the few freckles she had by her nose.

How had I not noticed this before? Her skin looked so soft but I had enough self-control to stop myself from touching her cheek.

"I understand," I said and my mouth felt dry all of a sudden.

"So, are you thirsty? I could do with a cup of coffee before our walk." Alisha grinned and I nodded, like she had read my mind.

"I know a few places," I said, leading the way and we both fell into step with one another. There were a few coffee shops nearby, so it didn't matter which one we would go into as they were all good. We picked one called *Ski fahren und Schleifen (Ski and Grind)*, which lived up to its name as it was full of ski photos, many celebrities had gone there and had signed their posters too. The baristas always made delicious coffee, some with aromatic spices. One of my favourites was the spiced chai latte so I would order one today. Alisha hadn't said much else to me as we entered inside the coffee shop but I was hoping we would engage in conversation once we were sat down.

"I'll get us the drinks. What would you like?" Alisha asked me. She had beaten me to it as I was going to offer to pay for us both.

"Spiced chai latte for me please, medium," I said, shrugging my coat off. There was a soft buzz of chatter around us and a few children were sitting in the sofa area, drawing pictures with their crayons.

"I didn't know you liked that. That's my favourite coffee. Or one of them." Alisha grinned. I knew I needed to keep making her smile like that throughout the day, as it made me feel like I achieved something good. Her smile always seemed genuine, I liked the way crinkles would form around her eyes.

"We might become best friends at this rate," I said, and I wasn't particularly joking. I knew I wanted to be a little more than friends though.

"Or soulmates." Alisha gave me a wink, and I was thankful that I was now sitting down otherwise I'd have toppled over. *Soulmates.* I didn't believe in them, never had.

I sighed and shook my head, the negative thoughts were not going to take a hold of me today. Definitely not today. I refocused my attention back on Alisha who was now at the front of the queue, she had grabbed a blueberry muffin which caused me to smile. She really did have a sweet tooth.

I drummed my fingers on my table as I tried not to stare too much. My phone pinged, signalling I had a text. Probably my sister checking in on me, as she usually did.

Mira: Hello, big brother. How is your morning going?

Felix: Good morning, little sister. Just in Ski and Grind with Alisha. We stopped for coffee before going for a walk. How's your shift going?

Mira: Oh, coffee ;) I haven't even met her but I'm already rooting for the pair of you. It's slow this morning but it will pick up in afternoon, just having a coffee myself but on my lonesome

Felix: Take care of yourself, you work too hard. I'd like to see more of you

Mira: Don't worry Felix, I'm okay. I'm going to see if I can request some annual leave, then maybe we can plan something together but I don't want to get your hopes up, as it's nearly Christmas and lots can happen

Felix: I get it, always here if you need me. Anyway, talk later

I put my phone away as Alisha placed a tray on the table, presenting two cups of coffee and her blueberry muffin. It did look delicious.

"I'm very jealous of your muffin," I said and that caused Alisha to laugh as she sat down in front of me, scraping her chair forward to rest her elbows on the table. She raised one eyebrow and I realised how that may have sounded.

"Oh, um, I meant that it looks delicious…"

Stop talking. Now.

"I'll share it with you, if you want," Alisha said, an almost innocent tone to her voice.

"Are you sure? I'm happy to go and get one myself," I said, hoping I hadn't made things awkward.

"Absolutely sure. Sharing is caring." Alisha picked up her knife and cut the muffin into two, offering me a piece. As I took a bite of the sweet but succulent treat, our eyes locked for a moment and it felt as though we were the only two in the room. All I could feel was heat. And then, alongside the scorching heat, I felt desire. I noticed the way her tongue darted out of her mouth, to swipe away any remaining crumbs. I wanted to taste her mouth if I could. But I wouldn't act on anything, nor do anything to make her uncomfortable. No matter how much I wanted it.

"That really is delicious." Alisha chuckled softly, wiping a napkin around her mouth. Her skin was lightly flushed.

Was she blushing?

"I never normally go for blueberry. But something tells me it's always worth trying something different," I said and Alisha nodded in agreement.

"It always is. Life is too short. Let's drink our coffee, before it gets cold. And then, talk to me about you. I want to know more." Alisha picked up her cup and blew softly over the top of it as it was still steaming.

She wanted to know more. I needed to be careful with what I would tell her today.

"Well, I'm quite close with my sister Mira. She checks in on me every day. We had a...rough start in life." I paused on the last sentence and took a long sip of my coffee, thankful I had that to distract me from panicking. Thinking about my past still affected me; it was the fact that my sister and I had parents who didn't care about us. Growing up, we didn't think we had been worthy of love. We'd found it difficult when our aunt took us in, and it took about six months before we fully trusted her and her sons. If I were to have kids of my own one day, I'd never abandon them or leave them to fend for themselves. I'd never let them feel the way me and Mira felt: unwanted and unloved. I wouldn't be the best father in the world, I'd make mistakes as any parent would but I'd make sure I did the best job I could raising my kids.

"You look lost in thought. Are you okay? Do you want to talk about it?" Alisha asked, looking a little concerned. I met her eyes again and all I could see was sympathy in them.

She was worried about me.

It was hard to believe that anyone would show a hint of care about me but I wanted to trust in Alisha. So I continued to speak.

"I won't talk about it today. But there's a lot. My past is still a lot to get my head round. I'm the person I am today because of it," I admitted.

"I completely understand. But thank you for telling me a bit about you. You're pretty cool, Felix," Alisha said. My heart raced when she said this, knowing that she thought I was cool. In return, I thought she was pretty phenomenal.

We continued to talk until we had finished our coffees and it was time to get going for our walk. The sun was beaming outside, and as we took a step outside into the fresh air, I reflected on what I'd said about my past. There was this saying, that the past shouldn't define you. Maybe I needed to listen to that.

Chapter 14

Alisha

Felix clearly had trouble opening up, more so than I had. I needed to tread carefully with him, I didn't want to lose his friendship or trust. It was clear he had been through it all, even just mentioning the word 'past' seemed to affect him deeply. When he was ready to talk about it, I would be here. Ready to listen. Ready to be a friend.

Felix and I were now walking side by side in a comfortable rhythm. The weather was stunning today, a slight crisp in the air but not too cold. I had removed my jacket and was thankful I changed my clothing into something more comfortable.

I couldn't ignore the way his fingers would curl up into his palm and the way he lightly bit his bottom lip as he concentrated on the path ahead of us. The scenery was certainly stunning and so was Felix. I had enough self-control to stop myself from grabbing his hand and holding it in mine. Yes, it was very clear I desired the man.

A gentle breeze wafted through the air, tickling the back of my neck and twisting through my hair. I was grateful for it as my skin still felt on fire. Felix and I hadn't even touched and all I could feel was heat. It was crazy that he was having this effect on me. I hadn't felt like this in a while.

"The view is stunning," I finally said after a few minutes of walking. As we were walking higher, you could see Iscghl in its glory, the cars driving down the roads. Felix turned his head towards me and my insides did a somersault. His expression was stoic but it was enough to affect me anyway.

He was so bloody attractive.

I could see a five o'clock shadow on his chin, his hazel eyes were twinkling in the sunlight and fuck, he also smelled good. *Sweet and spicy.* I tried to ignore the heat pooling between my legs.

"It is. But just as beautiful at night too. I feel lucky to live here," Felix said, and it sounded like he meant it. I wondered whether he ever ventured away from here.

"Well, I'm certainly going to mention this walk in the article," I replied and soon, the two of us came to a stop. I wished I had brought some water with me as now I was parched.

"You can interview me, if you want. It's always good to get some insight from a resident. I've never left Ischgl, so I know tons about it." Felix gave me a wry smile but even the smallest of gestures made me weak at the knees.

"If you don't mind. Maybe you can come back to mine after this? I'll cook us something. Ophelia will be there, she's very eager to meet you." I grinned, knowing exactly how my friend would react upon seeing Felix.

"I'm eager to meet her too. A friend of yours is a friend of mine," Felix said.

Could he get any cuter?

I'd noticed he had gradually become less grumpy, over the few times I had met him. I wondered what the change was. He seemed to notice I had forgotten to reply and edged a little closer, so that he was nearly towering over me. He looked ethereal as the sun beat down on him and I looked up at him through hooded eyes. If I stepped even closer, our bodies would be touching and our breaths would be mingled together.

"I, um," the words wouldn't come out all of a sudden. My mind was screaming to just take the plunge and kiss the man, but I didn't feel quite brave to conquer my thoughts. Felix took a step back and cleared his throat.

"Let's keep going. Tell me a bit more about England," Felix said, taking the lead and I fell into step beside him.

"Well, I think I told you a bit about my family. My parents are very supportive, they've always encouraged me to achieve my dreams. Do what makes me happy, you know?" Felix nodded and then I continued.

"Where I live in England, it's busy but comfortable. I have a cat called Chou, he keeps me company since I live alone," I said. I hoped my little buddy was okay but I knew Kiya would be taking good care of him.

"Do you like living alone?" Felix asked. The truth was, no I didn't. I wanted to share a place with someone in the future, ideally a partner. It wasn't terrible living on my own but I did want to come home to someone who adored me one day and collapse into their arms.

"Not really, no. Sometimes I wish I had a housemate. I'll admit to you though, I almost ended up living with my ex. But I'm thankful I didn't," I admitted. I felt comfortable to share this with Felix, he seemed to be a man of no judgement.

"What was he like, if you don't mind me asking?" Felix questioned. I took a deep breath before answering.

"Charming, at first. He won me over quite quickly and I'd say that I did love him. I used to have a friend called Felicity and she'd usually hang out with Caden, my ex, and me. We'd been together for nearly a year before I found out he was cheating on me with Felicity," I told Felix and his eyebrows raised, shock evident on his face.

"Shit, I'm sorry. That's horrible what he did to you. And also your friend. How did you handle that?"

"Happened about six months ago, so I'd say I'm pretty much over it. He does still try to contact me but I ignore his texts. Felicity, on the other hand, apologised once and that was that. It hurt, losing her friendship, but she lost my trust and I don't ever want to see her again. You don't do that to your so-called best friend, you know?" I realised I had been biting my bottom lip, probably due to nerves. I released my lip from my teeth, and focused on some deep breathing.

"She wasn't a true friend. Do you ever miss him though?" Felix was asking all the questions I'd been asking myself, but I had one clear answer.

"No, not anymore." I smiled, and for the first time, I felt relief. That I had ridden out the worst of the storm and now there was a rainbow waiting for me.

"I'm sorry, I forgot to bring hot chocolate. And the promised picnic," Felix said as we took a little break.

"Don't be sorry. I'm happy just walking with you," I told him.

If anything, food was the last thing on my mind.

After about twenty minutes or so of walking, I had grown rather tired and it was time for us to head back. My stomach was growling for food, and I was thankful we had done a food shop as there was plenty in the fridge for a late lunch. Grayson texted me to schedule a video call for tomorrow. He wanted to see how things were going and if I had a draft I could send him, so he could get a feel of what I was writing and perhaps provide some advice. I knew I needed to get something prepared this evening, and Felix thankfully offered to be interviewed so at least I had some things to note down.

It didn't take long to get to the chalet, and as soon as we entered through the front door, we were greeted by Ophelia.

"Well, hello." She smirked, her green eyes full of mischief. I hoped she wouldn't say or do anything that would embarrass me.

"Good afternoon," Felix greeted her, offering his hand to shake. Ophelia took it, giving it a firm shake. She then released it and crossed her arms.

"Finally good to talk to you. This girl has been talking my ear off about you and I wondered when I'd actually get to see the said man." Ophelia chuckled.

Here we go. Operation Embarrass Alisha is in action.

"Oh, has she? I hope all good things." Felix seemed to find this amusing as he met my gaze. I tried to relax my features as I was glaring previously at Ophelia.

"Oh yes. Well, at first, she called you Mr Grumpy. I don't get that vibe off you at all. You're very charming and it's a pleasure to meet you, Felix," Ophelia said and then gave me a wink, before mouthing *he's gorgeous*. Thankfully, Felix hadn't noticed this as he was glancing around the room.

"Can I make you something to drink? I was about to put on some hot chocolate," my friend offered.

"If you're making one, I'd love one too," Felix said politely.

"My wish has come true," I said, exchanging a look with Felix, who smiled warmly at me.

"Okay, great. Ali, come and help me. I'm guessing the two of you haven't eaten either, so we can get something cooking. Are you a fussy eater, Felix?" Ophelia asked. I didn't think Felix would be, he seemed to enjoy whatever he ate and drank.

"Not at all. I'll eat whatever." Felix smiled but he wasn't looking at Ophelia anymore. He was looking at me, and there was an expression I couldn't quite make out.

"You can take a seat on the sofa. Make yourself comfortable, I'll just be in the kitchen," I told him and he nodded, walking toward the living room. He had removed his coat and hung it on one of the hooks by the front door.

Ophelia and I hurried to the kitchen to get started but the minute we got there, she ambushed me.

"Do you see what I see? I think he likes you," Ophelia questioned.

"No. I don't think it's like that, Lia," I told her. Yes, Felix and I had shared a few looks. But nothing happened and he hadn't done or said anything that would make me think he actually liked me.

"But you like him, right?" Ophelia pushed and I knew she wouldn't let it go until I admitted the truth to her.

"I might do. But I'm happy just being friends, a relationship isn't exactly what I need right now," I told her, grabbing the cocoa out of one of the cupboards and some milk from the fridge.

"Hey, I'm making that. You're shit at making hot chocolate, sorry babes." Ophelia grabbed the cocoa from me and placed a pan on the hob.

"Ouch, you bitch." I stuck my tongue out at her and she giggled, greeting me with her middle finger. I did love the banter between us and I really was thankful she had joined me on this trip. Even if she was going to embarrass me for the next few hours.

I grabbed a few ingredients from the fridge, as I decided I would make us all a carbonara. It was quick to make and always delicious.

"He's not Caden, Ali. I think he's into you. You just need to trust that not all men are like your ex. But whatever you decide, I am here for you. I support you with whatever you choose." Ophelia stirred the cocoa and milk together in the pan, which was starting to bubble.

"Thanks, Lia. But I can't forget that I'm here for work. Grayson is going to call me tomorrow, so I can't afford to get distracted," I said, grabbing my own pan to start boiling the spaghetti.

"Okay, I understand. I already spoke to Grayson today, and he seems quite happy. He is thinking perhaps of coming up here soon with his family," Ophelia told me. It made sense, as Grayson always loved to travel, especially with his family and it wasn't long until Christmas. This was one of the best times to come.

"Oh, that's cool. Felix offered to be interviewed so hopefully, that will help with the article." I started to chop up the pancetta into smaller pieces and then fry it in a flat pan.

"That's kind of him." Ophelia switched off the stove as the hot chocolate was now ready and poured an equal amount into three mugs.

"I'm just going to ask him if he likes cream and marshmallows. Can you keep an eye on the pancetta please?" I asked, and my friend nodded before I made my way to the living room. Felix was glancing at his phone, before he noticed my presence and he put it back into his trouser pocket.

"Everything okay?" he asked, his eyes scanning me up and down.

"Yep. Hot chocolate is ready. Do you like cream and marshmallows?" I clasped my hands in front of me, suddenly feeling quite nervous in front of him.

"I do, thank you. Can I help in there at all?"

"No, we're okay. You're our guest. Feel free to put the TV on. I'll bring you your hot chocolate," I said, smiling chastely at him before heading back to the kitchen.

Ophelia had sorted out the carbonara sauce for me, which I was grateful for.

"You know what, let me handle all this. Go back in there and talk to him. Here's both of your hot chocolates." Ophelia ushered me away.

"Are you sure?"

"One hundred percent." She grinned and I knew I didn't have to ask her twice. She was very serious. I obeyed her, carrying two steaming mugs of hot chocolate topped with cream and marshmallows back to the living room where Felix was now channel hopping on the TV.

"Here we go." I held out his mug in front of him, which he took. A jolt of electricity sprung through me as the tips of our fingers touched through the exchange.

"Thank you." Felix smiled, taking his first sip.

"Ophelia took over from me. She's sorting out the lunch," I said, taking a seat beside him on the sofa.

"Fair enough. This is a nice chalet. Are the two of you paying for it?" Felix asked.

"Accommodation is being covered by the company. Ophelia and I offered to pay, however our boss Grayson insisted on sorting it all for us," I said, taking a deep sip of my hot beverage.

"He seems like he cares about his employees. That's good." Felix licked a bit of cream from his lips. This simple action sent me into overdrive, and I could feel myself getting hot again.

"He's a good boss," I said, trying to distract my heated thoughts with another sip of hot chocolate. As I placed my mug down on a coaster on the table in front of us, Felix was gazing at me rather intently.

"Have I got something on my face?" I suddenly felt worried and touched my nose. Perhaps cream had ended up there. How embarrassing.

"You just have a bit of cream on the top of your lip."

"Oh, okay." I tried to lick it away but this caused Felix to chuckle and he edged a bit closer to me. My heart was pumping fast and he lifted one of his fingers to gently touch my upper lip.

"Here. Let me," he spoke, a slight roughness to his voice. I took a sharp intake of breath, as his thumb gently swiped the stray cream away from my lip. I squeezed my thighs together, as he then licked his thumb, never breaking eye contact with me.

Maybe Ophelia was right. Maybe there was an attraction forming. But whether I was brave enough to do anything about it, that was the question.

"T-thanks." My voice was shaky but in a good way. I felt nervous but elated all at once. I welcomed these feelings but tried not to let them consume me entirely. I needed to appear composed.

We were startled by Felix's phone vibrating in his pocket and he seemed to dislike this.

"Sorry, I better answer it. Probably my sister." Felix said and I nodded. I took this as an opportunity to head to the bathroom and splash my face with cold water, so thankful that Ophelia hadn't seen what had happened.

As I looked at myself in the mirror, I could see how flushed my skin was, my breathing was erratic and my pupils were dilated. I gripped the edge of the sink and tried to convince myself to calm down.

"Get your shit together," I told myself in the mirror, glaring back at the image. I knew from this point on, it was going to be very difficult to mask my true feelings for Felix. I had slight hope that perhaps he felt the same too. For now, I needed to return back to him and see where the day would take us.

Chapter 15

Felix

I was thankful for my sister ringing, as it stopped me from doing what I wanted to do. Kissing Alisha. I didn't know if the moment would have been right, especially with her friend cooking in the kitchen. If I was going to kiss Alisha, I wanted it to be special. Our first kiss wasn't going to be here. I was a man of many romantic gestures so I'd do it when the time was right.

After speaking with my sister for a few minutes, Alisha returned and seemed calm in her demeanour. She finished the remainder of her hot chocolate and I mimicked. Her friend did make good beverages, probably one of the best I'd tried. I had been a bit nervous meeting her but there had been no awkwardness. Ophelia seemed genuine and made the effort to get to know me. She also seemed like a true friend to Alisha, who told me she had been through a horrible break-up.

Dealing with a break-up was always tough, but having someone you thought you loved and trusted cheat on you? Now, that was another thing.

Alisha and I both had dealt with heartbreak and she had been brave to share her story with me today. I needed to pluck up the courage and be honest with her too. I really admired the woman next to me. Fuck, she was the definition of beauty itself.

Do yourself a favour Felix and kiss her. Fuck the rules.

I argued with my conscience however, as this wasn't the right time. We needed to get the interview out of the way and then, maybe I could ask her out for dinner again. This time, I would admit that it's a date. That would be a perfect opportunity.

"Food is ready!" Ophelia's voice sang and just like clockwork, my stomach growled.

"Finally. I am starving." Alisha smiled, offering me her hand to pull me up from the sofa. With no hesitation, I took it, enveloping her fingers through mine. I loved how small her hand was and how soft her skin felt. I would hold her hand forever if I could, just to remain close to her. To my surprise, she didn't let go, even as we sat down to eat and Ophelia had served us. Maybe she felt the same way. Just maybe.

***

Lunch had been the chef's kiss, and the three of us were now satisfied. Ophelia had decided to get some work done, so left Alisha and I sitting alone together on the sofa. We were in a comfortable silence, as we watched an episode of Friends. I didn't mind watching this, as every so often, Alisha would laugh and fuck, I loved it when she laughed. I felt bold enough to intertwine our fingers again, and she smiled at this, giving my hand a squeeze.

"Are you okay?" she asked me, her brown eyes wide with slight concern.

"Yes," I breathed, squeezing her hand back. I could get used to this, feeling her touch. I could happily sit here, just holding her hand and watching Friends episodes. But I knew that time was ticking by, and she wanted to get some work done. I wouldn't hold her back from her job. I would do what I could to help her write the best article. I wanted her boss to give her that promotion she craved.

I wasn't an expert at writing but I knew how important it was to Alisha. And whatever was important to her was now important to me.

"Well, this article won't write itself. You up for some questions and answers then?" Alisha asked me, turning the TV off with the remote.

"Fire away, my lady," I said, noticing that as soon as I said the last two words, a faint hint of pink was tainting her cheeks.

"I'll go get my laptop," she said sheepishly and practically raced away to go and retrieve it. I had a good view of her ass as she did so, and fuck she had a good one. Her whole figure was amazing but the best feature? Her eyes. I could get lost in them if I wasn't careful. Well, on a few occasions I had. Couldn't help it.

Yes you could, and if you don't stop, you'll end up getting hurt.

The deeper part of my brain was telling me that stepping over the barrier between Alisha and I would be a bad idea, given the experience I had in my previous relationship, but your brain wasn't always right, was it?

Alisha interrupted my thoughts as she returned, shifting close beside me.

"You know what, it's more comfortable in my room. Would you like to join me?" Alisha asked. *Wow, already inviting you to her bedroom.*

"O-of course," I fumbled for words but this was enough for her to pull me up from my position and lead us toward her room. My heart was pounding and blood was rushing to my ears. I knew nothing would happen in there, that we were just going to work. Then I would go home.

When I entered Alisha's room, I could see how neat it was. She had arranged her dressing table with an array of body cream, perfume and make-up. The bed itself, which had pristine white sheets on it with a grey throw on top, looked comfortable and big enough for two people. I was glad she was sleeping comfortably.

Alisha sat down and gestured for me to join her, placing her laptop in front of her.

"So, I've got some questions. But I'll let you take the lead too. Don't mind me if I go quiet, just because I'll be taking notes. You'll see how fast I can type. I have magic fingers." Alisha grinned, her gorgeous smile was infectious and I couldn't help but smile back at her. Smiling no longer felt foreign to me, this woman seemed to have this effect on me.

"No problem," I said and watched as her fingers danced across the keyboard. She then lifted her eyes from the screen and cleared her throat.

"So, tell me about your life here in Ischgl. What's so appealing about it?" Alisha questioned. Interesting that she hadn't asked me about my family but I was grateful for it. I didn't want to dive into my sad childhood.

"Well, a lot of people think this town is just for skiing. But there's so much more to it. The people, the atmosphere, the nature. Once you're here, you don't want to leave. I haven't plucked up the courage to step outside of Ischgl yet. Does that sound crazy?" I paused as Alisha continued to type but she gave me an answer anyway.

"Not at all, it's understandable. You remind me of myself. I'm usually comfortable staying in one place," Alisha said.

"Do you feel glad you came here?" I asked, and I felt a sudden pang knowing that she would be leaving in less than two weeks. All the more reason to act on my emotions and ask her on a date. So, why was I here sitting like a lovesick puppy, unable to ask her the very words that had been swimming in my mind for the past twenty-four hours?

"Yeah, I'm enjoying my time here. I've met some great people." As she mentioned the last two words, she met my eyes and there was a softness within them.

"So, I'd love to know more about your family and how you celebrate Christmas," Alisha asked me, and it felt like a more personal question, maybe one she really wanted to know the answer to rather than just for the purpose of the article.

"I'm not sure your readers will want to know about my family life," I said. To be honest, my past had been documented in the past all those years ago and it had been hard, knowing that people knew exactly what me and Mira had gone through. They pitied us and I hated it. Aunt Brenna had tried to prevent us from seeing the daily newspaper but she'd been too late. As soon as I saw our names within an article, I wasn't able to stop reading. I still had a copy of that article somewhere at Aunt Brenna's, whether I'd read it again, who knows.

"Well, I think they will probably want to know what a traditional Christmas is like in Ischgl. So tell me, I'm all ears." Alisha smiled softly at me, but her eyes were telling me that it was okay if I didn't want to talk about it. However, I was thankful I had some good stories to tell about Christmas so as I spoke, Alisha would make notes and flash me a smile that made me almost lose my breath. Another barrier that was breaking away, which maybe was a good thing. Honesty was a good thing.

"My sister and I love to go skiing usually on Christmas Day, then our aunt prepares us a late lunch for us. We usually eat an array of things, ranging from bratwurst, to turkey and weihnachtsgans which is christmas goose," I told her and I didn't miss the way her tongue darted out to lick her bottom lip. This caused my cock to twitch in my trousers and I internally groaned, telling myself to stop becoming aroused by just a simple motion.

If only I could have taken that lip of hers between my teeth and swiped my own tongue across it.

"Wow, sounds delicious," she said in response, then looked back up at me from her laptop screen.

"What about you and your family?" I asked her. She told me previously her parents were from India but not much about their traditions.

"Well, we love Christmas. Back in India, it is like a wonderland with all the lights and decorations. We recently celebrated Diwali, the five-day festival of lights. It's a form of worship to the goddesses of India. It's amazing seeing everyone get together," Alisha told me, and I didn't know much about the festival but I certainly would find out more about it later. I wanted to learn more about her culture.

"Do you spend Christmas in India normally or in the UK?" I wanted to know more about her family and their traditions.

"For the last few years, we've celebrated in the UK. My aunts and uncles usually like to come down for it. We all stay at my parents place and a delicious meal is cooked. We have a lot of things to eat, like masala smashed potatoes and then for dessert, mum likes to bake a carrot cake or maybe an Indian dessert board which has nuts and fruits on it. Gosh, even thinking about it is making me hungry." Alisha smiled, getting lost in thoughts of home I would imagine.

"Sounds really great. How is your sister doing?" I pretty much wanted to stop talking about myself and learn more about Alisha, fuck the interview.

"Kiya, yeah she's alright. I always look out for her, she's very sweet and she has a good heart. Unfortunately people have taken advantage of that." Alisha let out a sigh. I could sympathise as I knew how that felt. It's what made it hard to trust people, but I felt as though I could trust Alisha, and it sounded like her family was trustworthy too.

"It's the same with my sister. Heart of gold which people are very quick to tear apart. We do what we can for our siblings, don't we?" I pondered on this comment, thinking back to the past few months where Mira picked up the pieces of my shattered heart, she really had been there for me and although she didn't have the instant solution of healing my heart, at least her company had done me good. I owed her a lot and I would do my best now to be a good brother.

"My brothers are a little different to me. Both stubborn but they mean well," Alisha said, scrunching her nose slightly.

"I bet it's nice to have a big family though," I said and she smiled at this, nodding in agreement.

"Oh, yeah. They have my back and I'm very lucky." Alisha flashed me another heart-stopping grin before getting back to typing.

She really was a quick typer.

"Sorry. I'm distracting you with my questions," I said, realising that really we were here to talk about me and my traditions.

"Not at all. It's nice to talk to someone who's genuinely interested in me and my family," Alisha said. I wondered who wouldn't be interested, she already had me in the palm of her hand and it'd only been a few days. Absolutely crazy. Originally I'd felt conflicted about my growing feelings for her, whether I was kidding myself or not. But the more I spent time with her, the more I felt like myself. The lost version I didn't think I'd get back. Maybe I was starting to become less afraid of the idea of liking someone again.

As if she could read my mind, Alisha's eyes met mine and I couldn't find myself looking away. I didn't want to.

I got lost in the abyss that was her deep brown eyes, deep and inviting. I didn't want to stop talking to her, to admire the way every so often she would wet her lips as if she was parched. This feeling was indescribable but I wanted more. The question was, how was I going to make the first move?

Chapter 16

Alisha

There was no denying now that I was under Felix's spell. The feelings I harboured for Felix were bordering on intense and I barely knew the man. This was only the second date, if you could call it that. I almost didn't want to go back home in a few weeks. I was beginning to like it here, to like how I felt with Felix. Conversation was easy—it didn't feel forced. I felt a sense of belonging I hadn't felt in a while, but did I truly deserve this? I'd been unlucky in love before but I couldn't blame myself for someone else's actions. I wasn't the one who cheated.

I tried to shake this thought away and remind myself that Felix didn't seem like the type to hurt someone. He looked like he had been the one who got burnt, and maybe he'd tell me soon, but I wanted it to be on his own terms. For him to feel truly comfortable and trusting of me.

I wanted so desperately to make the first move and yesterday had been the perfect opportunity, but I froze. I had all the words and actions in my head but actually doing something about them was as if I was super glued to the ground. I didn't miss the way he had a hint of yearning in his eyes and how every so often, his pupils would dilate as they looked at me. I reminisced the way his fingers were a mere few inches from my own and it had been tempting to intertwine them with my own, to drag them down my exposed skin.

The evening had been amazing too, once I had finished my interview with Felix we decided to get some dessert nearby and just talk. I didn't want the night to end but it had to at some point. I'd told myself that there was tomorrow and that time was really precious, to make the most of it whilst I was here.

I then decided in the evening, once Felix had left, to note down all my thoughts, since I was always better at writing than speaking. The first thing I did this morning was read the page I'd written and the hunger and lust I had felt resurfaced.

I'd never felt like this before. One of us was going to need to make the move. Maybe it would be me today.

Taking the lead in something always made me anxious, I avoided taking charge in most cases. My skiing lesson had gone very well again, and Ophelia treated me to a hearty lunch after. I needed to use the afternoon though to write, as Grayson would be calling me soon. He'd want to see what I'd written and give some feedback. I always valued his input and how supportive he was. He didn't shy away from giving constructive criticism, as any good boss would. He was straight to the point and I needed that.

With the notes from Felix's interview, I had plenty to use for the actual article and so far, I was pleased. I had a section about the food, as well as the places to visit and opinions of the residents. I wanted to market Ischgl in the right way, to show how wonderful it was. I wished I had come here sooner, to partly have gotten out of my comfort zone quicker but also as I would have met Felix sooner. To help fix whatever had caused him to break. I was going to try my best now to help, even if I only had less than two weeks left. Yes. It would be my mission to heal Felix as he was starting to heal me.

***

"You look beautiful," Ophelia had told me, as I was tying my dark hair up into a high ponytail. I was about to start a call with Grayson and wanted to look presentable, so I ditched my casual clothes and put on a smart shirt and trousers.

"Thanks. And you do, too. As always," I paid her the same compliment which caused her to smile, her pristine white teeth on display. She placed her laptop on the coffee table as Grayson's name popped up on my own screen. I accepted the call and was greeted with the calm expression of my boss. He was donning a grey, smart jumper and holding a mug of what looked like tea in his hands.

"Hi Alisha. How's everything?" Grayson asked with a stoic expression, taking a sip of his hot beverage.

"Absolutely fine," I replied, turning to see Ophelia give me a thumbs up.

"Good, you do sound happy. And the photos you shared look great. So, how's the writing coming along?" he asked, and this prompted me to forward the draft to his email.

"I've sent you the draft," I said and he nodded, tapping his fingers on his keyboard.

"Okay, great. Got it. So, let's discuss it and then we'll think of a plan," Grayson said and I nodded, hoping he would like what he saw. As he shared his screen, he started to highlight a few things and add a few comments which I could address after the call. He was always very efficient and thorough like this, which is again exactly what I needed to improve.

"You repeat this word often," Grayson pointed out and I realised I'd said 'though' more than three times. It caused the flow of my sentences to sound awkward.

"I like what you said about the coffee. The name of the cafe is very cute. How have you found skiing so far? I think it'd be a good idea to mention it, since it's a true experience and people always love to hear the author's account," Grayson told me, and it made sense. I was just afraid that he would ask me to scrap that if I'd written it.

"Skiing is a lot more fun than I'd anticipated. I'm learning very quickly," I said.

"So, definitely write about it. I'd love to see it. So far Alisha, it's looking good. Couple of descriptions could be better but I've added some comments here that you can look at after the call. A good first draft, well done." Grayson offered me a chaste smile, which signalled to me that this was a success. Ophelia silently clapped next to me and I smiled back at her. We definitely needed to go out for a drink later.

"Thank you so much, Grayson. I'll take your feedback on board, I always appreciate it."

"And I appreciate you. And Ophelia. Hope she's also doing okay," Grayson said and in response, Ophelia moved closer to me and said hello.

"I've got some things I'll send you as well, Grayson. Would love your opinion on it," Ophelia said.

"Ping it my way. Hope you two enjoy the rest of your day. Keep up the good work and enjoy the rest of your day."

"Thanks, Grayson. You too," I said, and then ended the call. I was met with a stifling hug from my friend and I squeezed her back in response. The video call couldn't have gone better.

"Ali, that's so amazing. He *liked* it." She grinned and it was clear she was truly delighted for me.

"We should go out for a drink to celebrate. You up for it?" I nudged her, and she released me from the hug.

"Oh hell yeah. Can't say no to a few cocktails with my girl. What time and where?" Ophelia clasped her hands together, practically bouncing on the sofa. I admired her energy and just her overall.

"Let's go for eight o'clock and how about a more lavish bar? There's one called Fire and Ice, it's amazing inside. Drinks are on me," I told my friend and she smirked at this. It wasn't often that I would suggest this.

"It's a girlie night then." Ophelia winked. She was right. I wanted to spend time with my best friend and make some crazy, funny memories. We had a few hours to kill and after the call, I felt a sense of fatigue so a nap was definitely needed. Ophelia felt the same too so we agreed one of us would wake the other up when it was time to get ready. When I retreated to my room, my phone was lighting up with a few texts. *Felix.* He was asking me how I was.

> **Alisha:** I'm okay, how's your day been?

> **Felix:** Really good actually x I'll be finishing work in a few hours, was wondering if you wanted to do something?

> **Alisha:** I'm glad you had a good day and I hope work is going okay too x well tonight, Ophelia and I are having a girls night x

> **Felix:** That sounds good, well I will leave you girls to it x enjoy your evening, I hope to see you soon

> **Alisha:** Thank you x and of course, text me

And after that, my phone went silent and perhaps because Felix was now preoccupied with something at work. I shrugged it off and rested my head on the pillow, falling into a deep sleep and thinking of gorgeous hazel eyes.

***

"You look absolutely stunning, Lia," I'd said to my friend, as she spun around slowly to show off her sparkly purple dress. It hugged her figure nicely and she was wearing a matching pair of heels. The dress suited her, especially as she had purple streaks in her hair anyway. Since we were going to be inside for the evening, our attire was appropriate.

"Thanks. And you look so beautiful yourself. Look at that dress." Ophelia motioned for me to spin around myself. I was wearing a velvet black bardot dress which ended a few inches above my knees. It wasn't too short or too long, which was perfect. I'd outlined my eyes with kohl eyeliner and dark eyeshadow which was bold for me. My hair itself was wavy and cascaded down my back.

"Now, have you got your purse?" Ophelia asked me, holding her own in her hands.

"Yes. Driver's licence and extra money just in case they don't take our cards," I said.

"So we're good to go. Let's have a great night. Let's celebrate you." She smiled.

"No. Let's celebrate us," I responded and she winked.

"Touché," she replied, linking her arm through mine as we left the house to make our way to Fire and Ice. We'd hired a taxi to take us, since walking in heels wouldn't be a good idea. It was waiting outside for us and we were greeted by our young, friendly driver with blond hair and green eyes, who engaged in polite conversation throughout the journey.

When we pulled up to the bar, we couldn't contain our excitement.

"You've picked the right place to go for drinks. Hope you enjoy your evening," the taxi driver said and I noticed his German accent was not as thick as Felix's.

"Thank you. Keep the change," I told him and he thanked me before driving away. Ophelia and I were like excited teenagers, linking arms again and walking up toward the front entrance. As we entered, we were taken aback by the decor—plush tables and chairs with fancy lights hanging from the walls. We didn't have to wait long before we were greeted by the host. Her name tag read *Bindi*, and she had kind, hazel eyes that reminded me of Felix's.

"Welcome, ladies," Bindi greeted us in English—to be honest, most of the people we came across spoke English.

"Hi," Ophelia said tepidly, as if she'd lost all confidence. She was still eyeing up the room and the furniture.

"You can come right through and take a seat at one of the tables. We offer food here too, so let us know what you'd like. You ladies look like you are celebrating so we want to give you a great experience. Anything you need, just let me know," Bindi said with a warm smile.

"Thank you so much," Ophelia said with full attention, as Bindi was now leading the way to our table. The bar was quite full with couples on dates and some single people too by the looks of it. It seemed a calm vibe but also quite sophisticated. I didn't mind how much we spent tonight, I'd happily pay the tab for both of us.

As we took our seats, we both looked through the menu and decided to order some fruity cocktails as our aperitifs. When they were placed in front of us, the glasses looked pristine and once we took our first sips, we couldn't stop. Peach and vodka coated my tongue with every gulp. I knew I was going to feel tipsy soon.

"So, any update on you and Felix?" Ophelia asked me, swirling a straw in her glass.

"We texted earlier and he hasn't messaged me since this afternoon," I said.

"Ah, look at you. So love struck. Why don't you send him a text now?"

"No texting tonight. He can wait. Tonight's all about us." I grinned, bringing my glass to my lips again.

"Tonight's all about *you*, Ali. You're pretty damn great, don't forget it."

"Back at you. Cheers." I clinked my glass with hers and then drained the rest of my drink.

"Another round? And then we'll order some food. I'm craving some pizza," Ophelia said and I agreed, the pizza did sound and look good. My stomach growled in response and I knew I didn't want to drink anymore on an empty stomach. I switched to water for the time being and Ophelia decided the same.

"You having a good time?" Bindi asked us as she took our food order.

"Oh, absolutely. Where are the toilets, if I may ask?" I questioned, trying to sound as polite as possible.

"Just to the left. I'll put this order through for you." Bindi smiled and then left us.

"I'll look after your purse," Ophelia said, reaching her hand out so I could pass her my purse.

"Thanks. Won't be long. Dying for a pee." I giggled and she waved her hand at me to go. I walked at a steady pace to the toilets, admiring the scenery around me. I noticed a few men glance my way, attention that I didn't necessarily want, but the look I returned was enough to tell them I wasn't interested.

Once I did my business in the toilets, I ran a tissue under my eyes as a bit of the eye shadow had fallen from my upper lids. As I stared at myself in the large mirror, I got lost in lustful thoughts of Felix appearing behind me, placing his firm hands on either side of my hips and pulling me to him. I imagined him pressing his lips to the flushed skin on my neck and then dipping his hand lower and lower until it met my—

I was interrupted by someone entering the toilets and I cleared my throat, adjusting my dress which had somehow ridden up my thighs.

Fucking hell.

I realised I'd probably take longer than expected so I needed to return to my waiting friend as it would be rude. I smiled at her as I strode toward the table, feeling a sudden burst of confidence. I took my seat next to her and she raised one eyebrow at me in curiosity.

"You okay there, pal?"

"Totally. Wonder when the food is coming," I said, taking a swig of my icy water. Definitely needed that to cool down. My thighs were still burning.

Ophelia's gaze moved away from my own to stare at something or rather someone that had caught her attention. Her eyebrows scrunched up as she was concentrating and then she opened her mouth.

"I think that's Felix over there." Ophelia's eyes met mine, full of curiosity. I quickly averted my gaze to where she was looking and my heart was pounding like mad in my chest.

He was here.

He looked amazing, in a smart white shirt and trousers. He'd also shaved and his hair was slightly ruffled. I looked to the left of him and could see he wasn't alone. He was speaking to a beautiful woman, who seemed as though she was confiding in him about something. The conversation looked serious. I could only see one side of Felix, as he stared ahead of him rather than at her. *Like he didn't want to be there.*

Then, just like clockwork, or maybe he could read minds, he turned his head and his eyes met mine. His expression went from angry then switched to what looked like excitement. Without looking back at the woman next to him, he made his way over. The woman looked fed up but didn't do or say anything to stop him.

Shit, he was coming over to me.

Chapter 17

Felix

Work had been okay today, I'd made the odd phone call here and there to potential clients as well as interact with my colleagues. The thing that got me through the last few hours was knowing I'd be able to see my sister, since she was coming over tonight. Probably to keep an eye on me and maybe even suggest going out. For the first time in a while, I didn't mind this.

I texted Alisha earlier and she told me she was having a girls night, which was good for her. I couldn't deny the slight pang of need I felt for her in that moment, to almost want to ask if I could come along, but I'd learned from my past mistakes, how reliant I had been on my ex. I wasn't the boyfriend to follow her around and ask what she was doing every five minutes but I cared about her day, what made her smile and frown. I cared about her wellbeing, but perhaps that had been too much. So, I stopped texting Alisha and ignored the desire to go and find her, press her against a wall ,and infuse her lips to mine.

Once I clocked out of my work, I practically sped home in my car and was very lucky not to be stopped by the police. I was usually a sensible driver but home was calling for me desperately. Pulling up into my drive, I switched off the engine and made haste towards my front door. I'd noticed my sister's car was already here and she'd let herself in. I didn't mind her having a key as she always respected my boundaries and private space.

"Hello!" Mira greeted me with a cheeky smile, clearly she was in high spirits as she was bouncing on the balls of her feet. Her eyes were gleaming with something I couldn't quite work out. Nonetheless, I was happy she was happy.

"Someone's happy," I said, shrugging my coat off to hang on one of the pegs by the front door. It had been a little colder today so I was wearing a dark grey jumper with black slim trousers.

"Well, I've managed to book some time off work. I want to spend some time with my big brother so I thought tonight, you and I could go out." My sister was still beaming at me, running one hand through her silky hair.

I walked past her to grab a mug from the kitchen which was only a mere few yards away and I answered my sister.

"Okay," I said, having pondered on the idea. I didn't want to backtrack on what I had thought earlier. I really wanted to turn a new leaf. To try and heal from the hurt and pain. I couldn't keep beating myself up like this, and it'd be great for me to have a night where I could take a break from my lustful thoughts of Alisha.

"Okay? So I don't need to drag you? Fucking finally!" Mira exclaimed and threw her arms around me in a tight hug.

"Are you okay?" she asked me after some time, one eyebrow slightly arched.

"I would tell you if I wasn't. Come on then. I'll make you some tea and you can tell me about your day. We'll also make some plans for Christmas," I told her. Christmas had always been fun and myself and my sister had only really started properly celebrating it when we moved in with our aunt. I tried to not think about the times where Mira and I weren't able to celebrate. We were incredibly lucky now to have a special meal to eat as well as presents to share and receive.

"Alright. One sugar for me please, and also you have no choice in what is going to happen now. We're going to talk to me more about this mystery woman. She's somehow changed you and I am here for it." Mira grinned and then took a seat on the sofa, grabbing one of the cushions to hug against her chest.

"Uh oh," I groaned in response, because really I *did* have no choice.

Whilst the kettle boiled, I grabbed another mug for my sister and placed the teabags in our mugs. I wasn't much of a tea drinker before but since getting to know about Alisha and the UK, I knew that most of the British loved what they called a 'cuppa'.

"Here we go." I passed Mira her mug and took a seat next to her. She'd turned on the TV and was watching an episode of *Grey's Anatomy,* which was ironic since she worked in a hospital. She loved to comment on the roles the characters played as well as the scenarios that took place. She'd seen a lot of things during her time and sadly witnessed some deaths. She had always known it would be a tough job but she loved it. I just always hoped she'd take a break every now and then, to focus on her own health.

"Mm, so tell me then big bro," Mira said after a while of comfortable silence and tea sipping. I knew she wanted to get me talking about Alisha and whether I was interested in pursuing something with her.

"She's a great person. She makes you want to also be great. I mean I've only known her for a short time so it's too soon to say if there's anything there," I said. Well at least I on my part felt something.

"I know you said the other day that it probably wasn't a good idea to start something. But I don't know now, seeing the way you are right now is making me think differently," my sister said truthfully, tapping her fingers gently against her ceramic mug. I supposed she could see how much of a good impact Alisha was having on me. I was eating and drinking properly, getting enough sleep and even being more social. I was even tempted to call up some of my old friends and see how they were.

"I want to make my move on her but I'm afraid," I said, nibbling at my bottom lip slightly.

"Afraid of what?" Mira questioned, raising one eyebrow. Nothing ever really made her afraid in life, she was very bold and took a lot of risks. Maybe I could do the same.

"Being rejected. You know, ever since Ev—"

"Fuck her! It's been nearly seven months now, I know it still hurts in some ways but that woman isn't worth your time or even a passing thought. Don't let her dictate the actions you want to make right now. I think you should go for it, and I also think Alisha feels the same," Mira said. What she said did make sense, it had just taken months of gruelling pain to realise it.

"Okay. So, should I invite her out tomorrow or something?" My mind was now being filled with thoughts of Alisha and I, me closing the distance between us and doing what I wanted to do for days.

"Invite her here for dinner. I think it's always a nice touch to cook a home-made meal for someone you like," Mira suggested and it didn't sound so bad. Cooking a three course meal would surely impress Alisha and I already had ideas swimming in my head of what I'd prepare for her. I'd do my research a little later and make a list of food to buy. Tomorrow, I'd go shopping, proper shopping.

"Okay. Can you help me?"

"Of course I can. Anything for you, you know that." Mira touched my cheek gently and I smiled at her, grateful for her presence right now, and then I opened my mouth to say the next words.

"How do you feel about going out tonight for drinks? My treat." As soon as I said this, Mira let out a howl of delight.

"Hell yes. We deserve a good night, it's been a while hasn't it? Where do you suggest?"

"I was thinking of Fire and Ice, I know the host there and she will be able to get us a nice table. I can get us dinner too," I said, realising how hungry I was. Work had really been quite busy today, with people booking last minute holidays and then getting feedback from past clients.

"Ah yes, Bindi. I know her too, she's lovely. I would love a cocktail, so you've picked the right place Felix." Mira smiled softly, seeming pleased. It was now six o'clock so the best time to leave would be in about two hours or so. I needed to get changed into a fresh pair of clothes and do something about my hair which was a little oilier than usual. Mira could read my expression and placed her mug down to grab my hands and pulled me up from my seated position.

"We'll pick something nice for you to wear. And you can help me too. I have some spare clothes in the room I usually sleep in," Mira said, which didn't surprise me or bother me in one bit. We just had that kind of relationship which was comfortable and within reason.

"Okay, thanks," I said. I let out a deep breath I'd apparently been holding and reminded myself that tonight was going to be good. There was nothing to worry about.

***

The clock had struck eight o'clock and we were on our way to Fire and Ice. Luckily, Mira had booked us a taxi since if we were drinking, it wouldn't be wise to drive ourselves. I was extremely hungry now and knew I'd order at least two main courses to satisfy my hunger. Call me crazy, but that's what I wanted.

As we paid the taxi driver, we could already see that it was busy and I spotted Bindi at the entrance with her usual warm grin.

"Hello guys! It's been a long time," she greeted us, ticking our names off the list she had in front of her. It was incredibly lucky we'd managed to get a table, given how popular this bar was. We were at the peak time of the year, where restaurants, bars and hotels were starting to become full with tourists. Ischgl was one of the best places, in my opinion, to have a good holiday. I was glad Alisha had decided to come now. I hoped she was having a good night herself, whatever her and Ophelia had decided to do.

"Nice to see you, Bindi," Mira said.

"Thanks, Bindi. Fire and Ice is one of the best places to be, thought I'd treat my sister tonight," I said and Mira in response hooked her arm through mine. She looked lovely tonight, wearing a dark blue dress with a pair of wedge heels. She'd styled her hair up in a loose bun. I was wearing smart black trousers with a white shirt, which I hoped I wouldn't spill sauce or drink on tonight. My hair

I had washed and added a little bit of gel to it. I'd even put some perfume on, which I'd bought about a year ago.

"That's sweet of you. Well, follow me. I've got a great table for you. And the first drinks are on me tonight, as a welcome," Bindi said. Her hospitality was very welcome and we proceeded to follow her. Lots of people were at the bar and as we walked past, a few women glanced my way. I didn't care for their attention as I wanted someone else's. I wished she was here.

Bindi stopped in front of a table by the corner which was decorated nicely. We thanked her and took our seats, pouring ourselves a glass of water which was on the table. Bindi took our drinks orders as well as our food at the same time, since we both knew what we wanted.

"Cheers to us," Mira said as soon as our drinks arrived, hers was an espresso martini and mine was a rum and coke, something simple but pleasing to my taste buds.

"Cheers." I clinked my glass with hers and took a long sip. Delicious. Not long after, our food arrived which was one large mozzarella and pepperoni pizza for me with fries and for Mira, she had ordered a steak and chips with peppercorn sauce and tomatoes. It didn't take long for us to polish our plates and then we were in need for another round of drinks. I was aware that table service would be a little slow so I stood up to go and order at the bar.

"Same again for you?" I asked my sister who was wiping her mouth with her napkin.

"I'll have a passion fruit martini please. Do you want me to come with you?" she asked.

"No, you stay here. Have a look at the dessert menu. I think I may still have room for something sweet," I said.

"I've been eyeing up the lemon tart. Okay, be back soon," she said, picking up the menu in front of her to glance at the options. I strode up towards the bar, nodding at the several bartenders. I waited my turn, not too fussed that maybe it would take a few minutes to be served. As I looked to the left of me, I cursed internally as I focused on the person I hadn't seen for months.

Evie was here. Of all places, she just had to be here. I quickly turned away, hoping she hadn't noticed me, but of course she fucking did. And she was coming over. I kept my gaze ahead of me, I could pretend I didn't see her but I'd be lying. Conversation had to be short and sweet, I'd decided. I didn't owe her a thing.

"Felix. Hi." Her voice was as soft as I remembered but it didn't make me surrender like I used to.

"Evie," I said with a slight grunt, angling my body a little more towards her. I didn't want to be entirely rude, that wasn't my style but I really didn't want to talk to her for long.

"How are you? You look...good," Evie said, leaning against the counter as she wanted to get a better look at me.

"I'm fine."

"Look, I've been meaning to talk to you about things. The way everything happened, we were both rushing I think. The time wasn't right," she said. Bullshit. It had nothing to do with time. It was to do with her and I wasn't what she really wanted. I needed to find an excuse to leave but she kept talking.

"I know you probably don't have much to say to me. And that's understandable but I'm honestly sorry. I really hope you're happy now and that you can move on—" I blocked out her voice as I turned my attention elsewhere and my eyes met the one woman who was worth everything and more. Everything felt still but right. She was the calm in this crazy fucking storm and I wanted her right here, right now. So I made the move, not caring that I was leaving Evie behind.

As I was walking, Alisha had of course noticed me and stood up from her seat to walk towards me. She looked amazing, she always did, and I needed to tell her that, show her that too.

"Felix," was all she said but it was enough. I pulled her toward me and I forgot the world around me as I pressed my lips to hers, sighing as she locked her arms around my neck in response. She pulled me closer and deepened the kiss, as my grip tightened around her waist. My world crashed and then was born again as her lips moved against mine. Feeling brave, I slipped a tongue into Alisha's perfect mouth and she groaned in response which was music to my ears. At that moment, it was just the two of us and nothing else mattered.

Chapter 18

Alisha

*H*oly *fuck, fuck, fuck.* I didn't want this kiss to end but it had to, since Ophelia was waiting at our table. Probably shocked or maybe proud, who knows.

Felix didn't seem to want to let go either as his grip had tightened on my waist, but I was so proud of him for making the move, for being so bold. Especially in front of a load of people. My lips were going to be swollen but I didn't care. I was so drunk off of Felix, the alcohol I had forgotten about as this man here was addicting himself.

Felix's lips left mine far too soon and I practically groaned. However, he didn't let go of me, want and need glistened in his eyes.

"You look beautiful," Felix said and I melted at this, he could have said anything and I would have.

"And you look handsome. Are you alright?" I scanned his features, but found there was nothing I should be concerned about as his expression was relaxed. I had worried because the woman he was standing next to could have been his ex and I hoped his night was ruined.

"I am now," Felix replied and just as he was about to kiss me again, someone cleared their throat. Ophelia.

"Sorry, Lia." I blushed and was met with the smirk of my friend.

"Not at all. Please continue. I should be the one who is sorry." Ophelia chuckled. *Phew, I was glad she wasn't upset.*

"Do you want to go somewhere?" I turned back to Felix and he quickly nodded, removing his hands from my waist but then slipping his hand into mine, gently tugging me forward.

"Lia, I'll be back shortly," I told her.

"Take your time." She winked, lifting her glass to take a sip and wiggling her eyebrows. I needed to thank her ten times later as she was such a good friend.

"Let's go outside," I told Felix and he led the way. He took us outside where it was less noisy and there were a few other couples too, but that was fine. They didn't pay us any attention as we stood near one of them.

"I didn't expect to see you here. When you said you were having a girls night, I presumed it was maybe at home. But I am glad you're here," Felix said, stepping closer to me. I didn't hesitate to intertwine our fingers together, merging our palms together. It felt so right.

"I'm glad you're here. I hope you don't mind me asking but who was that woman you were with?" I said, with a hint of jealousy to my voice. There was no denying that the woman was beautiful.

"I don't mind telling you. That was my ex fiancé, Evie," Felix said. Fiancé? I couldn't deny that I felt a little shocked.

He was going to get married at some point, but what had actually happened between them for the wedding to not go ahead?

"We were about to get married about nearly seven months ago. I thought we were in love. It was the day of the wedding and I had arrived early at the church. I waited for her," Felix said, then looked down at his feet. I hated seeing him look like this, not being able to meet my eyes.

"It's okay," I told him. He didn't need to tell me anymore but he opened his mouth to continue. I was so glad he could trust me.

"I waited and waited. But she didn't show up. She left me standing at the altar. Apparently she didn't love me anymore, maybe she never did. It ruined me so much that I couldn't leave the house for nearly two months." Felix was now looking back at me and then took my other hand in his.

I've got you.

"I'm so sorry," I said. The shock had now turned to anger and if Felix wasn't holding me, I would march back in there and find the damn woman to tell her she'd made a huge mistake. That Felix was worth ten times, no scratch that a *billion* times worth more than her.

"It's not your fault. It's hers, I've only just come to realise it. I blamed myself for months up until I met you. So I should thank you, really. You've changed my life and it's only been a week." Felix traced his thumb across my cheekbone. His words felt sincere and the yearning look he was giving me confirmed it too.

"I don't think time matters. When you meet the right person, it's so wonderful. But I don't have long left here, Felix. Should we really start something?" I dared to ask the question but it was better that I did. Felix deserved honesty and I didn't want to hurt him.

"I know. We don't need to put any pressure on it. I want to make the most of the time I have with you. So, how do you feel about coming to mine tomorrow for dinner? I'll be cooking and I want to share more about myself with you," he said, his hand now cupping the back of my head to pull me closer. I admired his boldness and that he wanted to bring me closer to him.

"I'd be delighted. What are you going to cook for me?" I asked. It was such a sweet gesture and made my heart sing.

"It's a surprise." Felix grinned and then closed the distance between us to kiss me again. My earth shattered once more and the stars aligned again, as our lips moved in the same motion. I loved the taste of him and the way he groaned into my mouth as I slipped a tongue into his. He was a brilliant kisser and his ex was absolutely crazy. I really hoped Felix was healing from the pain she had caused and I would try my best to make him forget about her. I wanted to be his safe haven, as he was starting to become mine.

"Maybe we should head back indoors," I suggested, as Felix pressed his forehead against mine. My insides were going to be like mush at this rate, I wanted to keep kissing him but I couldn't leave my friend waiting.

"You're right. My sister's here too. I'd like you to meet her." Felix smiled softly. He didn't let go of my hand as we walked back inside and as we found his sister who was sitting at a table not far from mine. Her eyebrows raised as she looked at Felix and I, and then our joined up hands. A smile stretched on her face and her eyes lit up. She looked so much like Felix when she did this.

"Oh my—hi! I'm Mira, it's so nice to meet you." She got up from her seat and pulled me into a hug. I relaxed and my anxiety levels lowered as she gave me a gentle squeeze. I was now completely relaxed, knowing that she liked me.

"Nice to meet you too. Felix speaks very highly of you," I said, giving him a gentle nudge with my elbow.

"Well, he always talks about you, sometimes he can't shut up. He's right when he said you were beautiful," Mira said, and this caused me to blush. She was picture perfect herself, with similar eyes to her brother and soft, blonde hair that was tied up in a loose bun. She was shorter than he was but she was bold in her posture and oozed confidence. She seemed really genuine, just like Felix. I felt like we could be good friends.

"Thank you. What else has he said about me?" I couldn't help but grin, and then Felix cleared his throat.

"Oh I could give you a long list but we'd be here all night." Mira laughed and it was the kind of laugh that was genuine, not forced. I turned to Felix, raising one eyebrow. He looked like he was blushing and I couldn't help but do the same.

Did he really talk about me that much?

"Well, let's go and see your friend. We can join tables together," Felix suggested and that sounded like a good idea. The night seemed like it was far from over and I still wanted to celebrate my success with my boss. Still holding onto Felix,

I marched us over to Ophelia who was sipping a new drink. I felt quite bad that I had made her wait and needed to thank her massively.

"Sorry, Lia. I didn't mean to leave you behind," I whispered as I took my seat next to her and she shook her head, waving her hand as if to dismiss my apology.

"Don't apologise. You two looked like you needed some time alone. Hi, I'm Ophelia," she said, sticking her hand out to Mira who decided a hug was better. Ophelia didn't mind this, she was an affectionate person herself.

"Mira. I like the fact that the three of us have names that end in an 'a'. I think we'll be the best of friends." Mira let go of Ophelia and offered us both a smile. I hadn't actually thought about that but it was pretty unique.

Luckily, Bindi had noticed we were all together and brought two extra chairs over for Felix and Mira. We ordered another round of drinks and soon got to chatting. I was so happy, that honestly nothing could ruin my night.

As we were speaking and sipping fruity cocktails, I rested my hand on Felix's thigh and then turned my head towards him. Ophelia and Mira were in a deep conversation so it gave us an opportunity to talk to one another.

"Is this okay?" I motioned to my hand and Felix nodded, his eyes darting to his thigh.

"Yes," Felix said, mirroring my action with his own hand. I immediately felt hot and wished his hand would move higher so he could feel how wet I was for him. I needed a release but I realised that perhaps it would be too soon for us to become sexual with one another. But that kiss signalled that he wanted me as desperately as I wanted him and if I wasn't wrong, he looked like he had a raging hard-on right now.

"I wish I could take you back to mine right now," Felix lowered his voice so only I could hear, but to be honest, the girls weren't paying attention anyway.

"I want that too." I suddenly felt shy and wished I could say more. I wanted to tell him how much I wanted that pretty mouth of his moving down south of me, to feel his hot breath against my core and then his gentle tongue inside of me, ruining me completely. I had to squeeze my thighs together and bite my lip with all the intense thoughts I was having. It didn't help as well that his fingers were tracing circles on my thigh, daring to edge closer.

Please do.

"Alisha, Du wirst mein Tod sein," Felix said. I wished I was fluent in German and so my plan tomorrow was to hop onto one of those language learning apps and learn some more vocabulary. I knew some phrases already but I wanted to set myself a bigger challenge.

"Could you translate please?" I giggled and Felix gave me a crooked smile.

"I'll let you find that out yourself." He winked at me and my heart spasmed at this simple motion.

Fuck, he was like sunshine and I'd been craving a bit of light in my life for a while.

"Well, I'm completely exhausted guys. Do you mind if I head back home?" Mira said and we all shook our heads.

"Don't worry, I'm shattered too. I think maybe we need to give these love-birds some space." Ophelia grinned.

"Are you sure?" I asked my friend.

"Absolutely. Go spend the night with him, it'll be worth it. Make the most of your time here, you know what I always say as life is too short." Ophelia's voice dipped in a low tone so only I could hear. She was right. Time was so precious and I really wanted to be with Felix tonight. Nothing had to happen but just being with him was exhilarating enough.

"How will you get home?" I asked her.

"I'll get a taxi. Mira, do you want to share one with me?" Ophelia asked her, and she nodded quickly.

"Good plan. Let me just head to the bathroom and then we can go. I am so glad to finally meet you, Alisha. I'd love to hang out with you and Ophelia, so let's plan something," Mira said as she stood up and I copied, pulling her into a hug.

"So glad to meet you too. Yes, let's organise something," I said, and she smiled before whispering something to me.

"We so should, I don't get out very often," Mira said.

"Because you work too hard," Felix replied, his sister sticking her tongue out at him in response. Their dynamics reminded me of my own siblings and I realised how much I missed them now.

"Right, give me a hug then big brother," Mira said and Felix obeyed, towering over his sister. I smiled at the pair of them and it reminded me of my own relationship with my siblings. I needed to call them tomorrow as I really missed them.

"Get home safe, please. Text me," Felix said to her.

"Of course," she said, reassuring her brother. It was time to also say goodbye to Ophelia and she engulfed me in a massive hug, pressing a kiss to my cheek.

"Right, you better tell me about everything tomorrow. I want all the juicy details, absolutely everything young lady." She grinned and I promised her I would.

"Right, you go. I'll sort out the bill here," I said, not taking no for an answer. She smiled in appreciation. She also gave Felix an embrace and warned him to take good care of me otherwise she would hunt him down. She did always follow through on her threats so he was right to look a little scared. She meant well though.

Then, it was just Felix and I. I knew in my head I wanted more to happen between us but I would go at the pace he wanted. Fuck, I was crazy about him and if he wanted to wait, then we would. I didn't have any more time to think as he pressed his soft lips to mine again, his tongue brushing mine.

I could get used to his lips.

"You can sleep in my bed if you want," Felix said. He didn't have to ask me twice.

"You don't mind?" Stupid question to ask but I was feeling nervous.

"I'd rather you be in my bed than not," Felix said in a matter-of-fact tone.

Well, that's sorted then.

"I don't want to scare you away when I just got you. Tell me if we're moving too fast and I'll back off," he continued, scratching the nape of his neck slowly.

"Felix, you could never scare me away. I want this just as much as you. I didn't think you felt the same but I'm over the moon, honestly," I reassured him, and he tilted my chin upwards and bore his gaze into me.

"I'm taking you home," he said firmly. It wasn't long before we got into a taxi and rode back to his place. I didn't know how the night was going to end but either way, I couldn't stop grinning and jiggling my legs up and down. When we finally pulled up to his place and paid the taxi driver, I realised that I didn't have any of my things with me apart from my phone.

"Could I borrow some pyjamas please and maybe a toothbrush?" I asked, as Felix let us in through his front door.

"Of course you can." He smiled and as we walked inside, I realised how neat and spacious his place was. I was quite impressed but perhaps because my ex's pad was always a mess and I'd have to pick up clothes from the floor all the time.

"Nice place," I observed and Felix gave me a soft smile, as he closed the door. He placed his keys on the dining table which wasn't too far from the kitchen and then turned to face me.

"I'm just going to get you some clothes," Felix said and I nodded. I couldn't help but stand in one spot as I looked around me, taking everything in.

Shit, I am in Felix's house.

Chapter 19

Felix

I felt like a cat who had got the cream, knowing that Alisha was waiting for me in the lounge. As badly as I wanted her, I would try to take things slow since it would be our first night sleeping in the same bed. That didn't mean we wouldn't kiss and cuddle, because I knew I didn't want to let go of her tonight. As I looked at myself in the bathroom mirror, I realised something. I looked like a changed man, a happier version of myself. The part of me I had lost months ago. I didn't want anything to ruin this happiness but a pang hit me as I knew Alisha would be leaving Austria soon. I had to make the most of my time with her.

I couldn't keep the beautiful woman waiting, couldn't waste any more seconds standing in this bathroom whilst she was waiting for me. I wondered whether she was nervous too. It was the first time having her in my home.

When I found her sitting on the sofa, she was an absolute vision. Her shapely legs caught my eye and very quickly I got lost in erratic thoughts of them locked around my waist. I imagined what it'd be like to feel them locked with mine in bed, feeling her warm body against me. To be honest, I'd imagined it for days and now it would come true.

"Thank you," Alisha said as I handed her a pair of pyjamas and a toothbrush. Her fingers brushed mine as we made the exchange and yes, I nearly fucking lost it at the simple touch.

"Are you sure you're okay being here? I can always drive you back home and—"

"Sh, stop talking." Alisha silenced me by placing her luscious lips on mine. She didn't have to tell me twice as I brought my hands either side of her face, pulling her closer. I loved the way she let out a small gasp as our tongues touched. I wanted to taste her, all of her.

Especially down there. I wanted to make her squirm with my tongue, to push her legs apart and make her scream my name.

I didn't need to look down at my crotch to know I had an erection right now. I wouldn't do anything without her consent though. All she had to do was say the word, and I would grant her whatever she wanted.

The kiss was divine and I couldn't help but grab the back of her neck, angling her even closer to me so that our bodies could almost merge into one. Her fingers dug into my hair, tugging gently which caused me to groan. In response to this, I rested my hands on the small of her back, just shy of her glorious ass. As if she was reading my mind, Alisha let go of my hair to grab my hands and guide them towards her ass.

"You can touch me there," she whispered against my lips.

"I'll only do whatever you are comfortable with, sweetheart," I said, hoping she knew that. I was a man of honour and wanted her to fully trust me, to know that I'd take care of her. Give her the world if I could. But only at a pace that didn't scare her. It was early days but this was special. I could tell she was a diamond and I didn't want to lose her.

Finally, our lips left one another and I took her to my bedroom, every step causing my heart rate to increase.

She was going to be in my bed.

I hoped she wouldn't mind me sleeping with no shirt on, as that's how I usually slept.

"Very nice room," Alisha finally spoke as she spun in a slow circle to take it in. Her eyes scanned the wardrobe I had in the corner and then to the bed, which thankfully I had made earlier today. Simple, grey sheets with extra pillows and a dark green throw just in case it got cold. To be honest it was December, so it was pretty cold.

"Thank you," I said, slipping my shoes off. I could see she was clutching the pyjamas closely to her and found it adorable how she hadn't let go of them.

"Do you mind if I use your bathroom? I just need to get out of this dress and wipe off my make-up," Alisha asked, pointing to her face.

"Of course, just turn right and you'll see it. There's toothpaste in there and some face wipes if you want to use them. I have extra for my sister, since she likes to come here a lot," I told her. In fact, I had quite a few of Mira's things here but honestly, it didn't bother me.

"Won't be long. Be back in a bit," Alisha said and then turned to leave. At least I had time to compose myself and smooth out my hair that was now standing up on all ends. I removed my clothing until I was only in my boxers but then I decided to put on a t-shirt as again, I didn't want to make Alisha uncomfortable. This was our first night together-I wanted it to go smoothly.

I placed my phone on charge and slid under the duvet, sighing as my head hit the pillow. I was quite tired and knew I'd get a good night's sleep. I still wanted to cook dinner for Alisha tomorrow and also since she was staying the night, breakfast too. I really wanted to impress this woman and also treat her like a queen.

Within a few minutes, she arrived back in my bedroom and looked even more beautiful than before. I admired her hair which she had tied back into a ponytail and the way my pyjamas looked perfect on her. I beckoned her to join me and she did, letting out a little shiver.

"Cold?" I asked her, taking hold of her hands and rubbing them between my palms. *Shit, she was freezing.*

"I'll warm up next to you. You exude warmth." Alisha smiled, pressing her body closer to mine. Her toes were freezing as they touched my bare legs and this only made me bundle her up more in the duvet.

"I hope you sleep well, sweetheart," I replied, pressing a soft kiss to her cheek. She let out a small yawn and then kissed me gently on my lips.

"Honestly, your bed is really comfortable so I think I'll be out like a light." She chuckled and I didn't blame her. I loved my bed too. But I loved it even more with *her* in it.

"I'm glad you're here," I told her.

"Me too. I like you, Felix."

"I like you too," I admitted, but I knew my feelings were growing even deeper and I could tell I was starting to fall for her. I still felt a little guarded with my emotions and I hadn't yet told Alisha about my past, with my birth mother. I was hoping she wouldn't run for the hills when I told her, that she wouldn't see me as a fuck up, but I tried not to focus on that now, when I had her here with me. She had already fallen asleep, her hands resting on her chest. She looked so perfect and I couldn't help but grin, knowing I'd get to wake up next to her tomorrow morning. This was heaven, but did I deserve it?

"Goodnight," I whispered and then closed my eyes, falling into my own peaceful slumber.

Chapter 20

Alisha

That sleep was absolute bliss, and even more so since I was cocooned with Felix. His arms were wrapped around me as he spooned me, our legs had intertwined in the night. It must have been the best sleep I'd had in a while.

I checked my phone, careful not to wake Felix, and could see it was only 7:30 am. I realised I needed to get up soon, and then head back to mine to get ready for my skiing lesson. It would feel like a rush but to be honest, nothing could break my mood today.

As I scrolled through my phone, I could see a text from Ophelia who asked if I was okay. I quickly replied back to her, telling her everything was fine and I'd be home soon. I then opened a message from my mum, who wanted to talk to me later. I was guessing she wanted to talk about plans for Christmas and how I've been finding Austria so far.

Felix's hold on me tightened, his fingers splayed on my bare stomach as my top had ridden up. I only wished that he would dive those fingers into my trousers and touch me where I wanted him to. To tease him, I pushed back gently against him so my ass was against his crotch and I nearly squealed when I felt his already hard cock press against me.

"Carry on like that and you'll be under me in seconds, sweetheart," Felix grumbled and I bit my lip, wishing that would come true. Honestly, I felt like a confident sexual goddess right now and I really wouldn't mind if he acted on his words. It had been a very long time since I'd been taken care of down there.

"I dare you," I teased and giggled as he did exactly what he said he'd do. Felix was hovering above me and smirking.

Gosh, I really hoped I didn't have morning breath.

Felix looked so gorgeous and rugged, a five o'clock shadow evident on his chin. He didn't hesitate to devour my mouth with his, pinning my arms above my head so that I was trapped under him.

"Schön[1]. You. Are. Perfect," Felix said in between kisses and I moaned, as his lips travelled my lips, to my neck.

"Is this alright?" he asked and I nodded, completely lost for words. With one hand still keeping my arms locked in place, his free one dipped into my trousers and gently cupped my throbbing pussy. I knew my knickers were going to be soaked and I gently hissed in pleasure, as he traced his index finger up and down.

"You are so wet, sweetheart. Tell me what you want." Felix waited for my next words patiently and honestly, I wanted everything and more. I wanted to go all the way but part of me felt it may be too soon. That didn't mean I didn't want to receive a mind-blowing orgasm.

"Fuck me with your mouth and fingers," I said, or rather, begged. Felix nodded, releasing my arms which I rested on his head as he moved further south of my body. He discarded my trousers very quickly and then my knickers so that I was totally bare. Slick and ready for him.

"I'm going to treat you so nicely, sweetheart. You deserve it," Felix said and started to gently massage my pussy with one finger.

---

1. Beautiful.

"Oh god, please," I whined, and he slowly edged his finger inside of me. I felt his hot breath on me and he edged my legs further apart. With just one swipe of his tongue, I was almost done for.

At first, he was gentle and then became more rough which is just how I liked it. He replaced one finger with two, and picked up his speed as he fucked me with his glorious tongue too. His fingers pumped in and out of me at a delicious speed, his tongue mimicking these movements. With his other hand he cupped my breast, his thumb brushing over my nipple. I wanted *more*.

"Baby, you taste so good," Felix mumbled. I couldn't reply because I was in a state of eternal bliss so I let him work his magic. Felix's hand left my breast to rest on my thigh, keeping me wide open for him.

"Harder, please," I begged. But I wanted his cock to replace his tongue now, because if oral sex was this good, then I could only imagine that his cock would be better. Felix seemed to listen as his tongue movements became rougher. My eyes rolled into the back of my head as this amazing man licked and sucked me. *Holy shit.*

I knew I was coming to the edge, as the pressure built up and up and I was rocking my hips into Felix simultaneously. Nothing could compare to this, I was literally seeing stars and the whole galaxy as I came hard. Felix's tongue lapped me up and his fingers came to a halt as I came down from my high.

It definitely had been too long.

"Oh, wow," was all I could say as I was breathing hard. Felix removed his fingers from my quivering pussy and then laid down next to me. I wanted to take care of him now, if he'd let me.

"Good?"

"More than good. How about I take care of you now?" I trailed my hand down his chest, stopping just short of his boxers. I could see a few tufts of pubic hair and I wondered how big he actually was as his cock was bulging already.

"All in good time, sweetheart. First, I want to make you something to eat as I bet you're hungry," Felix said.

Yes, hungry for you.

But damn it, my stomach rumbled so he was right. *A girl's gotta eat.*

"Thank you, it's like you know me." I smiled, pecking his lips quickly before he got up to leave. I couldn't help but check out his ass as he walked away and I got a glorious view of his hardened cock in his boxers as he turned to give me a little wave. I could tell he was going to ruin me one day. But I was ready for it.

***

I moaned in delight as I scraped away the remainder of my breakfast. Felix had outdone himself with the delicious breakfast he'd prepared. He had rustled up some eggs benedict with toast and cheese, accompanied by some delicious raspberry yoghurt. A pot of coffee had been brewed and after two cups, I was much more alert and ready to tackle the day. It was now about 8:30 am, meaning I had an hour and a half before my lesson. Felix had offered to drive me back which was very sweet.

"After your lesson, I think we should go skiing together. I'll ask your instructor though, just to see if you're ready. I know Hilde quite well," Felix said.

"Okay, sounds like a plan." I smiled at this, getting to spend more time with him was what I wanted. I remembered he had mentioned that he was going to cook dinner for us too, so I was getting the full on treatment today. I needed to remind myself that I did deserve to be happy and that this wasn't too good to be true. Felix had proved he was true to his words and that he wouldn't mess me about. I trusted him. Way more than I had with Caden. Was I scared that things were escalating between me and Felix? Especially as we only knew each other for nearly a week. The answer was a simple no. I felt more alive than I had done in months.

Then again I couldn't judge this situation as my own parents had fallen in love quite quickly. Their love was what I craved and they always had the utmost respect for one another. I was thankful to have been raised by them.

Felix started to clear up our plates in the kitchen whilst I couldn't help but watch. The way his muscles in his arms flexed as he washed the plates with a sponge and his peachy bum. Later today, he was going to ski with me. There was never a man that wanted to spend so much time with me like Felix.

"All done," Felix finally said, he was now leaning against the kitchen counter and watching me with a deep level of intensity. I could have melted to the ground with that stare of his. He was so gorgeous and he definitely needed reminding of that.

"Perfect. Thank you again, for an amazing night and morning." I blushed a little as I said the last two phrases and Felix walked over to me so that he was towering slightly above me. He placed his two fingers under my chin, leaning down to press a soft kiss to my slightly chapped lips.

"Anytime." He grinned, his mouth lingering above mine for one more kiss. Gosh, I could kiss this man forever if I could. But time was passing by and I really needed to get home. Felix could tell I was getting a little anxious about this so grabbed his car keys from the kitchen and then slipped on his shoes.

"Luckily, I'm not working today so I'll be doing a bit of skiing whilst you're having your lesson. I'll meet you when you're finished and we can get some food," Felix told me and it sounded like a good plan. I needed to remember though to call my mum later and then get some more writing done. Grayson was waiting for some updates and I didn't want to let him down.

"Okay, sounds good. I hope I can be as good as you one day," I said, putting on my own shoes which didn't exactly go with my pyjama outfit but it would have to do. Luckily, I would be sitting in a car rather than going on public transport so I didn't have to worry about how I looked. I had grabbed my outfit from last night as well as my phone and walked over to Felix's car with him.

"Sweetheart, you're doing brilliantly. Don't ever underestimate your achievements," Felix said. When he said this, it reminded me of my mum and how she always told me to look at my achievements with fondness, to be proud of them.

It didn't take long for him to drive me home and we spoke a little along the way, mainly about the plans for tonight. Felix mentioned he would drop me back home after skiing and then pick me up for dinner later this evening. Honestly, I felt like I was being spoiled and I told him that I didn't mind taking a taxi or even a bus to get to his, but he insisted so I accepted because he probably wouldn't take no for an answer.

Once we pulled up outside, Ophelia was waiting at the door and started waving like crazy. I knew she would start badgering me as soon as I got through the door.

"I'll see you later," Felix said, pulling me in for a much needed hug.

"Can't wait," I responded, pressing a kiss to his stubbly cheek and then exiting his car. I gave him a wave as he drove off and then turned to face my friend who grabbed my arm and pulled me inside.

"Right, sit down young lady and tell me everything," Ophelia practically begged and I obeyed, taking a seat on the sofa. After this conversation, I needed to get changed and probably have another coffee before leaving.

"Well, we got back to his and we were both quite nervous. Nothing happened during the night, which I was fine with," I told her and she nodded, waiting for me to continue.

"But this morning, well let's say I was very satisfied," I said. I didn't want to go into the nitty gritty details with my friend, she would know what I meant anyway.

"I bet you were. So, is there a relationship on the cards then?" Ophelia pushed for more information. Felix and I hadn't actually discussed that and I suppose neither one of us wanted to put that pressure on, since I would be returning home soon. I think what was important was embracing the present and the good times we were having with one another.

"I'm not quite sure, if I'm being honest. I think we both want to tread carefully, to not get too attached since I'm leaving soon," I admitted, playing with the hem of my top.

"I get that, I do. But I also think that the two of you are perfect for one another. I think you could make it work, if I'm being completely honest. He's not like Caden," Ophelia said. She was right. Felix was far better and his words matched his actions.

"We'll see how it goes," I replied and Ophelia nodded. I knew she wanted the best for me and though she wasn't an expert on relationships, her opinion mattered.

"Whatever you want, Ali. It's your life," she said and then lifted up her mug of coffee to her lips to take a sip. We spoke a little more before I really did have to get ready and go to my lesson.

I made sure to leave the house in good timing, so I wouldn't be panicking to get to my lesson. Ophelia decided to join me in the cable car and we chatted about work, some ideas that she had and then what we would be doing for Christmas at home. Ophelia would be going to Greece for a few days before returning to England to celebrate New Year's Eve.

"I can't wait to go home. I miss my mum's cooking," Ophelia said, her gaze following the moving mountains as we travelled higher and higher.

"You should try and replicate her cooking style."

"She always says her recipes will die with her. Fancy that, not even telling her own daughter," Ophelia said, but there was a slight sadness to her tone. She loved her mum but found it difficult to communicate with her at times. I was lucky to have a good relationship with mine, I could talk to her about anything.

"See you later, then!" I said to my friend as we finally got to our destination.

"Text me," Ophelia replied, enclosing me in a tight hug before releasing me. As she left, I adjusted my ski goggles and then made my way over to the ski school.

Hilde was already waiting for me with a smile on her face.

"Let's go, partner," Hilde said, giving me a high five. She knew about my anxiety and how often in these moments it would flare up. So she did whatever she could to help make my experience easier. I appreciated that about her, how patient and understanding she was.

I wasn't sure what she had planned for me today but I was ready for a fun lesson—whatever movements she'd teach me today I was ready for. My limbs would be sore by the end of it but I didn't mind. I was quickly becoming a fan of skiing and could see myself doing more of it in the future.

Chapter 21

Felix

I skied for about an hour, relishing the way the wind swept by me as I twisted and turned my body. Small flecks of snow fell on my face but I didn't mind. I was used to the feel of it. Skiing was always a great escape for me, the adrenaline rush was amazing and I was so glad that I was a pro at it as it meant I could go down difficult slopes. I felt a little smug about it of course but I had done this for years. I loved a challenge.

I finally skied to a stop at the end of a black run, and then checked the time on my phone realising that I had about ten minutes to get to Alisha. I couldn't move quick enough as I skied towards the cable car that would take me down to the ski school where Alisha would wait for me, or perhaps I would wait for her, if I got there a few minutes early.

However, there was a bit of a queue at the cable car so I knew I'd be a little late. I decided to send her a text to let her know.

Felix: Might be a bit late, but I'll be there :) xx

I removed my ski goggles and helmet as finally I took a seat inside the cable car, my skis were placed just outside of the car securely. A few others had joined me as well, which didn't bother me. I said hello to them before looking out of the window to gaze at the beauty of the snow dusted mountains. I could never get tired of this. I loved Ischgl wholeheartedly. I couldn't imagine moving away from here.

"Mama, können wir nächstes Jahr wieder hierher kommen?[1]" a young child, a little girl who looked about seven, said to her mother who was sitting next to me who laughed and pressed a kiss on top of her daughter's head.

"Ich wusste, dass ich deine Meinung ändern würde,[2]" the woman replied, giving her daughter a squeeze. I didn't want to be nosing in their conversation and thankfully, on the next stop they got off so I could relax a little in my seat. I had one more stop before I'd be with Alisha and I couldn't help but feel overly giddy. She had this effect on me, profound and deep already. I didn't want to let this feeling go away, nor her, but I knew I'd have to let her go soon, which I realised was going to be hard. I knew that I needed to make this trip for her the best one she'd ever have and that we'd stay in touch.

This morning had been incredible with her, the way she felt against my tongue as I fucked her pussy with my tongue and watched her come undone. I wanted to do that again and again with her, to make her scream my name and only mine. My cock hardened at steamy images of her, the way her pussy was perfectly glistening and pulsating for me.

If she felt that good in my mouth, I could only imagine she felt better sliding down my cock.

As the cable car neared to my stop, I placed my helmet back on my head with the goggles resting on top. I grabbed my skis and poles and trudged my way to the ski school, I had about two minutes to spare before Alisha would be there. It

---

1. *Mum, can we come back here next year?*

2. *I knew I'd change your mind.*

had only been a few hours since I last saw her, but I missed her. Was that insane to admit?

I came to a stop at the ski school and waited patiently, watching a few instructors helping some kids put on their skis and consoling a few who were in tears. For some people, skiing was natural but for others, it was scary and very much out of their comfort zone. I hoped Alisha was enjoying her lessons and I wanted to try and teach her what I'd learnt in my lessons as a child, but one step at a time.

I spotted her approaching, Hilde just behind her who was laughing at something she said. She was a great instructor, highly recommended and very chatty to her clients. I was glad she was teaching Alisha and clearly she looked comfortable. Alisha skied to a halt in front of me and gave me a cheery grin, one that caused my heart to flutter. I loved her smile. Everything about her was wonderful. Her ex was a fucking joke, breaking her heart like that. I hoped she had forgotten about him and had room now for me in her life. In her heart maybe.

"Hi, Felix," Hilde said to me, and I shook her hand to greet her.

"How are you doing?" I asked, hoping that she was well.

"Very good, thank you. Alisha here is quickly becoming a pro, I think she could be ready for a blue run. She could even try today, if she wants," Hilde said and to be honest, that sounded perfect. It was exactly what I was thinking.

"You've read my mind, I was thinking of taking her down a blue run if you think she is ready?" I proposed and Hilde nodded enthusiastically, whilst Alisha suddenly looked nervous.

"Don't worry, you're in good hands with Felix. I've always said he should become an instructor, given he is a natural and is very patient," Hilde said, giving me a warm smile.

"Okay, if you guys think so," Alisha replied, a slight hesitancy in her voice, which was understandable, but I wanted to reassure that she was safe with me. She always would be.

"Absolutely. Well, I'll leave you both to it. Have a wonderful day and see you tomorrow, Alisha." Hilde gave Alisha's arm a gentle squeeze and then bid me a goodbye before skiing off to meet her next client probably.

"Are you ready then?" I turned to Alisha, who was holding her hands together nervously. She nodded and looked at me with wide eyes before slipping her hand into mine.

"I think so." Alisha nodded ever so slightly. I could tell she was feeling anxious and I stepped closer to her.

"Breathe, baby. You've got this," I told her. I believed in her and I'd look after her in case anything happened.

"You'll save me, right? If I fall?"

"I'll catch you. Don't worry about it, sweetheart." I gave her hand a squeeze and decided not to let go as we made our way to an easy blue run, which wasn't too busy thankfully. Alisha still held my hand tightly in hers but I didn't mind. It made me very happy, knowing that she wanted to keep a hold of me as I wanted to of her.

***

"You're doing amazing!" I called out to Alisha who was now skiing on her own, her knees bent and arching forward. I was so proud of her, as the first five times I had to guide her down using the poles as support, with me skiing in front of her.

"I feel like I'm flying!" Alisha squealed and then came to stop just a few centimetres away from me. The huge smile on her face proved she was having a great time and that she really felt she was making progress.

"Well done, sweetheart," I told her as she barricaded me with a huge hug, both arms squeezing me tightly. I felt my heart swell at this and couldn't help but lean down to kiss her beautiful lips, to relish in the warmth and softness of her. She felt slightly cold, her cheeks had a soft rouge to them and she was breathing erratically. It was definitely time for a hot chocolate and a bite to eat so unwillingly, I stopped kissing her.

"Let's go get our hot chocolate and something to eat." I adjusted her helmet as it had fallen slightly off her head.

"I can't wait to eat, I'm starving," Alisha said as we took off our skis and placed them outside. The restaurant was called Idalp—Pardorama and I had been there a few times already so it never disappointed me.

It wasn't too busy inside, since it wasn't yet the lunch hour but hot meals were being served along with salads and sandwiches. I was in a spaghetti mood so I grabbed a bolognese and also some carrot soup with bread. Hot chocolate seemed to be the drink I'd get now with Alisha—it felt like it was our go-to drink, and I hoped to share many more with her.

When we finally paid for our food, well I did since I insisted, we took a seat at a quiet table in the corner, away from prying eyes. I knew though that within half an hour, it would be very busy so there wouldn't be a lot I could do. At least we weren't sitting in the middle of the restaurant, I always hated that.

"Gosh, this is so delicious." Alisha let out a moan as she chewed her panini made with melted cheese and ham, a dollop of Caesar dressing on her plate too. An interesting combination but I didn't query it. I liked my fair share of food combinations myself, especially with cheese. We liked our cheese over here.

I took a sip of my steaming hot chocolate, letting out a small sigh as the hot liquid ran down my throat. Perfect.

The two of us enjoyed our lunch and spoke about the skiing progress Alisha had made, and then dinner plans for this evening. I had made a list on my phone of the ingredients I needed. I was going to make chicken dopiaza, which was a tomato-based curry with caramelised onions and cream. I was also going to make the parathas, which was a flatbread. For dessert, I would make kheer which was a type of rice pudding. I was really hoping I wouldn't mess up the cooking, I wanted to make this perfect for Alisha. So, after lunch and dropping Alisha back to hers, I would go to the shops and get what I needed before sprucing myself up.

"Thanks for lunch, Felix," Alisha said, wiping her mouth with a blue paper napkin.

"You're very welcome. I'm glad you had a good ski session today too," I told her, finishing the last of my food.

"Could we make it a regular thing, you and me skiing after my lessons?" Alisha asked. *Abso-fucking-lutely.*

"Yes, sweetheart. There's more I want to show you. But let's get you back now," I said, although really I didn't want to say goodbye.

"Yeah, you're right. Ophelia has already gone back and is waiting for me, she wants to work on some things so I said I would be back by one pm," Alisha admitted and I realised it was now noon on the dot, just as it was starting to get busy in the restaurant.

I held out my hand for Alisha to take and we walked side by side back to the cable cars, where one was already vacant for us. On the journey down, Alisha rested her head on my shoulder and I couldn't help but smile to myself. I didn't want anything to ruin this, to ruin us, but a part of my brain was telling me this was too good to be true. I just didn't know whether I could ignore it.

# Chapter 22

Alisha

The temperature dropped by the time I arrived back at the chalet and I was thankful I'd worn my beanie and gloves today. One thing that had sprung to mind was how I needed to get some work done. As much as spending time with Felix was wonderful, I couldn't neglect the reason why I had come to Austria.

When I got in through the front door, Ophelia was hunched over at the dining table with some papers in front of her and her laptop. She was deeply engrossed in typing until I cleared my throat and she lifted her head to glance at me.

"Hey, Ali," she said simply before returning back to her laptop screen. I didn't want to disrupt her, so I headed to the kitchen to make us some coffee and cut us a slice of cake that I had bought from the local shop, chocolate fudge, which was one of Ophelia's favourites. I knew it would make her smile and I wanted to show her my appreciation for everything over the last few days. For being such a good friend. Cake wouldn't exactly suffice but it was a nice gesture I could offer at least.

Ophelia gave me a smile as I placed a plate of cake in front of her and slid a mug of coffee too next to the plate. I then proceeded to get my laptop from my room and start writing some more, since I had more inspiration. I wanted to write about my skiing experience and how nerve-wracking it was at the start.

As I sat down and started eating my slice of cake, my fingers danced away on the keyboard. I had to hit the delete button several times as there were some sentences that didn't quite flow and I even read them aloud to check.

"This doesn't sound right," I observed, deleting a couple of words I had typed.

"Just needs a bit more structure but you'll get it," Ophelia reassured me. I liked her honesty.

After adding a few more sentences, I felt a bit happier with what I'd produced. Reading it aloud loud was a way of checking too.

"Ischgl is one of the best places to go skiing and the locals are incredibly friendly. I've met some wonderful people so far and they've been helping me in many ways," I read aloud and Ophelia looked up from her laptop to listen.

"It's nice but maybe it sounds too much about you rather than Ischgl itself. Don't get me wrong, you can write about yourself but the readers will want to be convinced to go to Ischgl. You could write about the apres skis and the Christmas markets," Ophelia told me.

"I could also mention the ski school too, to give them some publicity," I replied. I'd also add some rhetorical questions in the article because these would capture people's attention. I also realised that maybe my sentences needed to sound more natural, more from the heart.

After about an hour and a half of working, I decided to take a break and call my mum who was eagerly waiting for me since she texted me about half an hour ago. I entered my bedroom and clicked on my mum's contact.

I was greeted by her beaming face as her picture appeared on the screen and my dad had also popped up, waving at me.

"Hallo priye[1] ,"my mum said, I had missed her voice and of course, her. She looked well and so did my dad. They were snuggled up against one another in their living room, and I could hear the faint noise from the TV.

"How are you both?" I asked, shifting into a more comfortable position on my bed.

"We're okay, thanks. Are you having fun?" Dad queried, his dark brown eyes twinkling.

"Yeah, quite a lot actually. I've been skiing a lot and getting some work done," I said, crossing my legs.

"As long as you are having a good time, then we're happy. Your brothers have been asking about you too. Especially Zane. He doesn't like to admit this, but he does miss you," Mum said, and I chuckled at this. My brother had a lot of pride and never liked to get deep into his emotions, but I knew he loved us all, just in his own way. Our other brother, Aadi, was a little bit more open. Kiya on the other hand was just a full on lovebug. Willing to do anything for anyone and wouldn't hesitate to drop her plans and be there for her family.

"I miss them too." I smiled and talked to my parents a little more before they needed to go, as they were heading out with a few of their friends. They were quite social and were friends with most of their neighbours, often hosting dinner parties. They felt part of the community which was important to them. Me on the other hand, I usually liked staying indoors and not interacting with people in my building.

"Get some good rest, jaaneman[2] ," Dad told me before saying goodbye.

As I rested my head on my pillow after hanging up the call, I felt my eyelids flutter and soon I was drifting into a much needed sleep. My mind was filled with images of Felix and only him.

***

---

1. *Hello, darling.*

2. Darling.

I stretched my whole body after a pleasant two hour nap and picked up my phone which was on the bedside table. Felix had already sent me a text message, letting me know what time he'd be coming to pick me up in two hours. As it was just a casual dinner at his place, I decided not to dress up. A pair of jeans and a jumper would be perfectly fine.

"Do you want tea?" Ophelia popped her head through my door and I was thankful she had as my throat was quite dry.

"Yes, please. I'll come and join you in a few minutes," I said, getting out from the covers and walking over to the mirror to assess my hair and face. All I needed to do was give it a quick brush and then just wipe away some of the mascara that had smudged underneath my eyes. Once that was sorted, I joined my friend in the living room who handed me a mug of piping hot tea. A packet of biscuits was on the table and the TV was blaring an episode of *The Walking Dead*, a series which Ophelia really enjoyed.

I swiped a biscuit from the packet, a chocolate digestive, and munched on it as I glanced at the TV, wincing as I saw a zombie being slayed, blood splattering out of its neck.

"Yes!" Ophelia shouted and I shook my head, as really I didn't find it appealing. But it was nice to sit next to her and spend some time together.

"I bet you are looking forward to tonight then," she finally said, turning the TV volume down.

"He's cooking dinner for me, which is very sweet," I said and I was curious as to what Felix had decided to cook.

"That is. Are you going to stay the night again?"

"No, I'll come back. He's also got work tomorrow, so he needs to be up early." I picked up another biscuit and bit into it, this time it was a ginger snap. I took a swig of my tea, turning the biscuit in my mouth to mush.

"Okay, fair enough. Maybe you and I could go out of town tomorrow, I can hire us a car," Ophelia suggested.

"Yeah, that's a good idea. We need to explore a bit more," I agreed.

"We'll go after your lesson," Ophelia said. A day out with one of my best friends sounded perfect and I couldn't wait. Honestly, this trip was one of the best I'd been on, and I'm glad I decided to step outside of my comfort zone. I was seeing another side of life and the beauty of adventure.

***

Two hours later, Felix arrived and I excitedly ran to greet him as he got out of his car. He looked absolutely amazing, wearing a soft blue jumper as well as some grey trousers. His hair was tousled and he had a cheeky grin on him, which caused my stomach to dive.

As soon as he said hello, I melted in his embrace and couldn't help but press my lips to his, hungry for his taste, his tongue to touch mine. His kisses caused explosions inside of me, exactly what I needed.

"Mm, sweetheart. I could kiss you all evening but we should get going. Your food awaits you." Felix grinned but placed his hand on my thigh to my delight and he kept it there all the way back to his.

"So I've prepared the starter and main course. I'll make the dessert a little later," Felix said as he switched off the engine and removed his hand from my thigh.

"You really didn't have to go to all that trouble, Felix." I was in awe of this man and the effort he had gone to, all to make me happy. No man had ever cooked a three course meal for me before.

"You deserve it. I want to make you happy," Felix said, determination etched in his voice.

"You're adorable," I told him. I needed to do something nice for him in return and I had a few ideas but needed Ophelia's opinion later. Felix led us inside his house, where immediately the smell of spices and tomato greeted my nose.

On the dining table, I could see that Felix had written out a menu and there were two unlit candles either side of the table with silver cutlery neatly set up. I turned to look at Felix, who gave me a nonchalant shrug.

"Right, take a seat. I'll bring out our starters shortly." Felix ushered me to the table where I waited patiently.

After about ten minutes, he returned with two bowls and placed one in front of me. I recognised that it was sweet potato soup, a speciality that my own mum liked to cook- a comfort meal she'd make whenever I was feeling down. The consistency of the soup looked creamy and smooth, just how it should be. I couldn't wait to taste it.

"I hope you enjoy it. I know you like soup, as I do too," Felix said, picking us his spoon and settling into his seat. I couldn't wait to tuck in and as soon as the liquid touched my tongue, I was in heaven.

"Felix, this is delicious," I told him, taking another spoonful. I knew I was going to finish this in less than two minutes with how amazing it tasted. The spices were not overpowering but you could just about taste them. True to my thoughts, I finished my bowl and scraped the spoon around the edges to get any remainders.

"So you liked that?" Felix asked, his lips quivering into a smile.

"Absolutely. I loved it, thank you so much. My mum loves cooking this back home, so it gave me some good memories," I said, patting my stomach in satisfaction.

"I'm glad, so are you ready for the main course?"

"More than ready, I bet it'll also be amazing." I had no doubt about it, if the starter was that good then the main had to be too. I couldn't help but watch Felix in his kitchen as he started to prepare the main, which took a little longer but I didn't mind. I admired the way he started to hum and chop at the same time, it looked like he was making some sort of curry.

My phone suddenly pinged and since Felix was in the kitchen, it wouldn't be rude of me to check it. It was from an unknown number.

> **Unknown:** Hi. How are you? It's been a while but thought I'd let you know I'd changed my number. I miss you, I really do Alisha. I hope we can talk so that I can explain things to you x

Felicity. The friend who also broke my heart. I tried not to let this bother me tonight and put my phone back in my jean pocket. I'd maybe deal with that later but for now, my focus was Felix and the amazing human he was. Giving me his time and attention. Proving to me that this was one hundred percent worth it. I knew I needed to talk to him about us tonight and lay the cards on the table.

Chapter 23

Felix

The starter and main courses were a success. Alisha even said that I almost surpassed her mother's cooking. I took this as a compliment because I knew how much she adored her mother. Honestly, it was just great to see her having fun with me tonight. We spoke about the day we had as well as Alisha's plans with her friend Ophelia tomorrow.

Alisha had gone a little quiet at some point in the evening and I wondered what was on her mind. I didn't press as she would talk to me when she felt ready and I would be there to listen. I started to make the dessert, all I needed to do was boil some milk and rice mixed with some sugar in an instant pot. Alisha had decided to keep me company in the kitchen and sat on the counter top, watching me curiously. I loved having her there, and every so often I would glance at her luscious legs that I wanted wrapped around me very soon. I imagined them locked around my waist as I pumped into her, fucking her senseless. If she'd let me, I'd give her another orgasm tonight with my mouth since I loved hearing her unravel underneath me. Completely at my mercy. Completely *mine*.

Something had been on my mind for the last few hours though. We needed to have a conversation about us and where it was going. I, of course, wanted more, to be exclusive and maybe even call her my girlfriend, but I wanted to ensure we were both on the same page, that we knew where we stood. If we were going to get into a relationship, we needed to think about how long distance would affect us. I felt scared because I didn't want to push her away, but I needed to tell her how I felt about her. My feelings were only going to get stronger the more time I spent with her. She'd already turned my world upside down in the space of a few days. Imagine what she could do within a few months. I wanted more of her though. I wasn't afraid of what was ahead, only afraid that I wouldn't have her in my life.

The kheer was pretty much done and I took two bowls over to the dining table, with Alisha following at my heels. The two of us dived into our delicious dessert, which honestly was now my favourite dish of the evening. Alisha let out another one of her moans which caused my cock to twitch in my trousers. I knew I needed a good release later tonight.

"Well, I am utterly impressed Felix. I think you should be a professional chef, with the way you cook." Alisha placed her empty bowl in front of her and licked her lips.

"Maybe I should quit my job." I let out a throaty laugh. I actually thought about it, maybe trying something else that I was more passionate about. I did enjoy cooking but knew it wasn't an easy profession to get into.

There were other things I could try, perhaps I would ask my sister when I saw her tomorrow. She wanted to take me out for dinner along with our aunt Brenna and then perhaps Christmas shopping at the weekend.

"Well, this was a lovely evening Felix. I know I've said thank you so many times but I really mean it. No one has ever gone to this much effort for me before," Alisha admitted. This woman really deserved queen treatment and I cursed her ex for being the dick he was. I hoped I would never cross paths with him. I wasn't a violent man but I could be harsh with my words, especially with people who deliberately hurt good people.

"My pleasure, thank you as well for your company," I replied, my voice had suddenly gone quiet as I knew I needed to talk to her next about us.

"Let's move to the sofa," I suggested, we'd be much more comfortable there. When Alisha sat down, I offered to make her some coffee but she declined politely. I also didn't want any so proceeded to sit down beside her, pulling her into me so that her head rested on my shoulder. She laced our fingers together, rubbing her thumb along my palm which sent tingles through me. She smelt like peaches today as I breathed in her scent and with my other hand, I placed this on her thigh.

"Sooo," Alisha drawled.

"Sooo," I mimicked, drawing lazy circles on her jean clad leg.

"Felix, what do you think about me?" she asked. I could answer this with full honesty, to tell her that I thought about her every hour, every minute, every second. Images of her consumed my thoughts, and I couldn't control them, nor did I want to. If she wanted to, I would make her mine and do whatever I could to prove she was worth it.

"What do I think of you? I care about you and I really like you. I want this to go further but I also don't want to put any pressure on you. I'll do whatever you want, at your pace," I said and Alisha relaxed into me, gripping my hand a little tighter. I could hear her heartbeat racing fast against me too.

"I really like you too. And I do want more, it's just if we decide to be exclusive then it'll be hard when I leave," she replied. She wasn't wrong and maybe we really just needed to see what happened in the next week. Maybe we really didn't need to put a label on it just yet. It was still early. I was happy just being with her, kissing her, holding her and getting to know her.

"I know. I think we should just keep doing what we're doing, no labels and no expectations. Just feel how we feel and we'll be alright. I want to cherish every moment I spend with you," I told her and she nodded in agreement, her lips curving into the smile I adored. Everything about her was so beautiful.

Things were becoming intense as we became more touchy with one another, hands pressed against skin and my lips pressing kisses against her neck, her collarbone and then finally her lips. Her fingers travelled into my hair, tugging me closer and I lifted her onto my lap, resting my own hands on her ass. I wanted her to feel how rock hard I was for her and it didn't help that she started to move against me as we deepened the kiss.

"Wenn wir jetzt nicht aufhören, werde ich dich ficken, Schatz[1]," I said this in German as I knew she wouldn't be able to translate and I wanted to keep her guessing.

"I imagine that's dirty talk." Alisha blushed. It had been a long time since I'd last had sex. After the break up with my ex, I didn't want to go sleeping around, and even the idea of jacking myself off at the time wasn't of interest, but now my libido was back and all I wanted to do was sink myself into Alisha. I wanted to pound hard into her, edge myself deeper into her world and come undone with her.

"Felix, take me to your room," Alisha said with a stern voice and of course, I couldn't say no to her. I hoisted her from my lap, leading her toward my room, and as soon as the door closed behind her, I pulled her body to mine and meshed our mouths together. Quick breaths escaped her as I kissed her with passion, nipping her bottom lip with my teeth gently. I wanted her underneath me now and I knew that was what she wanted to, her eyes were telling me and her body language too.

With one quick movement, she was on my bed and I was hovering above her, my left hand tugging down her jeans with her underwear following suit. I wanted to curl my fingers inside her again and watch her writhe. I looked at her glistening pussy and couldn't wait to taste her again. The way she clenched against my fingers and mouth this morning almost made me come myself.

"Sweetheart, I want to make you come. I loved watching you this morning, it was fucking sexy. So, I'm going to take care of you again," I told her, if anything I wanted to make her come ten times better than she had this morning. I wanted

---

1. *If we don't stop now, I'm going to fuck you, sweetheart.*

her to go home tonight thinking about it, to know that no other man could make her feel the way I would. Tonight, she was mine. If she could be forever, even better. A man could hope and want.

I had kept Alisha waiting far too long as she dragged my hand to cup her pussy, which was slick and ready for me.

Anything for you.

I gently eased one finger inside her as I pressed a firm kiss to her neck and then to her chest.

"Too much clothing," I said, wanting to remove her jumper so I could see her beautiful chest. I bet she had amazing breasts. She pulled her jumper off over her head and then unclasped her bra, revealing her perfect tits. I kept the pace with my finger inside of her and with my free hand cupped her left breast, swiping my tongue over her erect nipple.

"You are beautiful," I murmured and Alisha moaned in pleasure as I edged another finger inside of her, teasing her clit and her folds. I licked and sucked her nipple before giving special treatment to the other breast, enjoying the way she arched her body into me.

"Your mouth. Please," she begged, signalling for me to go down on her. I obeyed, wanting to taste every last drop of her. I dragged my tongue up and down her throbbing clit and at the same time, teasing my fingers in and out of her. The sound of her cries almost sent me over the edge as she came, her legs shaking as she did. I lapped up her release, relishing in the sweet taste of her. She was my own dessert and I could eat her out for days if I wanted to.

"I- wow. You're so amazing at that." Alisha giggled as I laid down next to her, catching her breath. I loved the effect I had on her and pulled her body against mine, to gaze deeply into her eyes.

"I want to go down on you now," she said. I wasn't expecting anything in return but the bulge in my trousers was very evident and she was eyeing it up, her eyes wide at the size of it.

"We don't have to if you don't want to. I just wanted to make sure you were satisfied tonight," I told her, brushing away a strand of hair that had fallen against her cheek. Her skin was flushed but she looked excited and desperate to take control. Fuck, I would let her. I was completely hers tonight, whatever she wanted.

"It's your turn, gorgeous." Alisha gave me a gentle push as my head rested against my pillow and her hand crept through my trousers to cup my balls through my boxers.

"Okay," was all I could muster and closed my eyes as she pulled down my trousers along with my boxers. She gasped and I opened my eyes to find her staring at my thick cock which yes, was slightly bigger than average, but I was hard for her and one day, I would fuck her senseless with it.

I waited for her to make her next move and bit down on my bottom lip, when her breath fanned over the tip of my cock and her fingers wrapped around me. My cock twitched in her hand and I knew that I wouldn't last long when she would finally place her lips around my length. My wish came true as she licked the tip of me and then her whole mouth enveloped me.

"Sweetheart, keep going like that, and I'll burst in your mouth," I groaned as her tongue started to flick up and down my pulsating cock.

Shit, I really wasn't going to last long. I needed to hold on, I would try to. But fuck, the way her tongue felt against my cock...

"Mm," Alisha let out as she sucked me, her head bobbing back and forth. She was a natural at this and I felt incredibly lucky that she was in front of me, looking as gorgeous as ever. All I wanted to do was bury myself in her because if her mouth was this amazing then her pussy wrapped around my cock would be even better. I needed to be patient though, for her to say the word.

As I fucked her mouth I knew I was reaching my release and I needed to let her know.

"I'm going to come," I said and she kept her speed, chasing my release quicker. With short and quick spurts, I came down her throat and let out a deep groan, gently tugging at her hair.

"Fuck, Alisha," I said through gritted teeth as Alisha swallowed every last drop of me and then licked her lips before resting beside me.

"Now we're both happy." Alisha grinned, pressing a kiss on my shoulder.

"You are incredible," I whispered back to her.

"Now, I'm going to cuddle you before I need to go home," Alisha said, tucking her head underneath my chin and wrapping her arms around my torso.

I wished she wouldn't have to go back to hers tonight, to spend another night with me. I dreaded going into work tomorrow, but luckily I'd be going on annual leave in a few days so I'd get to spend more hours with Alisha. As I held her in my arms and my heart resumed to a normal rate, I came to a realisation. Well, it had been dawning for some time but only just bubbled to the surface now.

I was falling for Alisha.

Chapter 24

Alisha

I hated having to go back home but Felix needed his beauty sleep and I needed to finish a few work related things. Ophelia was already asleep by the time I returned, a head resting on a pillow on the sofa. I grabbed a spare blanket and put this over her as I didn't want her to be cold. She'd probably wake up in an hour or so anyway and then move to her actual bed.

I tiptoed into my own room, careful not to make any noise and once inside, I left my clothes in a heap and sauntered into the bathroom, not caring that I was stark naked. If Ophelia was awake, she wouldn't be bothered anyway since she always did the same.

I hopped into the shower, relishing in the heat and patter of water down my body. I trailed my fingers down my body, circling my belly button. I imagined that Felix was standing behind me, his fingers enclosing around mine and then trailing further down my skin. It was enough to get me hot and bothered but

I didn't want to end up looking like a prune so after five minutes, I felt pretty clean.

I wanted to plan something nice for him next since he had prepared a wonderful three-course meal. I still couldn't get over how amazing the curry and dessert was but I wouldn't mention this to my mum, otherwise she'd get jealous. The fact that he had made all the effort to cook for me and also make one of my favourite dishes made my heart melt. He really cared enough to learn about Indian dishes and how to cook them.

I felt completely clean so stepped out of the shower and swiped the towel off the hook nearby, wrapping it around my body. I wrung out my hair to get rid of excess water and then decided to let it air dry.

Next, I needed to pamper my face since it was in need of attention. I had some facial cream on the sink basin and squeezed a pea drop size on two fingers. Once my face was lathered, I headed back to my room to get into my night clothes and dive under the covers with my laptop.

It was nearly midnight but I wasn't tired yet. I started to write, the words flowing out of me like lava. I was in a zone that I didn't want to get out of. I reflected on my boss' feedback too, how I needed to add a bit more detail and vividness to my words. Once I'd written quite a bit, I saved it and decided I would send this off to Grayson in the morning. Sleep was calling for me now and I wouldn't ignore that.

***

"Wakey, wakey," a chirpy voice sang and awoke me from my slumber. I squinted my eyes and my vision refocused on the silhouette of Ophelia who was holding a mug in her hand. I gratefully took it and took a large sip, as I was very parched.

"Thanks," I said after a few more sips, placing the mug on my bedside table. Tea always made me that extra bit ready for the day.

"Sleep okay?" Ophelia asked, taking a seat on the end of my bed. She was still wearing her pyjamas, a pattern of blue and white stripes.

"Like a baby. Did you move back to your room eventually? As when I came home, you were asleep on the sofa."

"I woke up about three in the morning and then moved. I think I got too comfortable, I'd worked quite a bit in the evening, so I was shattered," Ophelia said, tapping her fingers against her mug. She had painted her nails a different colour again, this time bright orange. They were perfectly manicured too, not too long or too short. My own nails weren't in the best condition but at least I wasn't biting them anymore.

"Glad you're alright though," I told her and I could tell she wanted me to talk to her about last night, as she shifted in her position and gave my leg a shake.

"Right, young missy. How was your dinner?"

"He cooked us a three-course meal, which was so sweet of him. It's like he knew what I liked. Then, some things happened." I blushed and Ophelia hummed, seeming satisfied with this knowledge.

"So, is he big?" Ophelia smirked, wanting to know all the finer details.

"Y-yes. But we didn't go all the way, just oral," I said very casually but nothing was casual about the act itself.

"But you wanted to." Ophelia nodded.

"Yep, I think it could have escalated but we were both conscious of time. I guess I didn't want to keep him."

"Girl, you should have stayed the night again. Don't worry about time, if you want each other then go for it," Ophelia said and maybe she was right. Maybe there really didn't need to be any barriers or reasons why Felix and I shouldn't sleep together yet. The desire and need was there. I supposed I just wanted to get to know him a little more before having sex with him.

"I can tell you're thinking. Anyway, it's your choice so I won't judge any decision you make. It's been a while since this old gal has had the D anyway but nothing my trusty toy can't fix." Ophelia winked and I laughed, appreciating her confidence in sexual freedom and self pleasure.

"I'm surprised you haven't broken it yet," I teased her.

"Me too. It's really been there for me when I needed it." Ophelia giggled. She then mentioned she would use the morning to do some work and then go and pick up the hire car for us so we could go on our adventure. I couldn't wait to spend some time with my friend, one of the best I'd ever had.

***

"Good progress today, Alisha. Felix taught you some tricks then." Hilde was skiing to a halt beside me, as we stopped just outside the ski school. It was rather busy today, with lots of children skiing with their parents and then some new adult learners taking the plunge. I had about two more lessons left with Hilde and I felt a little sad that they'd be over as I'd really grown to like my instructor. I needed to give her a special shout out in my article for sure.

"Yes, I feel so much more confident," I breathed, a mist of air escaping my mouth. It was extra cold today so I was glad I was bundled up, but skiing did create a sweat, so I definitely needed to take off this jacket soon.

"I can tell you are. Felix is a lovely man, by the way. I think he'd be a great instructor here, maybe you could talk to him about it," Hilde told me. Felix had spoken about the fact that he didn't enjoy his job and wanted to try something different. Being an instructor sounded right up his street; he was patient too and had the skills to teach.

So maybe yes, I would mention this to him. I wasn't sure whether I'd be seeing him today since I'd be going out with Ophelia but I'd send him some texts. Maybe even call him as I wanted to hear his voice.

I still remembered the text that Felicity had sent me last night and debated on whether to reply. I hadn't actually told Ophelia yet either, so I would wait until I got back before I even thought about replying.

Of course, I wondered how Felicity was doing and if she was truly sorry. I didn't know if we could ever be friends again, she had destroyed that trust and respect I had for her. It would be hard to bounce back from that. But I hadn't yet heard her side to the story, so maybe I owed it to myself to get some closure.

I shrugged these thoughts away for now and focused on Hilde.

"I'll talk to him," I replied.

"Tomorrow, we'll be going up a different slope. It's a little higher but I don't want you to be afraid. Remember, you are in control," Hilde told me before we said our goodbyes. In order to do something, you had to believe in yourself and I needed to keep reminding myself of that.

I got straight into a cable car which took me down to the bottom level, where I would place my ski gear in my locker that I'd hired. I sighed in relief once I took my boots off, as they were rubbing a little against my feet. I put on my normal shoes and then made the short journey back to the chalet, desperate for a cup of something hot and a few slices of toast. As I approached the chalet, I could see a dark grey car which must have been the one Ophelia hired. It was in excellent condition and I hoped it hadn't been too expensive. If we could use it for the next few days, then it would be very helpful.

Ophelia was nowhere to be seen as I entered through the door but I presumed she was either taking a shower or had gone back to sleep. I knew either way she'd be with me soon as we needed to set off for our trip.

Two slices of toast and a tea later, I was ready to go. I slipped into some more casual clothes and tied up my hair into a loose bun. I made a start on a draft email, making sure it was ready to send to Grayson with my work so far. My sister Kiya also texted to ask if it was okay if she brought a friend around to the flat. She always liked to double-check with me first before inviting people around, which was honourable of her. I texted back that it was fine and if she could send me a few photos of Chou as I was missing him. His purrs and head butts especially.

"Right, are you ready for an amazing trip?" Ophelia's voice barricaded the living room and I could see she was wearing a bright pink jumpsuit, donned with a gold belt and silver flat pumps. Her hair was curled and bounced as she walked over to me.

"I'm so ready!" I wanted to match her enthusiasm and she clapped her hands before grabbing the car key and then her duffle bag which looked full to the brim. I wasn't sure what she had packed in there but didn't question it regardless.

The two of us locked up and bundled inside the car, which had enough leg room thankfully. Ophelia launched the satnav to our destination. We would be travelling to Bregenz, known for its rich cultural and historical heritage. Sadly, it was too late to see the festival which took place there in July and August but we would be seeing the medieval old town as well as visiting the Kunsthaus museum. Ophelia and I both loved art and history so it would be a real treat.

If we were lucky, the journey itself would take less than two hours but I wasn't betting on it. I wasn't sure what Austrian traffic was like, especially around the Christmas period. England right now would be a real nightmare.

"Thanks for driving us," I said to Ophelia who gave me a soft smile.

"Anytime. Now let's rock and roll," she said, reversing the car and then joining the main road. I couldn't wait to see more of Austria and its beauty, especially with my best friend.

Chapter 25

Felix

I could have almost fallen asleep at work, given how slow it had been and how boring it was too. Surely, there was something better than this—could I really stay here for another year? There was only so much I could discover about working for a travel company. I really was starting to think about quitting and listening to my sister, who told me to take charge of my life and go for what I wanted.

It made me think of Alisha, and the love she had for her job. She loved writing. It had become second nature to her. I wondered what she was doing today too. She texted earlier to say she would be out of town until this evening. I would have loved to have joined her and Ophelia, but bills had to be paid and clients had to be spoken to.

My boss popped her head in a few times to check in on me and ask me to complete a few extra tasks. I didn't complain and did them as best as I could.

When it was time for my lunch break, I went into the staff room and grabbed the sandwich I'd stored in the fridge along with my orange juice. There was no one else in the room with me, not that it mattered as I didn't really have a friend here. Maybe that was my own damn fault.

After finishing my sandwich which was a lot more delicious than expected; cheese and pickle, I finished the rest of my juice and then pulled out my phone to endlessly scroll. My sister had asked me to go round to hers after work, where our aunt would also be. Dinner was booked for tonight and I wasn't sure if my cousins would be coming along. I'd be surprised if they did, since all they liked doing was playing games and watching sports on TV.

I had about twenty more minutes of my break before I was needed back at my desk. Thankfully I was clocking out a little earlier today, an hour earlier than usual. I couldn't wait to start my annual leave soon. I needed to make a start on my Christmas shopping and then have a think about my future at this company. If I would leave, I would have to give two weeks notice and as gruelling as that was, I would work my notice.

"Right, back to it," I muttered to myself as time was up and I could only stare at my phone so much before it would become tedious. Wanting time to hurry up, I finished every task I could and then did some copying and file organisation to keep me occupied.

By the time it hit 3:30 pm, I was ready to clock out and signed out of the computer I was working on. I said goodbye to my boss and in response, she dismissed me with a wave of her perfectly manicured hand. I'd never really spoken to her much other than talking about my performance and additional tasks to take on. As I left the building, I started to relax and drove to Mira's place, where I knew my company would be acknowledged and welcomed.

It didn't take too long to get to my sister's place, which was located at the end of her road. It was a simple two bed, with a small garden but she made sure to decorate it with flowers as she had a green thumb. Mira felt safe and comfortable here, and the rent was affordable. With her job and the hours she did, I supposed she could afford it. I could see her waving from the window as I parked and I couldn't help but laugh. She was always excited and I sometimes wished I could match that energy she had.

Aunt Brenna was also waiting for me and opened her arms for a big hug which I gladly granted her. I took in her familiar vanilla scent and she pressed a kiss either side of my cheeks.

"You look well, Felix." She scanned my features until she seemed content. Then I moved towards my sister who dived into my arms. Honestly, I loved my family and my heart would always swell with love whenever I was around them. I couldn't wait to spend some time with them, eat some good food and talk about anything and everything. Maybe I'd bring up Alisha to my aunt and I know that she'd be extremely eager to know more. She had wanted me to move on for some time, having picked up the pieces of my broken heart and shell. I didn't want her to worry anymore as things had changed.

"How was work today?" Aunt Brenna asked, leading me to Mira's living room. My sister had laid out some snacks on the table and poured us a glass of lemonade each as it was our go-to fizzy drink. The bubbles popped on my tongue as I took a long sip.

"Very boring, I must admit, but I go on my annual leave soon, so I can't wait," I replied, leaning back against the cushions to get more comfortable.

"I told him he should get another job, he's not happy there," Mira piped up, snatching a mini salted pretzel from one of the bowls. They did look delicious so I took a few as well.

"Oh, I'm sure he'll make the right decision Mira," Aunt Brenna replied with an almost warning tone, as if she didn't want my sister to bring it up again. My aunt had always taken a step back from my choices when I grew up and allowed me to make mistakes so I could learn from there. She did of course nurture me and teach me right from wrong. Clearly, she had done a good job with both my sister and I since we were well educated and both had paid jobs.

"I do have something I want to talk to you both about later, but for now let's catch up and I'll make us some tea," she said and Mira looked at me curiously, as if she thought I knew more than she did. I shook my head and shrugged but

I hoped it was nothing to do with my aunt and her health. Neither me or Mira wanted to worry about her, as she was everything to us.

"I'm sure it's fine," I reassured quietly to my sister but I knew in her head, she was starting to come up with possible scenarios. I did the same too but I had to trust that whatever it was, everything would be alright.

***

Mira had picked a very fancy restaurant called Restaurant Stiar, known for its flavours of Asian cuisine. I had eyed up the thai coconut soup on the menu before arriving so I knew I would order this. The chef was exceptionally talented here but I wasn't too sure whether we'd get the opportunity to meet him.

I was wearing the finest, crisp shirt I could find with a pair of black trousers and shoes to match. I had even decided to add gold cufflinks, ones that had been hiding away in my chest of drawers for some time. My hair had a little bit of gel but not too oily or too crunchy. Hey, I had to look classy since we were at an expensive restaurant.

The three of us were sat down at a perfectly decorated table, and were sipping glasses of crisp, white wine between us. We'd already ordered our starters—we simultaneously had ordered the soup. I remembered as well how much Alisha liked soup and how impressed she had been with my cooking.

"This is delicious," Aunt Brenna said, our starters had arrived and I moaned in agreement, especially with the way it slid down my throat and coated my insides with its warmth. I eyed my sister who was almost finished and tore off a piece of her bread roll to swipe around her bowl. Even the bread here was high class. I couldn't wait to try the main course; the homemade wild garlic noodles which would come with prawns with some grilled vegetables on the side. Wanted to be a little bit healthy tonight.

Our starters were shortly cleared away and we resumed back into easy conversation.

"So the boys didn't want to come out tonight?" Mira asked, drumming her fingers on the tablecloth.

"You know how they can be. There's a game they wanted to watch tonight. I suppose it's worked out, as I wanted it just to be us three anyway," Aunt Brenna said and I remembered that she had something she wanted to tell us. She didn't look too worried but I can tell there was a slight edge to her. She was easy to read—you could always tell when she was thinking about something.

"I care about the two of you very much, I hope you know that. I will always look out for you and be very proud of whatever you do," our aunt told the two of us, reaching across the table to take our hands. Now I was getting worried and I wasn't sure whether I'd be able to stomach my main course, especially if the news was bad.

"Okay, Aunt Brenna, you're scaring us a little." Mira let out a nervous laugh, meeting my eyes with hers. Her complexion was slightly pale and a few worry lines were stretched on her forehead.

"Is it your health?" I asked. I hoped it wasn't, I couldn't bear for my aunt to be sick.

"No, I'm healthy as a horse. It's not about me, kids," she drawled out and the anticipation was starting to become agonising. My heart was also skipping a beat and my palms were beginning to get clammy.

"You can tell us anything, we can take it," Mira said, squeezing Aunt Brenna's hand. Our aunt took a deep breath before speaking to us.

"It's your mother," Aunt Brenna said, her eyes darting between the two of us and waiting for our response. There was a silence as we processed this information. We never spoke about our birth mother. Ever. And I wondered why she came up in our conversation tonight.

"I saw her the other day in town. And she also saw me, so I couldn't ignore her," she continued and I nodded as of course my aunt wouldn't ignore her own sister. Believe it or not, at one point when they were kids they had gotten along well.

"Did she say anything, about us?" I dared to ask. I doubted my birth mother cared, she'd had years to get in touch. What was she even doing in town? She didn't live here or at least I didn't think she did.

"She wanted to know how you both were, what you looked like now. Whether she could see you too," Aunt Brenna said this with hesitation and she was right to. I would point blank refuse, like hell would I want to see the woman who abandoned me and my sister.

"Felix?" Mira turned to me, I knew she valued my opinion and wouldn't do anything without my input.

"I-I don't know. It doesn't sit right with me. Do you know how much trauma Mira and I went through as kids?" I felt my blood heat up as I said this, because I didn't want to think back to our difficult past.

"Of course I do and I did my best to shelter the pair of you from any further harm. You don't have to meet her at all, I completely understand," Aunt Brenna replied but I knew deep down she would want us to. I hoped she wasn't expecting us to play happy families with the woman, you couldn't undo the past.

"Maybe we need to think about it," Mira pondered and she was right. The two of us needed to speak on our own. Our main courses came within the next few minutes and I did my best to eat mine, but couldn't help but think about the possibility of seeing my birth mother again. Maybe I did need some closure but it would be ripping open old wounds that I didn't want to see or feel.

My aunt eyed the two of us for the rest of the evening with caution but spoke to us in a calm tone. I knew what she was thinking; she wanted us to meet our mother but she wouldn't push it. Her love for us overpowered her pride.

By the end of the evening, the three of us were full and ready to get back home. I knew before I'd go to sleep tonight that there were a lot of things I needed to think through. One of them being that I needed to talk to Alisha because leaving her in the dark wasn't fair. She deserved my full attention and I was going to give it to her.

Chapter 26

Alisha

The day had been extremely adventurous. Spending quality time with Ophelia was just what I needed. We were now just walking side by side, eating some vanilla ice cream, which was deliciously creamy. It reminded me of the 99p ice cream back home.

We'd enjoyed venturing around the town, taking photos and seeing the museum. The town itself was absolutely stunning and when the sun had started to set, there was a beautiful backdrop. It was a perfect photo opportunity, in fact, I had taken many today, and I wondered whether or not to include them in the article, as a few had me and Ophelia in them. I had plenty to write about later so I couldn't wait to sit down in front of my laptop and write until my heart was content.

The museum itself was unique, built with glass plates in the 1990s. There were a few exhibitions on, that showcased real talent and we were lucky to see them. After visiting the museum, Ophelia and I then grabbed dinner at Zum

Kornmesser, a hearty popular restaurant where I ordered a creamy risotto and Ophelia had boiled beef with fried potatoes. We exchanged hilarious stories about work and also about our favourite movies; I'd learnt that Ophelia was a big fan of Casper, something she hadn't told me about until now.

The sun was already set by the time we got back to the car and I was thankful I had taken a coat as it was definitely chilly. Ophelia turned on the heating in the car and then rubbed her hands together, blowing on them.

"I'm so tired but in a good way," she said as the car was starting to warm up. The ice that had built up on the windscreen was also melting away.

"Me too, it was nice to explore. Thanks again, Lia." I gave my friend's arm a squeeze, making a mental note to do something nice for her in return. We had a look ahead at the traffic on our phones and were relieved to see it was looking quiet on the roads. There was going to be snowfall tonight though, so we needed to try and get back before it got worse.

I hadn't heard from Felix since earlier this afternoon and I hoped he was okay, he had said he would be spending the evening with his family. Family time was important, I knew that much.

"Can't believe we have just a week left in Austria. I feel like there's so much more to discover," Ophelia said, keeping one hand in on the steering wheel as she drove at a steady pace.

"I know. I like it here," I said, with a hint of sadness to my tone. I knew I didn't want to leave, especially Felix just as we were starting to get closer. I felt ready to open my heart and maybe even give it to him.

***

I had made Ophelia and I some hot chocolate once we got in and the two of us decided to do some work. Grayson had replied to my email, attached with an updated version of my work and I could see he had highlighted and added comments. He mainly mentioned that my descriptions were better but that I needed just to work on some of my sentence flow, as some of my words ended abruptly. As I read through, it did make sense. To be a great writer, you had to accept your weak points and work on them. I had grown quite a backbone since working at Culture Horizon so any criticism now, I could take on the chin.

I had written a section about the history and arts that were available in Austria, but thought I'd add more to it. I wanted to plan a day out with Felix, and it would be perfect timing since he'd be on his holiday in two days. I wanted to try ice skating with him, as I'd never done it before, and it seemed romantic, a sweet moment for us to bond. I'd imagined it was similar to skiing, but the ice was harder and more of a chance of breaking a bone or two.

"Right, I am done," I muttered to myself and stretched my arms above my head as I'd been slouched for about an hour. A bubble bath sounded inviting. My muscles were now sore.

With the bath filling up and bubbling away, I discarded my clothes in a neat pile and took a moment to check out my body in the mirror. I'd never had a problem with my figure, I liked my shapely thighs, which had a few stretchmarks and then a huge birthmark on the inside of my left thigh. Originally, I felt insecure about this and Caden had made a few comments about it. I wished I'd realised back then how much of a douche he was. Too little too late but at least he wasn't in my life anymore.

Earlier in the day, I had spoken to Ophelia about Felicity's text and her response had been to ignore it. Felicity had had plenty of time to contact me and if she had wanted to, to even come and see me in person to apologise. She was a coward just like Caden and I had no energy for someone like that.

So, I deleted her text and moved on. Whether she'd contact me again, who knows. I'd probably choose a different outcome.

Happy thoughts now, Alisha.

I turned off the bath tap and sunk into the heated water, knowing my limbs would thank me for it.

Still no text from Felix when I last checked my phone but I didn't want to worry myself or seem like I was needy for him. I loved hearing from him though and always felt giddy when I saw his name pop up on my screen. As I scrubbed my skin with some body wash and a flannel, I sank a little further in the water and wondered whether he was thinking about me right now.

I imagined his firm hands cupping my breasts, circling my nipples with his thumbs. I loved it when he teased me, his hot breath mingling on my skin, hovering above my crotch. My pussy was starting to ache and my fingers had a mind of their own as they crawled down to the area that needed pleasing.

I rested my head back against the tub as my fingers rubbed between my folds. I wanted Felix's delectable mouth there instead but I'd have to settle for my fingers. If he was here, I'd beg for him to suck my clit and push my thighs further open as he dipped his head between them.

I was chasing my orgasm fast as I picked up the pace and I cried Felix's name as I came, gripping the side of the tub as I did, but this didn't compare to actually having him here.

I decided that I would text him once I got out of the bath and was dressed. I wondered what to say to him or whether to even call him.

No, just text him. He may be asleep.

I was lounging on my bed before plucking up the courage to send the damn thing I had typed.

I hit send quickly and then placed my phone on the bedside table, staring at it like it was a foreign object. I wasn't expecting him to reply fast, and I knew it wouldn't be a good idea to ponder or wait around, so I decided to make myself some chai before bed.

Ophelia was also in the kitchen and was on the phone to what sounded like her mum.

"Yes, I'll be seeing you soon. Don't worry," Ophelia said, giving me a wink as I reached past her to grab a mug.

Ophelia said her goodbyes to her mum before hanging up and then shoved her phone in her shorts pocket. She resumed making her drink, which looked like some kind of smoothie.

"Mum apparently has met a new man so she's really keen for me to meet him," Ophelia said, adding a dash of milk to her drink. Her parents had split up when she was ten and she'd spend most of her school holidays with her dad, who lived about two hours away from her. She had no brothers or sisters, which she didn't seem to mind. It meant her parents could give her all the attention and spoil her.

"Oh right, how do you feel about that?" I queried, boiling some water in a pan. I would add the tea leaves, milk and spices next. Ophelia scrunched up her nose and then crossed her arms, something she did when she wasn't quite sure about something.

"Well, mum has had several relationships over the years and they never seem to work out. They always end up disappointing her and she gives too many chances. I don't know what will be different about this one, so I'm not hopeful." Ophelia shrugged and I did sympathise with her, it must be a struggle having to watch your mum have their heart broken multiple times. It was probably a reason why Ophelia hadn't had a relationship for years, she didn't want to become invested and then give her heart away to someone who wasn't worth it. I valued that, her integrity and self respect.

"It's good that you look out for your mum," I told her, stirring a spoon in the pan as it was starting to boil.

"Someone has to," Ophelia replied and I decided not to talk too much about home with her since it was a tricky topic. She always liked to be positive and focus on the things ahead of her.

After drinking my cup of chai, the two of us decided to get some sleep but not before I looked out the living room window, to watch the snow fall. I was almost tempted to go outside but decided against it, as otherwise I'd be a snowwoman. I chuckled at this thought, remembering the time when Aadi and Zane barricaded me with snowballs when we were children. The two of them always liked to tease me and beat me at games, but as I was getting older I was starting to get the better of them.

Kiya had sent me a few photos and a video of Chou, which melted my heart. I missed my furry friend heaps.

When I returned back to my room, I hurriedly picked up my phone, expecting to see a reply from Felix. I tried not to be disheartened when I didn't. Maybe something had happened. Maybe he decided he wasn't into me anymore or perhaps realised he still had feelings for his ex.

I knew I needed to stop thinking this way but it was hard not to. I willed myself to sleep as there was no need to overthink when it could just be *nothing*.

I thought back to what he said to me the other day in German and after working it out, I realised what he'd said.

Du wirst mein Tod sein.

He was going to be the death of me too.

Chapter 27

Felix

Having three hours of sleep, I felt incredibly groggy and grumpy when I arrived at work. No amount of caffeine would change the mood I was in. I was just lucky today was my last day before annual leave. It was crazy how quickly the past twenty-four hours had gone. And there had been a lot to think about.

Of Mira and Aunt Brenna, to the news of my birth mother wanting to see us. And then finally, Alisha. I felt incredibly guilty that I hadn't responded to her text last night, as soon as I saw it I was desperate to respond. I didn't want to drag her into my shit though, so I did what I would do best and wallowed in self pity.

I hated myself, I really did, hated the way I couldn't manage my emotions properly and be brave.

I scratched my chin as I glared at the computer screen, after work I needed to go and do something proactive. Skiing was the only thing that would probably help my mood. And of course, seeing Alisha. I gave myself a reminder to call her later, to arrange to meet up. Maybe go for a late bite somewhere, I just missed her presence. She was all that was good and beautiful in this world and I needed that right now. I didn't want to fuck things up with her.

Leaning back in my chair, I closed my eyes and counted to three before opening them again. Just as I did, one of my colleagues brushed past me and then decided to talk to me. He was a polite person, with gentle green eyes and dark brown hair. His name was Charlie and he hadn't been at the company for very long.

"Felix, could you help me with something? No one else seems to have a clue," Charlie said, holding quite a large stack of papers in his hands. He looked hopeful and in need of some support. I wasn't one to say no, especially as I was in his shoes when I first started here. Charlie seemed genuine and he was about a year younger than me.

"Of course." I gestured for Charlie to sit down next to me and he spread the papers out in front of us.

"Some are complaints and then some are invoices, which I just can't seem to work out. I thought I was good at numbers, I was one of the top mathematicians in my year group." Charlie grinned as he said this. So, why did he need my help then?

"What seems to be confusing?" I questioned, glancing at one of the invoices which was dated from about a month ago.

"It's more so that the actual payments from customers are different from what's printed here, and I'm not sure why," he said and I already knew why. We had a select number of clients we offered discounts to, due to their loyalty to the company and service they would bring. I explained this to Charlie and he nodded, making sure to log it and then put the invoices away.

Next were the complaints, emails from customers who were not happy with the packages, some who had flight delays or cancellations and some who just wanted to moan.

"Sadly in any business, you can't please everyone and the best thing you can do is respond with hospitality and understanding," I told Charlie, having had lots of experience handling complaints.

"Right, well thanks Felix. I feel a little less stupid now." Charlie scratched the back of his neck and then offered me a warm smile. He didn't make a move from his seat and then decided to talk to me some more.

"I was wondering, if you wanted to come out for a drink one evening? I've asked a few of our work colleagues and they're keen to come along. Plus, I'd love to get to know you better. I've only even known you as Felix behind his desk," he said and the idea didn't sound too preposterous.

"Yeah, that sounds alright." I let out a nervous breath, as I hadn't hung out with other people apart from my own small circle in nearly a year. Maybe it was time to let down my walls I had built and have some fun. There was no harm in that.

***

Charlie and I chatted away for the rest of the shift and I'd learned that he was a twin, he had a girlfriend of two years and when he was eighteen, he was due to go to university, but he ended up in a car crash with one of his best friends, who sadly died. He was lucky to come out of it alive and didn't take anything for granted now. He said he was given a second chance at life and he was going to make the most of it.

"So, what do you usually do for Christmas?" I asked him as we were now on our lunch breaks, I had whipped up a swiss cheese and beef sandwich which was delicious. I was really starting to enjoy preparing food for myself and I'd even packed some fruit too. Very unlike me but my lifestyle needed changes.

"My twin and I usually do all the cooking, so our parents can relax. We've got quite a big family, all our cousins, aunts and uncles come down to celebrate with us. The house is big enough, thankfully," Charlie said, biting into his own lunch. He was halfway through eating a cream cheese bagel with a packet of crisps and some dried mango.

"That sounds great." I smiled at this. I'd imagine there was chaos but they probably all were used to it.

"What about you?" Charlie fired the question back to me. My Christmas tradition would be nothing compared to his but I loved it regardless.

"I have one sister, two twin cousins and then my aunt Brenna. We usually celebrate together at Brenna's."

"Ah, what about your parents?" I knew he'd ask this eventually and I couldn't really avoid the question.

"I don't know my father. Or my mother really," I admitted and Charlie seemed to understand that this was a touchy subject so I was grateful he didn't ask anymore. We changed the subject to the worst Christmas cracker jokes we'd seen before our break was finished.

It was nice to talk to another male and maybe I actually had a friend now. I was eager for the next few hours to speed by so I could get home and call Alisha, to find out how she was and apologise for my cold shoulder. She didn't deserve that. She deserved my undivided attention.

I would give her just that.

Charlie and I exchanged numbers as we clocked out of work and then I made my merry way back home, my heart racing every mile I got closer. It just meant I would be able to hear Alisha's voice soon. Even just imagining it sent shivers down my spine.

Fuck, you really are mad for her.

When I finally got home, my palms were sweaty and my hands shook a little, jingling the key in the door. I had only shut the front door about two minutes again when I heard two sharp knocks, which made me pause what I was doing.

It could be Alisha.

I strode over to the door, practically yanking it open with a grin on my face. However, the grin sloped into a frown when I focused on who was standing in front of me.

"Felix, I'm sorry but I had to see you. Can I come in?" Evie asked nervously.

Well, I couldn't slam the door in her face as it wasn't my style. I twisted my body so that she could slip through the door and then closed it behind her.

"I know I'm probably the last person you want to see. But I think we need a chat," she said and I let out a little sigh. We could have spoken months ago so why was she now about to pop my happy bubble?

"Evie, you could have spoken to me a while ago. I-I've moved on," I told her and I hoped I sounded convincing to her.

"Of course Felix, I understand that. I just wanted to say my piece and then I'll leave you alone. Is that alright?" Evie twiddled her thumbs, something she always did when she felt awkward. I had always noticed these tiny details about her, because I had *loved* her. Note the past tense. I didn't want her to be in my life anymore but I would hear her out on this occasion.

I motioned for her to take a seat on the sofa, which she boldly walked over to and sat down. I glanced at her features and she did look well, her skin was flushed but smooth and she had a gleam in her eyes. Maybe this new man of hers was really the one. Me being gracious, I hoped she was happy.

"Let's start from the beginning," Evie proposed and I grimaced a little, as I wasn't expecting to dive into the whole story of us. I only really wanted to hear about her going cold turkey on us, her reason for leaving me at the altar.

But I sat back and had open ears, all the time wishing the woman sitting in front of me was Alisha. I'd give anything to have her here instead of Evie.

Chapter 28

Alisha

The next morning was a little bleak, it was snowing quite heavily and the wind with it was causing the chalet to creak and groan. I didn't quite feel able to go to my ski lesson this morning, perfect timing as Hilde had also called to say *she* was unwell. So, I would spend my morning drinking coffee and working.

I needed to distract myself—there was still radio silence from Felix and to be honest, it was starting to irritate me. If he wasn't interested anymore, then he needed to be clear. He didn't seem like the type to play games but you couldn't always assume things about people. Eventually, they would show you who they truly were.

I was halfway through my meagre cup of coffee, which matched my overall mood, before I let out a huff and closed my laptop down. Nothing seemed to spring out of my mind.

I looked out of the window, I couldn't go out so there wasn't a great deal I could do to keep myself busy. Ophelia was still asleep in her room which I didn't blame her for, yesterday's endeavours had worn her out.

I just hoped the weather would let up soon, so I could do something active. I decided to call my sister, as her sweet face would cheer me up.

"Hello, didi. Everything okay or am I gonna have to fight somebody?" Kiya asked immediately, as we were so close she could read my moods, even through a screen.

"I'm just so bored. We're snowed in," I grumbled and Kiya seemed to find this amusing as she started to laugh.

"Isn't that like the dream though? I'm fricking jealous of you!!"

"Where's Chou? I miss my baby." My heart soared as Kiya flipped the screen so that I could see my precious boy, who was curled up in his bed, paws tucked in. He looked a little bigger than I remembered.

"Yeaaaah, I may have been giving him a few treats," Kiya said sheepishly, waiting for me to scold her. But as long as my cat was happy and being pampered, I wouldn't complain.

"Never mind." I shook this off and then propped my phone up against the vase on the table in front of me. I focused on my little sister's soft complexion and decided whether to get her advice about Felix.

"Bon, why are men so complicated?" I asked if I could have any superpower in the world, it would be to read minds. At least then I would stop worrying about what people thought. But there was a danger to that superpower, knowing everyone's thoughts.

Hm, maybe just settle being you, Alisha.

"I haven't had a relationship so I dunno, didi. Is there something I should know?" Kiya cocked her head slightly.

"I'm hung up on someone and I'm scared I've pushed him away."

"Why, what made you think that?" Kiya was puzzled at this. I hadn't really come up with a clear reason. I didn't want to think I was being ghosted.

"Haven't heard from Felix since yesterday, usually he texts me back but he hasn't responded." I flicked at a loose piece of skin by my nail bed before biting it off.

"So, call him then. That's your solution, you don't always have to wait for the man to call. Take charge, didi. Have faith in yourself, as you are that bitch," Kiya told me and it almost sounded as simple as she was making it out to be.

"Language, bon." I laughed at my beautiful but brilliant sister.

"Trust me, I know my shit. So listen to your little sister and follow that big and beautiful heart of yours. Then tell me all about it later, cause I've gotta go!" Kiya exclaimed.

"Hm, we'll see bon. Talk later," I said and then pressed the red button to hang up. I decided to hide my phone away for the rest of the morning, because staring at it for another few hours wouldn't help.

I decided after about ten minutes to cook something sweet and luckily, we had done a food shop recently so the ingredients I needed were here. I had a craving for gulab jamun parfait, a light Indian dessert that was relatively easy to make. Gulab jamuns were sweet round dumplings, made with paneer.

What I needed to do was fry the dumplings and soak them in a sugary syrup, which was the traditional way. After this, I would make a parfait with Greek yoghurt, accompanied by nuts and saffron.

My stomach grumbled at the thought of this and it would absolutely go down a treat with Ophelia. I would wake her up and surprise her with it.

Once I made the gulab jamuns, I thinly sliced about five of them and then cut the others into quarters. With the yoghurt, I decided to add some cream and mixed these together. On the hob, I boiled some milk, with a bit of water and saffron. Once everything was combined, I needed to chill the parfait in the fridge for about half an hour, which I left in a medium sized bowl. Usually, you could put them into small glasses but we didn't have these in the kitchen. I'd made enough anyway to just about halfway fill the bowl.

The sweet smell wafted through the room and made me feel warm inside, it reminded me of being back at my parents and I really did miss them. I couldn't wait to spend Christmas with them, like usual, but part of me wished perhaps I could stay here, to see the magic of the holidays in Austria.

I wanted to know more about Felix's family specifically. Mira seemed very sweet and I could see she was quite protective of her brother. I mean, who wouldn't be after watching him get his heart broken?

I thought back to his ex, who I had seen briefly the other night. I didn't know a lot about her but I had this sinking feeling that perhaps she still had a hold on Felix. Maybe he kissed me to make her jealous?

They were supposed to be getting married, for heaven's sake. How could I compete with that?

Stop the irrational thinking, you fool.

Well, you are a fool for him.

I couldn't believe I was having an argument with myself in my head but that's just what my brain always did. Sometimes I hated it, sometimes I loved it. Right now, I wanted to switch off and bury myself in between my pillows.

Kiya was right though, I needed to pluck up the courage and ring Felix myself. There was nothing to lose, I wouldn't be embarrassing myself or him. If he sent me to voicemail, then that would be my answer. Then, I could just try and forget about him.

But how could I forget about someone so incredible as him?

After picking and chewing at some more loose skin by my nails, I knew I needed to stop.

You can do this. You can do this. You can—

My erratic thoughts were interrupted by a sharp rap on the door and it almost knocked me off my seat. Me and Ophelia weren't expecting anyone so I was curious to who it was.

I trudged my way to answer it and opened the door without so much as glancing up at who was in front of me.

"Hi," a voice I had grown to adore greeted me and everything I had thought about went out the window. I lifted my head to gaze at him and take in his features. He looked tired with evident bags under his eyes but he didn't look away from me. His eyes looked as though there was a story to tell. I'd be willing to listen.

"C-come in," I told him, shuffling to the side so he could enter. I noticed that there was no car in the drive and my eyes widened at the realisation that he must have walked here. In this damn weather.

He must be freezing.

"Felix, bloody hell. You must be cold, did you walk here?" I asked a very obvious question but it was valid.

As I shut the door, Felix slipped his hand into mine and squeezed me gently. His fingers were so cold that I was worried he'd get frostbite.

"I couldn't drive here, and I wanted to see you," Felix said, a slight roughness to his tone.

He wanted to see me.

"Sit down and I'll make you a hot drink." I gestured for him to take a seat but he didn't budge, keeping a hold of me. *I loved that.*

"I don't need that. I need *you*." And my heart dropped.

I need you. I needed him too.

"Felix..." My voice trailed off, not being able to say anything else. So, I would just listen.

"A lot has happened over the past twenty-four hours, it's been crazy. I'm so sorry that I didn't reach out to you, I didn't want to freak you out or push you away. I've got a lot of baggage and I thought maybe you didn't want to be with someone that does." In his eyes, I could tell a war was going on. I needed to let him know I was here to help him through it, if he'd let me.

"Whatever has happened Felix, I'm here for you. You can always talk to me." I offered him a soft smile, reaching my other hand up to cup his cheek. My fingers grazed the stubble that was forming.

"Okay. Maybe I will take you up on that offer of a drink, I'm shit cold." Felix let out a laugh and I copied.

"Go and sit down then." I gave him a gentle push but he didn't let go of my hand. His fingers traced my cheekbone and then my trembling lips before leaning down so lips hovered above mine. All he needed to do was close the space between and make me his.

But I already was.

The kiss started off as gentle before becoming needy, as though we hadn't seen each other in months. The urgency for one another was real and the kiss became heated, his tongue edging into my mouth and his grip becoming tighter on my waist. All I could taste was him and I decided that that was my favourite now.

"Well, I'm just gonna go back to my room," a voice startled us, and I didn't need to look up to know it was Ophelia. Very quickly, she scarpered back to her room.

Poor woman, this must have scarred her for life.

"Maybe we should go to yours," Felix murmured. As much as I wanted to rip his clothes off, I needed him to get things off his chest first.

"Later," I told him, signalling that I would make his drink. Felix waited for me patiently, his eyes never waning from me. It made me blush with the level of intensity in his look.

I handed him his hot beverage, he had decided on a coffee, and then took a seat next to him. He held the mug between his hands, to heat himself up. There was still a few bits of snow on his jacket which I brushed off.

"First, I'll start off with the first news," Felix said. *Shit, it sounded like I needed to brace myself for whatever he'd say next.*

I wanted to ride through the storm with him, to crash through the erratic waves and be his anchor.

Chapter 29

Felix

Talking about my tragic childhood was always a sensitive topic for me, but I had huge trust in Alisha, as she waited patiently next to me. I knew I needed to be brave but the last time I had opened up to a woman about this was Evie. Her reaction at the time had been shock and now come to think of it disdain. Disapproval. As if she didn't want to know.

When Evie turned up at mine last night, it was all the confirmation I needed to keep her in the past and focus on my future. My future with Alisha. I wanted her in it, to create many more fun and exciting memories with her. And if I wanted to be with her, she needed to know everything about me.

I started to explain everything to Alisha about the tragic start in life that me and my sister had.

"I used to have two parents, we lived in a small house but it was comfortable. They would argue a lot in front of us, so much so that my dad just decided to leave one day and never come back. You can imagine the effect this had on my mum." I closed my eyes, reliving the horrible memory of my mother trying to get him to stop. Shortly after this, she turned to drinking and it was the only thing that she seemed to enjoy from then on.

Alisha took a deep breath, her shoulders were hunched and I watched the clocks set in motion through the expression on her face. She was clearly feeling sympathetic as she gave my hand a squeeze, her beautiful eyes willing me to continue.

"I remember the first night my mother didn't come back. Mira was very young and waited by the front door until she came home. She didn't eat because she was worried, neither did I." I kept my eyes on Alisha, watching her intake breath and exhale. I wondered what she was thinking in that brilliant mind of hers.

"Oh gosh," she gasped and if I wasn't wrong, I could see a few tears brimming in her eyes.

"The neighbours caught on, as they'd heard her come home and start yelling." I remembered this so vividly, I almost didn't want to but it was forever etched in my memories. My mother's cries were still so clear in my head.

"We were very quickly taken into care, but refused to be separated. Mira was all I had and we didn't have any other family members to look after us. Well at least, we didn't think we had anyone." I shifted in my seat, not wanting my body to go rigid. Alisha's hand had never wavered and she was invested in what I was telling her.

She was honestly so fucking amazing, I was definitely 'punching'. A term I had learnt from Alisha.

"What was it like, in care?"

"Rough. But we weren't there too long before our aunt found out about us. My mother had ended up in prison and my aunt caught wind of it. She immediately demanded to know where we were and she soon found us. It was the first time we'd ever properly met her and she welcomed us into her home, without batting an eyelid." I cracked a smile at this, as from that point in my life I had discovered hope. That someone would love us and keep us safe, as that was all we wanted.

"I'm so pleased she found you, she sounds wonderful," Alisha spoke gently and I nodded in agreement.

"Me too and she really is. Mira and I ever since have never gone without, we've got a family and that's all we could ask for," I said, but this wasn't the end of the story as now I had to tell Alisha about the possibility of meeting up with my mother.

"Thank you so much for telling me, Felix. I wish you could see how amazing you are. And I am here for you, whenever you need to talk."

"I need your opinion, Alisha. I don't know what to do." I looked down at my lap and Alisha didn't reply, rather waited for me to continue.

"My mother wants to meet up with me and Mira. She's in town." I still felt slightly angry whenever I mentioned the word 'mother', but at least for the first six years of my life, she had been there.

"Do you want to see her?" Alisha looked at me again with wide eyes, processing this information. I wondered what she would do in my position. Would she bite the bullet and go and meet the woman who had left me and my sister to fend for ourselves?

"I do and I don't. Part of me wants closure, to hear her out. Maybe she's changed," I admitted.

And maybe you do want a mother, after all these years.

"I get that. It's totally your decision and you wouldn't be wrong if you decided not to see her." Alisha had edged a little closer to me and I caught a whiff of her sweet scent.

"Would you come with me if I do?" I gazed back at her, feeling confident in what I had asked as really I didn't think I could go without her.

"Of course I can," Alisha said with no hesitation.

That's my girl.

"Thank you, for listening to me and being amazing. I do have more to tell you though and I'm not sure if you will like it." I mean if it were me, I wouldn't feel great knowing that her ex had turned up to see her.

"Try me," Alisha said and I let out a deep breath before telling her everything about last night.

***

Evie sat in front of me, perfectly poised and sparkly eyed as she'd always been. She wanted to talk about what had happened between us and how it led up to the break-up.

"I did love you, Felix. But I felt something was missing. I tried to fight for us and I knew you did too." Well, it was mainly me that had fought for our withering relationship. Evie would spend most evenings out with friends, some that didn't even care about her like I did.

"So, if you knew things weren't working then why didn't you call off the wedding?" I could feel my blood beginning to boil a little but I tried to remain calm and collected.

"I felt that maybe I could have given us that chance. I was dressed and ready to drive to the church with my bridesmaids. But then, I had an epiphany. I couldn't go through with it and I'd tried to get a hold of you, to let you know. I'm really sorry, Felix. I wish it hadn't ended this way." Evie looked sincere and I wondered if she really was telling the truth. Well, I'd have to believe it. Even if she finally told me seven months later.

"I thought we could be honest with each other. Evie, I would have built a whole new world for you to make you happy," I told her, she needed to know just how much I would have done for her. She'd trampled on my heart and my life. But now, I was taking both back. She had no power over me anymore. None.

"I know that now," Evie replied sadly and for a moment, I felt some sympathy for her.

"All we can do is move forward, focus on our own happiness." I saw her grimace at this which made me confused. Wasn't she happy with her new man?

"Of course, is there anyone on the horizon for you?" she asked. I didn't feel like she really needed to know but my feelings for Alisha growing and admitting them out loud to Evie would be clarity. I wanted to close that chapter, barricade the past with a tough brick wall and never look back.

"Yes, I am seeing someone." And someone pretty fucking great too. I just hoped I hadn't messed things up with her.

"Me too. He's French, very funny. He likes to make me laugh and cook me great dinners," Evie said. This would have bothered me months ago but it did nothing to me now. I didn't even blink.

"Nice," I said awkwardly. Sensing this, Evie stood up to make her leave and I was extremely thankful that she had read the room.

"I hope we can maybe be friends, Felix. But I understand if not. Maybe think about it? You have my number." Evie gave me a small nod before vacating my house.

I didn't have her number and I would never want it again. I decided there and then I didn't want to be friends or see her again. There was no place for her in my life and it felt fucking great to admit that to myself. This would be the end of thinking about Evie and what she was doing with her life.

***

"Wow," Alisha had finally said as I leant back against the chair. She then cleared her throat, running her tongue on her bottom lip and then teasing it between her teeth. My trousers tightened at this and now I realised how badly I wanted her. She was so close to me now, having moved a few centimetres on the sofa.

"I know," I breathed, a shaky laugh escaping from within me.

"I'm so bloody proud of you." Alisha squeezed my arms gently before pulling me into a much needed hug. I sank into her, resting my head in the crook of her neck. One of my favourite spots.

I needed to hear that, to know someone believed in me and I knew now that I needed to make Alisha mine. I couldn't lose her. I never wanted to.

"Sweetheart, I want to hear about you now. Are you alright?" I brushed a loose strand of her dark hair that had fallen against her flushed cheek, tucking it behind her ear.

"I am now that you are here." That was enough to scoop her up in my arms and carry her to her bedroom, placing her underneath me quickly.

"We have to be quiet, because of Ophelia." Alisha giggled as we were huddled under her covers.

"Hm, with what I'm about to do to you next, I don't think *you* can be." I palmed her perfect breasts through her shirt, wanting to rip it open and swirl my tongue over her nipples. She let out a soft whimper as my fingers were crawling through her trousers and moving her underwear to one side so I could access her throbbing pussy.

So wet for me already.

I knew I would tease her first before having my cock inside of her. But whatever she wanted from me, I would give her. I paused my teasing, waiting for her to tell me what to do.

"It's all about you, sweetheart. Tell me what you want."

"Fuck me now, Felix." Alisha's eyes were full of lust and I knew that after this, there would be no going back. *I didn't want to.*

I'd mark her as mine tonight.

Chapter 30

Alisha

I loved his fingers, the way they dived in and out of my pussy at a perfect speed. I wanted to withhold my orgasm though, to finally feel him inside of me. His trousers were bulging and he had a rabid look in his eyes.

"How do you want me to fuck you?" Felix was asking all the questions, which I found very sweet. But fuck, I really wanted him to take charge.

"Until I see stars, Felix. Don't hold back," I told him, firm in my words. I had never really had rough sex but I wanted to try it tonight with the man I was growing to adore. I trusted Felix and if he could make me come like that with his fingers and mouth, then his cock would be a whole other feeling.

I was a little nervous, since we'd be crossing another bridge together and there'd be no going back. I didn't want to anyway. I wanted this. *Him.*

I slipped off his shirt over his head, his coat he had discarded about five minutes ago, and tiptoed my fingers down his muscular chest, a few sprouts of hair were protruding from it but to me, that was extremely attractive. I loved a man with a bit of hair on his chest.

I dipped my fingers below his v-line, to help him take off his trousers and boxers. His breathing was deep, as I crept my fingers closed to erect cock.

Fuck, he felt huge.

I placed the tip of him in my mouth, licking a bead of precome. Felix tipped his head back and groaned deeply, as I lowered my mouth further and then dragged my lips back up with a pop.

"You're killing me, woman," Felix said through gritted teeth and then his hand found its way into my hair, giving it a tug.

"I love your hair." Gosh, he sounded so sexy and he looked so good too as I licked and sucked him, his hips also moving in time to my mouth. I couldn't exactly respond to him whilst I was trying to give him *the* blowjob of the century.

"Keep going sweetheart and I'll come in your gorgeous mouth. Do you want that?"

Holy hell, that would be hot.

"Mhm." I couldn't really reply as I had a mouth full of him. Seconds away from coming, he released himself from me and I almost pouted as I was really getting into it.

"Do you have a condom?" Felix asked, and I realised I hadn't.

Shit. Well, I didn't expect to be having sex on this holiday so I hadn't come prepared.

"No, but Ophelia might." I knew asking her wouldn't be a problem, these things didn't embarrass her and even though she didn't have sex regularly, she'd always have condoms with her.

"Sorry, normally I have some on me but it's been a while," Felix said.

"Don't be sorry, we've both been out of practice. I'll be back in a jiffy." I practically hopped off the bed but not before grabbing my nightgown to cover my naked body.

I knocked on my friend's door and she very quickly opened it, holding out a silver wrapped condom in front of her.

"Say no more. Thank me later," was all she said before closing the door. I was speechless but yes she was right. I would thank her later.

Perhaps she must have heard us fooling around.

I raced back to a waiting Felix, who had buried himself under the covers. He looked so adorable but there was no time for cuddling. I wanted to climb on top of him and act out all the dirty thoughts I had.

"You are beautiful," Felix said as he kissed me, untying the belt of my nightgown to reveal my bare body. I suddenly felt a bit self-conscious, covering my breasts with my hands.

"Don't hide from me, sweetheart. This body is beautiful. *You* are beautiful." Felix cupped my left breast with his broad hand and swiped his tongue over my perky nipple.

God, this was torture as I just wanted him inside me.

As if he read my mind, he took the condom from me and ripped open the packet. Slipping the condom on his cock, we took a moment to look at one another as if to check we were one hundred percent ready. No regrets. I wanted this just as much as he did.

He edged the tip at my entrance as he pinned both my arms down, taking full control. My legs locked around his hip as he brought himself closer to me. My heart was racing like crazy and slowly, he pushed himself inside me.

Of course, it stung a little as I hadn't had sex in months and perhaps I needed a bit more lubrication. I bit my bottom lip as he gently eased further into me. When he was completely inside me, I was full of him and my heart fluttered when he pressed a chaste kiss to my lips.

"Open your legs wider for me, baby. Let me make love to you," Felix said softly. I willingly obeyed and gasped as he delved deeper in me, into my soul.

The movements were slow but so good, he was stretching me and filling me up perfectly.

"You feel so good," I mumbled, my nails digging into his back as he picked up the pace. His cock was buried deep inside me and the way he was moving his hips sent me into overdrive. Our bodies became slick with sweat and I felt bold enough to switch positions, so that I was on top and in charge.

The grip on my ass meant that Felix was loving this and wanted me to be dominant.

"Take what you want, sweetheart. I am all yours." Felix started to thrust upward and fast as I threw my head back in pure ecstasy. He was also in bliss as he let out a low groan, his fingers gripping my hips tightly.

"I'm close, baby." Felix used his hands to open my legs wider. I had no words as my body clenched. I was close too.

I loved the way he watched me, his body writhing in time with mine. Almost like we were made for each other. *Maybe we were.*

My orgasm was blooming and with a few more rough thrusts, I lost all control and tipped my head back, letting out a loud cry. *So much for being quiet.*

He continued to fuck me until he reached his own orgasm, spilling himself into the condom and riding through the shock waves with me.

"Oh fuck, baby." Felix pulled me closer and pressed his lips firmly against mine. I fell back against him, wanting to stay like this forever if we could. His cock was still resting inside me but was becoming limp as minutes passed.

"Do you think your friend will be mad at us for making all that noise?" Felix chuckled underneath me, he looked completely sated and his breathing had returned to normal.

"No, she knew what was happening as when I knocked on the door, she had a condom already in her hand," I told him and a deep laugh erupted from his chest. I loved that sound, it was beginning to become one of my favourites.

I laid back down next to Felix, our faces side by side. I remembered that I had dessert in the fridge and I was quite hungry. I wanted to spend the rest of the day eating parfait with Felix and watching some Netflix episodes on my laptop. It sounded perfect. So that's what we did and nothing could burst our little bubble.

***

The parfait had gone down a treat with Ophelia and Felix; the three of us were playing Monopoly and we decided to invite Mira down for the evening.

Eventually, we'd hit the town together and maybe even go clubbing. I hadn't stepped foot in a club since I was 19, with my university friends I no longer spoke with. I used to go with Felicity too but most of our nights ended up with her head in a toilet and me holding her hair back. *Not my idea of fun.*

But hanging out with three wonderful people like Ophelia, Felix and Mira was enough to convince me to give clubbing another go, and if I didn't like it, I could leave. No pressure.

"Yes, I win!" Ophelia cheered, she had been wanting to beat Felix for the past half an hour so she rejoiced in the fact.

"I'll accept my defeat." Felix succumbed, leaning back in his chair and then gave me a wink. I felt my stomach somersault and under the table, I knocked his leg with mine. Over the last few hours, we had been very physical with each other and it didn't take long for me to be horny again.

We had time for *that* in the evening though and Felix had no curfew thankfully, since he had no work tomorrow and for the next two weeks. He told me a work friend of his called Charlie would also come out with his girlfriend, I had no problem with this. The more the merrier. Having a social life after years of being an introvert was surprisingly nice. I had really come out of my shell over the last week. Of course, my anxiety would never completely go away but I was managing it better. *Go me.*

"Right my friend, I think I'm going to go and get ready for tonight. Ali, want to join me?" Ophelia jerked her thumb behind her and I knew it'd be a perfect opportunity to talk to her about everything with Felix. I valued my friend's opinion and didn't want her to feel like I would spend less time with her now that I had Felix. There would *always* be room for her in my life.

"See you in a little bit." I pecked Felix's cheek and then told him he could watch whatever he wanted on the TV or help himself to a drink in the kitchen. I didn't know how long I'd be but I didn't want him to get bored. Mira would be here shortly too, so I guessed he wouldn't be on his own for too long.

Ophelia abruptly hustled me into her room and shut the door behind me. She motioned for me to sit on her bed, which was covered with a fluffy pink throw and multiple pillows. She always liked the extra comfort and bright colours. Just like her personality too.

I gingerly took a seat, not wanting to mess up her neatly arranged bed. Ophelia sat down on the stool in front of her dressing table and picked up her make-bag, full of cosmetics that she'd experiment with. She made a start on her eyelashes before talking to me.

"I must have saved your life earlier." Ophelia grinned at me through the mirror.

"Can't thank you enough, but I'm sorry if you heard too much." I blushed. She waved her hand in dismissal at this and dipped her mascara wand in another coating.

"Psh, don't worry about making noise. You haven't heard me yet. So, how was it? Did he rock your world as I hope he did?" I loved that she didn't hold back with her questions, nothing phased or freaked her out.

"It was the best I've ever had, Lia. If I'm being completely honest, nothing compares to that." I bit down on my bottom lip as I replayed the steamy images of Felix pumping into me, the way his cock pounded and how my pussy clenched against him. I wanted another round of him but had to be patient until tonight. *Good things come to those who wait.*

But is patience really a virtue?

"Mm, I can tell by just looking at you," Ophelia said with a wide grin, as she started to apply some lipstick.

"So, is it official then? Boyfriend and girlfriend type thing?" she continued. Again, me and Felix hadn't put a label or definition on us. But maybe we didn't need to. We knew we wouldn't be seeing other people. He'd made it clear that he had no feelings for his ex too. So I had nothing to worry about.

I realised I hadn't told him about Felicity yet but maybe I'd mention it later. I wanted no stress tonight, at least for a few hours.

"I think we'll just see what happens in the next week. Gotta remember we're leaving soon," I said, not wanting the reminder but having to be realistic. Would things really come to an end just as they started? Would it really just be a whirlwind holiday romance?

"I think the two of you will realise right at the last moment." Adjusting in her seat, she turned to me and gestured for me to take her place so she could do my make-up.

Maybe she was right.

I needed to just figure it out.

Chapter 31

Felix

My sister was getting along with Ophelia and Alisha like a house on fire, it warmed my heart to see it. The three of us were on a bar crawl before we'd try out a club called *Lebendig in der Nacht* which translated as *Alive At Night*. I'd never been as it'd only just opened but it was proving to be popular with people in our age category.

The bar we were in now was blasting cheesy Christmas tunes but I didn't mind. I was with good company and Gosser beer, which was rare for me as I never usually drank this type of alcohol. At 9:30 pm, it was neither too busy nor too quiet. Give it an hour though and it would get busier. By then, we would have left.

I had one arm around Alisha as I chatted to Charlie and his girlfriend Nora who was very sweet. She was originally from Manila in the Philippines and often took Charlie with her to see her family there. She had tanned skin and dark, long brown hair. Her smile was kind and so was her personality, as she was quick to get to know me and the others. Charlie seemed to worship her and so did she.

"Fucking hell, this song." Ophelia was already a little tipsy and had cursed at some of the song choices so far. This caused both Mira and Alisha to laugh until they started singing to annoy Ophelia further.

"Just join in." Alisha nudged her friend.

"No, otherwise you won't stop. Maybe I'll ask the DJ to change the genre."

"Bah, humbug!" Mira pouted, as she reached for her glass, causing herself to nearly tumble off her chair. I was quick to reach out and grab her arm before she could fall to the floor. Maybe I needed to be on the extra lookout for her tonight. Big brother duties.

"Thanks, big brother." Mira patted my hand and then took a swig of her drink.

"Anytime." I smiled back at her before turning my attention to the beautiful woman leaning against me. She smelt like cherries and all I wanted to do was get her in a room alone and taste every part of her.

The sex earlier had been absolutely sensational and now I was hooked. I wanted to be *that* man for her. One who would give her all the pleasure she deserved, to fuck her into oblivion and back. I'd noticed that tonight she gained a lot of male attention and the looks I gave them in return signalled *mine*. I didn't want to be the jealous type nor to be possessive but like hell would I be letting this woman go? *Absolutely not.*

I didn't just want her for days. I wanted her for longer. I had to bite that bitter pill though and accept that I'd be saying goodbye to her soon. She had a job and a family to get back to. If we had to do long-distance, then that's what we'd do.

I didn't want to grumble or feel sad tonight, so I relaxed into Alisha's embrace and appreciated the gentle pecks on my cheek that she'd give me every so often. It felt like we had been doing this for much longer than a few days.

In the back of my mind, I wondered whether we moved too fast, but then when it came to romance and love in general, there didn't have to be a time limit. If you felt something for someone and they felt the same for you, then what would be stopping you from pursuing what could be a great love story?

When I was little, I had always envisioned what my dream partner would be like. Kind, understanding and hopelessly in love with me. I wanted them to be a best friend as well as a partner. I already felt like Alisha was my best friend, even despite our cold start. If I could take back how I treated her initially, I would in a heartbeat.

In a way I was grateful, as it led us to now. I didn't want to feel any regrets, as at the end of it we are human and we make mistakes. I'd accepted mine, and maybe my ex had too. We all had our damages, our own shit to get through. It's what made us unique.

I took one more glance at Alisha, who was laughing at something Charlie had said and my heart swelled just watching her. I knew what was happening with my emotions and it didn't scare me. I wanted her to consume me, to take whatever she needed from me and in return, I would give her the same.

"I think we should get going, I'm ready to get my groove on. I haven't been dancing in a while." Mira was fastening on her coat and then placed her empty glass on the table. Mine, I had nearly finished but I'd be able to down it quickly.

"I think Nora and I will head home, since I've got work tomorrow. I'm so jealous of you, Felix. Lucky bastard." Charlie offered me his hand to shake but instead, I pulled him in for a hug. I was grateful for him even coming along and didn't blame him for wanting to go home and get a good night's sleep. Or maybe some alone time with Nora.

"Thanks for inviting us." Nora was the next one to hug us all but not before exchanging numbers with the girls.

"Get home safely," I told them before they headed off and six became four. Ready for wherever the night would take us, we made our way to the club which was a short taxi ride. I paid for the fare as it was just a few euros and had the cash on me.

As we got out of the taxi, we could see a small queue but it wasn't particularly moving slow. We didn't mind waiting, even if there was a chill in the air. At least it wasn't snowing anymore. I'd always been used to it anyway.

With our identification ready to show the burly bouncer, as he was checking, the girls were growing more and more excited. I didn't at all feel outnumbered and I was thankful Mira had Ophelia to talk to, so she wouldn't be a third wheel. My sister looked stunning, well she always did, but she had styled her hair differently, outlined her eyes with glitter eyeliner, and was wearing a deep red dress that flowed underneath her. Of course it was freezing outside, so she was wearing a coat which enveloped her. I'd also done the same.

Ophelia also looked lovely too, she had shaded her eyelids two different colours and was wearing a slip black halter neck top with sparkles and dark brown trousers that hugged her legs. But my full attention was on Alisha, her long hair flowing around her shoulders in loose curls, her beautiful brown eyes were smouldering, and her choice in outfit was perfect. She always looked perfect but the way this little black dress looked on her, I had to stop myself from pulling her to one side and lifting her leg up so I could pound my cock hard inside her. I'd either be going to hers tonight or she'd be coming to mine. Either way, I wanted her in a bed.

"You look hot," I whispered into Alisha's ear so only she could hear. I felt her shiver against me which I absolutely loved. I could whisper more things to her if I wanted but the queue was moving and I couldn't multitask. I'd save it for later.

"Finally," Ophelia groaned as we were let inside, identification checked until the bouncer was satisfied. I always grimaced at the photo and needed to update my picture, my twenty-year-old self was a lot different to my almost twenty-eight-year-old self now.

Alisha slipped her hand into mine, our fingers intertwining. I had a feeling she would keep hold of me tonight, as she looked a little nervous. Walking inside the club, we could see how busy it was, with a sea of bodies dancing to the nostalgic music. At least they weren't playing Christmas tunes. We then gave our coats to the man in the cloakroom, who gave us slips of paper with numbers on them so we could collect our coats later.

Mira was keen to buy the first round for us, diving into her glittery purse to pull out her debit card.

"Can you come with me, Ophelia? I don't want to go on my own and perhaps we can give these lovebirds some privacy." Mira smirked at us. Her observation of us throughout the night had been positive and at one point, she had pulled me aside to say that she really liked Alisha.

It was important for anyone I dated to get along with my sister and vice versa.

"Okay. Alisha, your usual?" Ophelia asked as Alisha nodded. Then she turned to me.

"Just water for now, please," I said. I didn't want to get too drunk tonight, especially since I'd probably have to be the sober one anyway and get the girls home safely. Plus, I didn't always see the fun in totally losing myself.

"Oh, I spy a handsome man at the bar. See you guys in a bit!" Mira practically squealed, a side I hadn't seen of her. I hoped people wouldn't take advantage of her good nature tonight. She was too good for anyone, in my opinion, but maybe I was biassed.

Arm in arm, Ophelia and Mira made their way to the bar which was a ten-second walk. Alisha and I decided to sit at a nearby table, taking in the view of the club. It was quite trendy and upscale; the lights weren't too flashy, but the decor and furniture was of good quality.

The seats were dark velvet and the tables were white and round, which counteracted with the seats. The music had changed to something smoother and the bodies in the crowd were swaying slowly to it. Whether Alisha and I would join, well I'd let her take the lead. Whatever she was comfortable with. I wasn't much of a dancer but it was a perfect excuse to be up close with the woman I was crazy about.

"Bloody hell, it's been a long time since I've been to one of these. I feel out of practice," Alisha said delicately. Her hand had never left mine and I could tell she was nervous as her palm was slick with sweat. If she wanted to get out now, she just needed to say the word and we'd go.

"Are you alright? Tell me if you want to go. I'll understand," I uttered, raising our joined hands to my lips to kiss. I always worried about her, wanted her to be okay more than anything.

"I'm totally fine. I've got you guys." Alisha beamed up at me. I didn't want to press on and knew she would talk to me if things became too much. We had that level of trust already. It was refreshing.

"Okay," I accepted and just as we were about to lean in for a kiss, Ophelia and Mira rejoined us.

"Oi, oi! Simmer down, you two!" Ophelia called, placing the drinks she was holding down on the table. I gratefully took my water, it was already starting to get warm in here. Alisha had Malibu and coke, which she'd said was one of her usuals.

"Thanks, girls. Bottoms up!" Alisha held out her glass so we could all clink ours together. We toasted to a great night. I secretly toasted to being given a new lease of life, newfound hope, and for crossing paths with Alisha. I was glad she had knocked into that first day we met and ever since then, she continued to knock the wind out of me. I felt breathless but floating at the same time. I didn't want to come down from the clouds.

Chapter 32

Alisha

One drink turned into two, and then by the third one, I felt very warm and fuzzy. I also felt much more relaxed and I let out a soft giggle as I moved my body to the music, with Ophelia and Mira dancing beside me. I think Felix had gone to the toilet or something. Hoped he'd come back so I could ravage him.

Mira was so sweet, and I felt like I could talk to her about anything. She was so much fun, just like Ophelia.

Wow, I needed to sit down. I was starting to get double vision.

"Just gonna get some water," I said, letting out a hiccup that I'd held onto for dear life. Ah, good release. But I was searching for a different kind of release in comparison to that.

"Might take you up on that, c-could you get some for me and Lia please?" Mira requested politely.

"T-totally. Go find a table and I'll meet you there." I hobbled on my feet, trying to walk in a straight line toward the bar where bottled water was waiting for me. I was thankful they offered that. I bumped into a tall figure on my way and I knew who it was due to the scent and clothes he was wearing.

I became a lovesick puppy around him and I loved it. I loved this version of me. Alisha 2.0 has awakened. And she ain't going back.

"Sweetheart, are you okay?" Felix looked concerned, but he didn't need to be. I knew he worried, he was an anxious person like I was so I understood.

"Just getting some water for the girls. Come with me as I need to hold onto somebody." I let out a shaky laugh before hooking my arm through Felix's own. His sexy muscular arms. Wanted him to pin me down with them later.

"Are you having a good time?" Felix guided us toward the bar, where a few people were waiting. I noticed the man that had caught Mira's attention earlier was there again and he'd hardly taken his eyes off of her. He seemed interested but hadn't plucked up the courage to go up to her. Maybe he needed a little push.

No, don't go there. Especially with Felix here. That's his sister. Don't meddle.

My inner self was right so I bit down on my tongue and listened. So glad I had some control, even with being quite drunk.

"Soooo good," I drawled, leaning into Felix's touch. Eventually the barman, who stood at six feet tall and had a permanent crooked smile on his face, asked what we wanted and raised one eyebrow when we requested just water. He didn't say anything though and grabbed three bottles of still water from the fridge.

"Nothing for you?" I asked my handsome man who shook his head.

"If I have any more drinks, I'll keep peeing," Felix chortled and the image of his penis flashed through my mind. I welcomed it as it was a perfect penis indeed.

The barman whose name I had worked out was Bastiaan took my card payment and then we said thank you to him before walking back over to the girls. They were losing themselves to the music and I would have joined them but my body was telling me it was tired.

I didn't know the time as my phone battery died but I assumed it was about one or two in the morning. I hadn't stayed out this late for a long time.

Man, I was going to feel groggy for my lesson in the morning.

"Water for you." I passed the bottles to Ophelia and Mira who looked ready to down them quickly.

"Thanks so much. I'm starting to feel sick so this should help." Mira twisted the bottle cap and took a few gulps. All three of us were satisfied once we had some water in our system and it wasn't long before the girls were tired like me.

"Definitely going to come here again. I didn't manage to speak to that guy though." Mira looked disappointed and to be honest, I thought the guy would have approached her after his longing stares. It reminded me a little of when Felix first met me. It seemed like a lifetime ago.

"Well, there's still time. He must be somewhere," I said. If Mira felt like it was worth it, she could go for it. We'd obviously be a few metres away from her but not far from her sight to keep an eye on her.

"Nope, it's okay. If it's meant to be, I'll bump into him somewhere. Or maybe he'll come into the hospital with a problem. Who knows? Let's go home." Mira offered us a smile, letting us know it was fine.

"So, who's going where tonight? Alisha to Felix? Or Felix to Alisha? Mira, you're welcome to stay over, there is a spare room," Ophelia offered and Mira pondered on this before accepting.

"Well, in that case, I'll go to Felix's," I said. I didn't want to make it uncomfortable for Mira, knowing her brother was in the room opposite possibly fucking my brains out. Well, I hoped there was no *possible* about it. I wanted him as soon as we got through his door.

"Good call." Ophelia winked. I still felt a little fuzzy and with Felix holding onto my waist, we walked to where the taxis were waiting.

"Okay, so see you in the morning," I said to my friend, pressing a kiss to her smooth cheek. "Goodnight, big brother." Mira leaned up to embrace Felix, her petite frame being enveloped by his big arms. I loved the relationship they had and now knowing Felix's backstory, I was grateful they had one another to get through that heart wrenching, difficult time. I didn't know how they managed to but they did. I have a newfound respect for the pair of them.

Going with Felix to meet his mother would probably be a little awkward, for both of them. But it was the kind of closure Felix needed, since clearly he was carrying a lot of demons. He seemed to still care about her, even if he didn't want to admit it. I think human beings would always have that curious side to ourselves.

I'd be happy to come along and let them do the talking. I'd be polite and if Felix needed me to, I'd say how great he was and all the wonderful things he had achieved growing up. But only if he wanted me to. I thought it was sweet he even asked me to come along. It meant that whatever was happening between us was more than just lust.

The journey back to Felix's was quite quick, since there was no traffic on the road. I almost fell asleep until Felix gently shook me on the shoulder, telling me that we'd arrived.

"Want me to carry you, sweetheart?" Felix teased as somehow my legs wouldn't move. But I needed to stay awake. Not when all night I'd been thinking of mind blowing sex with Felix.

"No, I'm okay," I said before paying the driver. I beat Felix to it this time.

We hustled inside the door once the taxi driver had driven off and I unfastened my shoes quickly, as they were starting to hurt. Once again, I didn't have any clothes with me but I loved wearing whatever Felix owned. I loved wearing his scent.

"Come on, let's get you some sleep. You looked exhausted." Felix slipped his warm hand into mine and I let out a yawn, somehow not being able to communicate verbally.

Felix's bed was so comfortable, I dived right into it. But then I realised I still had this dress on. So I slipped it off, exposing my bare upper body. No bra tonight.

"Sweetheart, are you trying to tempt me?" Felix laid down next to me, having taken off his own shirt and trousers. He was wearing nothing except his grey boxers. I admired his sculpted chest and the way his biceps flexed as he moved.

"Not at all. Do you have a shirt I could borrow?" I asked in a slightly sheepish tone. Felix got up to ransack through his chest of drawers before pulling out a dark blue T-shirt. I took this gratefully from him and quickly put this on so I could lay my head down on Felix's pillows again.

So, so tired, but Felix looks so good right now....

"We don't have to do anything tonight. Let's go to sleep. You need to be refreshed for your lesson." Felix nudged his nose against my neck which sent shivers down my spine. He was right, of course.

"Alriiiiight. Goodnight, handsome." I cocooned into his embrace and sighed into his chest. I knew I'd fall asleep in seconds, I felt safe with him and his bed was so soft too. But before I could slip away into dreamland, I could just about make out what he said next.

"I'm falling for you."

Chapter 33

Felix

I didn't regret what I said to Alisha last night, and I doubt she even heard me as she fell asleep pretty quickly. I had every reason to fall for her. Her kindness to others, her enthusiasm and passion for her work, the friendship she offered to my sister. She was the dream woman. *My* dream woman.

I'd finally found someone who was everything I wanted and more, and in six days, I'd be watching her get on a plane back to England. It was starting to kill me but there was nothing I could do. All I needed to do was enjoy the haven we had created together, appreciate every moment.

I woke up an hour earlier than usual as the sun was streaming through my grey curtains and then I couldn't get back to sleep after that. I needed to brew some coffee, so I quietly slipped away from my bed. My heart softened as I watched Alisha stir in her sleep, her gentle snores were so adorable. I pressed a kiss on her forehead, ever so gently so that she wouldn't wake up.

As I had time to kill, I guessed I would make a start on writing my resignation letter. I knew I didn't want to stay working at the travel agency, after nearly six years I knew nothing would change. I wouldn't be getting a promotion and I'd just continue to be miserable. I needed to choose what was right for me from now on.

I thought about potentially speaking to the Ischgl Ski School whilst Alisha had her lesson. When I was teaching Alisha the other day, I got such a thrill out of it and seeing her achieve what she initially found impossible.

Maybe it was what I was meant to do all along. I just hadn't realised it. Funny how all it took was one person to make me see sense.

Adding coffee granules to my mug, I poured the hot water in and stirred my teaspoon so that it could dissolve properly. I added a touch of milk and one sugar cube before I was satisfied. I liked my coffee piping hot so I didn't flinch when the liquid splashed my tongue.

I'd noticed some letters had come for me in the post, a couple of bills and then some advertisement for house sales. I was quite comfortable where I lived for now, it was affordable and I wasn't too far from where my aunt and sister lived.

But a question came to mind, would I live in Ischgl forever? All I knew was this place and the people I had crossed paths with over the years. Change would be scary.

Thinking about change made me realise I needed to talk to Aunt Brenna about meeting my mother. I knew she'd be surprised, she would expect me to be hostile to the idea. But a man could change. I wouldn't be doing it alone either.

"Hm." I was browsing on my phone, catching up with the latest news in Ischgl. I hadn't noticed someone creeping up behind me until they slipped their arms around me.

"I missed you," her voice said, it was quite husky as she had just woken up but fucking sexy too. I leaned back into her touch and as cheesy as it sounded, I felt butterflies. They fluttered like mad inside of me, as her hands dipped into my boxers. I let out a small groan as she touched my already semi-erect cock.

"Did you now?" I literally purred as she cupped my balls, gently massaging them. *Fucking hell.*

"Can't you tell?" Her voice was like gold and so was her touch. I could have come right here but it wouldn't have been sanitary. I needed to get us in my bed.

"What are you needing, sweetheart?" I redirected back at her, turning myself around and then tracing her bottom lip with my thumb. Her lips quivered as I brought my other hand to tilt her chin upwards.

Completely at my mercy.

"*You,*" Alisha saying one single word was enough. I literally swept her off her feet, gently smacking her ass as I placed her over my shoulder. I smirked as she let out a light squeal. If she wanted me to fuck her hard, I would, but I'd tease her first with my mouth, as I wanted to taste that delectable pussy of hers.

Once we were in my room, I was backed up by Alisha until my ass landed on the bed.

"So, you want to be in control then?" My hands made a move to grab Alisha's waist, pulling her onto my lap. She placed her legs either side of me and slowly started to grind herself on my erection.

This woman.

"Yes. Do as I say," Alisha breathed against my neck. Loved this so much, my girl taking what she wants. I was all hers.

"Take off my shirt," she continued. I did as she said, relishing when I saw her perky nipples. They looked desperate to be sucked and licked. But I wouldn't until she told me to.

"What else, sweetheart?" My hands itching to touch her, to curl my fingers up inside of her probably soaking wet pussy. Wanted to watch her come undone as I slipped my tongue inside of her.

"Mm, I'm gonna take off your boxers now. I want to make you feel good."

"You already do, baby. Just being around you makes me feel like I've won a billion euros," I told her. It was the fucking truth, I was a lucky man. And I wanted her on her knees. But it wasn't about me right now. Her pleasure was important.

"Me too." Alisha blushed, gently tugging down my underwear as my cock sprung free. Her beautiful eyes widened before she placed her heavenly mouth on the tip, her tongue swirling slowly.

"Oh, fuck." I let out a deep growl as she took me whole, gagging as she did. I was deep inside her throat and I hissed as she started to move her head. I knew I wasn't going to last long at all. I wanted to paint her throat with my release, marking her as mine.

But I almost wanted to come on her gorgeous tits, the work of art that she was.

"Come all over my body, Felix," Alisha said as she wrapped her hand around me, I was so big in her palm. If that's what she wanted, I'd grant her that wish.

As she sped up her movements, I was getting closer and closer until I couldn't hold it in any longer. With a deep grunt, my whole body jerked as I spurted my release over Alisha's neck and chest. She grinned and it was so damn hot, seeing her like this. Covered in *me*.

I had to catch my breath as I hadn't come so hard like that for a while. I reached over to grab a tissue and gently wiped Alisha, getting rid of the naughty evidence.

"That was..."

"Fucking sexy," I finished for her. She was still in charge though and I'd wait for her to let me take over. I so wanted to give her multiple orgasms but we were rushed for time.

"I want you to take control now, Felix." Alisha looked certain, kneeling on the bed and tracing one hand to pinch her left nipple.

"Good," I said. With one move, I had her under me and I was teasing her entrance with my once again erect cock. All I needed to do was grab a condom from my bedside drawer which I did. I was quick to slip it on and nudged Alisha's legs open so I could position myself between them.

Had to be inside her. I'd take her in as many positions as I could.

My girl was already soaking wet again, ready for me. I thrust into her hard, as I knew that was what she wanted.

God, she felt so good. I'd never get enough of this.

I squeezed my eyes shut as I pounded into her pussy as her nails scratched down my back, probably leaving marks. It didn't matter, she could mark me as much as she wanted. Taint my skin just as she'd tainted my heart.

"Oh, Felix," Alisha moaned, arching into me and opening her legs wider. I nipped at her neck then moved my mouth further south to taste her breasts, gently cupping them and squeezing.

"You like me fucking you like this, my cock so deep inside of you?" I watched as I drew in and out of her, her pussy had a vice lock grip on me and it almost made me blow my load again. I needed to hold on because I wanted her to come first.

"Yes," Alisha whimpered. She looked like a vision, so beautiful and so mine.

"This pussy is mine. *You* are mine." I wanted to make it clear who she belonged to.

"Yours," Alisha agreed. I threw her legs over my shoulder, which meant I could fuck her deeper and faster. Her breasts bounced with every movement and her body was growing slick with sweat. With her rapid breathing, I could see and also feel she was close with the way she tightened around me.

"That's it baby, come for me." I was reaching my second release too, which I had a feeling was going to be even better than the previous.

"I'm coming." Alisha practically mewled as my thrusts increased, hitting that spot until she was completely sated.

"Oh fuck, I'm about to—" Once again, my whole body shook and I threw my head back. I had never come near enough at the same time as another woman before. This was special.

I slipped myself out, pulling off the condom and chucking it in the bin near my bed. I laid down next to Alisha, pulling her into my chest as I wanted a cuddle. I always wanted one after sex, to feel close to my partner.

"We came pretty much at the same time." Alisha looked pleased and so was I.

"I know, that never normally happens." I pressed a kiss on the tip of her nose, noticing there were a few freckles there. I was learning more about her minute by minute, but there'd always be more to discover. I didn't want to scare her off but I was keen to meet her family already. Heck, I'd even get her to meet my aunt. Maybe for dinner tonight if she'd be up for it.

I wanted my days and nights to be filled with Alisha now. I wanted many more moments like these, but I knew the clock was ticking and there was nothing I could do about it.

Chapter 34

Alisha

Nothing could beat the way I felt waking up today. A beautiful, most perfect morning ever. I was on a high and didn't want to come down.

I was extra tired this morning and my body a little sore, mainly due to the earth shattering sex I'd had with Felix. But partly due to the dancing last night.

Shortly after my lesson ended, I grabbed a bite to eat but on my own as Felix was helping his aunt out with something this morning. Ophelia was still nursing a hangover, when I returned back from Felix's with just enough time to get changed, I checked in on her. She looked like she needed all the sleep she could get. I realised Mira was still there too, as her shoes were still at the doorway.

The sun was shining brightly in Ischgl and as I ate my apple strudel, which was incredible and the pastry was just the right consistency, I observed the people walking by, some with families and then some on their own.

I felt at peace, everything was calm. I felt like I was living my best life and I didn't want to turn away from it. I had less than a week until I'd be returning home and I knew it was going to be hard.

I thought about the last time I was lovesick, which was probably when I first started dating Caden. Looking back at it, there were red flags everywhere. With Felix, there were none. Only green flags and a huge neon sign flashing 'perfection'.

I was taken away from my thoughts by my phone ringing and could see that it was my brother Aadi, who didn't always call. I answered it in total surprise.

"Hi, Aadi," I greeted my brother and in the background, I could hear some rustling in the background. Probably my brother organising his paperwork, he had plenty due to his job at the hospital.

"Hello, I thought I'd check in on you. How are you?" Aadi's gentle voice spoke and I realised how much I missed him. Growing up, we loved to watch TV shows together and then play board games on Sundays when we were bored. It was nice as Aadi hadn't been that typical teenager, who wanted to spend most of his time on his laptop or phone playing games. It wasn't his style. Very different from Zane.

"I'm good, I'm glad you called. Are you okay? How's the hospital?" I traced my index finger around my mug of hot tea before taking a sip. It warmed up my body which was still slightly shivering.

"So busy, especially at this time of the year. You witness a lot, it can be hard. But it's what I want to do, I love helping people," Aadi said. That was true, he loved to help people. I remembered during secondary school, he was quite defensive of me, even being two years younger, and Kiya whenever we'd been bullied or teased. He also looked out for others around him, even if he didn't really know them. I admired him for that. I often wondered whether he'd seek a partner soon, he'd never been in a serious relationship and would say he didn't have time for one.

Maybe he just hadn't met the right person yet. Or maybe love just wasn't for him.

"I know, we're all so proud of you," I told my brother.

"So, Austria then. How are you finding it? I'm still quite surprised you went."

"I love it. I know, it shocked me at the start too. But something had to give, I suppose. Can't stay cooped up indoors all the time, doing the same thing day in day out," I admitted. Over the past week, I'd learnt so much about Austrian culture, winter sports, history and geography. I'd even experienced a holiday romance which definitely was not on my original cards.

I didn't know whether to mention that to Aadi though. Knowing he would slightly judge me, only because he cared and wanted the best for me. I knew he would worry that I'd have my heart broken again and that perhaps Felix only wanted me for sex. Which wasn't true at all. It was more than that. I knew I was falling hard.

"I hear you. I'm glad you decided to go, I think it's good for you. Bring me back something nice, you know?" Aadi chuckled, something he did when he wasn't being one hundred percent serious. He wouldn't expect me to bring him gifts, he never was into gestures. He was more into people's actions, how they really treated a person with no gimmicks. He just liked good company and honest conversations. He probably wanted that in his future partner too.

"Of course. I'll bring you back a teddy bear that says '*I love you*'. I know that'll make you cringe," I joked and could hear my brother scoff at this. He knew I was joking though as he didn't argue.

"Looking forward to seeing you when you come home," Aadi said.

"Me too. I hope work goes okay, take it easy sometimes as you work so hard." I felt like scolding him further but maybe it wasn't the time.

"People to save, you know? Anyway, talk soon, Sis," Aadi said, as I started to hear more noise in the background. Probably an emergency as my brother quickly hung up just as I said bye. It was nice to hear from him anyway, that he had made the effort to hear how I was. He didn't do that very often. It reminded me that I needed to call my parents later and double check the plan again for Christmas.

But I knew this Christmas would be very different and of course, I had given my heart away. Gladly, as cheesy as that sounded.

***

I made a start on improving my half finished article, over the last hour I had written a few paragraphs and fixed some of the formatting so it read better. Culture Horizon had published their latest article and hinted that the next one would be coming from me, their budding star in the making. It made me feel giddy, knowing that Grayson really valued me and my work. I felt very appreciated and I guessed that was rare so I wouldn't take it for granted.

I'd sent a few texts back and forth to Felix, some that made me laugh and then some steamy ones that made me clench my legs together.

God, the way he made me come this morning was incredible.

Mira had left in the early afternoon but texted to say that she would love to hang out again. I felt like she was quickly becoming a good friend to me and Ophelia. We didn't mind having an additional member in our circle, the more the merrier.

My tea was slightly cooler to drink now and I took a few sips before getting back to work. Once I was in a mode, I didn't want to get out of it. Work was important and I wanted my career to progress.

After half an hour, I knew I needed some downtime away from my laptop screen as otherwise, I'd get a headache. I felt like taking a walk and asking Felix to join me. If he was free. I clicked on his contact in my phone and pressed it against my ear, waiting for him to pick up. He answered in three rings.

"Hello, you. What's up?" He sounded happy and that was good, he deserved to be. I could tell he was still at his aunt's as she said hello in the background. Very cute.

"Totally fine. Just been getting on with some work but I need a break. I was wondering if you were free. We could go for a walk."

"Ah, I'm actually still helping my aunt here, so I can't come out," Felix said but then I heard his aunt say something else to him in German. I was unable to make it out.

"Oh, um, why not come here? My aunt said she'd like to meet you and has plenty of food. It'd be just us three as Mira's unwell," Felix offered and it actually sounded lovely. Finally, getting to meet Felix's aunt, who he adored. I knew I needed to set a good impression so I had to change my clothes. Wearing a hoodie and tracksuit bottoms wouldn't be a good look.

"Okay, if you're sure. I don't want to be a burden." I said.

"You won't be, sweetheart. I want to see you." Felix told me and it was enough to convince me.

Right, make yourself look presentable.

"Okay, I'll get a taxi or bus up to you. Don't worry about coming to get me, honestly," I reassured him, not wanting him to protest. Thankfully, he didn't and said he'd see me soon. Felix texted me the address, which I worked out was a short bus journey away. The bus station was about a five-minute walk from his, which I didn't mind.

When I hung up, I darted to my bedroom to comb through my wardrobe for a suitable outfit. After pondering on several options, I decided to go with a dark blue pair of jeans, a white vest top with a floral pattern and a soft purple cardigan with gold buttons. On my feet, I'd wear some comfortable lace-up boots. It was comfortable and not too flashy. I wanted Felix's aunt to see the real me, over dressing wouldn't be.

I added a touch of pink lip gloss to my lips and touched my cheeks with a bit of blusher. Feeling satisfied with my attire and face, I twisted my long hair up into a half-up, half-down style, leaving loose strands of hair to fall down either side of my face. I picked up a pair of silver studs too and placed these in my ear lobes. I didn't often wear studs; I was more of a hoop girl but the studs seemed more suited to this outfit. They were real silver too.

"Okay, let's do this," I told myself in the mirror and made a move to exit the chalet, not before grabbing my phone and purse. I had also picked up the unopened bottle of rosé that was on the kitchen counter and stuffed it into my bag. There was just enough space, thankfully. My card had plenty of money left, and it was easy to use with just a simple tap for transactions. I had the app too so I could see my purchases and the exchange rates.

I had change in my purse just in case the bus driver wouldn't accept my card, the fare was pretty cheap anyway. At almost 3:30 pm, the bus arrived, and I could see it was barely full, which calmed me down. I couldn't quite handle a full bus and having someone random sit next to me.

I placed my earphones in, clicking on Spotify so I could immerse myself into the world of music. It passed the time a lot quicker and before I knew it, I had arrived.

I thanked the driver as I got off, taking in the outside surroundings. The bus station on this side of the town was slightly busier and lots of children were hanging out together, some even smoking. It shocked me to be honest, whenever I saw this as things had really changed since I was a kid. Kids and teenagers nowadays are trying all sorts. I was thankful that I hadn't. Smoking just wasn't for me.

I accessed the maps on my phone and typed in Felix's address, the route worked out to be a five-minute walk exactly. I moved my feet and kept on listening to music but switched to some slower tunes, which matched the pace I was walking at.

As I turned a corner, my phone vibrated to let me know I was getting close. The houses in the area looked amazing, with well-kept front gardens, most of them growing an array of colourful, fresh flowers. It made me think of my own dream home.

The bottle of wine that I had bought for Felix's aunt was clinking in my bag. I hoped she liked rosé as it was the best brand I could find in our kitchen. Whenever I went round to people's houses, I always liked to bring something as it was polite.

I reached a large house with a gravel drive and recognised Felix's Range Rover immediately. I remember the first time I'd gotten into his car and how nervous the two of us were. So much had changed and feelings were stronger than ever. We had both grown as people. Felix had healed many parts of me and I was grateful for that.

Felix must have noticed me as I stood there admiring the house and hadn't moved. He was standing at the front door, a soft smile appearing on his face.

I loved the way he looked at me.

He was wearing a loose, dark blue shirt with the first few buttons undone. He looked absolutely divine, leaning against the door frame and gazing intensely at me. A look that could rupture me entirely.

Right, move your feet woman and go say hi to your man.

I did as my self-conscious told me, every step making me more and more excited. Crazy how we'd literally seen each other this morning, but I already missed everything about him.

"Hello. Your aunt's house is nice," I said nervously.

"Hello," Felix said in his sexy, husky voice and pulled me into his burly arms to capture a deep kiss.

As we were getting lost in one another, someone cleared their throat behind us. I felt a little embarrassed but this feeling dissolved quickly as soon as I saw Felix's aunt and her friendly smile. She didn't seem bothered, rather very happy for her nephew.

"Sorry to interrupt you. My name is Brenna, pleasure to meet you," Brenna said and I had a good look at her, noticing the similarities between her and Felix. Only slight but you could tell they were family.

"Nice to meet you too. Thank you for having me over at your lovely house. I brought you some wine if that's okay." I reached into my bag and pulled out the slender bottle, offering it to her.

"Oh, you didn't have to! Thank you." Brenna looked as though she was in awe and then pulled me into a tight hug as if I had given her a billion euros or something.

"Well, come on in. I've got some food cooking, I hope you like cheese as I've got a Brettljause prepared. Then we'll have my famous goulash soup, I think you'll like that." Brenna gushed and just on cue, my stomach grumbled. I already felt right at home.

This was so different from when I met Caden's family or rather I had to push him for months to finally meet them. Looking back at it, I could see he never wanted me to meet them as he hadn't been serious about me. Plus, add the cheating.

But that was then and this was now. I focused on the lovely woman in front of me, who started to show me around her house and ask me many questions about my life, my hopes and hobbies. Felix was trailing behind me and every so often, I'd turn back to look at him. It felt like he'd always be behind me, physically and mentally. It was just what I needed.

Chapter 35

Felix

Having two of my favourite women in the same room was wonderful. The way they were interacting was going well and occasionally, I'd jump in to talk about how Alisha was finding her ski lessons. Aunt Brenna was impressed with this and also with the fact that she was an aspiring journalist, as she had thought about dabbling into this career path many years ago.

"Well, I'm pleased you two have met. I could tell my Felix had changed, but for the better. It's great to see him so happy." Aunt Brenna met my eyes and then Alisha's. It felt like she had given her blessing in a way. Her opinion was very important and I could see she already liked Alisha. I could relax a little better now.

As promised, the food was waiting for us at the dining table. There was also some pickle sauce, which complimented the tangy, creamy cheeses. I loved my aunt's meat and cheese boards she'd prepare, and the bread was even made from scratch. She hated store-bought bread, always liked to make her own or grab one fresh from the local bakery. She had a particular taste, both in food and clothing. She tried not to judge people too quickly, but for herself, she wanted to look her best.

The goulash was also slow cooking in a pot but the gorgeous smell wafted through the kitchen into the dining room, wrapping itself around my body and tingling my tastebuds. I had actually helped her with this dish, chopping up the onions and dicing the potatoes once they had been peeled.

My aunt had asked me to come over on a phone call this morning, wanting my input about her sons and the tepid decisions they were making. I think she felt like it was a lost cause, motivating them to do more for the community. They had jobs but only part-time. She was expecting more from them and she had some money saved for them so they could put it down for a house deposit one day.

Both my cousins were great, I had plenty of time for them, but I understood where my aunt was coming from. She had high hopes for them and wanted them to fulfil their potential. It was why she had given me a house, as she believed that everything was stable for me.

Thinking about it, I would eventually move by selling the place and giving back the money to my aunt. I'd saved up over the years, not much, but perhaps enough to put down on a small flat. My aunt had helped me a lot financially too, and made sure I didn't go without. But I felt now at nearly 28, I needed to take charge of my future.

That included handing in my resignation, which was typed up and signed. I had worded it formally, with the help of my aunt until I was completely sated with how it looked.

I would be handing this into my boss tomorrow, no hesitation and no regrets. It was about damn time.

"This tastes absolutely delicious, Brenna." Alisha had taken a large bite of the homemade bread, which had a cheesy crust. She coated it with some butter and added a few slices of cheese—gouda and tiroler bergkäse which was a type of hard cheese. It went quite well with white wine but we settled for the bottle of rosé, which Alisha had brought. I had a generous glass of it in front of me.

I draped one arm across her chair, knocking my knee with hers. Once again, she smelled incredible. Cherries, which was now my favourite scent.

"So, you mentioned the article you're writing. What keeps you motivated when writing? I've always wanted to try it, but raising four kids kept me occupied." Brenna said this with a smile. I knew she loved being a mother first and foremost but part of me wished she had followed her dreams, as maybe she'd be happier.

Anyway, it was up to her and it was never too late if she decided to do it now. Alisha would be the right person to ask for advice.

"Well, I do experience this thing called writer's block from time to time. I hit a wall and it can be hard to jump over it. But what I tend to do is have a snack or two with me and then I chat to my friend to get her opinion." Alisha said, taking another bite of some bread and cheese. This time, she had added some ham.

"Are you pleased with your progress then?" Aunt Brenna was never shy with her questions, always wanting to know more about the person she spoke to.

"I feel like it's getting there, but it needs that magic touch. I'm sure something will come to mind soon. There's still so much more to discover here." Alisha pressed her lips together, swiping one finger around her lips to catch some stray crumbs.

I wished I could have done that for her with my tongue.

"Well, I think you should go to Vienna with Felix. I know it is typical, but there is so much to see there. The only thing is that it's more than a five-hour drive. The next place you could go to is the health and wellness park in See. It's great if you like to relax and see beautiful scenery." My aunt suggested. I had been to Vienna once, several years ago and it had slightly overwhelmed me with how busy it was.

A road trip sounded fun, but five hours behind the wheel there and back would probably wreck me. So I liked the idea of going to the park as we could have a picnic together. It would be romantic and I'd never taken a woman there before. Not even Evie.

"That sounds interesting. I don't think I've ever been to a park like that before. I'll look it up later. Thank you." Alisha seemed pleased with this idea and placed her dainty hand on my thigh. If she dipped her hand any lower, then I would be in trouble.

"You're welcome. Are you two ready for the goulash?"

"Absolutely. I can't wait to try it." Alisha gushed, picking up her napkin and timidly wiping her mouth for any residue of crumbs and cheese.

"How are you finding this?" I wanted to know what my girl was thinking, whether she was comfortable.

"She's so sweet. I can tell she adores you," Alisha said to me in a hushed tone, glancing in my aunt's direction, who was busy getting the bowls out of the cupboard. From the dining room, there was a clear view of the kitchen which was ginormous anyway. Sometimes I wondered how my aunt was able to manage a house of this size.

"She's been very good to me. I think she likes you." I circled my thumb around Alisha's hand which was still resting on my thigh.

"I like her too."

"And I *really* like you." I edged a bit closer to Alisha, nipping gently at her ear lobe. I wanted to give her a taste of what would happen later this evening, if she was coming back to mine or me going to hers. It felt like we were inseparable now.

"I really like you too. This feels right." Alisha's mouth hovered above mine and just as we were about to lock lips, my aunt bustled in with our food, humming a soft tune as she did. She held two bowls of hot soup in her hands, placing these down in front of us.

"Do you need a hand, Brenna?" Alisha twisted her head to the left to check on my aunt and see if she could help.

"Not at all!" My aunt's voice sang merrily as she rejoined us, a plate of more bread in one hand and her bowl of soup.

"Right, there is plenty more goulash if you want any. Guten Appetit." She said and we all picked up our spoons to have the first taste. It was creamy, with just the right amount of salt. I let out a small moan as I bit into a potato, it was neither too hard nor too soft. I had to cut myself a piece of bread too so I could dip it in the soup.

"So, do you have any siblings?" Aunt Brenna queried, scraping her spoon around the bowl as she was nearly finished.

"I've got three. Two brothers called Zane and Aadi and one sister called Kiya. We're all close," Alisha replied. I knew she was a bit homesick as she'd mentioned she was missing her family in bed this morning. I wondered about their relationship. Did they ever fight? Did they steal and hide each other's things growing up?

With Mira, all we had was one another so it was easy to get along. Being older, my goal had been to protect her and act in her best interest. When we arrived at the care home many years ago, we refused to sleep in separate rooms. I didn't want anyone to hurt my little sister and to this day, I felt the same. Call me slightly overbearing but I just cared.

"That's lovely. I'm not sure if Felix said but I have one sister. His mother. We were close growing up but things changed," Aunt Brenna's voice trailed off, I knew it was a touchy subject for her but she'd felt brave enough to mention my mother out loud to someone she didn't know.

Speaking of my mother, I'd spoken to my aunt about it earlier, confirming that I would meet her but only if Alisha could come. She didn't protest about it but pulled me into a tight embrace and said she was proud of me. It validated that it was the right decision I had made. Aunt Brenna still had love for her sister, that would never fade.

Alisha looked as though she was thinking what to say next but to make it less awkward, I stepped in.

"Aunt Brenna, thank you for the lovely meal. Do you want me to help with dessert?" My hand found Alisha's again under the table and gave it a squeeze.

"You're welcome. Well, I need to make a start on the Marillenkuchen," she said. Marillenkuchen was an Austrian apricot cake, the specialty was to add a bit of rum for that kick. But I decided to let my aunt sit back and rest, so Alisha and I would make it together. It was a perfect excuse to spend some alone time with her.

"Are you sure? I really don't mind making it." Aunt Brenna seemed a little hesitant, normally used to being in control and being the best host. But it was the least I could do for her.

"Sit back and relax, we've got this," I reassured her, stacking the empty bowls together and carrying them to the kitchen. Alisha followed behind me, having picked up the spare plates and empty wooden board which we'd had the cheese and meats on.

"You don't mind baking with me, do you?" I asked Alisha as I opened the dishwasher to start loading.

"You kidding? I love baking so much. Especially with you." Alisha hugged me from behind, pressing a kiss on my back. I loved feeling her petite frame pressed up against me, it made me feel all sorts.

"Good. I love having you by my side." I wanted to say so much more to her but for now, I'd hold it in. I wanted things to keep going smoothly. But of course, I wanted to give all of myself to Alisha. My heart didn't feel like it was beating just for me anymore. In fact, it didn't feel like my own anymore.

Was I in love already?

Chapter 36

Alisha

A couple of hours later, I was back home. Well, my temporary home. I really liked Felix's aunt, she made me feel very welcome and I could see why Felix adored her. She was stinking rich, very obvious once I saw her house, but she didn't let that affect the way she treated people. She was humble about it and did a lot for the community, which was the right thing to do if you had a lot of money. Invest in people and help others who need it.

"Thank you so much for helping Felix. I can see he's a changed man." Brenna had told me before we left and it warmed my heart, as to be honest it was Felix that had changed me. For the better. My world was a lot brighter since he crashed into it.

Felix was resting his head on my lap and I was playing with his hair, massaging my fingers into his scalp. He was going to stay the night and on the way here, had grabbed some extra clothes and snacks.

"Tell me what you were like as a kid." Felix lifted his head from my lap after some time, his eyes a little hazy as he had almost fallen asleep. I stretched my legs out in front of me, not wanting to get pins and needles.

"Quiet and reserved. I loved hiding in the library and reading. My sister would often join me to keep me company." I replied, resting my head back against the bed frame. I didn't have a lot of friends but it didn't bother me. Quality over quantity any day.

"That's cute." Felix was creeping closer to me on all fours, which was starting to turn me on. He placed both his hands on either side of me. I was trapped but I liked it.

"What about you? Any funny stories to tell?" My breath hitched as his left hand crept up my inner thigh.

"I had about three close friends. During our lunch breaks, we'd go to the computer room and play games. Could say we were total nerds. After school, we lost touch and didn't reconnect. Suppose that's just how it is." Felix said, pausing his current finger teasing. I could already tell my knickers were getting wet. One look at Felix and I could also see he wanted it too. We didn't need to exchange words to communicate this.

"Yeah, I didn't really keep in contact with people either," I said. It didn't affect me because I had one amazing best friend who showed up for me all the time. And now Mira was a good friend too. I hoped it would stay that way.

"And Ophelia? What's her story?" It was sweet he wanted to know more, it showed he was genuinely interested.

"She's from Greece. Parents are divorced, she doesn't like to be tied down to anyone. She's great to work with, has the most genuine heart ever." I gushed about my friend, I always wanted to speak highly of her as she was a literal queen.

"I like her. You can tell she is kind-hearted. Mira also likes her, it's been a while since my sister has found a good friend. I'm glad we all met." Felix was positioned a few centimetres away from me now and all he had to do was seal the deal with a kiss. I would surrender to him, I always would.

"Me too. Imagine if I hadn't come here."

"I don't want to imagine. I can't imagine a life without knowing you. Being able to touch you. Hearing a sigh escape from your lips as I kiss your neck." Felix's words mirrored his actions and he was right as a sigh released from me when he planted a kiss on my neck.

"Keep going," I murmured, closing my eyes as it became more passionate. But just as we were getting started, my phone rang and I mentally cursed. However, when I picked it up, I could see it was my mum and it would be best to answer rather than decline it.

"Sorry Felix, it's my mum. I have to take this otherwise, she worries," I said and Felix waved his hand at me, signalling that it was alright.

"Hello!" I greeted my mum as she appeared on screen. She looked like she was at the park as I could see people walking behind her and children playing football. Dad wasn't with her, probably on some conference call as he was a businessman.

"Hello, meri khubsurat beti.[1]" Mum always loved to compliment her children, but the real beauty was her, I would make sure I would remind her of this.

"Are you at the park?" I asked a question that was obvious and my mum nodded, angling the screen so I could see the outfit she was wearing. She looked like she was going on a run, wearing a sports bra and matching shorts with Adidas trainers. Mum liked to do her exercise at least twice a week, healthy body, healthy mind as she'd always say. It also helped her own mental health.

"My limbs were getting a bit stiff so I needed to do something about it. Plus, it's a beautiful evening. The sun will set soon, so I won't be out for long. How was your day?" Mum asked, pausing her walk to really look at me. I wasn't sure if she could tell I had company. But I wasn't quite ready to tell her yet. I knew she'd be nosy and start asking questions. I didn't want Felix to feel awkward. My mum always meant well but she could be pushy.

"Quite productive. I haven't yet explored the markets though so that's next on the list. I want to buy you and Dad something." I said, eyeing up Felix, who was scrolling on his phone.

---

1. My beautiful daughter.

"Bring us back some cookbooks or something useful. You know how we are, things we can use more than once." Mum had always been particular about gifts, she didn't mind food as it was quick to consume but anything like jewellery or knick knacks, she wasn't really into it. She didn't like clutter, as she called it, lying around the house.

"Sure. Is Dad working then?"

"Yes, hard as ever. But we've booked a restaurant for tonight, it's been a while since your father and I had a date night. We want to keep the magic alive in our old age." Mum chuckled, starting to walk again. I assumed back to home as she was walking in the opposite direction.

"You're not old, Maa," I told her. At fifty-two, she looked amazing and had a great attitude to life. She had a few wrinkles here and there, her hair had some strands of grey in it but she'd always be the same, warm mother who raised me. She had retired a little early from work, about a year ago as she wanted to focus on herself and her family. She had been a full-time teacher since the age of twenty-three, which was impressive as just two years later, she gave birth to Zane. Dad was twenty-four and did all he could to support his little family with the help of his parents.

We all went to the same secondary school that she worked at which in a way was a good and bad thing. She was keen and involved in our education but she couldn't be biased when it came to school results and other things.

"I feel it these days, priya[2] . Well, I won't keep you. You look tired, I hope you are getting enough sleep. Stop stressing and have fun." Mum scolded. I definitely was having fun, more than she thought but I wouldn't get into *that* over the phone. My mum was quite traditional. She'd waited until she was married before having sex. She'd had that talk with me when I was younger but said that it was my decision if I met the right person. I had given my virginity away to Caden, a part of me I'd never get back.

But now, I needed to look to the future. I felt that I had a deep connection with Felix. And not just sexual. It felt real and raw. I felt exposed, but I didn't

---

2. Sweetheart.

care. I wanted Felix to see all those parts of me and maybe to fall in love with them too. I wanted to be adored and already he was giving me more than I could ask for.

"I'm getting enough sleep, don't worry. Hope you and Dad have a good meal. Love you." I blew a kiss to my mum who copied. I missed her more than I was letting on and Dad too.

"Love you, too," Mum said sincerely, her eyes sparkling and her smile wide. We hung up after saying goodbye and I turned my attention to Felix who was looking at a photo he had taken of us last night. We both looked carefree, with toothy grins and arms around one another. We looked like a dream couple, one that had been together for years, albeit a few days.

"Sorry about that." I locked my phone and placed it back on the bedside table.

"No need to be sorry. She sounded happy to talk to you." Felix said.

"Yeah, she always likes to hear from us. I think she misses working but it was the right decision for her. Dad is supportive and they have plenty of savings to keep them afloat. I think it's easier since we've all grown up now." Talking about my family felt easy with Felix and he seemed to be listening as for the next half hour, he asked questions about each of my siblings, what their hobbies were and funny stories with them as a kid.

I told him about one of my favourites, which was when Zane, Kiya and I had set up a prank on Aadi, which involved shaving cream and lots of tears of laughter. So much that my little sister had wet her pants. We didn't let her live it down but Kiya had some dirt on us too.

"I've had one of the best days, Alisha," Felix said as we settled down for the evening, a bowl of chocolate raisins in front of us. We'd decided to order a takeaway, Margherita pizza with some garlic bread and chips. To quench our thirst, we each had a glass of Sprite and ice.

"Me too." This is the kind of life I'd be happy with and I wanted more days of this but I knew time was ticking by and there wasn't much I could do about it.

"I want more of this. I don't know if I can let you go, Alisha," Felix stated, his face was serious.

"I don't want you to either. I like things the way they are." I snuggled into him as I had finished my slice of pizza and now I wanted Felix cuddles.

"I'm not going to hold you back though, it would be selfish of me," Felix said. Of course he wouldn't and I didn't want to hold him back either. I wanted him to pursue the career he aspired for.

"We'll make this work. What about you? Are you definitely going to give your resignation in?"

"Absolutely. And I'm going to talk to the Ski School tomorrow during your lesson. I think I want to give this teaching thing a go," Felix mumbled into my hair, I could just about hear him and I was pleased with this information.

"That's amazing. And what about your mum? When do you want to meet her?" I didn't want to bring the topic up again, but we had to decide on a date.

"I spoke to my aunt earlier and she's going to suggest a time and a place. We just turn up and see if my mother does too. If she doesn't, then I'll know that it's not worth it." Felix shrugged and it ached my heart because what mother wouldn't want to see their child after twenty-odd years? I imagined she wanted to apologise and make amends but that was up to Felix if he wanted to accept and have her in his life. Either way, he'd be strong and loved by everyone around him.

"I think you're incredible. Please don't forget that," I told Felix, he was pretty damn special to me. I would be the person to remind him every day.

"You make me incredible. I am nothing without you now, Alisha." This sentence sparked a fire within me and all I desired now was to hold Felix close and feel his heart beating against mine.

Two hearts beating as one.

Chapter 37

Felix

You could say when you were extremely happy, time sped by too fast. I'd had an amazing past two days with Alisha, we'd spent yesterday afternoon at the park and now today, we were enjoying a lighthearted lunch in the mountains. We were at our usual restaurant, after a productive session of skiing. After Alisha's final lesson, I had a chat with Hilde and she joined us for coffee for the first twenty minutes.

Hilde was keen to get me on a week's trial at the ski school but she was confident I'd be a natural, given I was an expert at the sport already. All I needed to do was get myself a certificate, which would confirm that I was clear to work with children and adults, that would take a few weeks at least. I didn't mind waiting, I was making the right decision for once.

"I can never get over how beautiful the mountains are." Alisha was sipping another cup of hot chocolate, a small blob of cream was on her upper lip. It reminded me of our coffee date nearly a week ago, when neither one of us had admitted our feelings but the passion was evidently there.

"I can never get over how beautiful *you* are." And she so was. Her long hair was falling around her shoulders in gentle waves, her cheeks were flushed probably due to the cold and her eyes, ones I wanted to lose myself in forever, were sparkling brightly in the sun. I didn't think I'd ever seen true beauty until I saw her.

I would cherish the next few days as soon as she would out of reach physically and it was going to fucking hurt, I knew it. It was already starting to stab me like shards of ice and I could only imagine this feeling would intensify once I said goodbye.

"I love having hot chocolate with you, it feels like it's our thing." Alisha looked at me with pure elation.

"We can have many hot chocolates together," I replied. It sounded corny but it felt like it was one of the drinks that brought us closer, bonding over a simple beverage.

"How did you feel about your last ski lesson?" I cradled my mug in between my hands, blowing softly over the top of it.

"A little sad, Hilde was really great. But I want to keep skiing these next few days. I think I'm ready to go up a tougher slope. She said blue runs I'm definitely good to go down but I'm up for a challenge. Want to teach me to go down a red run?" Alisha proposed. I was surprised that the idea didn't freak her out, as going down red runs you needed to be deliberate and precise with your turning. I would make sure to see how she did down a blue run first before taking her up a more difficult slope. I wanted to make sure my girl was comfortable first.

"We've got to ease you in first, sweetheart. But I love your enthusiasm and I'd be happy to teach you," I agreed, as it meant spending more time with her and watching her achieve her goals made me want to do the same too. She was quickly becoming my reason to keep going.

"I know you'll *ease* me right in," Alisha joked and if we were alone, I'd bend her over and fuck her hard just for being a tease. I let my imagination run wild at all the sexual possibilities I could have with her later. I wanted underneath me, on top, riding my cock until she completely shuddered and coated me with her release. I wanted her to brand me and take whatever she needed.

"Earth to Felix?" Alisha waved her hand in front of my face and I hadn't realised I'd drifted off. But not for the wrong reasons.

"Oh, sorry." I dipped my head down, staring at my hot chocolate which was getting colder by the minute. I needed to finish it and then start my ski lesson with Alisha.

"I'd love to know what you're thinking." Alisha joined our hands together, her palm was a bit clammy and slightly red, probably from the tight grip she had on her ski pole during her lesson.

"Baby, you'll find out later. You have no idea," I said in a low voice so no one could hear. Not that anyone was eavesdropping but there were a few children around as well as an older, sweet couple at the table next to us.

"Hm, I'll take your word for it. Right, come on Mr Bauer. I'm ready to ski until my limbs are sore." Alisha downed the rest of her drink and then waited for me to finish mine. It didn't take me long and was just the right temperature to guzzle it down.

Alisha swung her legs round to get up from her seat and sealed up her ski boots again, as well as placing on her helmet. She looked utterly adorable in her gear and she looked invincible, ready to face whatever. I loved her attitude which was rubbing off on me.

"It's a little warmer outside now. So you might find you sweat a bit more. But that won't really bother you, as you'll be gliding and feeling the wind pass you," I told her as we walked out of the restaurant onto the crunchy snow.

Now midday, it was busy and we needed to grab our skis to connect them back to our boots.

"Can I lean on you? I don't always have good balance when I put these on." Alisha giggled.

"Of course you can. That's what I'm here for. I've got you," I responded and I didn't just mean helping her put her gear on. I would always be there for her.

My skis were clipped on with ease and Alisha finally managed to get hers on before letting out a triumphant laugh.

"On y va!" I told her, letting her take the lead. If I was behind her, it meant I could catch her in case she fell. I glided on the snow at a comfortable pace, moving out the way of people in front of me. When I skied, I felt free, and having Alisha here with me, well it felt like I was soaring in the clouds. I didn't want to land.

***

I'd never felt more proud of a single person until now. Alisha had just finished going down a blue run, this time without me skiing beside her. I knew she could do it but wanted her to believe she could too. I knew now teaching was in my bones, it felt exhilarating to guide someone who wanted to learn and reaped the rewards from it.

She was shaking but with excitement, a huge smile stretched across her face.

"Someone's happy." I skied to a halt next to her as she was catching her breath.

"On top of the world. Thank you so much!" Alisha exclaimed. I looked at the time on my phone and realised it was probably time to get back, she probably had some work to do and I needed to do some housework. I never normally did housework, as I didn't have the motivation to. Of course I didn't live like I was in a swamp but Mira had made a few comments in the past about tidying up and taking care of myself.

I felt like a lot of things had changed but for the better. I didn't want to revert back to the mess that *was* my life.

Work had accepted my resignation, which I'd given to my boss in person. She didn't seem to be surprised and said she wished the best for me. As I was still on annual leave, it meant that I didn't need to go back at all once it was over. I would collect my things, there wasn't much but I didn't want to leave it behind.

Charlie had texted to say good luck and to organise a meet up again soon. It was nice to know he cared to check in and that he didn't just want to be work colleagues.

"Let's get back, you must be tired," I told Alisha, it was clear she was exhausted as a few yawns escaped from her mouth.

"Yeah, I need a long bath," Alisha said. I thought about sharing one with her, soaking in some bubbles sounded perfect.

"And you're joining me," she finished. It was like she had dived into my mind but maybe I was just that easy to read.

"Good. And then after, I can do what I've been thinking about for the past two hours," I lowered my voice, in a tone that showed her I meant what I said. Feeling her silky, naked body against mine, being able to dip my head between her legs and taste her arousal.

"Me too. You're in for a rough ride, handsome." My girl was bold and confident, I loved it. I wanted her to keep talking but actions spoke louder than words. We skied back to the cable car and hopped into an empty one, locking our lips as soon as the door shut, I didn't care who saw but I wanted her soft lips against mine for hours. All the way down the lift, my trousers were tight and my cock was straining to get out. Patience was key and by the time we got out of the cable car, our lips were swollen. It made us both laugh and walk as if we had our tails between our legs, as a few people had seen us making out as we came to a stop at the station.

It had never been like this with my ex. I felt like I could just be myself, not pretending to be someone I wasn't. How did I get so lucky?

The universe had its way of connecting two people together, two souls that had endured so much pain and heartbreak. I knew that no matter what happened, I'd be grateful that Alisha had healed my broken heart. There'd be no one else for me but her.

Chapter 38

Alisha

Felix accompanied me back to the chalet, our hands were clasped together as we walked in unison. My heart swelled more than ever for him, how patient and kind he had been while teaching me to ski. Tomorrow, I'd be going down a red run and although it raised my heart rate a bit, I was determined to see it through.

The two of us bustled through the front door, taking off our coats and the rest of our winter gear. I sighed as Felix's hands found their way to my shoulders, giving me a gentle massage. *Wow, I needed that.*

No sign of Ophelia, I wondered if somehow she knew we were coming and was hiding away in her room. I turned to Felix and tilted my head up, to meet his hazel eyes.

"Can you run the bath? I'm just going to see if Ophelia's in her room," I told Felix, who nodded and understood. I wanted to check on my friend and ask how her day was. I didn't want her to feel like I had pushed her aside for a man, I valued her friendship and I always would.

I knocked on her door which was slightly ajar and then entered, to see that Ophelia was lying on her bed and snoring away. I smiled at this and then quietly backed up, not wanting to disturb her. I'd check on her in an hour or so. She seemed to be having a peaceful sleep, her head buried deep into her bright pillows.

I rejoined Felix in the bathroom, just as he was adding bath soap to the water. I pulled my shirt off over my head, to reveal my dark blue bra. It wasn't a push up one, those I didn't find comfortable. Just a standard bra. This still made Felix's eyes widen as he started at my chest. Usually I didn't like when men stared there but with Felix, he could look all he wanted. He had a perfect chest too and his own shirt fell to the floor, in a crumpled heap with mine.

"Is Ophelia okay then?" Next came Felix's trousers, revealing the V-line that made my mouth water.

"She's sleeping. I'll check on her again soon. How's the temperature?" I dipped my finger into the water and found that it was just right. The tub was half full but I'd get into it anyway.

"I added some of that rose scented bath soap, I know you like a lot of bubbles," Felix said, pulling down his boxers to reveal his semi-erect cock. This turned me on in no time and all I kept thinking about was bath sex. I'd never had it but something about it was hot. The only thing was we didn't have a condom.

I hadn't told Felix this but I'd been on the pill for a few months now, mainly for my periods to stop as they were quite intense. I had a clean record too, I'd only ever had sex with one other person until Felix. So I was healthy as a horse. I wanted to try bare sex with him, to feel him fully.

I slipped into the water once I was fully undressed, beckoning Felix to join me. He sunk into the water on the opposite side of the tub, he was a little too tall for it and it made me laugh.

"Pass me the flannel, I want to wash you," Felix said. I picked up the flannel that was lying by the gold bath taps, squeezing a little soap on it and passing it to Felix. I twisted my body round so that my back was against Felix and sighed when his lips kissed my shoulder and then my neck. My hair was tied up so he had more access.

We didn't exchange words as Felix massaged the flannel into my skin, starting from the small of my back and up to the base of my neck. It felt amazing and I relaxed into his body.

"You are fucking sexy, Miss Dutta," Felix grumbled into my ear as his flannel covered hand dipped in between the valley of my breasts and then in circular motions just above my belly button. *I knew where he was going and I wanted it badly.*

"Is this okay?" Felix moved the flannel lower, just above my pelvis.

"Yes. Please keep going." I bit down on my bottom lip as he obliged. His other hand found its way to tweak my right nipple, already hard and perky for him.

"You drive me insane, sweetheart. I want to fuck you in here." Felix's words sent me over the edge and his hand was now resting on my throbbing pussy. But now I didn't want to fuck in the bath, I wanted us on the bed as the idea of water sloshing around us didn't seem appealing. Especially when I wanted to feel all of his cock sliding in and out of me.

"I think we should take this to the bedroom, Mr Bauer," I half-whispered to him, cupping his face from behind. Felix finished cleaning me and then himself before picking up the towels I'd left on the floor for us. I stood up as Felix got out and he wrapped a crisp, white towel around my body.

"You look like a soft burrito. My burrito," Felix cooed and I rolled my eyes, blowing a raspberry at him.

"How rude. Just for that, I'll spank you." He feigned shock. *Yes please.*

"Do it. I deserve it," I teased and he hoisted me in his arms, lifting me out of the water. I was careful not to shriek, I'd never get over how strong he was.

He was dripping wet but he didn't seem to care as he carried me to the bedroom. I would drain the bath later but for now, my focus was on Felix. He had somehow picked up his trousers and as he placed me on my bed, he rummaged through his pocket to pull out a purple foiled condom.

"Felix?" I was going to tell him that we didn't need it but I wasn't sure how he'd react.

"Yes?" Felix was about to tear the condom open until he raised his head to look at me.

"Um, we won't need that. I'm on the pill. And I get regularly tested," I said, my body was tense as I waited for him to reply.

"So do I. Before you, it was only my ex. Are you sure you want this?" Felix placed the unopened condom packet on the table before hovering above me.

"Yes, I really do. I want to make love to you with no restraints in the way." Goosebumps were showing up on my skin and I could tell they were on Felix's too. This was going to be a new experience for me and I would have no regrets.

"Music to my ears." Felix cupped my face with his large palms, giving me a scorching kiss. His tongue edged in my mouth slowly and he let out a low growl as my hand wrapped around his steel hard cock.

His mouth trailed kisses further down my body and his tongue darted out to lick between my slick folds. He sucked hard on my clit, slipping in one finger at the same time. I needed to be lubricated before he fucked me with his bare cock.

Felix hovered his body above mine once his mouth left my pussy and his hands pinned mine into place above my head. *I loved it when he took control.*

As his cock slowly sunk into me, my legs latched around his waist. He pumped into me slowly until he was fully inside me and I gasped as a wave of pleasure came over me. My pussy fit around his cock like a glove but still, I wanted him closer.

"I don't think I will last very long, sweetheart. I can't wait to fill you up with my come," Felix muttered into my hair. All I could see, smell and feel was Felix.

His kiss was hungry as he hungrily took my mouth in his, easing in and out of me slowly. Whimpers eluded from me, ones I couldn't control as he felt so good, like he belonged only with me.

Every thrust became more desperate and it truly felt like we were making love, like we were starved of one another. Both my legs locked around him in a tight grip as his hands traced my neck and then my face. His eyes were closed but I kept mine open so I could watch him, how beautiful he looked whilst making love to me.

I felt so strongly for Felix now that I was close to tears but in a good way. I couldn't stop from falling out of my tear duct and down my cheek, as my mind was screaming to me that I'd be a thousand miles away from the man I was growing to love soon.

Felix had noticed and stopped his movements, looking very concerned.

"I didn't hurt you, did I? Please tell me I didn't." Felix wiped the tear away.

"No, these are happy tears. I don't want to lose this," I told him, holding him close against my chest.

"Do you want to stop?" Felix was about to slip out of me but I pressed a flat hand against his chest, shaking my head.

"No, I was so close to coming. I think you can get me there again." I giggled, gently pinching Felix's peachy ass. He let out a small yelp before moving inside of me again, his cock thickening. His thrusts were slow but firm and his mouth pressed warm kisses to my neck and breasts, branding me.

"Oh, Felix. I'm coming." He was hitting the right spot and as I announced this, his thrusts became rougher and deeper until he reached his own ending. I could feel his hot seed streaming through me as he let out a deep groan, head tilted back.

"Wow." Felix fell against me, his chest slick with sweat. I ran my fingers through his hair and listened to his heart beating rapidly.

"Felix, can you teach me some German?" I asked a few minutes later, when Felix had gone limp inside me and then pulled out to spoon me.

"You'll have to start paying me, sweetheart. Teaching you skiing and German is costly," Felix said and then laughed, as of course it was a joke. I loved that we could joke together, another sign that this was going well.

"Where do you imagine yourself in five years?" In a way, I was curious to hear if Felix could see me in his future. That was why I asked the question.

"I'm not sure if I could go down the altar again, given the first experience I had. I'm not sure. But with the right person, it is worth it. I also want kids, I'd be nearly thirty-two by then so having at least one would be great. How about you?" Felix started to stroke my hair, which was very smoothing. I could almost fall asleep.

"I'll be thirty by then, so I'd hope to be married and have had my first kid. I love the idea of spending fifty plus years with someone. Do you believe in soulmates?"

"I don't know. It's never been something I've thought about," Felix said. I didn't believe in soulmates, but I believed in true, everlasting love with the right person. Truth be said, I could see Felix in my future but I was worried he didn't see me in his. Now that he was pursuing another career, would there really be room for me in his life? Would he come and visit me in England? Would we keep the passion alive between us?

I couldn't shake these thoughts and endless questions away throughout the rest of the evening but I had to remind myself that it was still very early in our relationship, all I needed to do was appreciate the present and worry about the future later.

Chapter 39

Felix

The next morning was frostier and snow was falling slowly, decorating the windows like a work of art. I had woken up before Alisha and was looking out of her icy window, contemplating on what to do with myself because I didn't want to wake up the sleeping beauty in her bed.

I reflected back on yesterday evening, the questions Alisha asked me about the future and whether I believed in soulmates. With the experience I had walking down the aisle and then being left at the altar, I wasn't sure whether marriage was on the cards. I didn't want to feel embarrassed again, to have people whispering about me and saying things like 'second time lucky'.

But looking at Alisha, I knew she would never intentionally hurt me. My trust was building up and my walls were almost knocked down. I didn't want to be defensive of myself but naturally, I would be. Truth was, I was scared, scared of allowing myself to fully fall in love again. I wanted it to be the last time that I would.

I was falling fast for Alisha and there was nothing I could do to convince myself otherwise. Making love to her bare last night opened up another part of me, one that I had locked away.

I needed to talk to someone other than Alisha about this and who better than my sister, who had already sent me a text this morning. I would arrange to meet her for an early lunch and then pour my heart out to her, like I always did.

Aunt Brenna confirmed with me too that she spoke to her sister and mentioned the time and place. What would happen is I would turn up tomorrow afternoon at Baeckerei Konditorei Kurz, a popular cafe in town that I hadn't been to in years. Mainly because it'd be hard to get a table in there. But tomorrow, it would be calmer since there was a sports event taking place locally. Whether my mother would turn up, well that was the burning question. At least I would have Alisha with me, to calm my anxiety.

She stirred in her sleep and turned her body to face the other way, her chest rising and falling in a steady pace. I liked mornings like these, where I could stare at her and revel in her beauty, her presence.

I didn't want to leave her, for her to wake up alone but I also needed to get back to my place and get onto some admin work, specifically for the ski school as soon I'd be starting my trial.

I had some training I needed to complete both online and in person, but it'd be easy to pick up. In the bag I brought to Alisha's, I packed a cosy, cream cross stitch jumper and a pair of dark grey trousers. I got dressed, careful again not to make noise but almost lost my balance a few times when I put on some socks.

As I stood back up, Alisha was sitting upright in bed, knees tucked under her chin. She was looking at me curiously.

"Sorry sweetheart, I didn't mean to wake you." I walked over to her to kiss the tip of her nose and then her mouth.

"Are you heading out?" Alisha asked innocently and it sounded a little like she was disappointed.

"Just back to mine. Mira wants to meet later, I'm guessing to talk about me meeting our mother tomorrow." I replied, which was true as Mira was just as nervous as I was. If the meeting went well, then Mira would be the next to meet her.

What the heck would I even say to my mother? Hey, you fucked up my life for years but now I am finally starting to be happy. Or, why did you abandon us when we needed you the most? Why did dad even leave?

"I understand. I've got a ton of work to do today, too. Grayson has scheduled a video call later, so I can send him my next draft." Alisha picked up a hairbrush that was on her bedside table and dragged it through her hair.

"I bet you he'll love it. Do you think you can show me some of it later?" I plopped down next to her legs, giving one of them a squeeze.

"No, that's cheating. Read it when it's published." Alisha winked, wrapping her arms around my neck. I could have made love to her again and again this morning but knew I needed to get going. As hard as it was. I knew that Alisha wanted to spend time with Ophelia too, as she cared about her deeply.

"Fair enough. I'll see you later. My place or yours tonight?" I had the idea of taking her out to the cinema tonight and then going back to mine for a late dinner. And then lots of cuddles and love making.

"Happy to go to yours. I feel like we need to alternate," Alisha said, resting her head back on her pillow. She still looked tired so probably needed another hour or two. I could imagine so as her muscles would have been sore. I didn't want to wear her out today with more skiing, so rest was what she needed.

On the other hand, I wanted to be as active as I could be today. I left Alisha begrudgingly and on the drive home, I regretted leaving her and maybe she'd hate me a little for it but tried to shake off this negative feeling. I refused to suck myself into the abyss of self-pity again. That was uncharted territory.

***

Me and my sister were just finishing our lunch at a small cafe called *Frisch gebrüht*, translated as *Freshly Brewed* in English. It was discovered by my sister, who was always on the hunt for cute, independent businesses. It was only about a ten-minute walk from mine but it was worth it. The aroma of coffee and sweet delicacies filled the air and there was a gentle buzz of chatter from the customers sitting around us.

The two of us were enjoying a cup of coffee each, a splash of milk added and one sugar each. In terms of our food and drink choices, they were similar. But our outlook on life wasn't. I liked that we weren't practically joined at the hip, that we had our own opinions. Mira definitely liked to give hers vocally and it's why I wanted to see her today.

"Something's different with you today, Felix. Everything okay with you and Alisha?" Mira popped a question, her eyes were sincere and her face stoic. I knew she didn't want to express her concern to me but I grew up with her so it was easy to tell.

I let out a sigh before speaking, "I really like her but I'm scared that things will go wrong again. What if she can't make room for me in her life?"

"From what I've seen, I think the girl's mad about you too. Relationships long distance are tough but if the two of you are committed, you will make it work. Is that the only thing you're worried about?"

No, it wasn't.

"I'm worried about allowing myself to love again, of what people may think. You know how people were when they heard about me and Evie."

"Absolute crap Felix and you know it! If anything, people were talking shit about Evie more than you. You are the most amazing human I know, Felix. Don't let anything or *anyone* convince you otherwise," Mira said firmly, her tone ridden with slight annoyance. She hated whenever I put myself down and maybe she'd heard enough of it. Maybe I needed to think like her too.

"Don't be afraid to love again, Felix. The way you and Alisha are, I think it's so worth the heartache. I wish I had someone, you know. I feel incredibly lonely sometimes." Mira looked down at her coffee cup. She was a romantic like me but had been quite unlucky in her matches over the years. The men she had dated were idiots and couldn't keep up with her busy lifestyle. She needed to meet someone who matched her, who would be able to support her ambitions. My sister deserved the best and I wouldn't say otherwise.

I had all the validation I needed from my sister but now, I needed to convince myself.

"So, the big day tomorrow. Meeting Valerie." Mira grabbed my hands so she could hold them in hers, sensing my anxiety rise. Mira wasn't quite comfortable with calling Valerie 'mother' yet. She barely remembered her or maybe just didn't want to.

"Wish you were coming. I don't even know if she'll turn up," I said, picking up one of the muffins we had bought from the counter. Raspberry and white chocolate. *Wow, it tasted good.*

"If she doesn't, then we need to fully wipe our hands of her. To move on." Mira took a bite of her own muffin, a traditional blueberry one.

"You're right. And if she does turn up, I owe it both to you and me to hear her out. I wonder what she has to say after all these years." I finished chewing the piece of muffin I had placed in my mouth and looked at my sister who shrugged nonchalantly.

"Ever wonder about Christian as well?" *Our dad.* All Mira could remember was his name, as she was so small when he left. I could remember the arguments he'd have with mum. I didn't really know him either, as he never spent much time with me until he left for good.

"Of course. Part of me thinks he's dead now. I think I wouldn't want to see him if we had the choice."

"Right? Well anyway, we should be proud of ourselves as we've come so far. They both made their beds and they should lie in them. But I hope tomorrow goes okay, Felix. Maybe then I might consider meeting her," Mira told me and I nodded, completely understanding her reasoning. She didn't feel comfortable until I did. She'd wait until I told her everything after the meeting before making a big decision. She wanted to protect herself and that was absolutely fine. Me on the other hand, I wanted to face this woman who disrupted my childhood.

But like hell would she disrupt my current life.

Chapter 40

Alisha

My plan for today was to go skiing but I couldn't go without Felix, as he was teaching me now. His methods were slightly different to Hilde's, she always encouraged me but with Felix, he just knew what to say and do with me. He was a good teacher. No scrap that, a brilliant teacher and I knew he'd have so much fun with this new role.

I hoped he was okay today, I wanted him to stay in bed and lie in but he was keen to see Mira. When it came to his family, I knew I needed to step aside. Give him some space. He had so much on his mind right now: his new job, and meeting his mum tomorrow. All I needed to do was remind him I was there for him. I was very nervous for tomorrow, meeting a woman I didn't know anything about and being unsure whether she'd even come.

I didn't want Felix to be disappointed if she didn't but I knew part of him still cared about his mum, even if he didn't want to say it out loud.

I'd pondered in the kitchen for about five minutes, wondering what to do with myself before my phone rang. *Felix.*

"Hi," I breathed, elated to hear from him. *How cheesy.*

"Hello, you. How's your day going?" Felix's gorgeous voice rang through the phone and sent tingles down my spine. His Austrian German accent was strong and I loved it. Very quickly, my mind showed multiple images of him, a few of them steamy but some very sweet ones of us too.

"Bored out of my mind. Want to go skiing?" I'd checked the time and it was still decent enough to go skiing for an hour. I wanted to try a red run today at least.

"I'm ready whenever you are. Just got back after seeing Mira," Felix replied and I could hear him place his keys down on a table. It was sweet that he made time for his sister as well as me.

"Okay, I'll meet you at the cable car. I just need to get something warm on, the temperature's dropped outside again." I observed the weather over the past hour and every so often, it would start to snow. That's what was great about Austria, it was guaranteed to snow at some point. Especially at this time of the year. I thought about the weather back in England, especially in London. It would usually be very cold but not enough for it to snow and set on the ground.

If I could come to Austria for next Christmas, then I would, or Felix could come to me. I was hoping we'd still be together by then. I really wanted this to work as he was my everything. I definitely could fit him in my life, that was paramount and my siblings would really like him. Kiya kept asking about him whenever I spoke to her on the phone too. My parents didn't mind who I dated, they wanted me, my brothers and sister to be happy with whoever we ended up with. I'd break the news to them when I got back.

Thinking about my parents, I knew I wanted to be as happy as they were, to build an amazing life and have at least three children. It would take some saving but I was getting there financially. I wouldn't be living in my apartment forever and if I got a promotion after this article, I didn't want it to seem far-fetched but it was my dream, I'd want to move somewhere bigger.

Grayson had contacted me this morning to say that he was excited to see the completed draft of my article in two days time. I always made sure I met my deadlines and by tomorrow, I wanted everything to be written up and finalised. The edits would come after but I needed the main body to be complete at least.

I glanced at the first few sentences, reminiscing about the first day Ophelia and I arrived in Ischgl.

To step outside of your comfort zone, you have to face your fears and fly a couple thousand miles. I'd never heard of or been to Ischgl but as soon as I saw the beautiful town, I felt right at home.

Home felt like wherever Felix was now, his gentle embrace, his kisses and calming words. Life without him now seemed impossible. There was no going back. Everything that I knew about love had gone out the window. I'd discovered so much more about what a relationship should look and feel like. I was lucky to have found someone like him. I needed to let him know that. So, my plan was to do so on the last evening before I'd leave to go back to England.

Felix didn't know as well that I'd start to write another piece, just for him. I hadn't actually shown Grayson this either so I was nervous. I'd never written so deeply from my heart before so this was going to be received in a different way. I hoped it'd be a nice surprise for Felix, a reaffirmation for him to see how strongly I felt. Writing was how I expressed myself and I'd put it to good use.

Now, I was excited for my future writing. I wanted a more senior position at Culture Horizon and if this article could help me get there, at least to be one of the regular journalists that Grayson wanted, then that would be my dream come true.

Realising the time, I sprinted to my room to put on my skiing gear. A new pair of gloves were waiting for me, the ones I normally used were a bit tattered as I had borrowed them from Ophelia. I was ready to go within a few minutes until my stomach let out a low grumble. I'd make sure to grab an apple before going, to settle my stomach.

Fruit wouldn't fully satisfy my hunger but it'd do for now. I had a gorgeous man waiting for me.

It wasn't long before I approached the cable car after a short walk and Felix was already waiting, in his blue puffer jacket and ski poles in one hand. I could see some stubble dusted around his chin and above his upper lip. His hazel eyes were glistening in the afternoon sun and he had a cheeky grin on his face. Of course, my heart and stomach turned to mush when looking at him.

There's your knight in shining armour. And he's looking at you like you're his everything too.

"Hi." I grinned back at him, and couldn't contain my excitement at seeing him.

Was it always going to be like this with him? It felt like a honeymoon period.

"I like your scarf." Felix pointed, I was wearing a new pink scarf as well as my new gloves. The scarf felt so soft against my neck, no itchiness at all.

"I like your hat." I looked up at his head, he was wearing a dark blue beanie with snowmen holding hands in a circle. *So bloody cute.*

"I like *you*," Felix fired back, taking a few steps closer to me so that he towered over me. I felt so small compared to him. His hand wrapped around my waist as he leant in to kiss me and time stood still when he did. It was just us two, locked in our embrace.

His lips were full and needy against mine and I could taste a hint of raspberry when my tongue touched his. *Delicious.*

Before it got way too heated, especially as there were people walking around us, we paused the kissing and walked toward the cable cars. At this time in the afternoon, it was nowhere near as busy.

Good, as I wanted a cable car all to ourselves so we could kiss again.

"After you." Felix let me get inside first, giving me a crooked smile. There was a '*je ne sais quoi*' about him today and whether he wanted to tell me about it, well that was up to him. I just hoped he felt he could communicate with me, about anything.

As we both sat down in the cable car and it was moving upwards at a steady pace, we looked at one another. I wanted to say what I was thinking to Felix, that this was more than just a holiday romance. But I had to bite my lip and wait until the time was right, which wasn't now. I wanted an afternoon of fun and laughter, to learn some new skiing tricks if I could.

"What's your impression of Ischgl?" Felix finally asked me as we were halfway up, we had at least two more stops though. We wouldn't be getting off at the ski school like usual.

"I am in love," I told him. That was the truth, but it wasn't the only thing I was in love with.

***

"Look at you!" Felix was clapping his hands and cheering as I skied down the slope, in a quick zigzag. People around me looked impressed and fuck it, I was too.

"Damn, should have taken a video." I mentally cursed but I still had some time to do one more ski run.

"I'll film you for the next run. I'll skill alongside you," Felix said. This wouldn't phase him as I know he had good posture and balance when it came to this sport. Skiing was like breathing for him, completely natural. That was what writing was like for me. But I was now able to merge this passion with skiing, to see what Ophelia had been gushing about with me for months.

I wished I had done this sooner. But I was here now and it was wonderful. Truly magical.

And Felix was here too, a proud look on his face as I made my way back to the ski lift with him, so I could have another go. I loved sharing these moments with him, to see these emotions flicker on his face. They mirrored my own, as if we were in sync.

I didn't need to convince myself otherwise that my emotions were strong for him. I wanted to vocalise all of this to him, to make him see how utterly perfect he was.

"Felix, you're pretty damn special to me." I slipped my hand into his own as we took a seat, the bar coming down to keep us locked in. I always had a fear of falling from one of these but I had conquered this.

"You're a gift to me too, Alisha," Felix responded. There was a wave of emotion coursing on his face and maybe he wanted to say more. But these words were enough for me at this time.

After twenty more minutes of skiing and laughing until our lungs hurt, we headed back to get ready for the evening. Felix had mentioned we were going to the cinema, to watch this film both him and I had our eyes on. Funny how we had the same tastes in films, Felix hated anything horror related but didn't mind a bit of action.

We invited Ophelia and Mira to join us, both of them accepted but said they would sit in front of us, not to get in the way of our 'smooch session'. It made me laugh, as Felix and I weren't that bad surely? *It was hard to resist those lips of his though.*

The four of us were paying for our tickets and grabbed a few snacks from the sales booth. Me and Felix decided to share some sweet and salty popcorn and the girls bought a range of chocolates.

"This film better be good, Felix or I'm never coming to the cinema with you again," Mira teased her brother and then gave me a wink, popping a piece of chocolate in her mouth. She handed a piece to me which I gratefully took and relished the creamy goodness on my tongue.

Once we got inside and took our seats, the cinema was half full and there was some dull chatter filling the room. After about two minutes, the screen turned on and sadly, we had to sit through the adverts. Couldn't avoid them in Austria, let alone in England too.

When the film finally started, I became more comfortable and rested my head on Felix's shoulder. His lips kissed my hair and then my forehead and finally he wrapped his arm around me.

The film was actually okay and once the credits rolled, I had been on the edge of my seat. Even Mira and Ophelia were astounded.

"Okay, I take back what I said." Mira held her hands up as we walked out of the cinema.

"Good choice in film, I was so invested that I didn't notice the couple making out behind me. Or did I?" Ophelia raised one eyebrow, giving me a gentle nudge with her elbow. She had tied her colourful hair up into two space buns and was wearing an oversized pink jumper paired with dark skinny jeans.

"Ha ha," I mock laughed. The four of us decided to grab something to eat, since stomachs full of sugar wasn't something to sleep on.

A local Italian restaurant grabbed our attention and there we resumed our conversation, talking about the film we saw and plans for Christmas. Tomorrow was going to be a big day though and I could see that Felix was thinking about it, as he had gone quiet by the end of the evening. I held his hand tightly in mine and squeezed it reassuringly. I'd be right by his side, through thick and thin.

Chapter 41

Felix

The day I had been dreading was finally here. An uncomfortable wave of nausea overtook me and this morning, I'd already been close to throwing up a few times, but I *had* to do this.

Alisha was sitting patiently next to me and she made the effort to keep me calm, talking about anything other than my mother. I needed this woman more than ever. Throughout any difficulty I'd face, I wanted Alisha there with me.

We are all fools in love. This quote from Jane Austen rang true. I'd never read her books but it was a quote I'd stumbled across recently. I knew Alisha loved her too, she said *Pride and Prejudice* was especially her favourite. She told me about how much she loved reading before falling asleep last night and listening to her describe her favourite authors made me want to love them too. I didn't really read, never got into it, but maybe I would now.

I definitely was a fool for Alisha. I would choose her a hundred times over. I had completely changed for her and I just needed to find the right moment to tell her that if she wanted forever with me, I'd offer it to her.

I focused back to the present, my pulse racing every time the cafe door opened and closed. Would I recognise my mother after all these years?

After about ten more minutes of waiting, Alisha stood up and offered to get us both another coffee.

"Same again? I might go for something different, maybe a caramel latte this time," Alisha said casually. I knew she was also trying to stay calm but it was obvious she was just as nervous as me, her hands twitching by her side and her body swaying slightly back and forth.

"Yeah, please. Thanks." My knee bounced up and down as I watched her make her way to the small queue at the front of the cafe. I noticed her also eyeing up the array of colourful cakes and cookies, before picking two for us. A small smile stretched on my face, feeling grateful she was here.

My attention diverted when I heard the door bell jingle and I twisted my head to look at who was coming in. Despite it being over twenty years, I knew instantly who it was. *My mother.*

She looked around nervously as she closed the door behind her, scanning the cafe floor for someone. Until her eyes landed on me. It felt as though time stood still and I'd forgotten how to breathe. She knew it was me too as her face fell and her lips wobbled as if she was about to cry.

Was she feeling remorse? Was she happy to see me after all these years?

Feeling brave, I stood up, scraping my chair as I did on the floor and standing tall as my mother walked towards me. She looked...well. Up until now, I only remembered the drunk, torn version of her. Now, her hair was neat and falling in waves around her shoulders. She had strands of grey hair but still looked young. Well, she had me and Mira quite young, at the age of twenty-one and then twenty-three.

When she finally reached me, I had a better look at her. She was wearing a comfortable blue one piece outfit with a small belt. In her hand, she held a small purse and I could see her nails were freshly manicured. She looked like she took good care of herself, that she was.. happy.

"F-felix," her voice stuttered as she looked at me. Her voice had aged of course and it was ridden with what sounded like guilt.

Good, I hoped she felt guilty, but now was not the time to be angry.

"Hello," I responded, not quite sure whether to shake her hand. A hug was definitely out of the question though. There was a lot that needed to be discussed and trust to be rebuilt if we were going to have a relationship.

"You look so tall and.. handsome. You look like your father," Mum said, her voice was now edged with sadness. Probably because she realised she lost out on all these years. Watching me go through puberty, having my first kiss, my first relationship. Aunt Brenna had been the one to give me advice growing up, she'd taken on the role that my mother should have.

"Do I?" I said in disbelief. I didn't want to look anything like Christian but you couldn't fight genetics. I hoped I would be at least ten times the man in personality. Scrap that, why should I compare myself to him?

"Yes, I almost thought it was him I was looking at. How are you?" She gingerly took a seat opposite me, placing her purse down on the table. I took a moment to look at her eyes, which were similar to my own. Yet, hers had more of a hint of green. She had long, full eyelashes and slanting cheekbones. She looked like she hadn't touched a drink in years as her complexion was clear, no bags under her eyes and her composure was normal.

Maybe she had changed. Maybe I owed her a chance to make amends. But first, I'd need to talk to her.

"I am okay. How are you?" I fired the question back to her and she blinked twice before answering.

"I'm very good these days. I work in an art gallery, as an assistant. I know you remember me when I was a drunk but I haven't touched a drink in years. I don't want to be that version of myself ever again," she said calmly. I decided to let her keep talking but now I was wondering how Alisha was doing, as she was taking a little longer than expected.

"You...left us," was all I could muster but I needed her to hear it.

"I know and I'm so sorry. I hate myself for that. I know I did wrong but I'm here for another chance. Do you think you can give that to me?" Mum's face was crestfallen and it seemed her words were sincere. Just as I was thinking of what to say next, Alisha was walking slowly towards us with our coffees and cake. She paused, giving me a look to check if it was okay she could join us. I nodded and my mother's attention diverted from me to Alisha.

"Hi, I'm Alisha," Alisha said in a chirpy tone, placing the tray down and plopping next to me. Her hand found its way in mine and I instantly relaxed, her soft skin against mine helped me to calm down.

"I'm Valerie, nice to meet you. So, are you two together?" Mum had started speaking in English and then flicked her finger at the two of us. Alisha remained calm beside me as she opened her mouth to answer.

"Yes. We met not that long ago. I'm here on a work holiday and I'm leaving in a few days," Alisha said. My heart tore a little at hearing her say she'd be leaving soon because I really couldn't face saying goodbye to her for who knows how long. We were both going to be busy with work, especially now I was working for the ski school. Could we really make this work? I wanted to, so badly. I wanted to fight for us.

"What do you do for work?" My mum seemed very interested in getting to know Alisha and probably because she wanted to prove she was genuine about making amends. I lifted the coffee cup which was steaming and took a sip, the milky liquid splashing against my tongue.

"I'm an aspiring journalist. I'm hoping this article I'm writing will get me a permanent position at the company I work for as a journalist. It's what I've always wanted to do." Alisha gushed, her face lit up whenever she spoke about her job. It was cute.

"That's impressive. I hope you get it. What about you, Felix? What do you do now?" Mum turned her attention back to me.

"I was working for a travel agency but I quit. I'm training to be a ski instructor at the ski school," I said.

"I can see that. You always loved adventure as a little boy. Much more than your sister." She tucked a piece of her blonde hair behind one ear and then wet her lips.

"Mira works in a hospital. She's had a few days off but goes back to work tomorrow," I told my mother ,who again looked impressed. Maybe proud too.

"That's very brave of her. Is she coming today?" My mum's voice was laced with a little hesitancy, probably because she knew it'd be much more awkward with Mira. Mira didn't really remember her and it would take a little longer to gain her trust.

"Not today. But she has asked about you. I think she just needs some time," I said and my mother nodded, not pressing for any further information. It was something she'd have to accept for now.

"I understand. All I can say is that I'm very sorry. Over these years, I've thought so much about the pair of you. What you were doing, whether you were healthy and settled down. When I bumped into Brenna, I felt as those my prayers were answered. I know I need to do all that I can to prove to you all that I'm serious and if there's room for me in your lives, I'd like to be a part of it," she said, clasping her hands together tightly. I scanned her features for any sign of dishonesty but couldn't find any. Maybe she truly meant what she was saying.

"You don't have to give me an answer now but I'll give you my contact details and where I live now. I won't blame you if you decide not to speak to me ever again. But seeing you now, I want to be the mother I should have been," she finished, taking a card out of her purse to hand to me.

Valerie Huber. So she kept her maiden name then. Me and my sister had decided to take our aunt's surname long ago because we didn't want any further attachment to our mother. I didn't really imagine myself as anything other than a Bauer now.

"Okay." I didn't know what else to say but perhaps it was time to head back.

"I'll leave you both to it. I've got to head back to the gallery. Maybe you should come check it out soon?" Mum suggested and I nodded.

Before she left, she looked at me and then said her final words before leaving.

"I'll always love you, Felix. Never stopped." When she left, I pondered on her words and then came up with my own response in my head.

Part of me always loved her too, I just hadn't realised it until now. Funny how the heart works.

But when I turned to the gorgeous woman sitting next to me, eating her slice of chocolate cake, I realised it was a different kind of love. And the love I was feeling for Alisha was indescribable. Satiable. I couldn't breathe without her and was totally enamoured with her. I knew I needed to tell her soon but for now, I finished eating cake with her and reflecting on the meet-up with my mother, which had gone better than expected.

"Do you think you'll contact her?" Alisha was just finishing her final piece of cake.

"I think so. I'll talk to Mira about it though. I feel like we still need to talk about the past and about my dad, what happened between them," I told Alisha. There was so much more to discover and it scared me, but at least I had jumped over the first hurdle. With Alisha now in my life, it was going to be easier to jump over more hurdles but I wanted her to tackle them with me.

Chapter 42

Alisha

Meeting Felix's mum had been a success and it was clear how much the woman cared for her son. She'd given him her details as well as asking him to come and see her where she worked. You could visibly see she was sorry. It was up to Felix to fully forgive her and I knew he'd also want Mira's input on it all. That was why shortly after the meeting, we pulled up at her house and spilled the details.

"She looked healthy then?" Mira was making us all a cup of tea and had set down a plate of Apfelradln, which were deep-fried apple rings dusted with sugar. I took my first bite and was in absolute heaven.

"Yeah, she said she didn't drink anymore. You could tell," Felix responded, picking up an apple ring himself and taking a large bite.

"Hmm," Mira let out, placing our drinks on the table. Her house was quite cosy, perfect for one person. In terms of her decor, she kept it simple, dark brown wooden chairs, a soft, grey velvet sofa with a throw on top and a medium sized TV hanging on the wall in the living room.

"She also said she loves me. That she always has," Felix continued and this caused a flicker of emotion to appear on Mira's face.

"Right," Mira said. From what I could see, she would probably be a little bit stubborn about the exchange and rightly so. But now that her brother had met up with Valerie, she could make her decision. I knew Felix and Brenna wouldn't push her to it either.

"Is that all you can say?" Felix asked and Mira shrugged. I gave Felix a warning look, because Mira clearly didn't want to get into it. Plus, I didn't want these two to argue. So Felix slouched back into his seat and brought his cup of tea to his lips.

We didn't talk more about Valerie and after about an hour at Mira's, we decided to let her get on with things. She said she had a list of things to do today before going back to work.

Me and Felix headed back to the chalet, to talk about our plans for tomorrow. Felix would be starting his first day on trial and I would be on a call with Grayson and some other colleagues in the company. We needed to discuss the February and March issues, and hopefully with my input, I'd be able to create more exciting articles for them. Now that I'd travelled to Austria, I wasn't afraid to go to other places. I'd thought about Spain, perhaps. Somewhere warm. As much as I loved the cold here in Austria, I was keen to wear a different attire.

Felix had been silent on the drive to mine but I didn't blame him. He had just seen his mother and it was a huge deal. I admired him, he had been calm and collected throughout the entire meeting and didn't for once let his true feelings take over. That was strength, and being a part of that with him meant so much to me, that he trusted me and wanted me to be there. It convinced me that I really was in love with him. I'd fallen hard.

"Right, I'll make us some food and you sit back and relax," I said to Felix as we got through the door. Ophelia was sitting on the sofa, giving us a wave as her other hand was poised above her keyboard. She looked as though she was in the middle of typing an email. She was also still in her velvet pyjamas.

"Making us some food. Do you want any?" I asked my friend, shrugging my coat off to hang up on the hook near the door. Felix did the same and took his boots off, arranging them neatly next to mine.

"Well, if you're offering." Ophelia turned her head to give me a chaste smile. She looked more tired than usual and I hoped she wasn't working herself too hard, but she did love her job, talking with people and doing lots of research. She was dedicated and the company was lucky to have her.

In terms of food, I'd make us all Käsespätzle which was pasta mixed with cheese and topped with fried onions. The fridge was still fully stocked so me and Ophelia really needed to cook these last few days so that we wouldn't waste anything.

"I'm going to keep your friend company," Felix announced. Perfectly fine with me. I liked it when they got along and the fact that I didn't need to even ask him to join her was adorable.

"No problem." I grinned, starting to ransack through the fridge to grab the cheese and a bit of milk. The pasta was in the cupboard and onions were already lying on the kitchen counter. I would try to make enough so we could have leftovers and have a late night meal if we needed it.

I realised I was cooking so much more here than back in England, I'd usually have ready meals or my mum would cook and freeze food for me so that I was covered for days, sometimes even weeks.

I thought about my grandmother too, on my dad's side, how much I missed her cooking but she was miles and miles away in India. She lived in Kanpur, the largest city of Uttar Pradesh in North India, with my grandpa. They only came to England once or twice a year and I wondered whether they'd be coming this Christmas. I missed them a lot. It was always wonderful when the Dutta family came together. I thought about Diwali and how a few years ago we had spent it in Kanpur, how gorgeous it was. I also thought about taking Felix one day, to see my extended family. There were so many exciting things ahead that I wanted him to be part of.

With our early dinner finally prepared and bubbling in the oven, I rejoined Ophelia and Felix who were in mid conversation. I just about caught what they were talking about, giving their opinion on the TV show *The Walking Dead*. Ophelia was a die hard fan but Felix had never watched an episode so he was nodding along with whatever Ophelia had told him.

"Normally, I don't like guts and gore. But if there's a storyline, I can try it," Felix said. He shared the same sentiment as me when it came to TV shows, I didn't like watching programmes that didn't have a good plot. The only ones I really liked to watch now were *Friends, Bridgerton* and *The Fresh Prince of Bel Air*. All three made me laugh and cry when I needed it.

"How are you holding up anyway, Felix?" Ophelia asked, shutting her laptop lid down. She was bold to ask him outright but that's just who she was. Straight to the point.

"Today was an interesting day. I think I'll meet my mum again, and maybe go and visit this art gallery she works at. Just need to see what Mira decides next," Felix replied, scratching his chin. The stubble there was growing thicker and I hoped he wouldn't shave it all off. I loved a man with facial hair. Especially *this* man.

"Yeah, Mira texted me earlier. She's not one hundred percent sure, you know. Guess she's got a lot on her mind, going back to work and then the idea of seeing her mum after all this time. You both have been through so much," Ophelia said sadly. She was probably thinking about her own parents and how it hadn't worked out between them. Several months ago, she had told me she wished they would talk but they hadn't seen one another in years. Ophelia would find it a struggle going back and forth, listening to them complain about one another from time to time.

It was probably a reason why she hadn't fallen in love yet. Seeing what happened between her parents would be enough to turn you off the idea. If she was happy the way things were, then that was perfectly okay.

Her sparkling green eyes met my own dark brown ones and she silently let me know she was alright with a squint of her eyes. Sometimes, the two of us didn't need to exchange words, we just knew each other.

The timer went off on my phone to let me know the pasta was ready to take out of the oven. I dished our plates quickly and we ate comfortably together, reminiscing about the last few days in Ischgl and then about our flight plans.

We'd be travelling back in the afternoon, which gave us enough time to tidy the chalet, hand back the keys and then get a bus back to Innsbruck Airport. I knew once I returned back to England, life would be very different and I'd feel like a part of me would be missing. But sometimes in life, you had to have a little distance for the heart to grow fonder.

If Felix and I were meant for one another, we'd gravitate back to each other.

Chapter 43

Felix

It felt like the last few days had flown by and there was nothing I could do to freeze time. It was Alisha's last day today before she'd hop on a plane tomorrow, putting thousands of miles between us.

But there were lots of good things happening in my life: my trial at the ski school was going very well, my mentor was especially pleased with my efforts and I'd passed all my training. I was now working toward my level two ski instructor qualification. In a couple of weeks, I'd be ready to teach.

Aunt Brenna was slowly rekindling her relationship with her sister, they'd met a few times over the last few days. Mira, on the other hand, was still not ready. She was hard to crack but we didn't want to force her. When the time was right, she'd meet her. That didn't mean she didn't ask about her though.

I couldn't believe these last two weeks and how much had happened. How much my heart had thawed. At the beginning, I had been frosty with most people and refused to let people in. Now, I was thriving. Everything was finally looking up for me. Did it sound too good to be true? Perhaps, but I didn't care. It was a life I'd always craved and I'd treasure it.

After my training, I would take Alisha down some slopes because I wanted her to keep her learning fresh. She clearly loved it, the triumphant smiles she'd give me when she took off her skis and then jumped into my arms for endless kisses. Just yesterday, we visited the Christmas markets and Alisha had gazed at the handmade ornaments available on display. We also dived into some seasonal treats and drank some warm mulled wine. It was perfect.

We also had gone ice skating and I'd never seen Alisha laugh as hard as she did when the two of us fell over in unison on the ice. We were lucky not to break a bone or end up seriously injured. My heart only swelled more with love for her when she took my hand in hers and brought it to her lips, the world slipping away from us as we stared into each other's eyes. Into each other's souls.

To end the perfect day, we went back to mine and made cookies. Flour had ended up everywhere but we weren't phased. With one look in her eyes after tidying up, I knew what she wanted. She didn't have to communicate as her body language spoke for her. She very quickly ended up in my bed, clothes scattered on my bedroom floor and then I was inside her, where I belonged.

The love making as well had been intense, watching her crumble underneath me as she met her orgasm and then me following shortly after. We'd made love in many positions and then exchanged sweet declarations of how much we meant to one another. I still hadn't told her yet though. The three words that were on the tip of my tongue. Itching to be spilled. I wanted to pour my soul out to Alisha, for her to know that she was it for me. That for me, this wasn't just a two-week romance.

Tonight, Alisha was going to take us out for a romantic dinner just outside of Ischgl. We had a few hours though before that, so I was currently with my twin cousins. They convinced me to go grab a beer with them and catch up. We were drinking our second round of beers and playing foosball. Currently, I was winning against Elias whilst Jakob was cheering me on.

The bar was quite lively at four o'clock but it was a level of loudness I was comfortable with. Jakob patted me on the shoulder, as it was now his turn to play against me. I'd already won against Elias who didn't look too happy about it.

Oh well, he'd have to get over it.

"How's that gorgeous girlfriend of yours?" Jakob asked me as he grabbed the handles to start twisting them, knocking the mini ball in my direction.

Girlfriend. I hadn't exactly called Alisha that but maybe that's who she was to me now.

"He scores!" Elias shouted, raising one fist in the air. Jakob had managed to score a goal.

"She's good. You two met anyone yet?" I was determined to win this round so kept my eyes firmly on the prize.

"Nope, don't want to settle down just yet. Loving the single life," Jakob replied and then looked at this twin who was nodding in agreement.

"Gotta find the right person, there's no one here I like anyway," Elias said. Maybe that was because he slept with quite a few women and didn't want anything else. He was a good looking man and had plenty going for him. I supposed the only turn off was that he spent his weekends playing video games with Jakob and hanging around in bars.

"Do you want to get married one day?" I asked them both. I'd never actually asked them that before but now I was curious. For me, marriage was the end goal.

"Well, after seeing what happened with you and your ex. Maybe not. Sorry to be harsh, Felix. But that's the truth," Elias replied first.

"Elias! That *is* a bit harsh!" Jakob scolded his twin who murmured an apology to me. It didn't sting me like it would have done months ago. I was over that situation now.

"Don't worry. I won't cry about it." I winked at my twin cousins, who let out a sigh of relief and then resumed talking to me.

"Anyway my point is I have to really meet someone who's like me, for me to change my mind," Elias said. I didn't share this ideal, what was unique about me and Alisha was that we had different ideas and opinions but we respected one another. We listened and didn't judge. We were so in tune to one another, maybe to others it was sickening. But to me, it was heaven.

The music in the bar changed to something more soulful and a few people started to dance in the middle of the floor. I didn't mind Austrian bars, it was very rare for fights to happen and most people wanted to have a good time with friends and partners.

"He's got a point." Jakob pretty much agreed with anything his brother said, the two were joined at the hip. There was not much else I could say to change their minds about relationships so they would just have to discover real love themselves. Aunt Brenna had wanted me to try and give them a push but if they didn't listen to her, then of course they wouldn't to me. They were stubborn like their mother.

"If you marry this girl, I want to be the best man this time," Elias announced and this caused a rumble of laughter to erupt from my chest. He could be cheeky at the best of times but he sure did make me laugh.

Jakob obviously won this round and it was my turn to buy the next round of beers. It was nice to spend time with family but I couldn't wait for later this evening.

***

I was waiting patiently for Alisha, as she was getting dressed. I drummed my fingers on my knee and glanced around the room. It had been the perfect choice of accommodation for the girls and from what I'd worked out, not too expensive either. The host seemed friendly enough and said they were always welcome back.

I stopped drumming my fingers when my girl walked into the room, looking absolutely breathtaking. I felt as though my heart was in my mouth as I looked at her, and I mean really *looked* at her.

Alisha was wearing a dark green cocktail dress, with small frills at the bottom. It fit her body snugly and cinched at her curves. Her legs looked toned and on her feet were a pair of pair block heels with straps. Her long hair was tied up into a loose bun, adorned with a small rhinestone hair vine.

"Wow," I breathed but wanted to say so much more to her.

"Do I look okay?" Alisha held her hands in front of her and tugged her bottom lip between her teeth. Her lips were painted a dark red and this colour definitely suited her.

"You are so beautiful. I am lost for words, sweetheart." I took her in my arms and wanted to hold her here forever, to never let her go, but tomorrow afternoon, I'd have to. And I knew I'd go home and collapse into my bed, which smelled of her and held many memories. I knew she wouldn't want me to wallow though, to carry on living my life and enjoying myself out here in Ischgl. But how could I when she wouldn't be here to share memories with me?

"And you look so gorgeous too, Mr Bauer. Look at that bowtie." Alisha touched it, giving it a gentle pull. It was a fake one though, because I hadn't quite mastered tying up a real one.

"Wanted to look my best for you," I told her, my lips gently touching her smooth forehead. I inhaled her scent, trying to savour her in any way I could. *Cherries as always.*

"You always look handsome, Felix. Ready to go?" Alisha slipped her petite hand into mine and led us toward the door.

"So, do I get a hint where you are taking me tonight?" I asked her as we got into my car. She would enter the details into the satnav and asked me not to look.

Once she coded in the details, the satnav indicated that it would take about a twenty minute drive. Alisha had a mischievous look on her face as she buckled in her seat belt and said nothing more as I backed out of the driveway, turning my car to face the main road.

"So no hints at all, sweetheart?" I wondered if she'd let up during the journey but she shook her head vigorously.

"Nope. Just wait and see, Felix." Alisha at this moment wasn't easy to read but she must have had something up her sleeve. Whatever it was, I was excited and a romantic night with her was what I needed.

"What's Ophelia up to tonight?" I'd noticed her friend hadn't been around and Alisha chewed her lip before answering.

"She's...with Mira I think. They wanted to go to the markets again. Ophelia loves antiques but I told her not to buy anything too massive otherwise it won't fit in her suitcase." I loved it when she rambled, especially when she was nervous. I could tell she was as her voice was slightly shaky.

"Oh, very nice. I'm sure they'll bring you back something," I said, keeping a firm grip on the steering wheel. The satnav announced to make a left in about five minutes. I didn't recognise the route.

"Yeah." Alisha smirked as if she knew more than she was letting on. *What was she hiding?* I so wanted in but I'd shut my mouth for now and be prepared for whatever she had planned.

That's what I loved about this woman, she was unpredictable but had a pure heart and the best of intentions.

Chapter 44

Alisha

*D*on't spill anything.

It was incredibly hard keeping tonight a secret from Felix, as usually I'd tell him everything. But this, no I wanted it to be a surprise. Tonight, I was taking him on a reclusive date with Ophelia and Mira preparing our dinner and dessert for us.

Mira told me about this gorgeous park about twenty minutes away and we talked to the owners who agreed we could rent a small space for the evening. Mira and Ophelia had been so kind to chip in with their own money, which I refused at first, but they both told me they wanted me and Felix to have an amazing last night together, as we deserved it.

I remembered when Mira also pulled me to one side for a one on one conversation. I didn't know if she was going to give me a drilling, to warn me that if I hurt her brother, I'd be for it. But the conversation had been a lot better.

"You love him, don't you?" Mira asked me.

"I really do," I told her honestly and this satisfied her. She wanted a happy ending for her only brother and I'd want to give that to him.

There was a nearby restaurant that had been happy to offer its utensils and stoves so that Ophelia and Mira could cook. The whole evening was planned to a T and now, sitting in Felix's car, I was a bag of nerves, or rather a whole hurricane of them. I had to keep swallowing as my throat was getting dry and as we got closer and closer to our destination, my heart palpitated.

This was all for him and I wanted to have an incredible last night with him. I didn't know when I'd see him next after leaving tomorrow. Maybe we'd make plans for the new year, he could come to see me and meet my family. The thought of this sounded wonderful. I imagined my mum would smother him in hugs but my dad would be slightly more reserved. Protective. My brothers—they would act like they didn't care, but deep down they did. Kiya, well she'd be very happy and would want to be best friends with Felix immediately. I'd never been more set on a man meeting my family before.

Everything had really changed for the better, I was much more confident in myself. I had partly Felix to thank for that but I also owed it to myself, for persevering and stepping outside of my comfort box. It meant I now had the courage to try other things, maybe snowboarding next.

Finally, the satnav announced we arrived and I told Felix to park up near the park. He looked a little confused and I placed one finger on my lips, signalling my silence. Still wasn't going to spill the beans.

"Take my hand," I told him as we jumped out of the car and locked up. The street was quiet, a few people walking up and down it. The night was clear and crisp. I led us toward the iron gates of the park, which were left open and I was thankful there were a few lamps above the gravel path as we walked down it.

"I thought parks had to be closed after a certain time." Felix walked at a steady pace beside me, and he still looked confused—bless him.

"Not this one," I replied. I could see our table about a minute's distance away. I knew Ophelia and Mira would have done a brilliant job setting it up. Finally, Felix clocked on and as we came to a stop in front of the table, his mouth gaped open.

"Surprise!" I exclaimed, holding my hands out in front of me to present.

"This is...so..." Felix couldn't quite finish so I did for him.

"Romantic?" I smirked and Felix nodded. His eyes were full of adoration as he couldn't look away from me and I couldn't look away from him either until someone cleared their throat and I turned to see my two friends grinning, Mira holding two wine glasses and Ophelia holding the wine bottle. They looked adorable in their outfits, crisp, white shirts and smart black trousers with shiny shoes. They really looked the part and I needed to thank them immensely later.

"Sit down, lovebirds. We'll be your hosts tonight. We hope you like what we've prepared," Mira said and Felix was slightly shocked to see her.

"Mira, you're in on this too? I thought you were at the markets." Felix took his seat, still in disbelief, but he'd better believe it.

"Nope. You should know they're not open tonight." Mira placed the glasses down in front of us whilst Ophelia poured the wine into them. It looked like sparkling wine as she generously filled our glasses.

"My mistake." Felix chuckled, picking up his glass and taking a slow sip. I did the same, relishing the coolness of the wine and the fizz bubbling on my tongue. *Very refreshing.*

"Sit tight and we'll bring your main meals shortly." Ophelia offered us a bow, which made me giggle as she was so serious about it.

"Looks like we're going to tip the hosts tonight." Felix leaned a bit forward in his chair, admiring the handiwork on the table, courtesy of his sister and Ophelia.

"Give them more than ten percent" I fiddled with my napkin, which had been folded into a love heart.

"Thank you for doing this. It's very sweet of you," Felix thanked me, reaching across the table to intertwine our fingers. Electricity shot through me as our skin touched, like always. I would spend another week here in Ischgl if I could but home was calling.

"I wanted to give you an amazing last night with me. I don't know when I'll see you again," I said sadly.

"We'll make plans for after Christmas. I want to be in your life, Alisha," Felix told me, rubbing his thumb against my palm.

"I want to be in yours too. Felix, I—" I was about to tell him but was stopped by the girls reappearing with our food. Maybe I'd wait until the end of the evening, when we were completely alone.

"Bon appetit." Ophelia placed my hot plate on the table and I gazed at what the girls had prepared for us. Salmon with cheese sauce, steamed asparagus with tomato and couscous. It smelt and looked delicious, I was almost about to dribble on my plate. Luckily, I had good reflexes. Salmon was one of my favourite fishes to eat and Felix's too.

We thanked the girls and they left us to it. My fork sank into the salmon with ease, which meant that it was cooked just right. I had no doubt about my friends and their culinary skills but fish could usually be tricky to cook.

When I placed the first portion in my mouth, I moaned in delight. The cheese sauce complimented the salmon too.

"It's very creamy and just the right amount of salt. Who do you think made the cheese sauce?" Felix asked me.

"I bet it was Ophelia, she loves her sauces and she'd have suggested it to Mira. If the main meal is this good, I can't wait for dessert," I said, placing another forkful of food into my mouth.

Fuck, this was so good. I'd hire them as chefs if they gave up their day jobs.

"Where are they doing all the cooking?" Felix looked around him, but it was only us two in the park. It'd be impossible to cook outside, especially with the chilly weather and possibility of flies and other bugs getting into the oil.

"They're using a kitchen in a local restaurant, just a minute or two from here," I said, just as I finished swallowing. I didn't like to talk with my mouth full. It was unattractive, and I didn't want to spew food on a table, or even on Felix.

"Very impressive. I think I'll triple tip them, just hearing that." Felix stabbed his fork into an asparagus, eating it whole. Me, I liked to cut mine up into smaller pieces. When it came to food, especially vegetables, I'd try to cut them down into smaller portions. The tomato though, I'd eat with no problem as it had a sweeter taste.

Our plates were completely clear by the time the girls came back and when they saw this, they exchanged proud looks with one another.

"For dessert, we've prepared a chocolate fondue, with strawberry and banana. We know how you both love chocolate." Ophelia stacked the plates while Mira picked up our knives and forks.

"Chocolate is the best. I definitely have room for that." I smiled at the creative duo. They gave us some privacy again, saying they'd be back in about ten minutes. It was enough time for the food to settle in our stomachs.

"What's the first thing you'll do when you get home tomorrow?" Felix asked me as he dabbed at his mouth with his napkin. Good question. There were so many things I needed to do but one was to give my cat Chou all the cuddles and kisses as I had really missed my furry friend.

"Well, I think I'll order a takeaway once I've unpacked. Ophelia might stay over but then she's got a lot to do at her own apartment. We don't live that far from each other, so if she wants to stay she can," I said, finishing the rest of my wine. The fizz had dissipated a little but it still tasted amazing.

"And then what about Christmas?" Felix continued. I'd spoken to him a bit about potentially my grandparents coming down from India but it hadn't been confirmed yet by my parents. Mum would prepare the usual meal, a traditional Indian one. What I needed to do once I got home was pick out a saree to wear; last year, I had worn a dark purple one with an intricate lace design. This year, I was leaning more toward silk.

"I'll go to my parents for a Christmas lunch and we'll exchange presents with one another. Then mum likes to give out Indian sweets, rose cookies and nevris," I told Felix, a smile painted on my face as I spoke about the traditions we shared as a family.

"Rose cookies sound delicious."

"They're very popular in South India, where my mum was born. It's translated as Achu murukku. In Tamil, murukku means twisted and Achu means mould, so we use a flower shaped one," I said.

"Which part of South India?"

"Thanjavur, in Tamil Nadu," I said. I'd only been there once, about five years ago but a lot of tourists liked to go there, especially to see the Brihadisvara Temple. Mum had lived in Thanjavur until she was eighteen, from there she decided to attend university in the UK. She met my dad not long after, they were studying the same course and once they set their sights on one another, that was that. They fell in love quickly but decided to have a long engagement, to get to know each other's families. Within two years, they were married. They didn't want children straight away, so focused on their finances and building a home.

My mum's parents visited more often than dad's, so it was more natural for me to talk with them more.

"I'd love to go there with you," Felix said and my heart softened. I loved hearing that he wanted to get to know my family more, my culture. I also wanted to get to know his family more too. I hadn't managed to meet his cousins yet but they sounded like a laugh.

"The best time to go is between November and March. The temperature is not too bad then," I said, running my fingers through my hair. I caught a waft of something sweet and turned my head to see Ophelia and Mira approaching with our dessert.

"Wow, look at that!" Felix exclaimed, sparklers were going off, planted inside the bananas. There was a medium sized pot of melted chocolate on the side of the plate and a helpful portion of strawberries. Mira handed us two sticks so we could stab the fruit with them and dip in the chocolate. It was really a nice touch and a simple dessert, enough to keep us sated.

"We hope you've enjoyed your evening. Please don't forget to rate and review, as we'd like to do this again," Mira joked, linking her arm through Ophelia's.

"Five stars coming from me straight away, you've done well tonight girls." Felix gave them a round of applause and I joined him, we probably looked like idiots clapping in the middle of a deserted park but that didn't matter. I couldn't be happier.

"Thank you," I said graciously. I'd help the girls tidy up after eating the dessert and then we'd all head home. Well, I'd go to Felix's to have one last sleep with him, and I didn't mean sexually. I just wanted to hold him and fall asleep to the sound of his rhythmic heartbeat.

Me and Felix devoured the dessert and laughed until our stomachs hurt. As the date was drawing to a close, I wanted time to freeze so I could savour this moment. But time was a cruel thing, it didn't stop for anyone.

Once we finished eating, we helped clear the table and Ophelia provided a box where we could store everything. The girls said they'd take it with them and let us get on our way. I'd pulled them both into tight embraces and thanked them again. I had the most amazing friends ever. And the most amazing man too.

Felix still wasn't familiar with the route so needed to use the satnav on the way back and all throughout the journey, I gazed at him. I wanted to remember his gorgeous face, his five o'clock shadow, his full lips that I had pressed mine against many times and the way his biceps flexed whenever he moved his arms. I didn't want to forget tonight.

I hoped there were many more nights like these in the future.

Chapter 45

Felix

The woman of my dreams was slipping off her heels when we finally got home. I was quick to lift her up into my arms, closing the distance between us and smashing my lips on hers. I didn't know when I'd next get to kiss these lips I'd grown so familiar with but I'd savour them tonight, in any way I could. I wanted to taste all of her but I'd take my time. Tonight had been so special and would continue to be.

I placed Alisha gently on my kitchen counter, the bedroom could wait but I needed to give her that sweet release now. I knelt down in front of her, tracing my hand up her left thigh. Her brown eyes were wide but full of want and need for me. She waited for my next move.

"I've been wanting this all evening, Felix," Alisha declared, her voice had gone a little husky. But she was bold with her statement. Tonight, her pleasure was the most important.

"Me too. I've been craving to taste you, here." I pressed a kiss on her neck, her weak spot I had grown accustomed to.

"And here," I continued, another kiss landing on her thigh. Yes, we'd eaten dessert but I was hungry for more.

"Oh, Felix," Alisha sighed and tilted her head back, hands pressed against the counter as I pulled her knickers down her legs. She was always ready for me which drove me insane.

As I ran one finger down her folds, I could feel how wet she was. I needed to give special attention to her clit, so I eased the tip of my finger inside her and curled it upward. Her legs clenched together as I did this but with my other hand, I separated them. I needed her wide open for me, better access to that gorgeous pussy of hers. I loved the way she clamped down on me, enough to make me almost come in my pants.

"Mm, just like that," Alisha moaned, as I entered a second finger and started to ease them in and out. Her pussy clamped down on them and I knew it wouldn't take long for her to come. I knew what she liked.

I had a glorious view of her as I was on my knees and now I wanted to lick her out. My tongue darted out between my lips as I sunk my mouth on her clit, causing her to gasp and arch her back.

"Relax, baby," I told her, as she had tightened up a little. Her own fingers wrapped themselves into my hair, pushing my head closer.

Fuck, she tasted sweet.

I licked and sucked at a rapid pace until her legs shuddered and she was coming, her release coating my tongue. I lapped her all up but it wasn't enough. I wanted my cock to be soaked in her too. I became hard just thinking about it.

"Yes," Alisha gasped, her eyes glinting with something I couldn't quite make out.

"Fuck me here," she practically begged and I tugged my trousers down with my boxers until I was bare on the lower half. I was ready for her and I could see she was waiting for me, no direction given. Without hesitating, I plunged my cock deep inside her and I could feel her already tightening around me.

As I started to move, her muscles relaxed and soft moans escaped her mouth. I needed to see those tits of hers, so I unzipped her dress and let it fall around her waist until she shook it off from one of her legs. So gracefully too.

"So beautiful," I told her, as she started to unbutton my shirt. When her fingers touched my skin, I let out a small shudder and picked up my thrusts inside her. I would go slow and steady, because I wanted to make love to her all night. We'd start in the kitchen and then I'd take her to the bedroom.

"You always tell me that." Alisha couldn't hide her smile, a blush creeping on her cheeks.

"I'll tell you every day, sweetheart. Until you're bored of me," I teased, nipping gently at her soft neck with my teeth, not enough to leave a mark.

"Could never be bored of you." Alisha pulled me closer which was a sign she wanted me to move more, but the kitchen counter wouldn't give me the best access to her so I carried her back to my room, my cock still positioned inside of her.

"I want you bent over," I whispered in her ear and she nodded. I slipped out of her, my cock glistening with her wetness. Alisha turned around so her ass was in the air and her hands gripping the bed sheets.

I entered her pussy from behind, as she let out a cry and I gripped her hips so I could slam harder into her. She started to move with me, her perfect ass bouncing with every movement. I had a glorious view of her, completely and utterly mine. Yet tomorrow, I'd be letting go of her.

I pummeled deeper inside of her, until all I could feel, see and breathe was Alisha. I didn't want it to be any different. My movements became harder as I was getting close to the edge. To drive Alisha closer to her own orgasm, I started to tease her clit with my fingers and simultaneously thrusting hard inside her.

In a matter of seconds, she crumbled around me and came on my cock. Feeling her pulsate and clench made me meet my own release, my load came in short spurts and I let out a deep groan.

"I'm so tired," Alisha said with her eyes closed as we fell back next to each other on the bed. I wrapped the duvet around us and then rested my head against her chest, trying to familiarise myself with the pattern of her heartbeat. Still beating fast. My own was erratic, all because I wanted to tell her I was in love with her, but the words wouldn't come out.

Maybe it was because I wanted to tell her with some grand gesture, or that perhaps she didn't love me the way I loved her. It wasn't healthy to think that way but I'd been let down in the past.

But I didn't need to compare my past with right now. I'd had the best two weeks of my life and nothing could take that away. Lots of possibilities were now waiting for me, being able to teach for one, and then, possibly allowing my mother to be a part of my life.

Aunt Brenna said she'd like to see her sister more, to make up for lost time. Of course, once upon a time they'd been close. Mira needed a bit more time, which we'd give her. But all I knew was that my mother was happy to wait for us, just a phone call away.

Before I could say something else to Alisha, she was already asleep. Well, she had a busy day ahead of her tomorrow so needed all the sleep she could get.

Myself, I didn't know if I could sleep tonight because I was dreading tomorrow. I held Alisha tightly against me for hours, until eventually I slipped off into a slumber.

The last thought I had was of telling her I loved her and her saying that she did too.

Chapter 46

Alisha

S leep always came easy these days. I woke up in Felix's arms, shattered, but the feeling of euphoria washed over me. Felix looked radiant sleeping next to me and I knew I'd have to say goodbye to him soon. I felt as though it was killing me, that I was losing one half of me.

But it was time to go home. People were waiting for me. Chou was waiting for me and I missed my little fur buddy, his soft purrs and gentle kneads. There was so much I missed about England too.

What was ahead in terms of my job excited me, the article was pretty much done and was going through a round of edits. Grayson had been really happy with me over the last few days, I remembered when we had our video call, he said he was proud of me and he could tell through my writing that I'd really enjoyed myself.

He was thinking of making trips a regular thing now, but would alternate between staff to make it fair. I'd come back to Ischgl, of course, but didn't have a date set in mind just yet. I needed to work out a few things back home.

It was time to get up, and as much as I wanted to stay in Felix's arms, I needed to return to the chalet and finish packing. The place also needed a clean too before we handed back the keys.

"I've gotta get up, Felix," I softly said to him, kissing his bare shoulder. As I made a move to exit the bed, his strong arm wrapped around my waist to stop me.

"Five more minutes," he grumbled.

Five more minutes then.

And what seemed like more than five minutes later, I needed to get up. I needed a shower, as my legs were a bit sticky from Felix's release last night. It made me blush thinking about it.

"Want me to help you pack?" Felix asked me once we were finally dressed. He'd made us a fresh pot of coffee and I was guzzling mine down, needing the caffeine to be more alert. Felix looked tired today, his hair slightly ruffed and visible bags under his eyes. His eyes were also sad and I knew why. He didn't want me to leave. I didn't want to either.

"Yeah, that'd be great," I told him. In a few minutes, we left his place to get back to the chalet. Ophelia had the front door open already when we arrived, as she was taking the bins out. I mumbled a hello to her on the way in and Felix followed closely behind me.

"I can take away leftovers from your fridge," Felix suggested, scanning the contents in our fridge. I was making a start on cleaning the cupboards, the stove and then the floor. We knew the host would clean up again once we left, but it was a decent thing for us to leave the chalet how we first saw it.

"Thanks, Felix!" Ophelia called out as she was walking toward her room. I scrubbed everything until it was practically shining and the floor was starting to dry. Felix had put all the leftover food in a bag and was wiping the shelves in the fridge with a cloth. It was sweet as I hadn't even asked him to do that. Another thing I'd miss about him; his willingness to help.

"I'd love to take some food back with me, but don't think security will be too keen," I said, once I scanned the contents Felix had packed. A few blocks of cheese, some sauces, milk and a couple of sausages. From the cupboards, he'd taken pasta, salt, some of the spices and some tuna cans. Me and Ophelia hadn't touched the tuna for some reason.

"Well, it saves me shopping tonight," Felix replied.

"True. I'm going to finish packing now," I announced, remembering Felix wanted to help with this too. I'd see what his folding skills were like in action. My room was half clean so I'd sort this out after packing.

I rummaged through the chest of drawers to take out my underwear and then the rest of my casual clothes. Dresses and smart outfits were hung up in the cupboard and they'd go in my suitcase last.

Once I had a wad of clothes in my hands, I set them down on my bed so I could start folding. Felix joined me and after I showed him my method, he managed to do it well. My suitcase was fully packed in twenty minutes and the next things I needed to get were my toiletries, shoes. Electrical equipment had to stay out of my suitcase and go in my hand luggage. Anything with liquid had to go in a clear bag, which luckily I had a few spare ones of.

"Finally." I let out a deep sigh once everything was sorted, but I had a few more jobs to do.

"What time are you getting the bus?" Felix asked as I was stripping the bed. The covers would go in the laundry basket which the host would take.

"About two o'clock." I checked the time and we still had a few hours. The bus to the airport would only take an hour, so we'd arrive before check-in opened. I was getting a little hungry, so perhaps after tidying, we could grab something to eat.

"Okay, maybe we can take a break now and eat. Ask Ophelia to join us," Felix said. I did just that but Ophelia was keen to keep cleaning and she still had a lot to pack. I underestimated how much she brought as I scanned her messy room.

"She's stressed," I told Felix as we headed out the door. We knew where we wanted to go, just a small cafe that did sandwiches and toasties. I'd bring back something for Ophelia because I didn't want her going hungry.

"I hope she's had a good time here," Felix said as our boots crunched on the snow. There was no sun in the sky and it looked cloudy. I hoped it wouldn't turn into a storm, as it'd made the flight more unbearable. I already had a fear of planes.

"We both have. Getting to work and having fun in this town. What more could we ask for? Just hope the bill hasn't been too big for Grayson," I said. My boss covered the accommodation expenses but Ophelia and I insisted that we'd pay for the food and other things. It was only fair. Grayson didn't argue with it, it meant he didn't have to dig further into the company purse.

Me and Felix ordered our lunch shortly after we took our seats and then suddenly, my phone pinged. I wasn't expecting a text from anyone in particular and I sighed in relief when it was just a text from my mum wishing me a safe trip home. I texted her a quick reply before resuming conversation with Felix.

"Remember our coffee date?" I asked him, trying to think of happy memories rather than sad thoughts. This seemed to spark a light in Felix, who had been looking slightly crestfallen.

"It's permanently inked in my mind." Felix smiled.

"I remember how nervous I was." I took a sip of my drink.

"Me too. But look where we are now," Felix replied. I leaned across the table to squeeze his hand in mine. I didn't know when I'd get to hold his hand again, so I didn't let go.

"I'm going to visit the ski school later. Meeting up with the group for a few drinks," Felix said as we had just finished eating our paninis. They had generously been filled with cheese and ham, with ranch dressing on the side. All we needed to do now was pay and get back to the chalet. I shoved Ophelia's own panini in my pocket, thankful for the paper wrapping.

"I'm glad you're doing what you love. I think you'll have so much fun with this job," I told him. I took out my card to pay for the meal before Felix could protest. I wanted this to be one last nice thing I'd do for him.

"My favourite student is you, though. I bet your family will be so proud of you when you tell them all the tricks you learnt." Felix smiled warmly at me, slipping his hand into mine as we left the cafe.

"My brothers still can't quite believe it. But when I show them the videos, they'll shut up." I grinned, imagining that the two of them would tease me at first but then keep their mouths shut once they saw how skilled I'd become. Then they'd never doubt their sister again. I'd win every argument from then on.

"I bet they can be a right laugh," Felix said.

"Hmm, when it benefits them," I replied. My brothers would tease but at the end of it, they meant well and they never did it to the point where I was in tears.

We got back within ten minutes and saw that Ophelia was cleaning the coffee table in the living room. Everything looked much better now, barely any evidence that two young women had been staying here for two weeks. I handed her the panini from my pocket and she took it gratefully with a hungry, wild look on her face.

"This couldn't come at a better time." Ophelia bit into her panini, which probably would have been cold by now. I guessed it didn't bother her as she was that hungry.

"Right, is there anything else I can help you girls with?" Felix shoved his hands in his pockets, leaning against the door frame.

"We're all set." Ophelia smiled at him, a mouth full of her food.

"Then, I'm just going to chat with Alisha if you don't mind," Felix announced.

"Don't get too frisky in there," Ophelia joked and I mouthed *shut up* to her before we entered the bedroom.

"I just wanted to hold you. There's so much I want to say but words won't cover how I feel about you, Alisha," Felix told me as we sat down on the stripped bed.

"I know, I have to tell you too. You've brought out the best in me and I'm so grateful to have met you," I responded, resting my head on his shoulder. A single tear escaped my eye but I brushed it away quickly. I didn't want him to see me cry because a whole waterfall would come out if he did.

"Alisha, you are the best thing that's ever happened to me. These two weeks, they've felt longer and I wish we'd had more time." Felix squeezed my hand in his.

"Make sure you call me every night." I poked my finger into his chest. I wanted to hear from him every day if I could.

"You know I can't avoid hearing that gorgeous voice of yours." Felix rested his head on mine. We sat like this for who knows how long until it was time to go. We begrudgingly let go of one another, shaky breaths escaping our lips as we vacated the room.

The bus was waiting for me and Ophelia, having arrived three minutes early. We'd said our goodbyes to the chalet, hauled our suitcases out the door and gave the keys back to the host, who arrived about five minutes ago.

Now, I had to say goodbye to Felix who was looking at me sadly, almost as if he wanted to cry. I'd never actually seen him shed a tear though. Maybe because he'd trained himself to be strong after everything he'd gone through.

"It's okay." I gently cupped his cheek and then pressed my trembling lips to his. We fell into the kiss like we always did. His hands squeezed at my waist, pulling me closer. His mouth moved slowly with mine, my whole body sinking into his.

I finally released him reluctantly as I couldn't keep Ophelia and the bus waiting.

"See you soon," I told Felix.

"It was nice to meet you, Felix. And your sister." Ophelia stood on the tip of her toes to hook her arm around Felix.

"Take care of each other," Felix replied, patting Ophelia on the back. I grabbed my suitcase handle and started to walk toward the bus door but not before turning my head back to look at the man I loved fiercely.

"Bye," I said one more time, my voice sounded as though it would crack. *I don't want to leave you.*

"Auf Wiedersehen," Felix replied, he looked crestfallen but there was nothing I could do. Me and Ophelia took our seats on the bus, once confirming our details with the driver. Out the window, I watched Felix, who hadn't moved from his spot. I kept watching him as the bus started to drive off and he was still standing in the same position, the same crestfallen look on his face.

And I silently cried on the journey to the airport, wondering when would be the next time I'd see him. I hoped there would be a next time.

Chapter 47

Felix

The first few days after Alisha left, I felt quite numb and lost. Mira had been quick to check in on me daily to stop me from going mad. I'd been grateful for her company, especially as her shifts were keeping her busy, and she was already exhausted. But family mattered to us Bauers. Christmas Day had been calm. I'd eaten a lot, and this year, I'd gone all out on presents. Aunt Brenna had been very grateful and now she was resting, as she had really ensured we had the best Christmas yet.

It was the 28th of December and every single day and night, I'd be on the phone to Alisha. We'd usually switch to FaceTime, talking about what we did during the day and then plans for the next one. It didn't stop me from missing her like crazy though. My feelings were beyond intense at this point. I still hadn't told her I loved her but I had my reasons. I wanted to tell her to her face.

I had just finished teaching my first official lesson and it had gone extremely well. I had taught a kid who was eight years old and his parents were really keen for him to ski so that he could join them eventually. I agreed that it was good to start young, having started my ski lessons when I was eight years old too. Aunt Brenna had booked the lessons for me and Mira. She had no problem spending money on us especially as it benefited us.

"Good job, buddy." I gave the child a high-five, whose name was Declan. He was from the UK and loved dinosaurs. He couldn't stop talking about them as soon as I asked him what his hobbies were. It was very cute.

"Thanks, Felix. I had so much fun!" Declan cheered, his blue eyes wide. He then ran into the arms of his dad, who proudly lifted him up in the air. His parents had booked him in for another two lessons before heading back to the UK. They thanked me and then made their way to a nearby restaurant.

I had a few more lessons to do today, and my mentor would be observing to see how I did. It was actually Hilde, as I already knew her and she had great advice.

A couple more hours passed until it was time to close up and Hilde said that I'd done well today, that I had just the right amount of patience and wit. It was good to hear and I felt ready for the next day.

"See you tomorrow, Felix," Hilde said.

"See you."

The ski school though would be closed after the 30th for a few days, to ring in the New Year. The staff deserved a break as they worked incredibly hard and wanted to prepare for a busy year ahead.

I clocked out from my shift, eager to just get back home and dive into my bed, but Mira was calling so sleep would be out of the question. I knew she'd want to meet up, to check in on me again. I hung up my ski jacket and gear in the locker room and then made my way to the cable car. It always felt weird now, travelling down in one alone.

By the time I got home, Mira was already waiting for me in her car. She must have just got here as she had a key for the house but didn't go straight in.

"Hey," I said to my sister as soon as she got out of her car, keys dangling in her hand. She was still in her scrubs and like always, pulled me into a tight embrace as if she hadn't seen me for days. She'd only just seen me yesterday.

"You look good today, Felix." Mira's eyes scanned my face and then she let out a deep breath, shaking her head slightly.

"You know I worry," Mira continued. I knew that, maybe others would call it overbearing but it didn't bother me in the slightest.

"Come inside," I told her, taking my keys out from my trouser pocket. I offered my sister some tea once we got inside and she accepted, flopping down on the sofa and propping her feet up on the coffee table.

"Wow, that was a tough shift." Mira rested her head on one of the cushions.

"What happened?" I asked her, as I took two mugs out of the cupboard. I'd add a little lemon and honey to her tea to make her relax. If she wanted to stay the night, I'd let her as well.

"Someone died." Mira wrinkled her nose and then turned to look at me. I didn't know how she managed to do her job but she loved it so much. She wanted to help people and in that process, sadly, people died.

"I'm sorry," I couldn't say much. All my sister could do was shrug and scratch behind her ear before replying.

"I feel sorry for the family, especially as it's Christmas and nearly the New Year. Can't imagine losing the one you love." Mira sighed. She was right.

Once the tea was made, I placed her mug on the table and then went back to finish making mine. I'd decided on chai, I liked the spice and cinnamon especially. It reminded me of Alisha, fucking hell I missed her so much. The distance between us was bordering on agony and I knew I really needed to see her soon.

Once I returned, I could see Mira was scrolling through her phone. Until something caught her attention and she swung her legs off the table to read whatever it was she came across intensely.

"What?" I furrowed my eyebrows, stretching my own long legs in front of me and resting them on the table. I was totally tired too but I kept my attention on my sister, who shoved the phone in my free hand.

"Read it. I think you'll cry. It's already made me," Mira said, sniffing her nose and visible tears were in her eyes. *What the hell?*

"Okay," I said hesitantly, angling the phone so that I could get a better look. It looked like an article and once I saw the name of the journalist who wrote it, I froze in my spot. *Alisha.* I'd already read her most recent article about Ischgl and it was very good. I especially loved the part where she spoke about meeting me and what she learned about a traditional Austrian family.

I started to read the first paragraph and I already felt winded once I processed what the article was about. *Me.*

> *I didn't expect to find someone on my travels to Austria.*
>
> *Until I met him.*
>
> *I really thought I knew everything about love, but I was wrong.*
>
> *The first day I arrived in Ischgl, I was hesitant about even being there and my best friend was the only comfort I had.*
>
> *When I finally had my first ski lesson, my limbs were so sore I felt like I couldn't move.*
>
> *I then crashed into the most handsome man I'd ever met and from then on, I was completely under his spell.*
>
> *We spent the most amazing two weeks together, getting to know one another.*
>
> *I met his family, who are one of the kindest and most welcoming families I've ever met.*
>
> *I discovered a new part about myself and I owe it to Felix for teaching me to believe in myself, because I didn't before. Skiing became so much more fun when he was guiding me and*
>
> *Felix Bauer is everything and more. He's kind, funny and makes you laugh until your lungs hurt.*
>
> *If he is reading this, I want him to know that this was so much more than a holiday romance. If he'll have me, I will do my best to give him the happiness he deserves. He knows that I express myself better with written words and there are three I want for him to read.*
>
> *I love you. Thank you for coming into my life, for teaching me so many things but most of all, how to love again when I didn't believe it was possible.*

"Isn't that adorable?" Mira had waited to speak to me once I had finished reading. My heart was pounding in my chest and all I wanted to do now was see Alisha. But not over a video call. No, in person. There was no point in staying here in Ischgl for New Year, not when I really wanted to spend it with Alisha. I didn't want to start the year without her, I wanted to begin it with her.

"I need to see her," I said in a firm tone. My mind was made up. This moment reminded me of the many cheesy romance movies I'd watched with Alisha the past week. I'd almost scoffed at them but here I was, in the same position as the movie characters. Fighting for the woman I loved.

"Yes, you do," Mira agreed. I was quick to move, grabbing my laptop so I could look up flight details. It would be difficult to get a last-minute flight and we had to look at a lot of comparison sights until we finally found one for the 30th of December. A perfect one too, as it meant I could still finish up at work and then get myself off to England.

"That was lucky." Mira let out a deep heave as I managed to check out and pay for the flight online. The next few days were going to be crazy but I was a determined man. I'd do anything for love. I'd do anything for Alisha.

And my family would help me do that. Mira supported me in my decision and once I told Aunt Brenna later in the evening, she cheered over the phone. All I wanted now was for the clock to tick faster.

"Where will you stay once you get there?" Mira asked.

"I'll book a hotel nearby, just need to ask Ophelia where Alisha lives. Do you think she can keep a secret?" I was hopeful she could.

"Yeah, she is very trustworthy. I've told her a lot of things and so has she. It feels like she's a sister in a way." Mira smiled.

"Okay. I'll text her, can you give me her number as I don't have it?" I asked. Mira provided me with the number and then announced she'd make another tea for us. She also asked if she could stay over and perhaps we could hang out in the morning since her shift didn't start until the late afternoon.

I made sure to text Ophelia when Mira was making the tea to ask for the details of Alisha's apartment and where she'd be for New Year's Eve. She was quick to reply to me and extremely supportive, saying that Alisha seemed quite down the past few days. Well, that would change. Once I had the details, my next task was to book the hotel where I'd stay for a few days. I'd also let the ski school know I'd be away, that I needed to see someone important.

We'd finally be together and I'd tell her how much I'd been thinking about her for the last two weeks, that there was no future without her and I'd move the whole galaxy for her if it meant we'd be together. I'd never be so spontaneous like this but it felt right. New Year's Eve couldn't come quick enough.

***

A few hours later, with the flight booked and accommodation sorted, I was struggling to keep it all a secret from Alisha. I wanted to hear her voice though so I decided to ring her. She picked up just as quickly as I called her.

"Hi!" she said rather excitedly, which warmed my heart. I loved that she felt this way about me; this caused my own feelings to become stronger.

"How are you, gorgeous?" I asked, eager to hear about her day and what she got up to.

"I'm happy now. I've just been heckling my brothers about something and they riled me up," Alisha said. I could almost imagine that right now, she was rolling her eyes. She'd told me that her brothers were her world but they weren't always mature.

"Want to talk about it?"

"Nah, I want to hear about you and what you've been up to," Alisha replied. Oh, if only she knew that I'd be with her on New Year's Eve. I couldn't wait to hold her in my arms and tell her exactly how I felt. The time was right.

"Teaching my first lesson was fun. I feel like I've finally found something I was meant to do." I smiled as I said this, but really, I had a lot to thank Alisha for. She was my motivation. My reason.

"I'm so glad for you," Alisha told me. In the background, I could hear some clinking and I could only assume she was either washing dishes or putting things away. It reminded me that I needed to tidy up. Mira had offered earlier but

I declined because I could see how tired she was. My sister worked hard and deserved a break.

"I miss you," I told her truthfully. It was like a whole other piece of me had been torn away and I would only feel complete once I was with her. Three days felt too long but I had to be patient.

"I miss you more, Felix. Maybe we can arrange to see each other after New Year," she suggested.

But little did she know that I'd be with her much sooner.

Chapter 48

Alisha

Being back home had been strange for the first few days but now having been back for more than two weeks, I'd fallen right back into my normal routine. Except now every day and night I'd talk to Felix. I'd fallen asleep often while still on call with him and there were times he didn't hang up when I did this. I'd wake up in the morning to find my phone halfway down the bed and pick it up to see Felix gently snoring on camera.

Work was a lot of fun these days, my article had been released and the reception from the readers had been positive. Grayson was keen for me to write my next article, so I presented the one I had written about falling in love with Felix to him. It was soppy but it was from the heart. I wanted to express that what I had with Felix wasn't just a fling, it was more. I wasn't aware if Felix had even seen it since I hadn't told him once it had been published. I'd told Mira though, in the hope that she'd pass it on to her brother.

A few days after returning from Austria, I had been half expecting to receive another text from Felicity to wish me. I was thankful that she hadn't contacted me and it was a sign that I was ready to forget about our friendship. In terms of my mental health, I was doing a lot better. Whenever I did have a bad moment, I'd either call my sister or Felix.

My parents gave us a wonderful meal on Christmas Day, and my grandparents really enjoyed seeing us all. They flew back after a few days and tonight, we'd be celebrating New Year's Eve. We'd be celebrating at our local restaurant, with lots of my parents' friends. My aunts and uncles would also be there. Ophelia would be joining us but the deeper part of me wished Felix would be here too.

Kiya was the only sibling who knew about him, I hadn't felt comfortable telling my brothers yet knowing how they'd react. Or even my parents, who may judge me slightly less but still have questions. I knew there'd be a lot of explaining to do, my parents liked it when I was honest and they'd feel a little hurt that I hadn't told them sooner. But that had been up to me.

"Eeeeeek, you look gorgeous didi." Kiya was circling around me, I was surprised she wasn't getting dizzy. But that was just her and her infectious energy. I was wearing a black off-the-shoulder dress, my eyes slightly smokey, and my lips a deep red.

"Thanks, bon," I replied. My sister looked beautiful too, in a dark red flowing dress and gold heels adorned on her feet. Her chestnut hair was flowing in gentle curls around her shoulders and she'd even painted her fingernails red to match her dress.

"Look at my beautiful girls." Mum walked into the living room, holding a plate of chaat dip. Good timing as I was starving. I couldn't help but eat a mouthful as soon as she placed it on the table.

"And my beautiful sons, too," Mum said as my two brothers walked into the room, looking very sharp in their suits. We all looked the part. The only family member we were waiting on was my dad, who ten minutes ago had a telling off from Mum for not being ready yet.

"Yeah, yeah." Zane rolled his eyes as Mum pulled him into a hug after setting down the food on the table. He would always say he hated affection but really, he loved it. Who could pass up a cuddle from Mum?

Aadi stood beside me, giving me a sloppy grin. He looked lovely but I knew he wouldn't want me to compliment him. He was far too humble. He'd managed to get time off work for this evening, which initially he grumbled about because he didn't want to let down his colleagues. But eventually, he came to terms with it and realised that family was just as important.

"I'm so glad the family is together again." Mum looked at us proudly. She looked at us as though we were her greatest achievements.

"I need to get back to mine though, I forgot something," I said. I also remembered Ophelia would be meeting me there but said she was running a little late.

"Okay, we can meet you at the restaurant then. Fireworks will be going off at midnight in the back garden," Mum said, just as Dad entered the room. All of us let out a whistle as we admired his attire. Dad didn't wear a tux very often, usually a sherwani but tonight he wanted to try something different.

"So, that's why you were taking so long!" Kiya giggled as she pressed a cheek on dad's cheek.

"Had to look my best for my family, pyraai." Dad tapped Kiya on her nose and then looked at us all.

"You always look your best, mera pyar." Mum gushed as she looked at her husband. My brothers groaned as she kissed Dad but it was a quick kiss. My parents weren't usually into public displays of affection but tonight was an exception. I liked seeing them happy.

"Oh wow, I really need to go." I looked at my phone and slightly panicked at the time.

"Go! We'll see you there," Zane said. I felt a bit guilty leaving them all but couldn't keep my friend waiting. Plus, I needed to feed Chou and change his cat litter. He had been really happy when I returned home and slept on my chest for most nights. He had been good company, as I needed some form of embrace.

"Bye!" I blew a kiss to my family and then closed the door behind me, holding my dress up as I went down the stairs. As gracefully as I could in these heels too.

I'd swap the heels once I got in the car for my driving shoes. Made me sound old but I'd rather be safe than sorry.

Driving back to mine was quiet, as it was New Year's Eve and the roads were quiet as people were celebrating either indoors or at events. I looked at the time to see it was eight o'clock, meaning I really needed to hurry. I stepped on the gas a bit more and sighed in relief as soon as I saw the road I lived on.

No sign of Ophelia, well her car wasn't here at least. I parked up as close to the curb as I could, turned off the engine, and hobbled out of the car. Again, walking in this dress wasn't easy but I managed to get up the stairs toward my apartment.

Chou was sleeping on the sofa when I came in but lifted his head when he saw me.

"Yes, hello, darling." I scratched him on his head and he licked my palm as if it was his own way of saying hello back.

"Want some food?" I raided the cupboard for a packet of his favourite food, which I squeezed into his blue cat bowl. He padded over but not before rubbing himself against my legs. He then gobbled down his food. I was happy he was happy.

"Come on, Ophelia." I sunk into my sofa, checking the time again. 8:30 pm. She said she'd be here by then, at least.

But once I heard a few knocks at the door, I immediately got up and knew I'd ask her what took so long. I swung open the door once I took the lock off the latch, ready to face my friend.

"Ophelia, what happened?" I said but the person I was looking at was not my best friend. My mouth gaped open as I scanned the person's body, from their feet up to their head. Those eyes I had lost myself in dozens of times. Those hands that had held me so gently whenever we made love and those lips that kissed me softly. I was lost for words.

Felix.

I couldn't believe he was here. He was breathing heavily, as if he'd run here straight from Austria. Which would be a true trek and I wouldn't expect anyone to do that for me. But the fact that he was here was enough.

"What are you—" I started to ask but I was silenced by Felix's lips, hungrily attacking my own. I moved my lips against his, sighing in pleasure as he pulled me closer to his chest. His scent enveloped around me, like a spiral I didn't want to unravel. *Oh, I missed him so much.*

"Alisha, I love you," Felix declared as soon as we stopped kissing. I felt like my soul had gone to heaven when he told me this but I needed to come back down to him. To tell him how I felt too. But this time, with spoken words. No hiding behind my writing.

"I love you, too." I cupped his cheek. No truer words had ever been said. Felix pressed another kiss to my near swollen lips, his broad hands on either side of my waist. We could kiss forever if we wanted to but I had questions for this man. So I asked them.

"How did you manage to get here? I thought the flights would have been fully booked. Or did you ski here?" I joked but knowing that wouldn't be possible. I knew he'd understand my sense of humour though. Skiing was what had brought us together.

"I managed to find a flight at the last minute, I got here yesterday. I knew I wanted to be here once I read that article you wrote about me," Felix said, linking his arms around my waist. Knowing that he read it and then decided to fly all the way over here validated how he felt about me. I needed to ignore the negative comments in my head from now on. The man *loved* me.

"You are amazing. What did you think of the article?" I nuzzled my head into his chest, inhaling his scent. I then lifted my head to observe his outfit. He was dressed in a white shirt with a black tie and a pair of smart patent lace-ups.

"You write so well. You caused Mira to cry." Felix chuckled and then placed one finger under my chin, tilting my head slightly upwards. His gorgeous hazel eyes gazed into my own, full of love for me.

"Didn't make you cry then?" I teased.

"Almost, baby. But I don't want to feel sad about us. Let's be happy. I want to spend forever with you, if that's what you want too," Felix told me. I wanted forever too.

"I do. It's what I've always wanted." I wanted to feel his lips on mine again, so I was brave and initiated the kiss, fire igniting inside of me again when his tongue entered my mouth. My hands turned into fists to grip his shirt but we needed to stop. My family was waiting for me at the restaurant.

"As much as I want to stay here and kiss you into oblivion, my family is waiting for me. Would you like to come?" I asked Felix nervously. This was big but I needed to put my brave boots on and introduce the man I loved to my family.

"Of course. I want to reign in the New Year with you all," Felix said.

"I can't believe we get to start the New Year together." I gushed, pulling him closer to me. The fact that he had come all this way to see me demonstrated that we were in it for the long haul. He *loved* me. He really did. And I loved him with my whole being.

"Wouldn't have it any other way, sweetheart," Felix added and we held hands all the way to the car and all the way to the restaurant too.

And tonight, we had chosen each other. Our future together was clear. And I was no longer afraid of it. I would choose Felix in a million lifetimes and I was thankful that I had gone on that trip to Ischgl. It was a true resort to romance.

Epilogue

Alisha

Five months later

A lot had happened over time but nothing could ruin my happiness. Felix and I would go back and forth, visiting each other over the last few months. We were committed and we'd fall back into our usual routine every time we'd first see each other.

My family had taken really well to him, Kiya especially. My brothers didn't want to know all the soppy details but were happy for me. At first, they asked Felix what his intentions were. I remember that conversation like it happened yesterday.

"So, you must love our sister then. Are you planning on marrying her?" Zane had asked so boldly that I'd almost spat out the water I'd been drinking. Fucking Zane.

"If you're with someone you love, the goal is to get married. So yes, I do," Felix had responded.

It had been the right answer and satisfied my brothers so they didn't drill him anymore after that. Kiya had been less of a problem but still wanted to make it clear to Felix that she wanted the best for me. My parents? Well, they couldn't have been more welcoming. I had let out a huge sigh of relief when they invited him to dinner and instantly said they liked him when he told them how he felt about me.

Nothing could go wrong. Felix's plane was due to land at any moment now, and I was waiting at gate five for him. I would always get nervous but once I'd lay eyes on him, the nerves would be replaced with love and excitement.

He'd be staying with me for two weeks this time and we were planning on going on a road trip to Scotland, to see as many places as we could. We'd take turns driving, it would be long but it'd be worth it. I'd never been on a road trip before but going on one with the person you loved would be a perfect adventure.

Ophelia was helping me at work, I was working on another article for the company as my last few had been really popular. I was now a regular journalist and I'd been given a generous pay rise. Enough to finally find a bigger place. Culture Horizon was on the up and if things kept going well, we could branch out in Europe. Well, that was what Grayson hoped for.

I'd celebrated my twenty-sixth birthday two months ago and it had been the best one yet. All my family, Ophelia, Mira and Felix together. I'd ended the day with a lot of cake and mind-blowing orgasms provided by Felix. Chou thankfully didn't see as he'd disappeared into the bathroom. Good for his sake too.

"Poor cat," Felix had said after we had finished our lovemaking and I giggled when Chou entered the room, as if he had known we'd finished.

The months after that had been busy but that was how I liked it. Now, I could take a long needed holiday and spend time with my wonderful boyfriend. I still couldn't believe it had been nearly six months since we'd met. But they had been the best, I couldn't imagine my life without him. I was lucky in love. Irrevocably smitten with Felix, the way he was and the way he would be in the future, especially as a husband and hopefully father.

Yes, over the last month, I had thought about that more and I felt ready for the next step in our relationship. We'd discussed moving in together, but it probably wouldn't happen quite yet due to our jobs. Felix was thriving as a ski instructor and always had a busy day's work with lessons. People liked him and seemed to only want him to teach them.

I had gone back to Ischgl two months ago myself and had some extra ski lessons with Felix. We had to keep it professional, especially with people around us and small children. But after every lesson, he'd take me back to his and have his way with me.

Some people would have wondered how we made it work, how we kept the magic alive, but we just did. We were two people deeply in love who *wanted* to make it work. Of course it was hard at times, when both our jobs kept us occupied and we'd have nights where we didn't pick up the phone. But that was the reality of relationships. We were mature enough to recognise that and didn't belittle one another.

Ever since that text from Caden months ago, I never heard from him again. He must have caught wind that I was with someone. I was glad because I didn't want to hear or see him again. He'd remain in the past, where he belonged.

I spotted Felix instantly and sprinted over to him, like I always did whenever I saw him.

"Hello, gorgeous." Felix beamed at me, placing his bag that was on his shoulder down. He had a large suitcase with him.

"How was the flight?" I asked him as we walked hand in hand to the car park.

"Bit of turbulence. I had a nap, still pretty tired. Can't wait for our trip tomorrow." Felix let out a small yawn.

"I've made sure you're insured on my car. Just don't crash my car please," I joked. But I knew Felix was a perfectly capable driver, he had driven us all around Austria when I last went.

"As if," Felix scoffed, miming flipping his hair. Speaking of his hair, he'd grown it out a little. I liked it as it meant there was more to grab when we were making love. He also hadn't shaved, something else I loved.

"Are you going to grow a full on beard at this point?" I reached up to gently scratch his chin, where most of the hair was.

"No, I'm shaving this all off as soon as we get to yours. Because I know how much you love my bare face," Felix replied with a hint of sarcasm. *Oh well, goodbye facial hair.*

"I've made you something sweet. I bet you're hungry," I said to Felix as we buckled up in my car. The walk to the car park hadn't been very long and luckily, I'd only paid for an hour. It wasn't too expensive but airports knew how to make that extra money.

"Hungry for you." Felix smirked and I knew exactly what he wanted. We'd had car sex plenty of times but I for one wasn't going to do it in an airport car park. The man would have to wait.

"All in good time, honey," I replied, reaching across the gear stick to squeeze his thigh.

"I love you," Felix told me. He always made sure to tell me and his actions always spoke loud too.

"I love you, Felix." I didn't miss the flicker of need in his eyes as I said this. I needed to get us home.

On the drive home, I couldn't stop smiling as things had worked out so much. I had an amazing job, supportive family, the best friend in the world and a man who loved me fiercely. I loved him just as much too and going on this trip with him would unlock many more memories.

Felix

Two months later, after the Scotland trip

I was extremely nervous today, more than I usually was. The reason being that I'd be getting down on one knee to propose to Alisha. Aunt Brenna and Mira had been the ones to give me that final push as a part of me was wondering if we were ready for that next step. We'd only been together for about nearly eight months. Maybe some people would say we were moving too quickly.

But when you were madly in love, did that really matter? I *wanted* Alisha to be my wife. I'd walk down the aisle again for her. And this time, I knew it wouldn't end the way it had with my ex.

I had already picked out the ring—an 18K white gold halo ring. It was expensive but I knew it was perfect for Alisha. I'd also asked for her father's blessing and he'd shaken my hand until it felt like my arm would pop out of its socket. Both her parents were happy and then started to tell me more about engagements and the wedding itself. We'd have a fusion wedding- a mix of both mine and Alisha's cultures. It was going to be magical.

Now, I just needed to ask her to spend the rest of her life with me.

We were currently relaxing at home which had semi-permanently moved in. What I meant by that was, whenever I came down to stay in England, this is where I came. All my stuff was here but I was hoping for the move to be permanent soon.

I loved teaching at the ski school but coming home to an empty house was tough. I wanted to come home to Alisha, to tell her about my day and then fall asleep next to her. My family understood but said it'd be a big change for them, of course they'd need time to adjust. But whatever I decided, they'd support me.

My own mother? I saw her every so often, and I found out that we had a lot of similarities. She liked to ski in her free time and bake. Mira had finally arranged to meet her three months ago and had asked me to come along. At first, it was awkward, but the second time we met, the conversation felt natural. My mum had made it clear she wanted to be in our lives but we needed boundaries.

It was a beautiful, sunny day today. Me and Alisha had gone for a walk; we were currently staying in Scotland. After our trip to Scotland a few months ago, we knew we wanted to come back. We'd taken a boat this morning to go to the Scottish Highlands and the scenery was absolutely stunning. It was a perfect location to get engaged.

"This is so beautiful." Alisha was gazing in wonder at the view around us. We were surrounded by a lot of greenery. As she looked around her, I unzipped my backpack to pull out the ring box. It was now or never.

I hoped she would keep looking ahead whilst I got down on one knee.

"Alisha?" I wanted her attention as I opened the ring box. My hands were shaking, maybe partly due to the wind as we were high up. But also because I had thought about this for the past month and now it was finally happening. The anticipation was real.

"Yeah, Felix?" Alisha whipped her head around and then gasped as soon as she saw me kneeling on the floor, holding the box out in front of her.

"Alisha, I've been so lucky to find you. The moments we spend together are incredible. You are one-half of me. I'm so glad we met and now I want to spend the rest of my life with you. Will you do me the greatest honour and marry me?" I asked her. Her gaping mouth transformed into a huge grin and then she knelt down in front of me, so she was level with me.

"Funny, because I was also going to ask you the same thing!" Alisha exclaimed.

"So, will you?" I gazed at the woman I was completely enamoured with.

"Of course I'll marry you, I love you!" Alisha let out a squeal and I cheered myself. She held out her hand for me to slip the ring on her finger and she cooed at it, twisting her hand in the sun to admire the sparkles.

"I love you," I declared. I realised that Alisha was the missing puzzle piece to my life, she was right for me and I was for her. Hand in hand, we continued our trek in the Highlands and I knew I'd never walk alone again.

About the author

Kacey is a young, British author who owns three cats. She is a lover of Jane Austen and hopes to marry her own Darcy one day. Her novella, An Artist's Dream, is her first book and she hopes to inspire those through her words.

https://www.instagram.com/authorkaceysophia

Acknowledgements

Well, where can I start? Publishing my third book has been so much fun but also challenging at times. Sometimes I have to take a moment and reflect on the past few years and how things have really changed for the better. I have so many people to thank, for helping me become the person I am now and for their support on my writing journey.

Thank you to my partner for his constant encouragement because there were times where I felt like I wasn't good enough. Thank you for taking me skiing in Austria for the first time in 2023 because there, I came up with this book and created a universe that I'm super proud of. There are moments in this book which are based on what I experienced whilst skiing and also going around Ischgl.

Thank you to my incredible readers for your support and love keeps me going. I have a huge amount of love for you and without you, I wouldn't be able to do this. And to my fellow author community, you have been so lovely and kind with your advice and constant reassurance. I especially thank N.M Patel for always being helpful whenever I dropped you a DM.

I thank my cover designer Tracy (@slimmwrites) who did such a wonderful job on the cover, when I first saw it I squealed. Thank you for making my vision come to reality. I also thank my editor Cassidy, helping me to perfect my writing and giving me advice on what to add and improve on. Thank you to A.J. Knight for designing the chapter illustrations; they add such a gorgeous touch. And thank you to Almu for the cutest character art of Felix and Alisha, I love the way you captured their first meeting.

A big thank you to my alpha readers- Victoria, Rosana, Maia and Sammie. Your feedback was honest and valuable, especially with the first draft. You made me laugh too. I also thank Maggie for her insightful feedback on my first draft.

I must also thank Kriti and Sanjana from Swipethebook PR. You have made an author's dreams come true. I am so glad to have been working with you.

Super huge thank you to my arc readers, I hope you loved the book and thank you for giving me a chance. Your reviews are so helpful and important to us authors.

Now, I've got to dry my eyes! Writing is something I'll always love and I can't wait to share more with you. Watch out for the next book in the Duttas series.